THE DOG SHARE

Fiona was born in a youth hostel in Yorkshire. She started working on teen magazine *Jackie* at age 17, then went on to join *Just Seventeen* and *More!* where she invented the infamous 'Position of the Fortnight'. Fiona now lives in Scotland with her husband Jimmy, their three children and a wayward rescue collie cross called Jack.

For more info, visit www.fionagibson.com. You can follow Fiona on Twitter @fionagibson.

By the same author:

FIONA GIBSON

The DOG SHARE

FSC
www.fsc.org

MIX
Paper from
responsible sources

FSC C007454

...ook is produced from independently certified FSC™ pa...
to ensure responsible forest management.

...r more information visit: www.harpercollins.co.uk/green

avon.

Published by AVON
A division of HarperCollins*Publishers* Ltd
1 London Bridge Street
London SE1 9GF

www.harpercollins.co.uk

HarperCollins*Publishers*
1st Floor, Watermarque Building, Ringsend Road
Dublin 4, Ireland

A Paperback Original 2021

First published in Great Britain by HarperCollins*Publishers* 2021

ISBN: 978-0-00-838599-6

Typeset in Sabon LT Std by Palimpsest Book Production Limited, Falkirk, Stirlingshire
Printed and bound in UK by CPI Group (UK) Ltd, Croydon CR0 4YY

For Caroline, Ratty and Moth with love

Prologue

'Dad,' I yell, 'look at that dog!'

I'm running across Silver Beach. I know it so well; every rock, the names of all of the shells, the best places to find flat stones for skimming. I know most of the people we see here – and their dogs – at least to say hi to.

But I've never seen this dog before.

I stop and wait for Dad to catch up. 'That's the kind I want,' I tell him.

'Are you sure?' he says, smiling. 'Last time we looked, you said you'd have *any* kind . . .'

He means the dog rescue centre websites. I'm always checking them out, seeing which dog I'd adopt if Dad would let me. Not that he will – I realise that. *It wouldn't be fair, I'm out all day, we don't have a garden, blah-blah-blah*. I've heard it all a million times. But it doesn't stop me looking . . . just in case.

I like reading about dogs too. I know loads of canine facts, like they only sweat from furless areas (their noses, the pads on their feet). And when they see a dog on TV, they actually *recognise* it as a dog. Some even have their

1

favourite programmes (my friend Lucas's whippet likes *Match of the Day*). Dogs are *amazing*.

I grab a piece of driftwood and throw it. The dog tears after it and brings it back to me. We do it again and again as Dad strolls about, looking for more sticks.

The dog's mostly brown, with a patch of white on his chest, and he's a bit scruffy and skinny. He probably wouldn't win any of those competitions where the dogs are paraded about in front of judges. I don't really like those competitions, but maybe the dogs don't mind. Obviously they can't say, 'God, this is boring, having to sit nicely and look neat. Can we go out and play now?'

I like thinking of all those competition dogs sending each other telepathic messages, planning a mass breakout. I mean, they can communicate through sounds, movements and by producing scents – so why not by telepathy too?

A dog is as intelligent as a two-year-old human, I told Dad recently.

That's amazing. But we're still not getting one, he said with a smile.

'I can't see anyone about,' Dad's saying now. 'Maybe he's run away?'

'Yeah, maybe.' I nod.

'We should take him to the police station,' he adds.

'Can't we play a bit more?'

Dad checks his watch. 'No, we really should go. We don't want to miss the ferry, do we?'

In fact, I wouldn't mind missing it this time. I don't really want to go back to Glasgow. And I definitely don't want to take the dog to the police station. I want to play here all day, like I used to, when it wasn't just me and Dad who came to the island, but Mum, too.

Sometimes I feel sad being here without her. It didn't matter so much when I was little – I'd been busy building sandcastles, filling my bucket with seawater to flood moats, all of that. But I'm not little anymore. I'm ten years old and sometimes the sadness seems to creep in, a bit like the seawater that seeps in through my trainers and wets my feet. And I can't do anything to stop it.

I miss her then. But I'm not missing her now that I have this little dog to play with. We run and run, and I pretend not to hear as Dad calls out: 'I don't feel good about leaving this dog on the beach by himself. If we hurry up now, we could drop him off at the police station and we'll still catch the ferry . . .'

'Aw, Dad!'

'He's probably run away. And someone'll be going crazy, looking for him.' Dad's looking serious now, properly worried. 'See if you can catch him. We can use my scarf as a lead . . .'

'Can't we take him home?' I stare at Dad, wanting him to say yes more than anything. 'Please, Dad. Please!'

'I'm sorry. You know we can't do that.'

'But he's lost! Or maybe he's been abandoned?' I look back round, expecting to see the dog sitting there, waiting for our stick game to start up again.

But he's not there. And when I scan the whole beach I spot a blur of brown in the far distance, growing smaller and smaller until he runs around the headland, and is gone.

Chapter One

Two Years Earlier
Suzy

The island had come clearly into view, illuminated by a shaft of silvery light. We stared, transfixed, from the deck of the ferry.

'So, what d'you think?' Paul asked.

'It's incredible,' I murmured. 'It's like one of those old religious paintings – like a Michelangelo or something. All it needs are some floating cherubs and a scattering of naked muscular gods . . .'

'Pervert.' He laughed and squeezed my hand.

I glanced at his handsome profile: long, strong nose; full lips; messy, wavy, light brown hair being buffeted by the wind. 'I'm so excited, Paul,' I added. 'Look at those mountains! And those little white cottages dotted along the shore . . .'

'And I think that's the whisky distillery over there.' He pointed towards the end of the town.

'Really? It's tiny!' I gazed at the purplish hills that scooped down towards the greener lower pastures. A little way along from the town – the only sizeable settlement on the island – lay a wide crescent of beach. It looked deserted. There would be no resort-style entertainment here, no shops crammed with souvenir keyrings and novelty booze that never seems quite so enticing once you cart it home. My heart soared with the anticipation of a whole week together, separated from the rest of the world.

My mother had been astounded when she'd first heard about our trip. 'Belinda said you're off to some island?' she'd barked down the phone. So she and my sister had been gossiping about Paul and me. Although I didn't know where my hackles were exactly, I was sure they were raised.

'Yes, we just thought it'd make a nice change,' I explained.

'A *Scottish* island?' she gasped.

'That's right, Mum. It's in the Hebrides.'

'The Hebrides! How on earth will you get there?'

'We'll drive up to Oban on the west coast and take the ferry from there. It looks amazing,' I added, to stir her up even further.

Mum paused, obviously figuring out how to fish for more information in a non-blatant way. 'Isn't that a bit . . . different for you two?'

Ah, the 'D' word, a favourite of Mum's, as in, 'Oh, is that a new jacket, Suzy? It's different!' I.e., 'If you're happy to go out in public wearing such a hideous article, then who am I to stop you?'

'We've been up to the Highlands plenty of times,' I reminded her, 'since Paul's dad bought that hotel. You know we love it up there.'

'Yes, but that was in *proper* Scotland, wasn't it?' You'd have thought we were talking the Arctic Circle. But then

5

my parents had spent their whole lives living within a few miles of York – where Paul and I also lived – and rarely ventured out of Yorkshire.

'Erm, it was on the mainland, yes,' I replied. 'But the islands are proper Scotland too, Mum.'

'That was in a town, though, with things to do.' Like we were a couple of kids. 'And obviously,' she added, 'now Paul's dad has, um . . .'

Died was what she couldn't quite bring herself to say. My boyfriend had lost his father the previous summer. Paul had only been ten when his mum had passed away, and apparently he and his dad had been a real team – inseparable really – as he'd been growing up on their Bradford estate. He'd taken his death extremely hard.

'We are still allowed in Scotland,' I said lightly, 'even though Ian's not there anymore.'

'I know that, love,' Mum said, in a softer tone. 'But d'you think Paul will enjoy it? I mean, don't you normally go to Majorca or Spain—'

'I'm sure he'll love it,' I said firmly.

'But what will he *do* there?'

'What everyone does on a Scottish island, I'd imagine,' I said, sensing a throbbing in my temples. 'Explore and enjoy the incredible scenery . . .'

'What if it rains?'

I couldn't help smiling at that. 'You're talking as if he's a difficult toddler who I wouldn't consider taking anywhere if there wasn't going to be a gigantic soft play centre or a petting zoo.'

'I'm sure there aren't any petting zoos there!'

Now I was laughing. 'Mum, he's a forty-eight-year-old man. He doesn't need a petting zoo. And if the weather's terrible I'm sure there'll be some jigsaws in the cottage.'

'I wouldn't have thought he was the jigsaw type,' she remarked.

'Oh, yes. Let him anywhere near a 2000-piecer and he can't keep his hands off it.'

'Hmm.' Mum paused, then added: 'It's not a bucket list thing, is it?'

'What, completing a 2000-piece jigsaw?'

'No! I mean Paul wanting to go to that island—'

'You think he'd only want to visit a designated area of outstanding beauty if he were about to cark it?'

'Of course not,' she blustered. 'Why are you so defensive? I didn't mean to upset you, Suzy.'

'I know that,' I said, impressed by my ability to remain cordial. 'Anyway, it sounds like there's plenty to do there. There's a distillery that does visitor tours, and you know Paul loves whisky . . .'

'You can say that again.' Mum never missed an opportunity to imply that my boyfriend was a useless drunk.

'. . . And then there's the smokery,' I added. 'They do incredible fish, apparently. Buckingham Palace has a regular order for kippers. In fact, the island's name comes from the Gaelic word for herring – *sgadan* – so Sgadansay actually means "Isle of herring" . . .' *A factlet I'm sure you're fascinated by,* I reflected, sensing Mum's interest dwindling now it had become clear that I would Not Be Riled. 'And we're planning to do loads of hiking,' I breezed on, 'up and down hills in our anoraks . . .'

'Do you even *have* an anorak?'

'I'll get one. And waterproof trousers. There are these amazing silver sand beaches and we don't want the weather to hamper us . . .' *And then there's shagging,* I yearned to add, keen to wrap up our chat now. *If it pours down all week – which I fully expect – I'm planning to cram the fridge with wine, draw the curtains and we'll shag each other senseless, in our anoraks. I might even ask Paul to smack me with one of those artisanal kippers.* 'And there's probably a church we can visit,' I added.

'Well, I hope you have fun,' Mum remarked tartly, and we finished the call.

In fact, although it pained me to the core, I could understand why she was so perplexed about our trip. As far as Paul was concerned, holiday heaven meant glorious sunshine and music blaring from beach bars – and he always wanted to make friends with *everyone*. We'd been together six years, and although I'd always enjoyed our jaunts, occasionally I yearned for wide-open spaces and for it just to be the two of us. Frieda, my daughter, had already left home and her brother Isaac would soon be flying the nest too. There was no reason, I kept telling Paul, why we couldn't have a few days in the country as well as our usual fortnight in the sun.

However, he'd never really 'got' the countryside, and became visibly twitchy if he found himself in it accidentally. We never even went to parks together, unless we were cutting through one to get to somewhere else. And now he'd booked a holiday that would be entirely focused on country walks, and require polo necks?

I couldn't ignore the fact that it was completely bizarre. But I was damned if I was going to admit that to Mum.

Those thoughts soon blew away on the cool breeze as the ferry approached the quayside. We'd have a wonderful time here, I just knew it. It was a beautiful blue-skied April afternoon, and my heart soared like the seagulls squawking overhead.

* * *

8

We stayed in a tiny whitewashed cottage close to the shore. Whatever the weather, we'd pack up hearty picnics and set off on hikes along the rugged coastline or up into the hills. Eagles soared above us. We saw red deer who stopped and glanced at us briefly as if to say, 'So, who are *you*?' before scampering away. We rolled up our jeans and paddled in crystal clear streams and fell back, laughing, onto pillows of springy heather.

Our holiday was certainly revealing a side to Paul that I'd never seen before. But I wasn't complaining. I loved the glorious beaches where we'd barely see another soul, and the wonderful bakery, the old-fashioned sweet shop and the cosy pubs in the town. As I photographed a terrace of impossibly cute cottages – each one painted a different pastel shade – we joked that they'd probably been natural, unadorned stone until Instagram had come along. Then out had come the paint rollers and the jaunty colours.

Not once did Paul grumble about the fierce winds or sudden downpours that soaked us to the bones. The local fish and chips were heavenly and seemed to taste even better when we ate them huddled together for warmth in a covered wooden shelter facing the choppy sea. One evening we treated ourselves to a vast seafood platter – everything caught mere hours before we devoured it – at an elegant art deco hotel.

'Is it because of your dad that you wanted to come here?' I asked that night as we strolled back to the cottage.

'Kind of,' he said. It made sense that Paul had been drawn to Scotland, which, in turn, had led him to researching the Outer Hebrides for our trip. Ian had been a ducker and diver, owning various ramshackle hotels in Yorkshire before making his final purchase way up north, in Fort William. He'd loved the Heather Glen Hotel so much he'd moved to Scotland permanently and spent his final years living in its annex of leaky attic rooms.

Like his father, Paul had never had a thought-out career plan. When I'd met him he'd been flogging spicy sausages from a fast food van close to York Minster – but that enterprise hadn't lasted long and there had been a string of ill-fated schemes since then. 'When's Paul going to settle down?' my sister asked a couple of Christmases ago at her place. She and her marathon runner husband Derek live in a vast modern detached house on the outskirts of Leeds. Their kitchen island probably rivals some of the smaller Scottish isles in terms of square footage. Child-free by choice, and with a law degree and a high-flying job with the civil service, Belinda has always relished her wiser older sister role.

'He's *fine*,' I replied, defensively. 'There are plenty of things he can do. He's very resourceful.'

'Hmm, is that what you call it? And you being freelance as well,' Belinda added. By a weird kind of fluke, I had become an in-demand writer of obituaries for newspapers. So much work had poured in – because people are *always* dying – I'd been able to quit my lacklustre job at a recruitment consultancy to focus on writing full-time. 'I don't know how you can stand the uncertainty, Suze,' my sister had added. 'Will he still be like this when he's fifty? Sixty? For the rest of his life?'

I don't know! I wanted to tell her. *Anyway, what does it matter to you what he does?* The thing is, I'd always reassured myself, you don't fall for someone on the basis that they're a settled option. At least I don't. Yes, Paul was certainly fickle and perhaps not your go-to person if you wanted advice on investments or domestic boiler maintenance policies. But I loved him, and during those long, blissful days as we explored Sgadansay together, I don't think I'd ever felt happier.

Paul booked us onto the whisky distillery tour where a homely lady in an Aran sweater and tartan trousers talked our small group through the distillation processes. We sampled the whiskies and met the master distiller, a rather gruff elderly man with a rangy build and neatly cropped silvery hair. Apparently, his main method of maintaining quality control involved an awful lot of tasting. 'It seems terribly unscientific,' someone murmured.

'It *is* scientific,' our guide said with a smile, 'but it's about instinct, too. Isn't it, Harry?'

He nodded and looked around at us as if wishing he could get back to work, instead of being forced to talk to visitors.

'But how d'you know when it's right?' asked a portly man from Texas.

'Experience,' Harry said with a shrug.

'Harry's been our master distiller for thirty-five years,' the tour guide explained. 'There's nothing he doesn't know about whisky.'

'I'm happy to apply for the job, if ever you want to step aside.' The Texan chuckled. Meanwhile, Paul kept pinging questions to the ever-patient guide: *What creates a whisky's distinctive flavour? Was it the water, the climate, or the casks in which the spirit matures slowly over several years?*

'When you strip it down to the basics,' she explained, 'there are three main components to whisky, and they happen to be the very ingredients that are essential to a healthy, happy life.' She looked around at us. 'Can anyone guess what they are?'

11

Paul cast me a bemused glance in recognition of her teacherly tone. 'Water,' someone piped up.

'That's right. And here on Sgadansay we have the best water in the world. Anything else?'

Paul shot up his hand. 'Barley?'

'Yep,' she said, nodding. 'There's malted barley, plus yeast, which we regard as the food element. And the last one?' She looked around again at our expectant faces. '*Love*,' she said finally, 'by which I mean the patience and care that's needed to make a distinctive whisky like ours.' She paused as a skinny young man handed around samples of amber-coloured spirit. 'And that's it,' our guide concluded. 'Water, food and love. Isn't that right, Harry?' I caught the master distiller's barely detectable eye-roll. I suspected he was too down-to-earth for that kind of flowery talk.

'That was so interesting,' Paul enthused as we left.

'It really was,' I agreed. 'And what a swot you were with all your questions! Are you thinking of distilling your own whisky at home in our bath?'

Paul grinned. 'Why not? I mean, how hard can it be?' I laughed, trying to shrug off a twinge of regret that we would be leaving the island tomorrow. The sharp, salty air filled my lungs, and Paul kissed the top of my head as we stopped to gaze out to sea. 'Um, Suze, I've been thinking,' he added. 'When we get back home . . . well, I'd like to do something different.'

I gave him a quick look. 'You want to take up hiking?' I asked with a smile.

'Not exactly. I mean, I've loved it but . . .' He wound an arm around my waist. 'I mean a kind of work project.'

Oh, Christ. For the past few months he'd been working

at a gig equipment hire company in York. I'd been relieved that he seemed to have 'settled down', as my sister would have put it. 'What d'you mean?' I asked.

'Well, um . . . you know my job's just a tiding-over thing, don't you?'

'Is it?' I studied his face.

'Well, yeah. I mean, it's not exactly what I want to do for the rest of my life.'

I cleared my throat. 'Yeah, okay, I get that. So, what're you thinking about?'

Dusk was falling and the sky was streaked with pink and gold. Paul pointed towards the cluster of buildings in the distance, their lights glimmering like stars. 'What would you say if I suggested buying it?'

'Buying it?' I stared at him. 'You mean the *island*?' I was laughing now, awash with relief. For a moment I'd assumed he was being serious.

'I mean it,' he said quickly, 'but I'm not talking about the island. Dad's inheritance won't quite stretch to that.'

I blinked at him in confusion. 'So what *are* you talking about?'

He looked at me, clearly fizzing with anticipation, like a child with a secret they're dying to share. 'See the white building over there, down by the shore?'

I nodded. 'The distillery, you mean?'

'Uh-huh.' A smile flickered across his lips. 'It's for sale, you know.'

'Is it?' My stomach shifted uneasily.

'Yep,' he said. 'And the hotel sale should complete next week, so I could go for it . . .' His father's Fort William hotel, he meant, of which Paul was the sole beneficiary; there had also been a sizeable financial settlement, which had come through recently. Given Ian's haphazard approach to business, Paul had been surprised that there had been anything at all.

'Paul,' I started, 'you don't really mean this, do you? I'm sorry, but I can't take this seriously—'

'Why not?' He frowned, looking hurt.

'Because . . .' I paused. 'Because you know nothing about distilling, do you? And it's a highly specialised thing. That Harry guy, the master distiller – hasn't he been doing that job for thirty-five years?'

'Yeah, but Harry would still be there,' Paul insisted, 'and I wouldn't need to actually do anything in a hands-on kind of way—'

'Please tell me you're not serious about this!'

'I am. I really am,' he said firmly.

'It's completely mad,' I exclaimed. 'You might as well buy a fishmonger's for all you know about—'

'I don't want to buy a fishmonger's,' he cut in. 'I want to buy a fantastic distillery that's been doing brilliantly for decades now. I mean, it can't possibly go wrong.'

'My God, Paul.' I placed a hand over my eyes moment-arily as my sister's question rang in my ears: *Will he still be like this when he's fifty? Sixty? For the rest of his life?*

He took my hand and kissed me gently on the lips. 'It'd be an amazing adventure for us,' he said firmly. 'Please, my darling. *Please* say yes.'

Chapter Two

Back at home in York, I decided that my best plan of action was to throw myself into my work in the hope that Paul's obsession would soon be forgotten. I wrote obituaries of actors, composers and a celebrated wine-maker who had established a vineyard in Sussex. Her niche English wines had garnered accolades until her death at ninety-two.

Since Sgadansay, everything I'd read about the drinks industry suggested *at best* the need for copious patience and experience, and at worst, that the wrong kind of booze can cause serious harm. For instance, I'd read that the first liquid to run off after distillation may contain methanol. Once ingested, this can turn into formaldehyde, which is useful for chemical loos and the preservation of corpses – but it's not something you'd want to be swishing around your insides while you're alive. *It can severely damage the central nervous system,* I'd read, *and cause blindness and death.*

I knew Paul would laugh in my face if I mentioned this stuff, so instead I was trying to *gently* persuade him to reconsider what to do with his inheritance. 'It could really make a difference to your future,' I ventured as we lay in bed one night.

'To *our* future,' he said.

'Well, yes. But maybe there's something else you could invest in, that's slightly less risky—'

'It's *not* risky,' he insisted. 'Okay, I might not be experienced but I'm committed and passionate. You know the owner's keen to sell up and retire . . .' I nodded mutely. We'd been over this already. 'And he's eager to pass it on to someone like me, who'll bring a fresh approach, rather than a big conglomerate that'll just gobble it up.'

Since when was Paul committed and passionate about the spirits industry apart from – and I hated to concede that my mother was right – when it came to drinking the stuff?

'I'm not jumping into this,' he added. 'I've been looking into it for months.' We had already established that he'd lured me to the island under false pretences. 'All I want to do is make more of the heritage and the island setting,' he insisted. 'And you'd be brilliant at handling the media side . . .'

'But I have a job already!'

'Yeah, but you could take this on as another strand.'

'What if I don't want "another strand"?'

'And you've got tons of newspaper contacts . . .'

'Yes,' I countered, 'but only on the obituaries side—'

'C'mon, Suze. Let's be daring and bold. Live a little!'

Don't you 'live-a-little' me, I seethed, resenting the implication that I was the one spoiling his fun. Suzy Medley: Trampler of Dreams. This was coming from a man who hadn't been able to sell his spicy sausages

16

without accruing a rack of debt – which I'd helped him pay off. 'Paul,' I said firmly, 'just leave it, will you? I can't talk about this anymore. I just can't.'

A couple of days later he found me in Frieda's room, which wasn't really Frieda's room anymore but my office. I'd had to admit, it was silly to keep it as some kind of shrine after she'd left for university. So I'd carefully packed away the curly-edged posters and heaps of battered old trainers and conducted a thorough archaeological excavation under her bed. There I'd found yet more trainers, a musty old sleeping bag, tatty school jotters and, startlingly, a half-eaten pizza in a greasy box.

I'd also rescued the withered cheese plant she'd refused to let me 'interfere with', as she put it, insisting it was 'fine' crammed into the rusting olive oil can she'd found lying in the street. I seem to have a lucky touch with houseplants. The first thing I'd done, when I'd come home from dropping her off at student halls in Cumbria, was ease it out of the can and re-home it in a roomier earthenware pot so it could breathe. I'd imagined it groaning with relief – like a woman ripping off a constricting bra at the end of the day.

'Can I show you something?' Paul asked now, laptop clasped to his chest.

'Sure,' I replied. If it was going to be a YouTube clip of a man being chased by a hippopotamus, I hoped it'd be quick as I had urgent work to finish off. He pulled up a spare chair and opened his laptop on the desk.

I read the document on the screen. It certainly went into far greater depth than any of his previous business plans, which had amounted to scribbled notes in tatty notebooks or, on one occasion, on a Pret a Manger lemon cake wrapper. This time he had acquired a full list of the distillery's employees, and their salaries, plus detailed costs of raw materials, bottling, transport, property maintenance, insurance, utilities and legal shenanigans; every overhead seemed to have been accounted for. He had also written an impressive marketing strategy with the aim of bringing the small distillery to the attention of the world.

'This is really thorough,' I remarked.

Paul nodded. 'My dad would be so proud,' he said, with a catch to his voice. Startlingly, his eyes were wet.

'Oh, darling.' I pulled him close and kissed him. 'This is all about your dad, isn't it? You're not over it, I can tell.'

He shrugged mutely and raked back his hair. It was still abundant, peppered with just a little silvery grey at the sides. 'You don't believe in me, do you?' he muttered.

'It's not that,' I insisted.

'Wasn't I supportive to you, when you gave up your job to write full-time?'

'Of course you were! I don't think I'd have had the courage without you—'

'Well, I thought it was daring,' he went on, 'and it made me love you even more—'

'I hated that job though,' I cut in, which was true. The atmosphere at the recruitment consultancy had been toxic and I'd been relieved to get out. 'And it felt like the right time,' I added.

'Well, *this* feels like the right time too,' he said firmly. 'What are you worried about exactly?'

'That you don't know anything about it.'

'It's only whisky, Suze. You saw how they did it. It's not difficult—'

'What about the chemicals?'

'What chemicals?' he asked, looking confused.

18

'The chemicals produced when you distil something! I'm scared you'll embalm yourself—'

'*What?*' he spluttered.

'It's true, Paul. I read about it.'

'I don't think that's likely, babe.' He was smirking now, infuriatingly. 'What about when you made that sloe gin? I wasn't aware of you performing a risk assessment then—'

'Sloe gin's just gin, with sloes in!' I sensed hysteria rising in me as we started to laugh.

'Fuck, Suzy, you're bonkers, you know that?' *I* was bonkers? Bloody cheek! 'Remember there's the master distiller,' Paul added. 'That Harry guy . . .'

'Okay, so why d'you want *me* to be involved?'

'Because you'd be brilliant,' he insisted, 'and because I love you.'

'I love you too, but—'

'Listen,' he cut in, brushing a strand of hair from my face, 'I want to do something amazing with Dad's money. But . . .' He paused. 'I'll only do it with your blessing.'

I smiled, despite everything. 'I know what you're like. You'll do whatever you want.'

'Oh, Suze. You know I'd never do anything to hurt or upset you.' He slid his arms around my waist and kissed me again. Even after six years I was still hit with a whoosh of desire whenever he touched me. Damn him for being so sexy and for always getting his way.

'Okay,' I said finally. 'I guess you should do what feels right for you—'

'For both of us,' he said, beaming now. 'I want this to it be *our* adventure.'

Six weeks later, Paul and I became joint directors of the Sgadansay Distillery. And two years after that, the once-thriving business had been royally fucked up.

19

Chapter Three

Now

I expected a grilling. I deserve it too. Yet it's still shocking to look around at all the stony faces and realise every single person in this room hates me.

It's like when you've run, panting, onto an aeroplane. As the last passenger on board, you've caused its delay and now it's missed its departure slot. Instead of jetting off to Lanzarote you now have to sit on the tarmac for two and a half hours. Everyone knows it's your fault and they are radiating hatred.

Only this is worse – *far* worse. It's not the start of their holidays that's been ruined, but their livelihoods. I feel sick with shame.

'Erm, if I could please just say something,' I call out, shakily, then wait for the hubbub to die down. We are all crammed into the wood-panelled reception area of the distillery. It was sunny half an hour ago but now rain is battering at the windows.

The dozen employees are all sitting on plastic chairs and staring at me with disdain. I inhale fully, trying to give the impression that I am calm and in control. 'I've tried to explain things as honestly as I can,' I start. 'That's why I'm here, so you'd all know the full picture and that I'm doing my best to try and sort things out.' My voice wobbles as I scan the room again. 'Please believe me when I say I'm deeply sorry about everything that's happened,' I continue. 'If there's anything at all that I can—'

'*Sorry?*' calls out a sturdy man in a lumberjack shirt. 'You think saying sorry makes things any better for us?'

'No, of course not,' I bluster. 'I just want you to know that—'

'Sorry's not going to put food on my table,' cries out a woman with a beanie hat pulled low down on her head.

'I realise that,' I start, 'and I wish things were different—'

'We deserve a full explanation,' thunders a ruddy-faced man in overalls, 'as to why it's been allowed to get into this state.'

'That's what I'm trying to give you,' I say, sensing my own cheeks flaming. I look down at the smart charcoal linen dress and glossy black heels that I borrowed from my friend Dee to wear today, in the hope that they would make me seem professional and calm; reassuring, even. But now I suspect the businesslike outfit is just alienating me even more – if that were possible – from everyone else in their jeans, thick sweaters and flat boots.

It's-Margaret-fucking-Thatcher, a man muttered under his breath as I walked in. He looked about twenty-five. I was amazed that she was even in his frame of reference at all.

'No idea what you were doing,' the lumberjack shirt man barks from the front row. 'It's a bloody disgrace!'

'You bought it on a whim,' snaps the beanie hat woman.

'A vanity project!' cries someone else.

'Thought it'd be fun to have it—'

21

'With no thought of what it'd involve . . .'

'Bloody idiots, the pair of them!'

I've lost track of who's saying what, and even if I could come up with something helpful to say – something to calm the simmering fury – I wouldn't be able to get a word in. The only person remaining silent is Harry, one of the few employees I know by name, and whom I hadn't expected to be here today. He's just sitting there, staring ahead, in faded jeans and a big grey fisherman's sweater. I can hardly bear to look at him.

'You didn't consider the responsibility of what you'd taken on,' announces a woman with spectacles perched low on her nose – and it strikes me now that it could be an animal she's talking about: a dog bought for Christmas with no thought as to who would be walking it and bagging up its poos. And now, as I stand here being shouted at, I'm transported back to a time when my daughter had begged for a dog.

She was almost ten, so it was over a decade ago. I'd explained that, as I was working out of the house all day, it wouldn't be fair to leave one all alone.

'We could get a dog walker,' Frieda suggested.

'Honey, I'm not getting a dog and then employing someone else to walk it.'

'What about *you*, then? You could come home for lunch—'

'Could I?' I laughed. I was working in the centre of York at the recruitment consultancy. 'It's too far from the office,' I added.

'You could run. It'd do you good, Mum. You were saying you need to exercise!'

'I'm not running back and forth to our house every lunchtime . . .'

'You could take him to work then!' So this dog was already a 'he' and not some imaginary, gender-less pet.

'I very much doubt it,' I replied, truthfully.

'Why not?'

I should add that this was long before the entire western world had become obsessed with dogs and started taking them to their offices and lying around on beanbags cuddling them. 'He might pee on the carpet,' I replied.

'Please, Mum,' Frieda begged. 'He wouldn't. We'd train him!'

I knew I was a soft touch. From what I'd gathered, I allowed far more impromptu sleepovers than any of the other mums. However, I refused to give in, and I think I made the right decision in opting for guinea pigs instead. I was still married to Tony then – our children's father – and he'd grudgingly agreed, adding, 'I hope they don't get tired of them, Suzy. You know how fickle kids are.'

We got two, partly so Frieda and Isaac could have one each; plus, I'd read that solo guinea pigs can get lonely. They named them Millie and Maisie (I suspect Frieda over-rode Isaac on that score) and loved them uncondi-tionally. Frieda never asked for a dog again.

I read once that, when you're in the midst of a terrible situation, it's not uncommon for your brain to spin off to a happier time to protect you from the awfulness that's going on. It's a kind of coping mechanism, I think. Perhaps that's why, as the lumberjack shirt man jumps up to shout, and is swiftly joined by almost everyone else until there's a cacophony of yelling and tears are flooding my eyes, I'm picturing that beautiful day – the morning of Frieda's tenth birthday. When I was just a normal mum, respon-sible for my own little family and *not the inhabitants of an entire island whose lives were about to be wrecked.*

23

'I love this icing!' Isaac, who was eight, had said as he lurched towards the cake I'd made the night before. I loved to bake and tend to our little suburban garden. How simple life was back then.

'Hands off, Isaac,' I said. Too late, he was already licking a swirl of chocolate frosting off a finger.

I turned towards Frieda, who'd wandered into the kitchen to see what was going on. 'There's a surprise for you two in the garden,' I said.

'What is it?' she asked.

'Go out and see.' Frieda grinned, then ran out through the back door. Isaac and I hurried after her.

'Mum!' she cried. 'Oh, Mum. Are they ours?' I nodded, too choked to speak for a moment. She and Isaac bobbed down to gaze at the two bundles of beige and white fluff inside the new hutch.

'Can we hold them?' he asked.

'Of course you can,' I said, feeling as if my heart might burst, 'as long as you're careful . . .' Frieda opened the hutch door and they scooped up the animals into their arms.

That's what I'm picturing now, as the shouting goes on and my gaze lands upon the only person in this room who has remained seated: Harry in the grey sweater. In his late seventies, he is by far the oldest team member – but he's not even employed by us anymore. He resigned a few months ago, apparently disgusted with how things were developing here.

I look at him and he gazes back at me, and I'm on the verge of rushing over to hug him. I don't, of course, because I can imagine how that would go down around here.

Who the hell does she think she is, coming out here, trying to hug people?

He's up on his feet now and wiping at his eyes with his hands. Oh God, I think he is crying.

The shouts seem to fade as I watch him striding towards the door. I'm seized by an urge to follow him, even though I know that's the last thing he'd want. So I just stand there, feeling helpless as he leaves; this dignified elderly man, whom I have broken.

It seems incredible that, once upon a time, everything could be made right with a couple of guinea pigs.

Chapter Four

No one wants to hang around and chat after the meeting. Understandably, of course; it's hardly a tea and cake kind of scenario. So it seems there is nothing else for it but to leave as quickly as possible and drive through the heavy rain back to the holiday cottage where I'm staying. I park up with a jolt and march – as much as I can march, in those teetering heels Dee lent me – across the gravelled garden and into the low-slung, single-storey cottage where I bolt the door behind me.

And what does a fully functional grown-up woman do when everything's screwed up? She kicks off her shoes and yanks the screw top off a bottle of wine and pours herself a massive glassful.

I sit at the kitchen table, sipping and sipping and telling myself it's fine, that 5.15 p.m. counts as evening and anyway, what else would I be doing here, all alone? The wind moans outside and rain streams down the small kitchen window. On Sgadansay it's still winter in March. At least I'll be back home in York tomorrow night and not feel quite so wretched and alone.

I've stayed on the island several times since that first visit with Paul, in much nicer cottages than this one. However, this time I booked the cheapest one I could find. I wasn't looking for hot tubs or a Nespresso machine. And at least it was well away from town, down an unmade single-track lane with no other houses nearby. Not that I'd expected anyone to find out where I was staying and egg the windows – but you never know.

Somehow, several hours have spun by. It's almost nine o'clock and pitch-black outside. I say 'somehow' because I'm trying not to admit that I've done nothing more useful than guzzle wine, change into my pyjamas and finally relocate from the kitchen table to the well-worn sofa in the living room. I must have dozed off here, clutching my greasy glass. Now I've woken with a jolt to realise it's still welded to my hand.

And then I hear a noise outside and realise that's what woke me. Something – or someone – is out there. I sit bolt upright, my heart hammering. *One of those angry employees has found out where I'm staying and come to get me.* Perhaps there's a whole bunch of them out there?

There it goes again; a sort of whine. It doesn't sound like a person, but a *thing*. It's high-pitched and plaintive. It stops, then starts up again. We've all seen those films where the scared woman ventures out into the dark – in pyjamas – to investigate. 'Don't be so stupid!' we implore her. 'Just leave it. Make this the one where the lone female in the holiday cottage stays indoors with the TV on and makes a cup of tea.'

So I try to ignore it and tell myself that whatever it is, it'll go away.

In an attempt to keep busy, I turn my attentions to the reams of paperwork I've brought with me in the hope of making some kind of sense out of the distillery's finances. Admittedly, numbers aren't my strong point, and it seems that the associates Paul had roped in on that side of things have turned out to be as flaky – and elusive – as he is. Calling the team together seemed like the most urgent thing to do. If nothing else, it felt important to meet everyone properly and to show that I cared, that I was trying to take control of things now.

I'd asked Paul about the team numerous times, but he was always so evasive. Whenever I was more forceful and demanded to know what kind of financial state we were in, he'd become defensive and more than once it had erupted into a row. Didn't I trust him? Couldn't I understand that he was giving the business his all? Although I hadn't invested any money I was still a director – because he'd insisted it would be a joint venture – and the situation had started to give me sleepless nights.

Of course I should have tried harder and *forced* the information out of him. Orders were being cancelled; loyal customers who'd stocked Sgadansay whisky for years were switching to other brands. There were technical problems that Paul wouldn't address, and a radical rebranding he'd 'masterminded', which had proved to be so unpopular as to be laughable. But still, everything was 'fine', he kept insisting – or we were 'just having a few hiccups'.

I fiddle about with spreadsheets, scribbling notes in the dimly lit living room. But the whining continues, making it impossible to focus. Perhaps it's trees blowing, or just the wind – or maybe I'm imagining it? Admittedly, I worked my way through the whole bottle of wine I'd bought at what was quaintly termed 'Mary's Store', having had no proper dinner. Whilst I'm not exactly staggering around, crashing into doors, I wouldn't like to operate heavy machinery.

Maybe I should try to knock together some semblance of a proper meal to mop up the booze? At least the noise seems to have stopped. I go through to the kitchen and peer around in the gloom. I've been here for two days, existing on food that needs no chopping, cooking or in fact any prep whatsoever, apart from being *opened*. There's a tub of paprika Pringles, a sliced white loaf, some cream crackers and a couple of packets of unexciting biscuits. They look like the provisions of a student who can't get it together to boil a pan of pasta, not a forty-eight-year-old mother of two.

I'm eating the Pringles disgustingly – cramming them in by the stack – when the whining starts up again. 'Sod this,' I mutter. I stride to the porch window and peer out. It's so dark out there, and still raining so heavily, I can't make anything out. And I find myself wishing – maddeningly – that Paul were here. Never mind that he's the very reason why my life's in this mess. At least he'd go out to investigate, and come back in to reassure me that there was nothing out there, nothing to worry about at all.

And *then* I could go back to hating him.

But Paul's not here. It's just me and jaunty Mr Pringles with his swirly moustache. 'Stack 'n' share', it says on the orange tube. No chance of that, even if there was anyone here to share them with. Back in the kitchen, I'm crunching them by the handful to try and sober myself up and drown out the noise of the thing outside (multitasking!). Now it's not only whining but scratching at the door as well – with *claws*, it sounds like. What kind of thing has claws around here?

In panic, I try to list the animals I've ever seen on the island: cattle, horses, red deer, sheep – and seals. It's none of them, obviously, so what the hell is it? I've heard that there are wildcats in the Highlands, but I didn't think there were any on the islands. Maybe one swam across? What kind of cat would do that? A deranged one, I decide, picturing it ploughing determinedly through the cold, black water, its fur slicked back from his face.

I peer through the porch window again. 'Hello?' I call out sharply, trying to give the impression that I'm a tough, no-nonsense islander rather than a feeble visitor. I wish I could phone someone, not for help or advice (what could anyone do?), but just to hear a friendly voice – another human being. But there's no mobile signal here. For that, I'd have to go down to the end of the lane, climb onto the big rock at the side of the main road and wave my phone in the air (I only know this because a previous guest was kind enough to write detailed instructions in the visitors' book). There's no landline either, or even Wi-Fi, which I'd viewed as a positive when I booked this place; a chance to clear the mental clutter. But really, what was I thinking? Anything could happen to me and no one would know.

Idyllic remote location, read the blurb when I booked this place, as if I were coming here for pleasure. *Glorious views over the bay.* Now I'm starting to imagine Isaac and Frieda being delivered the terrible news that their mother's body was found, mauled to death by some unnamed beast, and the autopsy revealed that she was entirely full of Echo Falls and Pringles.

How did I plummet from being a calm, capable, cake-baking mother to this? 'Get a grip on yourself,' I instruct myself, tipsily. After all, a wildcat is just a cat. It's simply a bit bigger, and more feral, than your average puss. So how scary can it actually be?

I stare down at the letterbox. It has one of those brushy things to stop draughts coming in. Every nerve in my body seems to be jangling as I wait for a paw to jab through it. I crouch down, lean in close and call out, shakily, 'Go away!'

That'll scare the shit out of it.

There's another scrape on the door.

'Just-fuck-off!' I bellow eloquently as I straighten up. I stand there and wait. Behind me in the kitchen, the fridge – which was possibly manufactured in something like 1967 – grumbles ominously. I try to transmit to whatever's out there that I am not to be messed with, and it must go away.

WOOF!

It barked. The thing actually barked like a dog.

Woof! it goes again. It barked like a dog because it *is* a dog! Why would anyone come to my door with a dog at nearly ten o'clock at night?

'Hello?' I shout out, more forcefully now. 'Who is this?'

Could they be lost, or having some kind of emergency? Maybe they need help. But surely they could *say* something, to show they're not planning to rob or attack me? There's a short burst of barking and another plaintive whine. It's a smallish dog, judging by the pitch. It doesn't *sound* like a robber's dog. I peer through the porch window and glimpse a wagging tail and a distinctly non-threatening face. Crucially, I can't see anyone with it. The dog needs help, I decide. I ease the door open a little.

A nose appears first, black and trembling, then a small, wet face – mainly a scruffy biscuit brown with lighter patches around the eyes. It's a terrier type, I think; possibly a mixture, with a white patch in its chest. Whatever it is, it looks terribly skinny and hardly seems like it's planning to tear me limb from limb. 'Well, hello,' I say cautiously. 'Who are you?'

31

The dog is shivering, obviously cold and scared. I glance around for a person but there's definitely no one out there on this bleak, wet night.

I look down at the dog. It stares back at me, not barking now but just standing there, looking hopeful. 'You poor little thing,' I murmur. 'Are you lost?' Maybe he – he's definitely a he, I realise now – ran off during a late-night walk, and someone's out there looking for him. 'Hello?' I call out. 'There's a dog here! Has anyone lost a dog?'

It's so quiet out here, and so dark – the kind of velvety blackness you never see in a town or a city. You certainly don't see it in York, or even in the small North Yorkshire market town where my parents live and where I grew up. Here, there are no street lamps or lights from other houses, or sounds from distant cars. There aren't even any stars visible tonight.

I bend down to pat the dog's head. He licks at my hand. Gathering courage now, I beckon him into the tiny porch where we shelter from the rain, with the front door open, as we wait for someone to show up looking for him. He has a collar, I notice – a smart red leather one – but no tag, no form of ID as far as I can make out.

I stroke him some more and tickle him gently behind his ears. Dogs usually like that, I recall now, although the only dog I've ever really known was Daffy, my Aunty Helen's huge, fluffy blonde pillow of a golden retriever who I'd loved to cuddle as a kid. But my mother had always warned me to never go near any dog that I didn't know. 'They're not all like Daffy,' she warned. 'They can snap with no warning. Never trust a dog that just comes up to you.' I study my visitor as he sits pertly, close to my feet, as if trying to demonstrate how unthreatening he is.

'So, what shall we do with you?' I ask him. My options

seem to be to send him away into the miserable night (clearly unthinkable), or to stand here in the doorway for God knows how long – or I could let him in.

When I booked this place, the owner was adamant about the no pets rule. She even messaged me just to make doubly sure I'd understood, even though it was stipulated on the website. *It's fine,* I replied, *I don't have any pets.*

You'd be amazed at how many people try to sneak a dog in, Shona had messaged back. I had wondered if she was being prickly because she knew who I was, even though I'd used my maiden name when booking (I've kept my ex-husband Tony's surname – Medley – simply because it matches the kids'). But then, on previous visits to the island, everyone I'd met around town had been friendly. *You're just being paranoid,* I told myself. *She just doesn't want dogs bringing in mud and chewing the soft furnishings.*

And now, as the dog peers at me expectantly, I'm thinking: never mind Shona and her rules. She'll never know. I'm about to beckon him in when he gets up and shoots past my pyjama-clad legs, straight through to the kitchen where he stands, wagging his short white tail and panting up at me.

'Oh, okay then,' I say. 'Do come in.' My God – my mouth has actually formed a smile! It feels like nothing short of a miracle tonight.

The past few months have been terrible. Today's meeting counts as one of the worst experiences of my life. But now this small, scruffy dog has shown up out of nowhere, and he's caused something to flicker inside me.

It's a tiny glimmer of hope.

Chapter Five

Ricky

'Dad, please calm down. Getting upset won't help anything.'

'Why should I calm down?' he thunders. 'She comes up here, lords it all over us, goes on about how bloody *sorry* she is—'

'I know, you're absolutely right. It's awful.' I am pacing about, phone pressed to my ear, in the hallway of my Glasgow flat. It's half ten and it's unheard of for my father to call me so late. While not drunk exactly, I can tell he's had a few.

'God knows what's going to happen to everyone now.' He exhales forcefully.

'I know, Dad. I know.'

'. . . in her high heels, clopping about like lady bloody muck—'

'It's terrible, but try not to get worked up about it. It's probably best to try and move on from it now you've—'

'Been sacked,' he says bluntly. 'Slung out on my ear.'

'*Left*, Dad. You resigned, didn't you?'

'No choice really. If I hadn't, I'd have been pushed. You know how things were going. Sod the bloody pair of them.'

34

I catch Meg's eye as she curls up on the sofa. She came over to my place straight from work after a full day of back-to-back appointments at her own alternative therapy practice. I'd just got home too, having picked up Arthur from after-school club as I had an after-hours group myself today.

At ten years old my son has reached the stage where he's distinctly unkeen that his school has been added to my rota, although he's fully aware that peripatetic music teachers don't get to choose where they teach. In the state system we're given our allocation of schools to visit, and that's that. We can't say, 'Sorry, my son finds me a bit of an embarrassment. D'you mind if I skip Corrybank Primary?' He was still a bit huffy when we got home, but I cheered him up with his favourite sausages and crinkle-cut oven chips, which he squirted liberally with ketchup from our plastic tomato-shaped dispenser and shovelled down as if stoking a steam locomotive. Meanwhile I made a prawn risotto for Meg and me (Arthur would never classify a 'pile of rice' – as he terms my girlfriend-pleasing speciality – as a proper dinner, and Meg would never ingest an oven chip).

I realise my mind has wandered as Dad reiterates, angrily, what 'that damn woman' said at the distillery meeting today.

'Maybe it wasn't such a good idea to go,' I offer.

'I just wanted to know what was happening,' he snaps; then, as if catching himself, he adds, 'Oh, I'm sorry, son.' I'm forty-nine years old and he still calls me son. 'It just got to me a bit today,' he adds.

'I know, Dad, and it's fine. Of course you're upset.'

'Not your fault, though, is it?' This twists my gut a little. It's so unlike Dad to apologise. I'm used to his gruff manner, so typical of the older men on the island. He's worked hard all his life, keeping his house and garden together and driving all over Sgadansay, delivering groceries to elderly people when the weather's particularly bad. Which, frankly, is a lot of the time out there.

'Got to look after the old folk,' Dad always says, as if he's a spring chicken himself when he's actually seventy-eight. Yet as far as I'm aware, there's never been a word of self-pity or dissatisfaction out of him, ever – not until he was pretty much forced out of his job. There hadn't been so much as a moan out of him when he was looking after Mum, who had emphysema, or when she died a decade ago. More recently, the whole island knew he was devastated when his beloved collie died peacefully in her sleep last year. But Dad wouldn't acknowledge that he missed their daily walks, even though he and Bess had been inseparable. Arthur was so upset, I guess he cried enough tears for both of them.

'Shall we come up, Dad?' I suggest. 'Me and Arthur, I mean?' Meg gets up from the sofa in her faintly equine way and strolls past me to the kitchen.

'But you've only just been here,' he remarks.

'Well, yes, but we could come again, if you're feeling a bit—'

'I'm fine!' he exclaims. 'You're coming in the Easter holidays, aren't you?'

'Yeah, but that's still weeks away. How about we head up on Friday straight after work?'

'Oh, there's no need for that. You'd never make the last ferry anyway.'

'Well, I could fly—'

'What for?' he gasps.

36

I can't help smiling at that. 'To see you of course. To check you're okay—'

'You'd fly up from Glasgow?' he splutters.

'Yes, of course.' *That is where I live, after all . . .*

'But it's a fortune!' The very thought of this seems to agitate him even more than the distillery woman. Dad's frugality knows no bounds. I feared that he'd have a coronary when I once let slip that I'd put the oven on solely to bake a jacket potato.

'Well, yeah, but I'm happy to come,' I tell him.

'No, that's just crazy,' he says firmly. 'Like we said, I'll see you in the Easter holidays.'

'Okay,' I concede. 'But you do remember Arthur's not coming this time, don't you? He's being whisked off by his mate's family to Alicante—'

'Of course I remember. I might've been given the shove, but I'm not senile, son.'

'I know that, Dad.' Would I dare to suggest that he's less than fully in control of his faculties? 'So it'll just be me and Meg,' I add. 'She's really looking forward to meeting you, Dad.'

'Aye, I'm looking forward to it too,' he concedes, and just as I'm thinking, that's better, I hope he's planning to dial down the grumpiness when we visit, he adds, 'but she'll have to take me as she finds me.'

For crying out loud, how else would she take him? She's hardly expecting a home cinema or an infinity pool. 'Yes, of course she will,' I say firmly. 'It's going to be great.'

I find Meg in the kitchen, about to make her special tea. She keeps a Kilner jar of it here, and another containing her toasted coconut granola. 'Meg's gravel,' as Arthur jokingly calls it, preferring Coco Pops himself (which she finds repellent). The appearance of these jars a few months ago seemed to mark a significant shift in our relationship.

With her own wooden scoop, she transfers hibiscus flowers to the teapot and sloshes in boiling water. She grows and dries these flowers herself, in window boxes, supplying upmarket delis across the posher part of the city where she lives. I'd never have imagined such an enterprise could make her a little extra money, but it does, although she's admitted she doesn't really need it. Apparently, her therapy practice is thriving. She just does it for the enjoyment and loves cycling about with her wicker basket full of cellophane packets of petals. Plus, it's all great 'content', as she calls it, for her Instagram.

'Sounds like Dad had a shitty day,' I tell her.

'So I gathered,' she says. 'It's really awful, what's happened up there. But maybe it's for the best . . .' She pours her pinkish tea.

'In what way?' I ask.

She blows across the rim of the pale blue mug she brought from her own place, having deemed my selection unacceptable. She requires a fine porcelain one with a white interior: not too big, she insists, because she 'can't get with this thing of drinking tea from a bucket'; and any other colour of interior and she literally can't drink from it. 'Well, he's quite old to be working full-time, isn't he?'

'Yeah, but it was his whole life really. I don't know what he's going to do with himself now.'

Meg pulls a sympathetic face. 'Maybe it'll just take him a bit of time to adjust.'

'I guess so,' I concede. When Meg and I met in a coffee shop just over a year ago, I couldn't believe this natural beauty was interested in me – although she says I was hard to miss as I was carrying a double bass at the time. When she'd started quizzing me about it, then asked if she could share a table with 'the two of you' (i.e. me and the bass) I thought she might be working up to asking about lessons.

'I hope I'm not playing gooseberry,' she remarked, glancing from me to the bass and back to me again.

'No, not at all,' I said.

'D'you normally hang out together,' she teased, 'in coffee shops?'

'Not usually,' I replied. 'But I've just picked it up from being repaired and it's so cold out there . . .'

'Aw, doesn't its case have a sheepskin lining?' My God, I thought, as her blue eyes kind of danced as she laughed, this woman might just possibly be flirting with me. I'd meant I'd wanted a coffee to warm myself up.

Bar a few short-lived relationships, I'd been pretty much single since Arthur was six, when the terrible stuff happened with his mum, stuff I don't like to think about, even now. For the first year or so without Katy it was all I could do to look after him and keep things together at home. I took some time off work, but as my meagre savings dwindled I had to ease my way back into teaching, first with private lessons and then back in schools. We needed money, after all. The years rolled on, and the women I met usually came to the conclusion that I was 'distant' and 'impossible to get close to'. They said they understood why but, of course, I was hardly brilliant boyfriend material.

Looking back, I realise a couple of these women viewed me as someone to be rescued – but the last thing I wanted was to 'talk about things' and rake over what had happened with Katy. Arthur had adored his mum. As a toddler he'd roared in protest if she so much as went to the loo. Mostly, Katy didn't mind, but occasionally she'd explode. 'You're like a parasite!' she yelled once, and literally fled from him, out of our flat, banging the door behind her. Arthur cried and cried.

As he grew older, he'd beg her to bake or paint pictures with him, and on the rare occasions when she agreed, he'd literally radiate happiness. So he certainly didn't want a replacement mother figure, and I know a couple of women were hurt when he seemed less than enthralled by their presents: the dinosaur T-shirt, the invisible ink pen, the Batman outfit that didn't quite hit the right note.

My last girlfriend, Paula, went all out to be Arthur's mate, constantly trying to haul him out to the park when he just wanted to lie on the sofa. One time she tried to teach him dance routines (not Arthur's scene *at* all). Then she persuaded a friend to dress up as Santa and show up at our flat on a 'special visit', long after Arthur had stopped believing that his presents came from a workshop in Lapland. My mortified son tried to look pleased, but lacked the acting skills and 'Santa' shuffled off into the rain like a rebuffed door-to-door salesman.

'What's wrong with him?' Paula exclaimed, when he'd politely declined a trip to the trampolining centre with her. *Nothing,* I wanted to say. *Just leave him be.* But she was trying so hard; she was a good, kind person and the whole thing made me exasperated with him, and also deeply, deeply sad. 'You can't say I didn't fucking try,' was her parting shot when we broke up.

Was I failing as a father? Or was I one of those men who's just useless at relationships? My track record suggested that might be the case, and for a long time I stopped seeing anyone at all. As women weren't exactly beating a path to my door, it wasn't difficult to remain single. I mean, it's not as if I had to build an electrified fence to keep them at bay. I was barely 'alone' anyway, having Arthur and a full work timetable, which had become more and more crazy over the years as budgets had been cut and there were fewer teachers to cover all the schools. So I was doing fine on my own, keeping things simple, with as few complications as possible.

Then along came Meg, and she didn't seem like a complication at all.

There was a sheen of self-assuredness about her that I found extremely attractive, and before I knew it an hour had drifted by in that coffee shop. 'D'you fancy a drink sometime?' she'd asked as we left.

Bloody hell! Of course I fancied a drink! 'That'd be lovely,' I said. We exchanged numbers and off I went, the double bass suddenly seeming like no burden at all, no more troublesome than a penny whistle.

As we started seeing each other, it became clear that Meg didn't view herself as my 'rescuer', even as details emerged about my past. She was sympathetic, but we didn't dwell upon anything, which suited me fine. And incredibly, Arthur seemed to like her – perhaps because, while friendly and sweet with him, she didn't go overboard on trying to be his best mate, which seemed like the perfect way to go about things. Clearly focused on her business, she had never wanted children. She didn't seem overly concerned about being *my* best mate either; from the off, there was a sense of aloofness emanating from her, and I figured that she was just used to doing her own thing. I meant it positively when I described her to friends as 'really driven and independent'. And when my friend Brenna asked, 'So, are you in love then, Ricky?'

41

I blustered, 'She's fantastic, yeah.' Which I guess didn't really answer her question.

'This might be a bit controversial,' Meg says now, still clutching her mug, 'but your dad could retire, couldn't he? I mean, that's what people do, isn't it?'

'They do,' I say, 'but unfortunately he's not the retiring type.'

Meg shrugs. 'Could he take up a new hobby then?'

I can't help smiling at this. Again, I find myself wondering what Meg and my father will make of each other when they meet in the Easter holidays. Like me, Meg is an only child, but there our similarities end. She was brought up in one of the smartest suburbs of Glasgow – where her affluent parents still live – and she enjoys treating herself to luxury yoga retreats on the Greek islands. Obviously, staying in a little terraced cottage with no central heating on a Hebridean island will be a little different. *I have been to Skye, you know,* she's reminded me. *I'm not a complete urbanite.* Yes, but she stayed in a boutique hotel and dined at a Michelin-starred restaurant. And Sgadansay is way smaller than Skye, with less than a quarter of the population. It's not quite 'everyone knows each other' territory, but most people do, at least by sight.

'He's not really the hobby type either,' I tell her.

'What about his garden?' she asks. 'Does he grow vegetables?'

'Just potatoes. Unfortunately that's the only vegetable he'll tolerate.'

Meg laughs dryly. 'I can see where Arthur gets it from then.' I decide to let this go. She's made it clear that she thinks I'm too easy-going with Arthur's meals, with my willingness to dish up oven chips and the fact that I have

42

given up nagging him to eat salad. 'Could your dad get another dog?' she suggests. 'Didn't you say he adored his collie?'

I shake my head. 'I've suggested that. He said he'd never have another one after Bess. He wouldn't admit it, because he'll never admit to having any emotions at all, really – but I don't think he could stand the idea of losing a dog again.'

Meg sighs. 'Okay, I can understand that. But there must be *something* he could get into.'

'Honestly, I can't think of anything.'

'How about chickens?'

I splutter with laughter.

'I'm serious, Ricky! Why not? He'd have eggs—'

'He's not a chicken-keeping kind of guy, trust me.'

'What about pigeons then?' she suggests.

'Why would he want pigeons?' I ask, genuinely baffled by this.

'Well, it's a thing, isn't it, with older men? Racing them, I mean. Our gardener was into it . . .'

'Your gardener?' I repeat with a grin.

'Yeah.' She shrugs dismissively. 'He was mad about his birds. He'd get some bloke to drive them to Penzance or something and release them and they'd fly all the way home to Glasgow—'

'Yeah, that's it! That'd take his mind off his job.' Despite the bleakness of my conversation with Dad, I'm chuckling now.

'I'm serious, Ricky,' Meg insists. 'When people lose their jobs they need something to give them a sense of purpose and structure.'

'How did your parents manage, when they retired?' I ask with genuine interest. I know her dad was something

43

pretty high up in book publishing and her mother ran an actors' agency.

'Mum set up her little catering thing,' she reminds me. 'You know – the grazing tables she does.'

'Oh, yes.' She's mentioned this, and described it as a kind of modern take on the party buffet. I gather it's somewhat more evolved than cheese cubes and chipolatas on sticks.

'And they went into party overload,' she adds with a grin. 'Barbecues, dinner parties – they're busier than ever these days.'

I think about Dad, whose idea of socialising is pretty much limited to a few pints at the Anchor.

'It's important to stay connected to people,' she adds. 'Otherwise it can really take a toll on their mental health, you know?' Suddenly, I don't like the way this conversation is going. 'You should suggest something,' she adds. 'Go on – suggest pigeon racing . . .'

I snigger as I start to load the dishwasher. 'Dad's barely left the island in years. I can't imagine him driving all the way down to Cornwall with some birds in a cage—'

'No, *someone else* drives them.'

'So what would Dad do then?'

She shrugs. 'Sit and wait for them to come home!'

'Like they're wayward teenagers out on the lash? He'd be no more likely to join the quilters' society.'

'I'm just saying—'

'Or crochet a hammock,' I add. 'Maybe that's what he should start doing? Get one of the neighbours to teach him to crochet and then—'

'Granddad's learning to crochet?' Arthur grins at me from the doorway.

'Hey,' I say, 'what're you doing up?'

44

'Nothing,' he replies. 'But you know my birthday?'

'Er, yes, I think I'm aware that it's coming up,' I tease him.

He crosses his arms and tilts his head. 'Could I have a dog?'

I splutter and turn to Meg. 'We go through this every year and he's been even worse since we met that stray dog on the beach . . .'

'And he always says no,' Arthur retorts, 'because he works all day and we don't have a garden—'

'Which, you have to admit, count as valid reasons,' I say.

'Your dad's right,' remarks Meg, glancing at the wall clock; she reckons I'm a bit lax about Arthur's bedtime too. 'Kids of his age need ten hours' sleep a night,' she adds when I've ushered him back to his room.

'Yeah. Well, he probably gets that most nights.' I try to push away the small niggle I experience whenever she tells me how to parent my own kid. And later still, as we go to bed, I wonder if it's me who's being oversensitive, with all the stuff about Dad. I'm not an angry person usually. Arthur exasperates me sometimes but I'm hardly ever properly cross with him. However, ever since it all kicked off on the island I *have* felt angry – with the people who handled everything so badly and let down Dad, his friends and neighbours; the whole community really.

Paul Leighton and Suzanna Medley. The couple who appeared two years ago, seemingly out of nowhere, and proceeded to destroy a distillery that had been doing brilliantly until then. So yes, I'm angry. But more than that, I just feel so helpless that I can't make everything all right.

45

Chapter Six

Suzy

At her dog-nagging peak, Frieda took to gathering facts about their characteristics. For instance, I learnt that your average dog is as smart as a two-year-old child, and that they are more similar to humans than any other animal – so really, it would be *just like having another little person in the house*. 'And you know how we have six million smell receptors in our noses?' she added. In fact, I hadn't known that. 'Dogs have 300 million,' she'd announced, as if that would swing it. 'Smelling is their way of gathering clues about their habitat.'

'Amazing,' I said. *But we're still not getting one, honey.*

I watch now as my visitor snuffles his way around the kitchen. 'Is that what you're doing?' I ask him. 'Are you gathering information for your little doggie brain?' Already, there are muddy paw prints on the pale green linoleum. 'Wait here a sec,' I add. Ignoring my request, he trots after me to the minuscule bathroom as I fetch my own towel in order to dry him off. I don't feel brave enough to use one of the house towels on a soggy dog who's not even meant to be here.

46

Back in the kitchen he stands obediently as I pat down his short coat and wipe his paw prints off the floor. 'Shona doesn't allow pets,' I explain. 'She emailed me about it. So we'd better not leave any evidence that you've been here.'

As we study each other it occurs to me that something peculiar has happened. Instantly, I seem to have slipped into being the kind of person who not only talks to unfamiliar dogs, but does so in a special *talking-to-dogs* kind of voice. Why has this happened? It's as if I'm assuming that, if I speak at a certain frequency, he'll understand mysterious concepts such as 'Shona', 'email' and 'evidence'. 'If you had a tag with a phone number on it,' I tell him, 'we could go down to the end of the lane, and I'd stand on that rock, waving my phone about until we got a signal. And I'd call your owner and tell them you've been found.'

Even more bizarrely – as if he can follow my ramblings – I'm now worried that in mentioning the lack of identity tag, I'm making him feel worse. *If your owner had cared for you properly then we'd be able to get you safely back home.* 'Have you been abandoned?' I ask, ruffing the top of his head. This strikes me as unlikely. The community here seems to be incredibly close-knit, and I'd imagine that any local dog would be recognised and returned instantly. It's more probable, I reckon, that he's strayed from his garden and his owner will come looking for him soon.

'Let's get you a drink,' I tell him, on high alert now for the sound of an approaching vehicle. In the absence of anything more suitable, I fish out a cereal bowl from a cupboard and try not to think how Shona would react as I fill it and place it before him. He laps at it noisily until all the water has gone.

'Wow, you were thirsty,' I murmur as I refill it. 'Bet you're hungry too.' He certainly looks terribly thin, but

47

maybe that's just his breed? Or perhaps these hardy islanders simply don't overindulge their pets, and what I'm viewing as skinny is actually a healthy weight? He whines pitifully, and for a moment my own bleak situation pales into insignificance compared to the pressing matter of what to give him. At nearly eleven o'clock there'll be no shop open in town. Even if there was, I've downed that bottle of wine so I wouldn't be driving anywhere. The dog barks sharply as if to emphasise that dinner is required urgently.

I scan the kitchen with its beige tiles patterned with wheat sheaves and milkmaids for something to offer my visitor. Remembering the small block of cheddar in the fridge, I glance at my phone on the worktop. The lack of signal and Wi-Fi is beginning to irritate because there are so many things I need to google:

Can dogs eat cheese?
Can dogs eat paprika Pringles?
Lost dog Sgadansay
Dog rescue Hebrides
Where to report a lost dog

He whines some more but seems to perk up as I take the cheese out of the fridge and cut off a sliver. He guzzles it down. I give him a tiny bit more, then offer him a Pringle. This too is wolfed. Remembering now that Aunty Helen would give Daffy buttered toast just before bed, I make a slice for my guest. He devours it with enthusiasm. Hoping that'll be enough to keep him going, we head through to the living room.

Here, he sniffs his way around the periphery, paying special attention to the gas fire, which I haven't dared to ignite for fear that it might explode in my face. There's intense exploration of the luridly patterned carpet, then it's onwards to the green corduroy pouffe, where perhaps he detects the whiff of previous guests' feet; all those couples on romantic breaks, like Paul and me on our first visit to the island two years ago, when I was still deranged enough to be in love with him.

As I watch my new friend it strikes me that perhaps Frieda was right, and that dogs are more similar to humans than I'd realised. For instance, what he's doing now is pretty much what I do whenever I arrive in a hotel room and need to check things out before I can settle. All this sniffing is his equivalent of investigating the minibar, the cellophane packets of biscuits, the tea sachets and minia-ture toiletries. On and on he goes, working his way around the sofa, then meandering back to the pouffe where he—

'No, no, don't do that!' I cry out. *We absolutely do not cock our legs against the pouffe when checking out our accommodation!*

Of course he doesn't halt on command. He just carries on peeing, the minutes seeming to stretch as I watch helplessly, too scared to try to manhandle him away from it – and where would I manhandle him *to*? He'd just carry on piddling a stream across the carpet and that wouldn't help things at all.

Christ, how much urine can a small animal actually contain? Rather than possessing such a thing as a bladder, it seems to me that this little dog is a hollow vessel entirely filled with wee. On and on it goes, with me trapped watching as if it's one of those YouTube clips Paul was so fond of: the acrobatic kittens or the lady's hat being eaten by a giraffe at the zoo. Only now, the laughter factor and thumbs-up emojis are decidedly lacking as the peeing goes on interminably, distorting time and space as I sense myself ageing rapidly, my face wrinkling and sagging until finally . . . the sprightly flow dwindles to a mere trickle, and then stops.

I stare at the sizeable wet patch. Seemingly unconcerned, the dog wanders off to inspect the bookshelf, where amongst the well-thumbed romances and thrillers I happened to spot a gnarly old copy of *Don't Sweat The Small Stuff*.

Oh, I'm sweating it all right. I'm sweating the big *and* the small stuff, thank you very much, as I grab the washing-up liquid and a spongy wipe from the kitchen and return to scrub at the pouffe. I scrub and scrub, silently testing out the various lies I could tell, in case I'm rumbled: *Oh, I'm sorry, Shona! I've no idea how your pouffe got wet. Maybe I spilt some tea? Or could there be a leak from the roof?*

Realising I'm starting to rub away at the corduroy's fluffy pile, I fetch my towel and blot away what I can of the wetness and washing-up liquid froth. I sigh loudly and push back my hair from my clammy forehead, now regretting that I hadn't bought more wine at Mary's Store. Or gin – yes, gin would be excellent right now. I'm not mad at the dog, though – not really. It was probably my fault, for giving him two bowlfuls of water and not letting him outside to pee it all out. Is that how dogs work? They drink, it literally shoots through their systems and you have to let them out pretty much straight away?

'I wish I could phone someone,' I murmur, giving him a reassuring stroke, to show that he's not in trouble. 'I'm probably not looking after you very well.' I think of Frieda, who's likely to be hanging out with her housemates in Cumbria over a few beers, with music filling their kitchen. They're a hearty, outdoorsy bunch, not averse to a party but still with the energy to hike up a mountain the following day. And then there's Isaac, who might well have a history essay due in tomorrow, but probably has a pile of friends round and has most likely decided to finish it 'later' (which, for him, usually means working through the night).

Whereas Frieda grafted steadily at school, determined to get on that outdoor leadership course, Isaac, although undoubtedly smart, was more chaotic. Tony and I had long since divorced by the time our kids had reached their mid-teens, and I was living with Paul. However, Tony and I still got along well enough to panic together over what would become of our boy with his exploding biros and illegible notes. We could still lament over the fact that he barely seemed to know when his A-levels were happening, let alone getting it together to revise for them. Incredibly to us, he pulled it out of the bag and gained a place at Liverpool University.

Sometimes – like now – I'm hit with a wave of missing them so much it causes an actual ache in my gut. They both love their student lives, which of course is brilliant for them but in practice it means I hardly ever see them. When I visit, it has to be carefully planned to fit in among their numerous social engagements.

I know this is healthy, and I'd never dream of guilt-tripping my kids by hinting that I'm lonely without them sometimes. But I am, and it's been happening more often since Paul walked out, leaving only a note and this colossal mess for me to deal with. Without warning, my eyes brim with tears. Oh God, what a soggy heap of self-pity I am these days. I perch on the sofa and rest my head in my hands as the tears pour out. Rain patters at the window, and I'm aware of the gentle nudge of a small snout against my leg.

I sweep my hands back from my wet face and look down. I can't help smiling at the dog's expectant expression. He seems to interpret this as an invitation to jump up and join me on the sofa, where he presses his small, warm body close to my leg. After the pouffe incident it hardly seems worth shooing him off. As he snuggles closer I realise it's highly unlikely that anyone's going to come looking for him tonight.

Which means he'll have to stay the night with me.

'You're like a little Boy Scout on a night hike,' I tell him gently, 'and you've lost your pack.' I sit in silence for a few moments, stroking his soft head. 'I'll call you Scout,' I add. It's probably not terribly original – but then I'm not terribly sober either (although, admittedly, the pouffe incident straightened me out a bit). Anyway, it's only a temporary name, and I'll have to call him *something* if we're going to spend the night together.

'You can stay,' I tell him, 'but don't do anything crazy during the night.' He blinks at me, then lets out a contented sigh as he rests his chin on my thigh. I look down at him, wondering why he chose to come to this cottage in particular, in the middle of nowhere. Does he know it? Or was it just a random thing? Or, with those 300 million scent receptors did he somehow sniff out my misery and decide to drop by to cheer me up?

His warm, thin body is rising and falling with each breath now. I think he has fallen asleep. I close my eyes, barely daring to breathe in case it disturbs him. Because I'm so honoured that, at the end of this terrible day, this dog has chosen to rest his weary head on my leg.

* * *

Milky morning light filters through the thin floral curtains. I lie still for a moment, remembering the events of last night: wine guzzling, Pringle gorging, that noise outside, and the dog—

The dog! I sit bolt upright in bed, remembering now that he hadn't seemed keen on sleeping out in the hall. And I'd been wary of shutting him out of the bedroom in case he took exception to that (do dogs take exception to things?) and did some protest peeing – or worse. So I'd let him sleep with me on the bed. But where is he now?

'Scout!' I call out. 'Scout? Where are you?'

Never mind that his new name will mean nothing to him. The bedroom door is ajar; did I leave it open last night? I can't remember. I swivel out of bed and hurry through to the living room – no sign of him there – then into the kitchen where he is standing, tail wagging as he looks up at me with what I can only interpret as delight. A jumper is lying on the floor. He must have pulled it off the sofa and dragged it through.

'*Here* you are,' I exclaim, bobbing down to greet him. 'I thought you were one of those guys who sneaks off in the night and calls a taxi.' He licks my face, which I might once have found a bit icky but now seems like an appreciation of my joke.

Pushing away my mother's warning from forty years ago – '*Any* dog can turn nasty, Suzy!' – I gather him up in my arms and cradle him. He seems to be quite happy about this. As I stand there, conscious of his beating heart against my chest, it occurs to me that something significant has happened to me. Compared to the achievements of the incredible people whose obituaries I write, welcoming in a lost dog and keeping him safe until morning might not count as much. However, something seems to have *shifted* since last night. Bright sunlight streams in through the kitchen window, chasing away the gloom. The cottage feels cheerful now – no longer depressingly dated – and befitting those glowing comments I read in the visitors' book:

Thank you, Shona. We loved our stay in your cosy home!
The perfect holiday house for us – the kids adored it.
Amazing hospitality on our favourite Hebridean island.
We'll definitely be back!

I lower Scout carefully to the floor. 'Not so bad here, is it?' I ask him. 'Shame we're not going to have longer together.' I make him a piece of toast and cut him off a sliver of cheese, then stride towards the front door and open it. 'C'mon,' I add, 'we'd better let you out.'

As Scout trots out into the gravelled garden, I stand for a moment and take in the view over the sparkling bay. It's just gone 7.40 a.m. on this clear, cloudless March morning. Checkout is at eleven o'clock; Shona asked me to leave the key on the table, and to simply close the front door behind me. However, my plan is to pack up and leave way before that, so that Scout and I arrive in the town just as the shops and cafés are opening up. I'm booked on the midday ferry back to the mainland, and the more time we have, the higher our chances of finding somewhere safe to leave him – or, better still, of taking him home.

I'm already thinking of us as 'we', I realise as I pick up the navy blue sweater from the floor. It's actually an old one of Paul's that I took to wearing for gardening and mucky jobs. I hold it up by the shoulders and study the hole Scout has gnawed in the middle of it. It's comically large – bigger than a human head – and I can't help chuckling as I toss it aside.

'Never mind, Scout,' I say. 'I never liked that sweater much anyway.'

54

Chapter Seven

Medley Family WhatsApp

Me: Hey, how's things? Hope all okay!
Frieda: Mum! You've got signal :) Yeah all good here. How did the meeting go?
Pretty awful but at least it's done. Relieved about that.
Frieda: So unfair you having to deal with this.
It's fine. Don't worry.
Frieda: Where are you now?
In town sitting on the harbour wall. It's lovely. Loads of gulls diving for fish. Isaac, are you around? How's things with you?
Isaac, after several minutes: Hey Mum, was just about to message you.
That's kind of you, love.
Isaac: Yeah I wanted to ask, is it normal for the microwave to spark like mad when you put something in it?
What?! What did you put in it?
Isaac: Just a burrito from last night.
Why did it spark?

Frieda: Erm, Ize, why are we talking about your burrito when Mum's got this massively important stuff going on?

Isaac: It wasn't the burrito that was sparking, it was the foil.

You put foil in the microwave???

Isaac: Yeah it was wrapped up in foil.

Never do that! It's very dangerous to microwave foil!

Isaac: Yeah Matis said that. Anyway I turned it off.

How did Matis know that and you didn't?

Isaac: Dunno. Better parenting? ;)

Please don't do that again, Isaac, that's all I'm saying.

Isaac: Yeah you already said that.

Frieda: You did A-level physics, Ize!

Isaac: But we never covered that.

Maybe you should have. It'd have been more useful than that thing you teased me about when I didn't know what it was.

Isaac: Geosynchronous orbit? Yeah you'd never even heard of it!

It's a wonder I've managed to keep myself alive.

Isaac: :D

Anyway I also have good news. Exciting news anyway. A dog turned up at the cottage last night! A lost dog with no tag on his collar. So I've come into town to try and find somewhere to take him before I catch the ferry.

Frieda: A dog! What's he like?

Hang on. [I take a picture]. Like this.

Frieda: Oh Mum he's so cute. I love him!!!!!!

Isaac: Have you bought a dog?

Are you reading my messages, Isaac? He came to the cottage last night. He seemed lost. I just wanted to tell you before I take him to the police station.
Frieda: Don't do that. Bring him home!
I can't do that.
Frieda: Why not?
Isaac: Go on, he'd keep you company.
I don't need company thank you, Ize!
Frieda: If he has no tag he's probably a stray. You should definitely keep him.
Maybe it fell off. He must belong to someone. His owner's probably frantic with worry.
Frieda: But what if no one's reported him missing?
Mum: I'll leave him with the police.
Isaac: Do they do that out there? Do they have some kind of dog-holding service?
I don't know! What else d'you suggest?
Frieda: Bring him home.
Isaac: Go on Mum. You know you want to. Just look at that little face.
I know, he's very handsome, love. I'll let you know what happens and PLEASE be more careful in the kitchen, okay?
Isaac: Message received Mum :)

Parenthood is a funny thing, I decide, as I grasp Scout's makeshift lead (we are improvising with a pair of my 30-denier tights). Forget the fact that I appear to be solely responsible for a failing distillery, will probably have to declare bankruptcy and might even lose my home.

Right now I'm thinking, fuck, my son could've burnt the house down.

Chapter Eight

Ricky

Friday morning, and I've arrived at my first school of the day. It's one of the bigger primaries in the area and, significantly, it's Arthur's school. I know he'd like me to avoid him (or, better still, be something else entirely like an engineer or a car salesman; anything but a teacher). But here I am, and there *he* is, sauntering along the corridor with his two best friends.

Ah, the joys of youth, I reflect as he joshes and laughs with Kai and Lucas. They seem to be engaged in some kind of game involving trying to pull at each other's ears, which is causing much hilarity. As Arthur hasn't seen me, his young life hasn't yet been destroyed. If I could, I'd vaporise into the slightly musty air in order to preserve his happiness. But as that's not possible, I carry on walking towards them, carrying a folder of sheet music and a flimsy music stand, which seems to have been twisted into something you might see displayed in the Tate.

'Hi, Ricky!' Kai spots me first. Kai, whose generous parents are taking Arthur with them on their week's holiday at Easter to Alicante. Both he and Lucas are unfazed to see me knocking about on school premises, because I am not their dad.

'Hi,' I say with a smile. However, Arthur isn't smiling. It's as if a shutter has come down over his face, like a shop closing at the end of the day – or perhaps in preparation for impending nuclear attack. He stares at me, his face drained of blood, as if I've strode into his school wearing a mankini.

The message *go-away-go-away-go-away* beams fiercely from his dark eyes. Sorry, I want to tell him, but I'm just doing my job to earn the money that pays for our food, the roof over our heads and the laptop you might be getting for your birthday, if you're lucky. The boys and I pass each other. Just as I sense him relaxing, my phone starts ringing. As I pull it from my pocket the music stand slips from my grasp, tumbling to the floor with a metallic clatter.

The boys glance back. 'Oops,' Kai says, wincing, as Arthur looks askance. I grab the stand and check who's calling; Ralph's name is displayed.

Kai's dad. The boys are marching away now and my phone has stopped ringing. Ralph owns a popular city centre bar and, although we're friends, it's virtually unheard of him to ring me during the working day. There's no time to call him back right now as the string ensemble's due for a rehearsal, and the classroom we use is always a tip.

I prepare the room quickly, rearranging chairs, setting up music stands and rifling through my folder for a simpler cello part, as the current version is proving too tricky for Joey to master. The cello has always been my main instrument. While I'd like to say I've always loved it, it's not quite as simple as that; at a certain point in my teens I wished the darned thing had never been invented. But then it opened up my life in ways I hadn't even dared to imagine.

At eighteen years old I left Sgadansay to study music in Glasgow. I fell in love with the city and made new friends from all over the world. There was a confidence about them, a breezy approach to life that I'd never encountered before. My friends who'd stayed on Sgadansay tended to work at the local shops and businesses, like the distillery, or for the ferry company or on their parents' farms.

I graduated and started working as a tutor in Glasgow schools with private pupils on the side. It was a bit of a scramble as I was still young and all over the place. But I loved living in the city and seemed to have aptitude for teaching kids.

My twenties flew by in a blur. Then, on my thirtieth birthday, something significant happened.

I'd been dragged to a club by some friends; a divey place with banging music. I felt too old, like I didn't belong there. I'd never been a clubber really. Maybe it's because of my island background but I'd always felt happier chatting with a few mates in the pub.

The night dragged on, and just when I'd been thinking of leaving I got chatting to a striking red-headed woman at the bar. Suddenly, I didn't feel too old anymore. I felt like a teenager. This chatty and animated woman turned out to be a pharmacist called Katy who came from London but had studied and settled in Glasgow.

We started seeing each other and fell madly in love. Seven years later our son was born, the image of his beautiful mum. We were thrilled with Arthur, our smiley baby with his shock of red hair, and I never imagined that anything would ever spoil our happiness.

How wrong I was.

In come the kids now, chatting and giggling, eating crisps, swigging from plastic bottles and banging their instrument cases against the furniture. We're prepping for a concert, which is way off in June, thank God, because before any actual playing can begin:

'Mr Vance! I forgot my music.'

'Don't worry, I have a new part for you, Joey . . .'

'Mr Vance! Look at my bow—'

'What happened to it, Natalie? Christ, look at the state of it.' It appears to have been gnawed by an animal.

'My dog got it. He thought it was a stick.' There's a ripple of laughter.

'If your dog can open a violin case,' I venture, 'you should film it and put it on YouTube. Can he play it as well?'

She giggles. 'He can howl along to "Help!" by the Beatles . . .'

'I'd have thought he'd prefer Bach,' I say, which elicits a collective groan. 'Okay, okay,' I add in a more serious tone, 'I'd love to spend the whole session chatting but we've got work to get on with . . .'

There's a scraping of chairs and a fluttering of sheet music falling to the floor. Anaya babbles an excuse about having not practised all week – 'Haven't had time, Mr Vance!' – and there's some raggedy sawing on the cello. And now *finally* Corrybank Primary's string ensemble is ready to make beautiful music. Or at least to batter its way through a Hungarian folk song and then, to lighten things up, *The Scooby-Doo* theme tune, arranged

61

for strings – which is probably more terrifying than anything Scooby and the gang ever found themselves having to deal with.

Session over, I troop out to my car, sitting in the driver's seat for a few minutes in order to scoff a sausage roll before setting off for my next school. Ralph, I remember now. Better call him back.

'Hi, Ricky,' he says. Immediately, I detect the strain in his voice.

'Everything okay?' I ask.

'Yeah. Well . . . kind of. Not really. It's about Easter, mate. The holiday, I mean.'

I frown. 'Oh, what's up?'

He exhales loudly. 'We can't take Arthur. I'm sorry. I mean, none of us are going to Spain. We've cancelled the holiday. Brenna's mum's taken a turn for the worse and we think she's nearing the end now.'

'Oh, God, I am sorry.' I know Ralph's mother-in-law has Alzheimer's and has been in decline for some time.

'Thanks, mate. It's, well, it's hard, you know? Bren says she couldn't forgive herself if she was away when, y'know, *it* happens . . .'

'God, yeah, I totally understand that.'

He clears his throat. 'We could still go, but I really don't feel like taking the boys away without Bren.'

'Of course not,' I say firmly. 'You couldn't do that. You need to be with her. And please don't worry about Arthur, okay? I'm just sorry you're all going through this . . .'

'Thanks,' Ralph murmurs. 'Um, look – we haven't told the boys we're not going yet. We only made the decision this morning and I wanted to speak to you first.' The Fergusons have three boys, Kai being the youngest. 'I didn't want Arthur to hear it from Kai, before we'd spoken,' he adds.

'Honestly, don't even think about that. Just look after yourselves. This is awful for you and Arthur'll be absolutely fine—'

'Will he go up to your dad's instead?' So typical of Ralph to worry about Arthur being disappointed when his mother-in-law is dying.

'Yeah, of course he will,' I reply firmly. 'He'll come to Sgadansay with me and Meg. He loves his granddad. It'll be great.'

Chapter Nine

Suzy

Sgadansay's police station is tucked down a back street and looks like an elderly couple's house. There's a pot of yellow pansies at the door and a cluster of pony ornaments on the inside windowsill. The door is locked. A notice on the wall details its opening hours.

Opening hours, as if it's a museum and not a vital community resource! 'It's shut on Fridays,' I tell Scout. 'Just as well I'm not lying bleeding in the street.' As if he even knows what day of the week it is. He sniffs at a chip on the pavement and scarfs it down (I've noticed that he seems to be on high alert for pavement food and had to whisk him away from a discarded kebab). The notice also says to call 101 in a non-emergency – but how could a call centre operative on the mainland help us?

We wander back to the main shopping street, Scout trotting obediently at my side. On a positive note, at least no one seems to have recognised me from the distillery. We encounter no hostility as we stop off at the butcher's, to see if anyone there knows Scout: 'Sorry, never seen him before,' says a bald man in a stripy apron. He offers him a scrap of ham as if to make up for being unable to help us. People are similarly sympathetic at the cycle repair shop, and at Mary's Store, where I bought my refined carbohydrates and cheap plonk.

When he hears of our predicament, the reedy young man at the till fetches a plastic carton of water for Scout, which he laps at eagerly. He won't accept any money for the box of dry dog food I want to buy. 'You know, a couple of customers mentioned they'd noticed a dog wandering about,' he says, tickling Scout under the chin. 'I think he'd been seen on the beach but he'd run off before they could do anything about it.'

'Poor thing,' I murmur. 'He did seem terribly hungry when he turned up.'

'Someone must know him,' the man adds. 'I'll ask around for you – and good luck.'

'Thanks so much,' I say, touched by his kindness. As I did in the other shops, I leave my number on a scrap of paper, writing 'lost terrier type dog', plus 'Suzanna', my actual name, which no one has used since about 1987.

We arrive at the bakery-cum-teashop where a smiling silver-haired woman comes to the door. 'Don't stand out here,' she insists. 'Bring him in.'

'Oh, if you're sure?' Although Scout has had plenty of opportunities to pee, after the pouffe incident I'm still cautious.

''Course I am, love. Sweet wee thing, isn't he?' Someone on this island is actually calling me *love*? It must be a dog thing, I decide. He seems to be sending out a signal along the lines of, *This lady likes dogs and therefore you can be reassured that she is a good person.*

'He is, yes,' I reply. 'I really hope I can find out who he belongs to.'

'Oh, me too.' She indicates his makeshift lead. 'What's this?'

'My tights,' I reply with a smile. 'I didn't have a lead for him.'

She chuckles. 'Let me see if we have anything in the back room. We get all sorts of stuff left behind.' She disappears briefly and returns with a red leather lead. 'I thought we had one lying around. Look, it even matches his collar!'

'Oh, thank you,' I say. 'D'you need it back at all?'

'Of course not,' she says, unscrewing the lid from a jar of dog biscuits on the counter. 'Can he have one of these?'

The implication that I am Scout's guardian, and therefore the one making important decisions regarding his nutrition, gives me a small glow of pride. 'I'm sure he'd love that.'

He crunches it down and I thank her profusely as we leave. 'You should try the vet's,' she calls after me. 'He's probably microchipped, isn't he? They'll be able to scan him and find out.'

'That *is* a good idea,' I say. 'I should have thought of that. Thank you so much.'

She gives us directions, and I check the time on my phone; almost 11 a.m., so an hour until the ferry departs – although car passengers are supposed to be there half an hour early. 'We'll be fine,' I tell Scout, hoping to radiate confidence. He looks up at me as we walk. My God, he looks as if he's actually smiling again. I try to push away the anxiety that's growing in me now as the veterinary surgery comes into view.

Scout leads the way into the bustling waiting room where a cheerful receptionist taps away at her keyboard, checking lost animal databases (no joy there), then asks us to take a seat. I perch on a chair and Scout sits pertly with ears pricked, as if keenly taking in his new surroundings.

I glance around, feeling a little furtive in the thick of the Sgadansay community with their assorted pets. There's an elderly man with a black and white cat mewling in its carrier, and a mother and daughter with what looks like a hamster in a cardboard box. A tough-looking man with bulging forearms has brought in a surprisingly decorative puffball of a pooch sporting a diamanté-studded collar. I'm aware now that we'll be cutting it fine to catch the ferry if we have to wait our turn.

However, I'm not prepared to ask to be seen immediately, not after the horrors of yesterday. *Distillery wrecker and now queue jumper at the vet's!* So we wait and wait as, one by one, the animals are taken into the consulting room.

The phone on reception trills constantly. More people arrive. A woman is talking about her son getting a job with a fire service and a man is reminding his neighbour about Saturday's pub quiz. I'm trying to stop obsessively checking the time on my phone as the receptionist greets another new arrival.

'Hello, Barney,' she says, addressing the woman's toffee-brown spaniel. 'Nice to see you again, lovely boy.' The newcomer's shiny black hair is cut in a choppy bob, and she's wearing skinny jeans and a buttercup-yellow waxed jacket. She smiles pleasantly as she sits beside me.

'He's a sweet little fellow,' she remarks, looking down at Scout.

'Thanks.' It seems a little dishonest to accept praise for 'my' dog, but I'd rather not go into the whole story now.

She pats her own dog, encouraging him to settle at her feet, then turns back to me. 'Lovely day, isn't it?'

'It is,' I reply.

'Are you from around here?'

'Erm, no,' I reply distractedly. 'Just here on a visit.'

'On holiday?' There's a trace of Geordie accent.

'Kind of, yes.' While I don't wish to appear rude, I'd rather avoid explaining precisely why I'm here in such a public setting. I'd just like to get this business over and done with and hand Scout over to, well, *someone* capable who'll agree to look after him so I can catch that ferry, drive back to Yorkshire and get on with sorting out my life. But now, an expectant hush has fallen over the room. Clearly, as the yellow jacket woman has admired 'my' dog, it's probably the done thing to praise hers.

'He's lovely,' I say. 'What's he here for?' I hope it's okay, etiquette-wise, to ask that question. Surely it is. It's a vet's surgery, not a sexual health clinic.

The woman grimaces. She has high cheekbones, striking grey-blue eyes and a smooth, creamy complexion. She's probably in her late thirties, and there's a vibrancy about her that whisks me straight back to toddler group days, when I'd spy a fellow mum across the church hall and think, *She looks nice. Maybe I'll try and make friends with her?* When all of us were eager to make new connections, thrown together in what was essentially a platonic speed-dating exercise.

'He's been pretty off colour,' she explains. 'He's a grand old age, though. He's fifteen.'

'Oh, I hope he's going to be okay,' I murmur.

She smiles stoically. 'We'll see. So, what about this little chap?'

'He just turned up where I was staying,' I reply. 'He seems to be lost. I'm hoping the vet can scan him and see if there are any details of—'

'Ah, is this the little lost dog?' I break off as a woman with curly hair piled up in a tangly topknot appears from the consulting room.

'Yes, this is him,' I reply.

She strides towards me clutching a small blue plastic device. 'So sorry to keep you waiting. I'm the veterinary nurse.' She crouches down to greet Scout. 'Hey, little man. I hear you've been on a bit of an adventure and this kind lady's been looking after you. Now, let's see if we can get you home.'

It turns out that Scout is not only unchipped but also something of a renegade hound. 'All dogs are meant to be microchipped by law,' the veterinary nurse explains, adding that, as there's no animal sanctuary on the island, it would be *so very, very helpful* if I could drop him off at the nearest dog rescue centre on the mainland. I'd mentioned that I was in a hurry to catch the lunchtime ferry, and would therefore be passing through Oban. 'You don't *mind* taking him, do you?' she adds with a hopeful smile. 'It's a lovely centre, run by a very kind couple. This poor little chap's a bit underweight but they'll soon nurture him back to good health. I'll call so they'll be expecting you.'

Of course I don't mind – and, anyway, what else can I do? So I say a brisk goodbye to the yellow jacket woman, and Scout and I speed-walk to my car. He leaps onto the back seat obligingly and I drive a little too quickly around to the port, causing another driver to gesticulate angrily.

'Sorry!' I call out. I park up with a jolt, just in time to see the ramp being pulled up and the ferry turning slowly, the solid hunk of black and red already chugging away.

Chapter Ten

Two hours, Scout and I have been mooching aimlessly around town. I know, in the grand scheme of things, it's not a major disaster. *Don't sweat the small stuff,* et cetera (obviously the book's author had never been saddled with a failing distillery, agitated creditors and a furious work-force). But right now, after the events of the past few days, it feels like the last thing we need.

There is a later ferry, leaving at 7.30 p.m., and thank-fully I've managed to book onto it. Scout and I have already watched the fishing boats chugging in and out of the harbour and the speckled seals, shifting position lazily on the rocks. I have called my friend Dee – lender of the businesslike outfit – to update her; whilst delighted to hear about my new canine companion, she sounded shocked that I'd missed the boat (I don't think she has ever missed anything in her life).

'Will you book a hotel on the mainland?' she asked.

'No, I'll drive straight home. I just want to get back.'

'You'll drive all night?' I got to know Dee at the school gates and soon had her sussed as an extremely capable single mother to her two daughters, both of whom have already sailed through medical school.

'I'll be fine, honestly,' I said, more to bolster myself than anything else. 'It'll be an adventure.'

I have also called my mother, to let her know I'm still alive, and the dog and cat rescue centre at Oban to let them know of our later arrival (thankfully, someone will be there to welcome Scout). But how will we fill the rest of the hours? I sit on a bench, facing the calm sea, and ruffle the top of Scout's head as I try to think of what to do next. He really seems to like me, but is that just because I've been taking care of him? Perhaps he's this friendly with everyone. I have no idea because, of course, I don't actually *know* him at all.

We make our way along the main street, where most of the shops and cafés are clustered together, a jumble of brightly painted signs and not a chain store to be seen. There's a tiny museum of Hebridean life and the old fashioned sweetshop with its jars of boiled sweets gleaming on shelves behind the counter. A customer comes out bringing with her a heady waft of liquorice and sugar.

I buy a takeaway Americano and a cheese toastie at a café, and Scout and I wander onwards to the beach. Here on the wide sweep of silver sand, I let him off his lead. There seems to be little point in phoning anywhere to report him lost, as the vet's receptionist took care of all of that – and anyway, he'll be at the rescue centre soon. He bounds off in delight, stopping to look round every so often as if to check I'm still there. I perch on a rock and watch him whilst munching my toastie.

As I take my last bite, a flash of buttercup yellow appears in the distance. It's the chatty woman with bobbed black hair from the vet's. Unaccompanied by her dog now, she trots lightly down the worn old stone steps to the beach. I send a silent plea for her to head off in the opposite direction. It's not that I'm unfriendly by nature; just that I'd rather just have Scout for company right now. However, she raises a hand in greeting and makes her way towards me.

'Weren't you rushing off to catch the ferry?' she asks as she approaches.

'We missed it,' I say with a grimace.

'Oh, God, did you? That's a shame.'

I sip my coffee as she perches on the rock next to mine. Her blue-grey eyes look a little puffy, I realise now – as if she's been crying. Perhaps they'd been that way at the vet's, and I hadn't noticed.

'It's not a disaster,' I add. 'I've called the animal rescue centre in Oban. The veterinary nurse asked if I could take him there . . .'

'Yes, I heard her asking you. That's really good of you.'

'Oh, it's no trouble,' I say briskly. 'And anyway, they can still take him, even though we'll be really late.'

She nods. 'That's good news. So, whereabouts are you from?'

'I live in York, so I have a pretty long drive tonight.'

'God, that is a heck of a journey.' She smiles sympathetically.

'D'you live here on the island?' I ask.

'Uh, yeah, but I'm pretty new, still finding my feet around here.' I glance at her, my interest piqued now. 'After you'd left the vet's,' she adds, 'someone said they thought you were connected to the distillery?'

It happens again – that judder of dread that I'm going to have to explain it once more, and apologise as I did at the meeting. Despite her cheery attitude, her pleasant, smiley face and being 'pretty new around here', she's probably close to someone who's about to lose their livelihood – and that's another life I've wrecked. 'Er, yes, that's right,' I reply, turning to Scout, who's wandered away to investigate a rock pool. 'Scout, c'mon, boy!' I call out. 'Well, we'd better get on our walk,' I add, as if it's a matter of urgency.

'D'you mind if I join you?' She straightens up, and seems to catch herself. 'Unless you'd rather enjoy a bit of peace and quiet? I know lots of dog walkers prefer that.'

I catch a glimmer of something – of curiosity, maybe – in her eyes. 'No, not at all,' I reply, figuring now that she can't possibly know about the distillery's troubles; or at least, that I am partially responsible. If she did, she wouldn't be this friendly and straightforward with me.

'You're welcome to join us,' I say.

'Great,' she says brightly. 'So, his name's Scout?'

'That's just his temporary name,' I reply with a smile. 'It was the first one that popped into my head. And I'm Suzy . . .'

'I'm Cara,' she says with a wide, warm smile, 'and I think his temporary name suits him perfectly.'

Perhaps it's the fact that I've spent so much time alone lately. Or maybe it's Cara's warmth and friendliness that makes my initial wariness dissipate into the salty air.

'I'd always loved the idea of spending time in the Hebrides,' she says, when I ask what brought her to the island. 'I'm from Hexham in Northumberland and I'd lived there all my life. I'd been here on holidays – not to Sgadansay, but to other islands – so I thought, why not do something bold and see if I could actually make a life here?'

'By yourself?' I hope it's not presumptuous to ask.

She nods. 'Yep, it's just me. Well, me and Barney . . .' She glances at me, perhaps registering my surprise. 'It felt exciting,' she adds.

'Well, I think it's brave,' I say, wondering why some people have the ability to just go for it, without considering all the things that could possibly go wrong. Of course, Paul does that; he once took a job as a York ghost tour guide, without considering that it'd involve tramping about at night in all weathers with tourists firing questions at him ('Why do I have to be working when everyone else is out having fun?').

As Cara throws a stick for Scout, I wonder why she hasn't brought Barney down to the beach. Maybe he's already had his big walk for the day? Or perhaps he's not well enough? Better not ask, I decide as Scout leaps over rock pools, retrieves the stick and drops it at our feet. 'He's so lovely,' she adds. 'Bet you don't want to let him go really.'

I smile, surprised to feel a small twinge of regret. 'You're right. My kids have already been on at me to keep him and they don't even live with me anymore.'

Cara chuckles. 'I don't blame them. How old are they?'

'Frieda's twenty-one and Isaac's nineteen. D'you have any kids?'

She shakes her head. 'No, it's just me and Barney.'

There's a pause, so I ask, quickly, 'So, have you settled in? What's it like living here?'

'It's stunning of course, but you know that.' I nod, remembering how I'd felt, when Paul and I had first stepped off the ferry here. How I'd been thrilled that he'd chosen such a wild and beautiful island for our holiday.

'What kind of work d'you do?' I ask.

'I'm an artist and an art educator. I have a house and studio in Hexham where I ran screen printing classes. But I've let it out now, and I'm renting a pretty bonkers place here. It's a bit of a state but it's just right for me really.' Cara stops and smiles. 'Sorry. I'm rambling on about myself. I've probably spent a bit too much time on my own lately.'

'Oh, me too,' I say, before I can stop myself. 'And you're not rambling at all. So, what kind of bonkers is it?'

'It was a tearoom with a little outdoor play area but it shut for business years ago. It was being offered to rent as a workshop or studio, and it just seemed perfect for me.' She grins. 'A wreck, but with potential. And there's still a rusty old swing and a roundabout outside so I'm never bored.'

I smile, impressed by her courage to come over here and set up a life on her own. She's petite in stature but I detect an inner strength about her. 'So you live there too?' I ask. 'In the old tearoom, I mean?'

'Yeah, there are a couple of rooms at the back and that does me fine.'

'It sounds wonderful,' I say.

We both turn as Scout darts towards the sea and springs in and out of the shallow waves. 'I wonder how he came to be lost?' Cara muses.

'No idea,' I reply. 'It's baffling. If your dog was missing, wouldn't you report it straight away?'

'Yes, of course,' she says vehemently.

'So I'm thinking he might have been abandoned,' I add.

Cara nods. 'Poor little thing.' We fall into comfortable silence as we stop and look out to sea. The mainland is visible as a hazy strip on the horizon, the afternoon bright

75

and sunny with a bite to the air. I'm thinking now that it wasn't a disaster to miss our ferry after all. Scout is loving his walk, and it's given us some extra time together. I've met Cara, too, and it strikes me now how much I've needed to talk, not about anything major but just to be normal with another human being, and not to be judged. And that's when she says it, just as I knew she would at some point: 'Anyway, that really is enough about me.' She pushes back her windblown hair. 'So, what's your connection with the distillery?'

I could brush her off. I could say sorry, we really must go now; we have things to do. But what the hell, I could do with talking, and something about her tells me that she won't assume I'm an incompetent fool. 'It's a bit of a story,' I tell her. 'Would you like to come for a coffee with me?'

In the cosy dog-friendly café I pour it all out. How Paul walked out, and I'd come to the island to meet the distillery team face to face and explain the true extent of the problems. 'So he left you,' Cara exclaims, 'with all that to deal with?'

'Yep, pretty much. He said he needed a bit of time . . .' I break off. Deciding we needed more than coffee, we're devouring platefuls of excellent fish and chips.

'Time to do what?' she prompts me.

'To think, maybe? Or to drink himself stupid or assume a new identity? Honestly, I have no idea.' It's gratifying, how aghast she seems, although I'm still amazed that I'm telling a stranger all of this. 'I'd been out visiting my parents,' I explain. 'I came home to find a note in the kitchen saying, "Sorry, Suze. Need to get away for a while".'

'My God, that's terrible! But it sounded like he'd just gone temporarily?'

'I thought so, yes. I assumed he'd just had a wobble or something. But then, when he wouldn't answer his phone, I started to panic and badgered all his friends. Finally I messaged an old mate of his, who lives in London, and he said Paul was with him but he wasn't around right now.' I pause. 'He'd gone out to lunch.'

'Gone out to lunch?' Cara splutters. 'The nerve!'

'Exactly. And of course, I pictured him feasting on seafood, a glass of chilled Chablis at his side . . .'

'Picking over a langoustine platter at a riverside restaurant . . .'

'Sunlight glimmering on the Thames,' I add. 'Yeah, exactly that. And I know this sounds awful but I started thinking about those pliers you get, you know the ones for crunching up crab?'

'Oh yes!' she exclaims.

'I'd happily have set about him with those.' I chuckle, immensely grateful now that she's here. The whole time, Scout has been dozing at my feet. 'But then,' I continue, 'I remembered I'd invented the seafood scenario, and for all I knew he'd just nipped out for a McDonald's . . .' We are both laughing now.

'You don't "go out to lunch" to McDonald's,' Cara observes.

I nod. 'No, you just *go to McDonald's*.'

As she pops her last chip into her mouth I find myself wishing we'd met in some other circumstances, and not at the end of a stressful trip. I check my phone, surprised by how the time has flown by. Dusk is falling as we leave the café, and the sea shimmers inky blue as we head towards my car.

'How about I take a photo of Scout and print off some lost dog posters?' she suggests. 'I could put them up around town. I'd imagine people'd be good about that around here.'

'Would you do that? That would be brilliant. Thank you so much.'

'No problem at all,' she says, whipping out her phone and taking an endearing close-up of his face. 'Shall I put your phone number on them?'

'Yes, that's probably best. And if anyone gets in touch I can direct them to the rescue centre.' As we exchange numbers it strikes me that it was always Paul who amassed the contact details of new friends we'd made on holiday. 'This has been lovely,' I add. 'I feel so much better, thanks to you.'

'It's been great.' She smiles but, startlingly, her eyes start to tear up. 'I'd had a bit of a day, actually, and you've really helped to take my mind off things.'

'Oh?' I say, frowning. 'I'm sorry—'

'It's Barney,' she says quickly, clearly trying to keep her emotions in check.

I look at her, feeling terrible now for going on about my own predicament. 'Is he going to be okay?'

Cara shakes her head as she strides on determinedly. 'Like I said, he's an old boy and he's had a lovely life. A brilliant life! So he's been lucky really, and so have I.' I open my mouth to speak but Cara charges on: 'So he's staying over at the vet's tonight. He's really unwell. He had surgery and that wasn't successful and it's probably best if he doesn't hang on and on for months. So I'll have to make . . . *that* decision soon. I'm sorry, I—' She stops suddenly, tears rolling down her cheeks.

'I'm *so* sorry,' I murmur, hugging her. 'This must be terrible for you. I can't imagine how you must feel.'

She nods and wipes at her face. 'A dog feels like family, you know?'

'Yes, I'm sure he does,' I say, at a loss for how to comfort this woman who seems so capable and has been so kind to me today.

'Look,' she says quickly. 'The ferry's almost in.'

I glance around and see its lipstick-red funnel shining out against the darkening sky. We have reached my car, parked close to the jetty. 'I feel terrible rushing off like this,' I add.

'I'll be fine, honestly. Off you go!' She smiles stoically, bobs down to cuddle Scout and plonks a noisy kiss on the top of his head. Then we are saying hasty goodbyes, and Scout hops into my car. There's a great metallic clanking as we drive over the ramp and onto the ferry.

I thought I'd be relieved to be heading home. But something twists in my heart as the boat turns slowly away from the harbour, and we leave Sgadansay behind.

Chapter Eleven

Ricky

There was a horrible incident a couple of years ago when Arthur was eight and used to go to Cubs. 'Your mum was a junkie,' a little shitbag told him. I was horrified when he blurted out what had happened. And of course, I told the Cub leader I needed a word. He was mortified – and the kid was told to never speak to Arthur like that again.

'Don't listen to anyone who says stuff like that,' I told him later that night.

'Don't worry, Dad,' he said firmly. 'He's a wanker.' It nearly broke me, how brave he was being, and when I picked him up from school today I was reminded a little of that moment.

'That's a shame,' he murmured after I'd told him that he wouldn't be spending his Easter holiday in Spain after all.

'Yeah. I know you were really looking forward to it.'

'I don't mean that,' he said quickly. 'I mean about Kai's granny. D'you think she's gonna die soon?'

'Um, well, it's not looking good.' I paused. 'It's sad

for him – for all of them. But we'll have a great time, won't we?'

Arthur nodded and raked at his outgrown hair. 'Yeah.'

I cleared my throat as we climbed into my car. The back seat was piled with instruments I was taking home for minor repairs. It's an unofficial part of being a music teacher; if we didn't fix the instruments, eventually there'd be none left for our pupils to play. I glanced at Arthur, almost wishing I wasn't going out tonight. It's not that he ever seems to mind – he's a huge fan of Jojo, his student babysitter – but I felt as if I should be home for him really, in case he wanted to chat about stuff.

He didn't seem to want to, though. He wolfed his dinner as normal and now, as I work on the beleaguered instruments on the living room floor, he mooches off to his room. I fix a violin's wobbly tuning peg and turn my attentions to the sticky goo on the neck of a cello. These instruments are cheap and basic but often the only means by which a child can learn to make music.

'What're you doing?' Arthur has appeared in the doorway. I really need to finish up as Jojo is due to arrive any minute now.

'Just trying to clean this stuff off it,' I explain. 'I think it's marmalade. It's got a kinda citrussy tang.'

He smirks. 'How does marmalade even *get* on a cello?'

I grin at him. 'Maybe it was hit by a piece of flying toast?'

Arthur sniggers and I try to gauge whether he's really okay, or just putting on a brave face. 'Hey, are you sure you're okay about the holiday?'

'Yeah.' He shoves his hands into his jeans pockets, and I get up from my cross-legged position and put an arm around him.

'What about Meg coming to Granddad's with us? D'you feel all right about that?'

'Dad, it's *fine*,' he insists, before pulling away and disappearing off to his room again, leaving me to consider our forthcoming jaunt. It'll be Meg's first visit to Sgadansay. The first time she'll have met my father, and our first holiday with the three of us – Arthur, Meg and me.

Which, now I come to think about it, is an awful lot of 'firsts' for one trip.

Meg's favourite restaurant is a casual, modern place with polished concrete floors and cheery, attractive waiting staff. She seems unfazed by the news that it won't just be the two of us going to Sgadansay.

'Did you honestly think I'd mind?' she asks, picking at a plateful of tofu, papaya and a sprinkling of seeds.

'No, of course not,' I reply. 'It's just not what we planned, that's all.'

'Well, it's not as if you could leave him at home by himself,' she teases.

I fork in the last of my pad thai and smile. 'I did think he might be okay with a few packets of those sausages he likes.'

'Ugh, those sausages,' she says with a shudder. 'D'you really have to cook something different for him every night?'

'I don't,' I say, slightly taken aback.

'Well, you do when *I'm* there. Last time it was sausages. The time before that, fish fingers . . .' Christ, has she been keeping a dossier on our meals? 'Why can't he just have what we have,' she adds, 'and save yourself the trouble?'

'But it isn't any trouble,' I reply, trying to keep a note

of defensiveness out of my voice. And it's true; it's hardly any effort for me to stick Arthur's favourites under the grill. It's not as if he's demanding lobster thermidor or a boar, roasted on a spit. But there it is again: a little dig about my parenting.

'I'm not trying to get at you,' she remarks.

'I'm not saying you are.' *You are, though, aren't you? At least, you're getting at something,* I think, wondering now if she does mind about our trip after all. I'm aware that it was a pretty big deal for her to agree to come to Sgadansay in the first place. Apart from it being a little different to her usual, more glamorous holidays, she's also had to arrange for a fellow alternative therapist – a friend with an 'ironic' moustache and a fondness for padded body warmers – to cover her appointments for the week.

'I think it's pretty normal for a ten-year-old to love fish fingers,' I add, keen to move on to another topic now.

She smooths back her fine hair with a hand. 'They're so processed, though.'

'I can think of things that are a lot *more* processed.' Why am I even getting into this?

'That doesn't mean they're good for him, Ricky.'

'For goodness' sake, they're just fish, aren't they? Cod or whatever, cut into rectangles—'

'Coated with crumbs and colouring and God knows what—'

'That's why they're delicious,' I say with unnecessary vigour.

'Why don't *you* have them then?' she asks sharply.

Because I wouldn't fucking dare! At least, not unless Arthur and I were alone, secretly scarfing down our illicit delicacies from the sea. 'Shall we change the subject?' I ask.

'I was only *saying*, Ricky.' The peculiar mood lingers on as she pokes away at the last of her papaya, but at least she lets the matter drop. 'So, how d'you think your dad and I will get along?'

'I'm sure it'll be fine,' I reply firmly. 'He can be a grumpy old bugger but he's a decent guy underneath.'

Meg smiles, and as our plates are whisked away I try to picture her at Dad's house on the island. In her line of work she specialises in ear candling (which sounds terrifying) and an even more mysterious treatment called 'rolfing', which I'd assumed involved making her patients throw up but is actually, she explained, 'About aligning their energy field with the gravitational pull of the earth.' I can't help wondering what Dad will make of that.

'It's a funny situation, though, isn't it?' she remarks.

'The meeting-the-parents thing, you mean?'

She nods. 'Yeah. At our age, anyway.'

'Dad'll love you,' I say firmly, remembering how apprehensive I'd been when her parents had invited me and Arthur over for dinner ('Of course they want to meet you!' she'd insisted). In fact Diane and Simon – a strikingly attractive couple in their early seventies – had been lovely and relaxed and different to any parents-of-a-partner I'd ever met before, not that there had been that many. Their enormous bay-fronted lounge was filled with jazz records, abstract art and poetry books, and Arthur had found the experience fascinating.

'It was like a mansion,' he murmured later, and I couldn't disagree.

Now a young, blonde waitress wearing bright red lipstick appears at our table. 'Would you like dessert?'

'Not for me, thanks,' Meg says automatically. On any other night I'd have been tempted by the chocolate pudding but all that fish finger talk seems to have dented my appetite. So I ask for the bill and, as we leave, I suggest stopping off for a drink on the way home. It's not yet ten o'clock and Jojo isn't expecting us back until after eleven.

'Actually,' Meg says, 'd'you mind if I just go home tonight?'

'Huh?' I blink at her in the street. It's full of restaurants and bars, and is bustling tonight, as it always is at the weekends. 'But I thought—'

'I was looking through tomorrow's appointments,' she cuts in, 'and there's some prep I need to do tonight. And I should get into work extra early in the morning to make sure I'm all set up—'

'Oh, are you sure?' I'm used to Meg working Saturdays but in the past year I have never known her to deviate from arriving at her practice at 8.30 a.m. Her life is managed with more precision than that of anyone else I have ever met.

'Yeah. Sorry to be such a bore, darling.' She looks up and down the street for a cab. I'm wondering now if we've had an argument that I've failed to notice. Surely this isn't about the fish fingers? I could try to persuade her, of course, but clearly, her mind is made up. Spotting a taxi, she hails it and kisses me briefly on the cheek.

'See you over the weekend, then?' I say, still a little bewildered as I can't remember the last time she didn't stay at mine after a night out.

The cab pulls up and she murmurs her street name to the driver. 'Yeah, of course,' she says, glancing back. 'I'll call you tomorrow. Bye, honey.'

As the taxi drives away I can't help thinking how weird this is, this sudden change of heart. Clearly, something has annoyed or upset her tonight. Or perhaps I'm just being paranoid and it's nothing to do with me at all? I start to walk towards the subway, trying to shake off the sense that something's not right – not just about Dad, and the whole terrible business up on Sgadansay, but closer to home, between Meg and me.

Something's wrong and I can't put my finger on what it is.

Chapter Twelve

Suzy

Oskar at the rescue centre brushes off my apologies for our late arrival. 'Hey, little man,' he says, first offering Scout the back of his hand to sniff before murmuring to him gently and tickling his ears. He stands back and seems to appraise him.

'I hope you haven't had to stay behind just for us,' I say. 'I felt so silly missing the earlier ferry.'

'No no, my partner and I live here on site.' He smiles kindly. He has striking brown eyes, thick dark eyebrows and dense stubble. We're in the reception area of the ancient stone building just outside town – it's a former coach house, apparently – and apart from the occasional bark, the premises are quiet.

'Well, I'm very grateful,' I say.

Oskar leads me over to a seating area and opens a laptop. 'It was good of you to bring him to us. So, he seems healthy enough, if a bit underweight. And he obviously has a lovely character . . .'

'Yes, he's been brilliant during the short time we've been together. The only thing that's upset him was the ferry journey. He was terrified on the deck, and when I took him into the lounge he lay there, shaking, under the table.'

'Poor little chap. Let's hope he doesn't have to go through that again. So, from what they told us at the vet's, he seemed to be lost or abandoned?'

I nod. 'I think probably abandoned. There's been no report of a lost dog like him.'

'Yeah, I'd say so too.' Oskar frowns, clearly touched by Scout's story. 'I've just done another search and there's still nothing.'

'Hard to believe, isn't it?' I say.

'Yes, but sadly it happens quite a lot. Obviously, we have people handing in dogs that they can't keep any longer, but there are quite a few strays here too.'

At the sound of a distant howl, Scout pricks up his ears. 'A friend on the island says she'll put up some lost dog posters,' I add, aware that it already feels natural to refer to Cara in that way. 'So obviously, I'll let you know if anyone contacts me through those.'

'Yes, please do.'

'I hope he hasn't just been abandoned,' I add. 'Why on earth do people do that?'

Oskar shrugs sadly. 'We can only go on hunches of course, but if there are obvious health or behavioural issues, then we assume that's why they've been dumped. It happens a lot with older dogs too, when the vet's bills can start creeping up.'

'That's awful.' I glance at Scout. He gazes back at me, pink tongue out, eyes shining. 'I wonder how old he is?'

'Pretty young, I'd guess,' Oskar says. 'Maybe around two? That's common too,' he adds. 'I mean, for dogs to be dumped during the first couple of years after puppyhood.'

'Why would anyone do that?' I exclaim.

'Well, by that stage they're not so little and fluffy anymore, and they need work and commitment so everyone can live happily together.'

I nod as Oskar turns back to his laptop. 'If I could start with your contact details . . .' I give him my landline and mobile numbers, plus my home address. 'So, apart from hating the ferry, there are no other issues you're aware of?'

I'm pretty confident gnawing a sweater wouldn't count as an 'issue'. 'No, nothing at all,' I say.

'Does he seem to be house-trained?'

I pause. 'There was, uh, one small peeing incident at the holiday house.'

'Oh, that's understandable,' Oskar says briskly. 'He was probably scared and a bit out of sorts. How does he behave around other dogs?'

'We haven't met any properly,' I reply, 'but he seemed fine at the vet's, and there were some there.' I think about Cara and how she's had to leave Barney at the vet's on Sgadansay tonight. And how she'll wake up tomorrow morning and the first thing she'll think is, did he die during the night?

Oskar gets up and takes a phone from a desk drawer. 'I'll take some pictures to put on his file.' As he snaps away, an extremely beautiful young woman strides in.

'Hi,' she says with a bright smile. 'You must be Suzy, with our new little friend?' She bobs down to greet him.

'Yes, that's right.'

'I'm Shalini. I'm Oskar's partner. We run this place together.'

'Oh, what an amazing thing you do here,' I say.

She straightens up and smiles. Her glossy dark hair is piled up on her head, and she's wearing a baggy red sweater and faded jeans. 'We can't imagine doing anything else, can we, Osk?' she says, and he shakes his head.

'Well, thanks for bringing him in,' he adds. 'We can keep in touch, let you know if he's adopted . . .'

'*When* he's adopted,' Shalini corrects him with a grin. 'He's such a cutie! I'm sure he won't be with us for very long.'

'That's good to hear,' I say with a catch to my voice.

Shalini meets my gaze and smiles kindly. 'He'll make someone very happy. And don't worry – we're super-careful before we agree to an adoption. We always have a face-to-face meeting to make sure they're suitable.'

'We always want an adoption to be successful,' Oskar adds, 'and we follow up with calls to make sure the dog's settling in.'

Shalini looks at him and chuckles. 'We might as well admit it, Osk. With some of them, we find it a little bit hard to let them go . . .'

'Oh, God, yeah.' He catches my eye and smiles.

'I can imagine,' I say truthfully. I look down at Scout, feeling a little peculiar now that the time has come to say goodbye. And now I'm thinking of Cara again, and how brave she was being about Barney. And it strikes me that perhaps that's why she was so eager to ask about *my* stuff; all the business with Paul and the distillery. It's as if she's wanted to talk about *anything* other than the imminent loss of her dog. In fact, she'd only blurted out how serious his condition was as I was about to catch the ferry.

'People often hold back the thing they really want to tell you until the last minute,' my friend Dee, the GP, explained to me once. 'They come to the surgery and it's all, "I've been feeling a bit tired" or, "I've got this rash on my little finger". You deal with that, and then, just as they're leaving – their hand is actually on the door handle – they'll blurt out, "Oh, um, there *is* another thing . . ." And they'll have a lump they're terrified about. Or they'll want help to stop drinking. And that's the real crux of it, that's why they really came in – because of the, *Oh-and-there-is-another-thing.*'

Barney was Cara's 'another-thing', I realise now. And if she can be so stoical and brave, and chat to a stranger so cheerfully, listening to me prattling on about Paul and chilled Chablis and crab pliers, then I can deal with what's happened to the distillery, and somehow make it all right.

I need to go home, I decide, and do all I can to rescue the business. I need to be as strong as Cara was on the beach today.

Shalini looks at me. 'Would you like a few minutes with Scout, just to say bye, before you head off?'

I nod. 'Actually, yes, I would. Thank you.' I catch myself. 'It seems crazy, I know. He's only been with me for twenty-four hours . . .'

Oskar chuckles. 'A little dog can make a big impression.'

As they leave the room together I glimpse their living quarters through the open door: a lounge with a sage-coloured sofa scattered with cerise and lemon cushions and the orangey glow of a wood-burning stove. It looks so cosy through there, and I'm sure the dogs' and cats' quarters are the best they could possibly be. I know Scout will be well cared for here.

I call him over and he trots towards me. I crouch down, and he sits comfortably at my feet. 'I'm going to miss you,' I murmur, stroking the top of his head where his fur is softer, less wiry, than on the rest of his body. 'But someone nice will choose you,' I add, my eyes misting a little. It's been a brief relationship – a one-night stand really – and if he's adopted by someone who'll love him, then at least something good will have come out of my trip.

I pull my phone from my pocket, intending to take a final photo of him, but my attention is caught by a text. It's from Shona, the holiday cottage's owner: *Thank you for leaving the house in such good order. I did notice some wetness on living room carpet. We've had a bit of dampness coming up occasionally and will be getting a builder to investigate. Hope this didn't spoil your stay.*

It was no problem at all, I reply. *I had a lovely time – thank you.* I turn back to Scout, deciding not to take a photo after all as Oskar and Shalini reappear. 'All okay?' he says.

I nod. It's almost 11 p.m. and I really should leave them in peace now.

'You have a long drive ahead of you,' he adds.

I nod. 'Around six and a half hours.'

'Wow, so you'll be driving most of the night . . .'

'You could stay here, if that's easier?' Shalini offers, giving Oskar a quick look. 'We have a spare room—'

'That's very kind of you,' I say, 'but I'll be fine, honestly—'

'But it's such a long drive on your own,' she says.

I muster a smile and glance down at Scout, then back at Oskar and Shalini. 'Look, I'm sorry if I've messed you about, but I've kind of . . .' I exhale loudly, barely able to believe what I'm about to say. 'I've actually changed my mind.'

Oskar seems to study my face for a moment, then I catch him and Shalini exchanging a brief glance, as if they half-expected this to happen. This is crazy, I tell myself. I live alone and I have never owned a dog; I didn't even give in after all those months of Frieda nagging. However, that was over a decade ago and now everything's different, and I'm thinking: Scout turned up in the night and lifted my heart when I truly believed I'd never be happy again.

Oskar and Shalini are looking at me expectantly. Then Shalini smiles. 'You want to take him home with you?'

I nod. 'Yes, I do.'

'Um . . . normally, we'd ask you to leave the dog with us for seven days,' Oskar says, 'just in case the owner turns up to claim him.'

I clear my dry throat. 'But he was found on Sgadansay, not around here.'

He rubs at his bristly chin. 'It's just a rule we have.' He shrugs apologetically. 'Normally, we'd say, if you feel the same in a week, and he still hasn't been claimed, then you'd be welcome to come back and collect him—'

'But Suzy lives way down in York,' Shalini reminds him. 'It's not exactly handy for her, Osk.'

'Yeah.' He nods and I suspect now that it's Shalini who's in charge around here.

'So it's not exactly a normal situation, is it?' she adds. 'And all that matters is that we make the right decision for the dog . . .'

'Yep,' he says, tickling Scout behind his velvety ears. 'That's what matters.'

Minutes later Oskar is fitting a makeshift grille in the back of my car, and Shalini is handing me a bundle of soft old blankets to fashion a bed for Scout's journey. Then I'm waving goodbye as I pull away from the gravelled driveway of the old coach house.

What the heck have I done? A mad thing, I realise – but I just couldn't leave him behind. After all, Scout came to me when I needed someone, and he seemed to need someone too. 'It's you and me now,' I tell him happily as we set off into the dark night, on the long journey to Yorkshire, to Scout's new home.

Chapter Thirteen

Medley Family WhatsApp

Hi, I'm home! Also I bring exciting news :)
Frieda: Hi Mum :) Did you sort out the distillery stuff?
Sadly no. But I have something exciting to tell you.
Frieda: What??
This happened. [I attach a photo of Scout].
Frieda: Is that the stray dog from the island?
Yes.
Frieda: He's so cute, Mum!
He certainly is.
Isaac: Aw is that the lost dog?
Yes that's him, love.
Isaac: Nice.
Notice anything else about the photo?
Frieda: ??
Never mind. So how are you both anyway? You haven't been microwaving foil again, Isaac? Or had any more kitchen emergencies?
Isaac: No but something funny happened. Rex bought us a kettle at last and it totally freaked him out.
Why? What happened?

94

Isaac: We switched it on and it started steaming like crazy then switched itself off!

Frieda: God's sake Ize, that's what kettles are meant to do!

Isaac: Is it?

Frieda: OMG. YES.

Yes Isaac. They steam – indicating boiling – then switch themselves off. What have you been doing since you left home?

Isaac: In terms of what? :)

Frieda: In terms of making hot drinks?

Isaac: Using a pan.

You've been boiling water in a pan for six months?!

Isaac: Only when we've needed boiling water.

Frieda: Didn't you notice our kettle at home does that? I mean the steaming, switching itself off thing?

Isaac: :) Course I did. It was only Rex who freaked out. Me and Matis were chilled about it.

Thank God for that. Anyway, now that excitement's over you might want to take a closer look at that photo and see if you recognise anything.

Isaac, after a pause: That's our yellow chair.

Frieda: That's our rug.

Correct. And that's the dog I met on the island so . . .

Isaac: I don't get it.

You don't think I carted our home furnishings to Sgadansay, do you?

Isaac: Have you brought the dog home?

Frieda: MUM!! You've brought the dog home with you!

Yes, love.

Frieda: I can't believe this!

Aren't you pleased?

Frieda: Pleased that you've finally FINALLY said yes to getting a dog when I've left home? :)

Sorry, darling. I couldn't resist him.

Frieda: I'm devastated!

Will you ever forgive me?

Isaac: Yeah we might.

Frieda: Eventually :)

Isaac: It's like guinea pig day all over again.

Frieda: But even better.

Will you come home and meet him soon?

Isaac: Yeah course!

Frieda: God yes next weekend I'm coming.

Isaac: Me too.

That's brilliant. Maybe I'll see both of you a bit more often now.

Isaac: Maybe :)

Frieda: Oh Mum I can't wait to meet him. You're the best!!!

Chapter Fourteen

The pet shop lady makes a big fuss of Scout as I select water and food bowls, plus a basket. While I've enjoyed the warm, comforting feeling of him cosying up to me on the bed, I'm wondering now if I should give him the option of having sleeping quarters of his own. I'm keen to take my responsibilities as his guardian seriously.

I also choose an assortment of rubbery toys, which the shop lady explains are beneficial to health ('Chewing exercises every single muscle in his body!') and, of course food, plus more poo bags on a handy roll dispenser, which perhaps thrills me more than it should. The woman has obviously marked me out as a Naive New Dog Person and therefore in the market for some enthusiastic up-selling. I almost let her talk me into buying a complicated lead with multiple straps, a gigantic velour floor cushion 'so he can relax in comfort in any room' and a packet of treats for training ('only one calorie apiece'). However, as she tries to flog me some pigs' ears – actual ears of pig, with hairs still attached – I judder to my senses and leave the shop with just the necessaries, which we load up into my car.

Back home, I unpack everything and then go to find Scout, who's still keenly exploring the house. I discover him in Isaac's room, gnawing happily on a pair of boxers that he must have found in a murky corner somewhere. How simple dogs are compared to humans, I muse, when it comes to entertainment. We need cinemas, restaurants and hobbies – oh, yes, hobbies! Paul was always a big one for the short-lived all-consuming passion, such as learning the trumpet and baking sourdough loaves (which was at least quiet and relatively cheap). There was also his wine connoisseur phase, when he insisted we went along to tasting evenings where you had to whirl your glass about and detect notes of apricot, cedar and, startlingly, cabbage. This business of dressing up a piss-up as something more worthy, almost *scholarly*; I should have spotted the danger signs years ago.

For a brief period, Paul was mad about cycling. For this, he had to kit himself out in top-of-the-range apparel. 'It's more aerodynamic,' he'd explain, when actually, he just thought his arse looked great in tight Lycra. Derek, my brother-in-law, has the same thing with his running gear. There's always some new, more breathable fabric he has to have, worn super-tight so as to show off his package. I always have to make a point of staring determinedly at Derek's face.

As Scout continues his gnawing, I pull my phone from my jeans pocket and scroll to Belinda's number. Although she's never practised, she studied law at uni and I have a faint idea that she might know where I should go for help.

'Hi, sis,' she says briskly. 'How was your trip?'

'Um, it was pretty tough actually.'

'God, yes, I'm sure it was. Horrible for you.'

I pause, wondering how best to put it and realising there's no 'best' way; it is what it is, plain and simple. 'Erm, I'm going to have to get legal advice pretty urgently,' I explain. 'I mean, I think I'm going to have to liquidate the company—'

'Oh God, really? Is it that bad?'

'Yes, unfortunately. And from what I've been able to find out, the best thing to do is appoint someone to—'

'Suze, who was looking after the finances in all of this?' she cuts in.

'Erm, well—'

'I mean, who was handling the accounts before you and Paul took over?'

You and Paul. Ouch. 'There were people,' I say, keeping my voice level, 'but he had a lot of disagreements about how things were being done, and he appointed his own people and, yes, it was all very badly handled—'

'Bloody hell, Suzy,' my sister murmurs, and I catch Derek barking something unintelligible in the background. 'I wish you'd said something before things got so bad,' she adds and, again, Derek's voice sounds out.

'What's he saying?' I ask, irritation fizzing up in me now.

'He says he's surprised there wasn't a proper plan,' she replies, and at this point I phase out, my brain screaming, *But there was! At least, it looked like one, from what I saw, however naive that may seem now.*

'Tell him thank you for that,' I say curtly, trying to ignore a prickling sensation behind my eyes. 'But, look, I actually wondered if you might be able to suggest someone who can help me. If you can't, don't worry—'

'Suzy—' She cuts off as Scout drops the boxers and starts barking urgently. 'What's that?' she exclaims.

'Erm, it's my dog.'

'That's loud isn't it—'

'Yeah, I think someone put a flyer through the letterbox. He's gone crazy . . .'

'God,' she says with a dry laugh, 'for a minute I thought you said *your* dog—'

'I did.'

'You bought a *dog*?'

'Well, no. I didn't buy him. He was a stray on the island. He just turned up at the house where I was staying—'

'You're not keeping him, are you?' she splutters.

'Yes, I am.'

I can virtually *hear* her eye-roll. 'Why on earth have you taken on a dog?'

'Because . . . I wanted to. He had nowhere else to go—'

She exhales loudly. 'Honestly, I worry about you, I really do. Don't you have enough on your plate—'

'You're right,' I cut in, sensing my cheeks flaring now, 'I do have a lot on, but this is actually the best thing that's happened to me in a long time, not that he's a *thing*, he's a lovely, sweet, affectionate dog, and we're having such fun together—'

'Suze, I just meant—'

'And yes, it might seem mad, but it felt like the right thing to do. So anyway,' I barge on, barely catching a breath, 'I don't suppose there's much chance of being able to talk to a legal person on a Saturday but I'm going make a plan, ask around, see who's recommended—'

'Suzy, please listen,' Belinda cuts in sharply. 'Look, I'm sorry. It's your decision whether you want an animal—' an *animal*? '—and that's nothing to do with me. Get yourself a wild bison if you like . . .'

'I don't want a wild bison!'

She sighs heavily. 'What I was trying to say is, I *do* know someone who might be able to help.'

'Do you?' I'm still smarting a little and experiencing a stab of envy for my friends who are close and vaguely *equal* to their siblings – like Dee the GP and her sister the head teacher. Not Belinda the high-ranking civil servant and Suzy the utter fucking failure who came home from Scotland to find a carton of solidified milk in her fridge.

Oh, I know that makes me sound like a self-pitying fool and I hate myself for it. Scout potters over and licks the bare bit of ankle that's exposed beneath my jeans. *That's why I've adopted you,* I decide; *because you don't think I'm a raving idiot. You like me enough to lick my leg.*

'Her name's Roz,' Belinda goes on. 'Rosalind Nulty. She's a lawyer specialising in insolvency, liquidation, that kind of thing. She really knows her stuff.'

'Oh,' I say quietly. 'How d'you know her?'

'From uni,' she replies, 'and we've kept in touch a bit over the years.' I frown. I'm pretty sure I know most of Belinda's friends from her university days and I've never heard of a Roz Nulty before. 'I could give her a call now,' she adds, 'if you like? Just to sound her out a bit?'

'Really? Are you sure?' I'd hoped she might have a name from her law faculty days, but hadn't anticipated this level of help: a virtual introduction.

'Yeah, I could try at least.'

I rub at my face. 'I'm just a bit worried about the cost, Bel. Is she crazily expensive?'

'You can worry about that later,' she says firmly, back to her usual clippy tone as we end the call.

I sit on the edge of Isaac's bed, feeling chastened now

101

that Belinda seems prepared to help me, and is actually on my side. Like Cara on the island, who couldn't have been *more* helpful, offering to make and distribute lost dog posters around town. I scroll for her number, wondering why it feels so tricky to compose a message when I'm supposed to be good with words.

Hi Cara, I start, *hope you're doing okay and Barney is getting better.* I pause before continuing: *I'm sure it's not easy. I just wanted you to know I'm thinking of you, Sx*

I slide my phone back into my pocket, not even sure if that was the right thing to do, or whether she'll reply. But it felt important to say something.

Later, after a walk, I stretch out on the sofa, making room for Scout as he snuggles close to me. First thing on Monday I'll call the council up there – and the police on Sgadansay – in case someone's reported him missing. That would be the best result; to see him reunited with the person – or people – who love him. But . . . I love him too.

My phone rings, making me flinch; it's Belinda. 'I've just spoken to her,' she says. 'Roz Nulty, I mean. She's based in Leeds – not far from us actually. And she can see you on Wednesday afternoon for an initial chat.'

'Great,' I say with genuine gratitude, although I'd hoped – perhaps naively – that she'd be available first thing on Monday morning.

'I'll text you her address,' she adds.

'Thanks, Bel. Thanks so much.'

'That's okay—' She breaks off as Derek starts hectoring in the background. 'Yes, Derek,' she says, a tad sharply. 'Yes, I'll tell her that.' I brace myself for further reminders about my ineptitude in the running of a business and the choosing of boyfriends. She exhales. 'Sorry, Suze. He's saying, d'you remember he's allergic? It's going to be very difficult for Derek to come to your house now you have that dog.'

What an almighty tragedy that will be, I think, as we finish the call.

And then a text comes, and I'm no longer thinking about my brother-in-law in his groin-hugging running attire. I've forgotten to be annoyed with him, and those ominous words – 'insolvency', 'liquidation' – have melted away in my mind.

Thanks for your kind message, Cara has written. *How lovely of you. I put lost dog posters up all over the place – has anyone been in touch?*

No, nothing yet, I reply, *but thanks so much for doing that.* My stomach seems to tighten as I add: *How are things with you?*

A few moments her later her reply comes: *I'm very sad but also trying my best to be happy because Barney is now running along the endless beach to the stars. Cx.*

Chapter Fifteen

Ricky

When you arrive at a party you can roughly gauge how long it's been going on, and it's clear that this one has gathered quite a bit of momentum already. At just gone eight, Meg's parents' garden and conservatory are decked out with fairy lights and milling with guests. The lawn is huge, even for the suburbs, the garden well tended with apple trees and tables bearing ice buckets filled with wine and champagne.

The biggest table is laden with an enormous array of charcuterie and cheeses, savoury tarts and piles of flat-breads, figs, olives and exotic fruits, all artfully arranged with fresh flowers and sprigs of greenery. It looks like a vast, edible sculpture and brings to mind an image of my own parents' parties – limited to Christmas and significant wedding anniversaries – where there'd be cans of lager, wine in a box and one of those divided platters with separate sections for peanuts (salted and dry roasted) and prawn cocktail crisps.

'So, *that*,' Meg murmurs into my ear, 'is what we call a grazing table.'

'Wow.' I chuckle. 'If I take an olive, will it wreck the whole thing?'

'No – just go for it. Give it an hour and it'll look like it's been ransacked by wolves anyway.' She plants a quick kiss on my cheek. It's pretty clear that she's got over her prickliness about Arthur's fish fingers or whatever it was that triggered that strange mood last night. He's staying over at a friend's tonight. It's Lucas's eleventh birthday and I imagine the lads will be up most of the night on the PlayStation.

Diane – Meg's mother – glides over to us in a floaty green dress and hugs both of us in turn. 'Sorry to spring this on you, Ricky,' she announces, 'but we woke up and thought, what a beautiful day! Let's make the most of it. We don't get many of these at this time of year, do we?'

'No, we don't,' I reply. 'This is really lovely.' If this is a spontaneous party I can't imagine what their planned ones are like.

'There was no stopping her,' announces Simon, Meg's father, who's looking dapper in a black polo-neck sweater, brown cords and chunky black-framed spectacles.

I'm handed a glass of wine and whisked over by Meg to meet a tipsy aunt in a red trouser suit, her lipstick already askew: 'Oh, we've all heard about you, Ricky,' she says. 'You're the music teacher, aren't you? Shame you didn't bring your cello!'

Meg laughs and squeezes my hand. 'Maybe next time,' I say with a smile.

'Oh,' Meg exclaims, 'there's Ellie and Tom! They're my cousins. I didn't know they were coming . . .' She pulls me across the lawn towards a wispy woman with cascades of crinkly raven hair, and a man with a substantial beard, who are installed at a wrought-iron table at the bottom of the garden. After enthusiastic introductions I learn that Tom is home on a brief visit from Madrid, where he runs a web design business. His sister Ellie, who's a lecturer in costume design in London, popped up to Glasgow to see him.

'That's my little one there,' Ellie explains, indicating a little girl who's running around in a rainbow-coloured dress, multiple necklaces jangling around her neck. The half dozen or so children present are all in a state of giddy excitement. 'There was no way she was staying with her dad this weekend,' she adds. 'She loves coming here.' The talk turns to how amazing Meg's parents are, with their famous parties, and then to children. Tom's two are back home with his wife in Madrid, and Ellie is separated and her daughter has numerous stepbrothers and sisters; it's becoming extremely difficult to keep up.

'So, it's just you and Arthur?' she asks.

'Yes, that's right.'

'Shame he couldn't be here too!'

'Yeah, he'd love it,' I say, wondering what he'd make of all these glamorous people, the hundreds of fairy lights and the grazing table.

Tom refills our glasses and I'm quizzed at length about teaching kids music, which I don't mind at all; these people are friendly and fun and, before I know it, a couple of hours have spun by.

We go to fetch food – Meg's prediction was accurate, her mother's artful display has been ravaged – and as the four of us drift back to our table I glimpse the pack of kids who are all chasing each other around a tepee. It's the kind that Katy, Arthur's mum, always yearned to buy for him; she'd show him pictures of them in those posh toy catalogues where everything is made of wood or gingham and is utterly charming. But our four-year-old Arthur hadn't wanted a tepee for Christmas. He'd begged for a garish plastic karaoke machine so she'd finally given in and we'd bought him that instead.

It had driven her mad, being subjected to the tinny backing tracks and raucous singing whenever Arthur had his friends round. 'I'm sorry,' she hissed eventually, 'but that bloody machine's got to go.'

I hadn't believed for one moment that she'd actually meant it.

'Anyway, Ricky,' Ellie says now, 'I heard Meg picked you up in a coffee shop!'

I laugh and turn to Meg. 'Well . . . we got chatting, didn't we? That's how I remember it . . .'

'Yes, I *did* pick you up.' Meg giggles, eyes shining, looking tipsier than I've ever seen her before. A couple of wines is usually her max, but tonight the four of us have worked our way through a few bottles of wine already. 'I saw him standing there,' she adds.

'Someone should write a song about that,' Tom quips.

'. . . looking so cute and a bit dishevelled,' she continues, 'with that whopping double bass. And I thought, oh, why not? Just go for it . . .'

'Good for you!' Ellie asserts, and I laugh, pretty tipsy myself now, although I'm trying to be sensible as the last thing I want is to seem pissed in front of Meg's parents and a whole pile of strangers.

Ellie pulls a mock-furtive expression as she extracts a packet of cigarettes from her bag. 'Just a little mummy cig,' she says with a chuckle, and Tom lights it for her. 'So,' she goes on, turning back to me, 'we still don't know much about you, Ricky. How about we play the secrets game?'

'Oh, God, do we have to?' Meg groans, but Ellie insists

107

that we do, explaining to me, 'Basically, you have to tell the group something that none of us knows.' She beams around at all of us, showing dazzling white teeth. 'That's harder for us. We know all our dirt, don't we, Megsy?' Ellie raises a brow and shoots her a knowing look.

'Shut up, Ells.' Meg sniggers.

It's not that I'm an anti-games person. But in this kind of scenario, with no shortage of wine and food and conversation, I don't really see the need for them. However, I try to get into the spirit as Tom 'reveals' that once, as a teenager, he stole his Mum's make-up and applied a full face of it, 'and I made such a mess of her stuff that I had to wrap it up in carrier bags and stash it at the bottom of the kitchen bin . . .'

'And Mum blamed me,' shrieks Ellie, 'because a *boy* wouldn't steal his mum's make-up, would he?'

Everyone laughs until Meg points out: 'That doesn't count, Tom, 'cause Ellie knew about it.'

He rolls his eyes. 'God, you're such a stickler for rules, Megs.' More laughter. 'What about you, Ells?' he prompts his sister.

'Um . . .' She frowns and bites her lip, and I'm thinking, actually, this has been fun but I'd like to go quite soon as it's just the two of us tonight, with Arthur being away on a sleepover. And also: what was the 'dirt' Ellie referred to, that Meg clearly didn't want to go into? 'Okay,' Ellie blurts out, 'I once shoplifted a box of those candied lemon slices you put on cakes.'

'That's so lame,' Meg declares.

'Well, what about you, then?' Ellie counters. 'We're all waiting, Meg.'

'No, it's Ricky's turn,' she insists, and they all turn to me.

'Erm . . .' I glance around the garden. The children

have been herded indoors and most of the adults are now congregating in the conservatory. 'Okay,' I start. 'I really don't know how you're going to take this, Meg.'

She looks at me, eyes wide. 'What is it?'

'Go on, tell!' Ellie demands.

I clear my throat. 'Well, um . . . often, when I'm working, and have to grab a quick lunch between schools, I . . . go to Greggs.'

'Do you?' Meg exclaims, looking genuinely shocked.

'Yes, I do. And I have a sausage roll or a chicken bake.'

'Ugh!' She shudders.

'Well, that's your relationship scuppered, mate,' Tom says, laughing, as Meg gets up suddenly, and grabs the table for support.

'Oh my God, it's a deal breaker,' Ellie announces. For a moment I think: is it really? Is she storming off due to my secret fondness for puff pastry and saturated fat? But no, it isn't that.

'Sorry,' Meg murmurs. 'I don't feel too well.'

'Aw, she's always been a lightweight,' Tom observes as I jump up and put an arm around her shoulders.

'I'll get you some water,' I tell her.

'I actually want to go home,' she announces, all in a rush. 'No drawn-out goodbyes, please. Tom, Ellie, would you tell Mum and Dad that we had to rush off?' She looks at me. 'Just say it's something about Ricky's son . . .' Then off we go, winding our way between glass-laden tables as I call a cab. It arrives swiftly and she leans into me on the back seat, murmuring, 'You were lovely tonight. Sorry, darling . . .'

'Nothing to be sorry for,' I assure her. Unusually, due to Arthur's social engagement, we're staying over at Meg's flat tonight.

'Did you enjoy yourself?' she mutters.

'Yeah, I really did,' I say truthfully.

She smiles squiffily. 'You didn't want to play that game, did you? The secrets game?'

'I went along with it, didn't I?' I tease her. 'But I did notice *you* didn't share anything . . .'

'Oh, I don't have any secrets,' she says as we pull up at her block. She lets us into her flat and zooms straight to the sink where she glugs an enormous glass of water. This, and the plain buttered toast I make for her, seems to straighten her out a little as we go to bed.

I probably shouldn't ask. It's not that I want to grill her, but still, I can't help being curious. I mean, we've been together for almost a year and I thought I knew her pretty well by now. I turn towards her in bed. 'What was that thing Ellie said? Something about some kind of—'

'Uh, she's just so vanilla,' Meg mumbles, shaking her head.

'Vanilla?' I'm assuming she's not referring to ice cream.

'Yeah,' she drawls, 'and anyway, it wouldn't have counted as a secret because she and Tom know.'

I stare at her, genuinely confused now. '*What* do they know?'

'Just about stuff I used to do,' she says blithely, and something shifts uneasily in my gut. I mean, I'm not judgemental. My upbringing might seem strange to her, so remote and cut off on the island, where the monthly disco in the village hall was as thrilling as it ever really got out there. But I have lived in Glasgow since the age of eighteen and met numerous musicians who often happen to be highly sensitive and extremely complicated individuals. And Arthur's mum was hardly straightforward, to put it mildly.

110

'Is it something you can tell me about?' I ask hesitantly, although what I really want to ask is, *What did you used to do? Are we talking some kind of fetish? Did you go to bondage clubs or whip people or throw cream cakes at naked men?*

She murmurs something I don't catch.

'Sorry?' I say.

'I said—' she reaches for the water glass on her bedside table '—I used to be Polly Amara.'

I stare at her. 'You changed your name?'

She turns back to face me, her lips set firm as if trying to trap in a laugh. 'What?'

'Is that what you said? That you were Polly-something?'

Now she *is* laughing. 'Oh, Ricky. You're so sweet! So naive. Jesus . . .' I sit up and try to unravel what's happening here. Am I missing something?

'I didn't say Polly Amara,' she says. 'I said I used to be *polyamorous*.' Her gaze meets mine as I try to fathom out whether I've interpreted the word correctly. I mean, I'm not an idiot – I don't think – but now I'm worrying that, during my young adult life, when other people were busy being polyamorous, I was too busy practising my scales and arpeggios and I kind of missed what was going on. 'D'you know what that means?' she asks.

'It means, er . . . you saw different people at the same time.'

'That's right.' I almost expect her to produce a 'well donc' sticker from the drawer in her bedside table. 'But the actual definition is having more than one intimate relationship at the same time, with everyone's knowledge and consent.'

'Ah, right.' I look at her, stuck for what to say next. After all, I knocked back quite a bit of booze myself

111

tonight. For a moment I wonder if I'm in one of those weird, drunken dreams and when I wake up, everything will be normal and there'll be no Polly-anything.

'Otherwise, it's just plain old infidelity,' she adds.

'Yeah, I guess so,' I murmur, trying to ignore the creeping wave of sadness that's washing over me. 'So, why did you have that kind of, uh . . . arrangement?'

'It was just *fun*, that's all,' she says, taking my hand and squeezing it. 'But that was years ago. It just felt right at the time, for me and the guy I was seeing.'

'Oh.' I pause. 'Who was that?'

'Just someone,' she says with a quick shake of her head. She tilts her face and looks at me. 'You did ask, Ricky.'

'Yeah, of course.' It makes my sausage roll confession seem – to use her word – pretty lame. 'But can I ask you something?'

She nods. 'Yeah, sure.'

I inhale deeply. 'Would you tell me honestly if that's the kind of situation you'd be happier with now?'

'Of course I'd tell you,' she exclaims, 'and no, it's not. Not anymore, not with you.' She sighs loudly to signify that she no longer wants to discuss it.

'I just wish you'd told me before,' I add.

'It's in the past, Ricky,' she says firmly, 'and, anyway, when do we ever get the chance to talk about anything in any depth? I mean, it's not easy when Arthur's around.'

I blink at her. What does she expect me to do, put him up for adoption? Oh, I know I'm swerving in the wrong direction here, and she's right – I did ask. 'Well, not when we're at mine, maybe,' I say, 'but we *do* go out . . .'

'Occasionally,' she retorts. 'Anyway, you hold things back from me too.'

I frown. 'What kind of things?'

'Important things. I mean, you're fine talking about trivial stuff. You'll tell me about your pupil's dog trying to eat her violin bow and your dad being outraged when he saw a bag of shop-bought ice in your freezer and couldn't believe you didn't make your own—'

'Meg,' I cut in, 'can we stop this now? It's late and we've had a heck of a lot of wine and—'

'You tell me all that,' she barges on, 'but the bigger things, the *significant* things, you keep tightly guarded to your chest. Don't you trust me?'

I rub at my face, wondering how the hell we've got into this. I'd thought the dog-biting-the-bow thing was funny; that's why I'd told her about it. 'Of course I trust you,' I murmur.

'Can I ask you about something then?'

I look at her as it dawns on me what she's going to say. But it's not something I want to go into now – not with Meg, not with anyone.

It's buried in the past and it's staying that way.

'Ricky?' she says, sitting bolt upright as if primed for burglars. 'Would you *please* tell me what happened to Arthur's mum?'

Chapter Sixteen

Suzy

'So, I should be back at around six,' I tell Dee, 'but I'll call if I'm running late. Everything's in the bag – food, bowls, poo bags—'

'Stop fussing.' She laughs. 'I am capable of looking after him, you know. Although I can ping you hourly updates if you like.'

I smile, realising I'm acting like a parent dropping off her child at nursery for the first time. Dee's day off coincided with my Rosalind meeting, and she insisted she'd be delighted to dog-sit on this blustery Wednesday afternoon. 'I hope he behaves,' I add, looking around her tidy yet inviting living room: stripped floorboards, slouchy pale blue velvet sofa, her two daughters' graduation photographs framed tastefully on the pale grey wall.

She grins. 'As long as he doesn't try and make chips when my back's turned. Anyway, just focus on what you have to do and don't worry about anything here.'

I nod and swallow hard. 'Whatever happens,' I say, more to myself really, 'the main thing is to hold it together and be strictly businesslike.'

'That's right.' Dee squeezes my arm. 'You can do it, Suze. You're being proactive and brave and I'm really proud of you.'

'Thanks so much.' I pause and glance down at Scout. 'I'm *not* going to get emotional,' I add firmly, giving him a prolonged cuddle and several noisy kisses before heading off to see if this old friend of my sister's – who's never been mentioned before – can actually sort out my life.

As I drive to Leeds I try to make the mental shift from soppy pet kisser to someone who is consulting a professional and must therefore be the epitome of professionalism herself. Although I have already emailed over countless documents and spreadsheets to Rosalind (I must *not* call her Roz, I've decided), there are also reams of paperwork neatly sorted in folders, sitting expectantly on the back seat of my car.

Even though I'll be close to Belinda's house, I'm not planning to visit today; not even after my meeting when she's likely to be home after work. The truth is, I'm not sure I could face Derek, who's rolled out his 'Paul couldn't organise a piss-up in a distillery' line too many times for my liking. Although he was correct on that score, it's not as if he does anything particularly meaningful himself, as far as I've been able to gather. He doesn't have an actual job as such. Instead, he has shares and stuff – investments – and makes a great show of conducting phone calls in a very loud voice. But I've always suspected it's a front and that, once Belinda has headed off to work, he lies about scratching his arse all day.

As I arrive at the outskirts of the city, I push away negative thoughts and allow the satnav to guide me towards my rescuer. Dee was right, I reassure myself; I'm being proactive and trying to sort things out, a shift that seems to have coincided with Scout arriving in my life. In fact, I'm a little surprised at how much I've managed to achieve during the past four days, since I arrived home from Sgadansay. There's been a flurry of notable people dying – a Seventies pop icon, a much-loved author and a celebrity hairdresser – and I've managed to pull together obituaries for all of them. 'They're like buses,' Paul once joked. 'You wait for one famous person to peg it and seven come along at once!'

On top of all that I took Scout for a health check at the vet's and felt inordinately proud as he behaved beautifully during his MOT. The vet pronounced him 'a little underweight but otherwise in excellent health'. I'd have been no more proud of my boy (when did I start thinking of him as my *boy*?) if I'd been given a glowing report at parents' evening.

And now, as I pull over to park, I try to picture things running just as smoothly at Rosalind Nulty's office. After all, she is a leading insolvency expert, according to Belinda. I'm picturing a bright, toothy, captain-of-hockey-team type who'll smile sympathetically and say, 'Okay, Suzy, I can see it's been a terribly stressful time for you. But now you can leave it all with me.'

I climb out of my car, gather up my files of paperwork and stride past a run-down computer repair shop and a nail bar with a young woman in a tunic smoking outside. And I think about all the things I'd rather be doing, like playing with Scout in the park or sharing a bottle of wine with Dee. Come to that, I'd rather be sluicing out the wheelie bin or having my spleen removed than this – but it's not about what I *want*, but what I *need* to do.

The grey concrete block comes into view. It looks like

116

a faceless government office or maybe a detention centre. Before going in, I pause and take a deep breath to steady myself. From the plaque on the wall, I can see that several businesses are housed here, none of which spark joy: PaydayLoans4U; J. Savage Debt Recovery; and: Nulty & Loaming Financial Solutions.

Can this woman help me, as my sister has promised? *Don't get emotional,* I tell myself firmly as I push the door open and walk in.

Chapter Seventeen

Rosalind has short, feathery dark hair and berry-like brown eyes. Her dainty face, plus the tiny hand that shakes mine, brings to mind a woodland mammal like a shrew or a vole (my animal identification skills aren't that hot – after all, I'd mistaken Scout's whines for the yowl of a wildcat).

'So, I've been through everything you sent me,' she says, 'and what struck me is how quickly things started to go wrong.' We're straight onto business without the offer of tea, coffee or even a glass of tap water to moisten my parched mouth. But never mind that. I'm here for help, not refreshment. We haven't even mentioned Belinda, our common link.

'Well, yes,' I say, feeling faintly scolded, 'although I didn't realise the full extent of the problems for quite a long time. I mean, Paul was pretty evasive. I know now that I should've been involved in every aspect. But that was never the plan. It was very much his baby. And for a while at least, I really believed he was on top of everything.'

Rosalind blinks at me across her desk, as if finding it

difficult to comprehend my levels of idiocy. *Don't get emotional. Just keep yourself together and find out what you need to do next.*

'So you weren't involved day to day?' she asks.

'No, not really.' *As I have already explained, on the phone and by email and actually two seconds ago.*

'So what role did you have,' she asks, quirking a brow, 'just out of interest?'

'Um, I wrote the press releases,' I reply, 'and the text for the brochures, that kind of thing. Anything that needed to be written, basically . . .'

'Ah, right.' She nods. 'Did you enjoy that?'

'I guess I did at first,' I reply, impatience rising in me now as I wish we could just discuss the matter in hand, as she'd seemed keen to do at first. 'I mean, it was fine when I could just write normally.'

She frowns. 'Normally? As opposed to what?'

'As opposed to . . . in the voice of a puffin,' I reply, aware of my cheeks reddening.

'You pretended to be a puffin?' Her eyes widen.

I glance down at the pile of paperwork I gave her, which she has shoved to one side of her desk. 'The distillery's old whisky labels had an antique-style engraving of Sgadansay harbour,' I explain. 'They summed up the history and heritage of the brand. But Paul decided we needed to be different so he asked a friend to come up with a new design. And, er . . . he drew a puffin.'

I detect a hint of amusement in her eyes, and no wonder. Paul's friend's artistic credentials amounted to little more than owning a packet of crayons, from what I could make out. 'They decided to call him Percy,' I continue, 'and he'd be our mascot and we'd have T-shirts and mouse mats and all of that printed with him on, and then Paul insisted that I should write all our marketing material as if it was actually Percy talking—'

'*That* must have been challenging,' Rosalind observes with a barely disguised smirk.

'It was,' I say, 'but, you know, my main concern now is what to do next. Because the whole operation is hanging by a thread . . .'

'Yes, I can see that.'

'Everyone's still being paid,' I continue, 'but pretty soon I'll have to think about laying people off and I'm dreading it. It'd be bad enough anywhere, but there's so little employment on Sgadansay. There are all their families to think about . . .'

Rosalind clears her throat. 'Yes, I can see you're in a very precarious position.' As she turns to her computer screen, I glance around her dreary office with its beige walls, a small grey fan in the corner and a white plastic pot on the windowsill, containing a few shrivelled leaves. I hope she's better at sorting out financial messes than she is at tending to houseplants. In any other circumstances I'd ask if she'd let me have a go at resurrecting it. But we're not here to talk about her plant. It's my business we need to rescue.

I shift position in the chair as she taps away at her keyboard. I'd pictured myself striding out of her office after twenty minutes – destitute, yes, and never again allowed to borrow a library book, let alone have a credit card to my name, but able to move on with my life.

She nudges her keyboard aside and turns back to me. 'Are you familiar with the term liquidation?'

I nod glumly. Naturally, I've spent countless hours reading up about it. 'Yes, I am.'

'And you understand that if that happens, the business

is closed and the assets are sold in order to pay the creditors?'

'Yes,' I murmur.

'. . . so we have your supply chain, your raw materials, your distributors . . .'

'That's right.' On and on she goes, listing every company and individual who needs to be paid; from the IT experts to the builders who refurbished the visitors' centre last year – unnecessarily, in my opinion, but Paul was all about image and making 'a big splash', as he called it.

Rosalind's jaw seems to tighten as she looks up at me. 'Okay, Suzy. I'm going to pull everything together and we can take a final look at the figures together. But it looks like voluntary liquidation will be your best option.'

I knew, deep down, that this was probably what she'd say. However, I suppose a tiny piece of me had clung to the hope that she'd smile pertly and say, 'Leave it with me and everything will be fine.' Like my sympathetic sewing teacher at school who'd baulked at my disastrous creation then kindly unpicked the seams and whizzed it back up for me, correctly.

Of course, this is a distillery, not a calico tote bag, and there's no kindly Miss Bostock on hand to make everything all right.

Rosalind is talking about the intricacies of liquidation now. I exhale slowly, feeling quite sick, and glance over at the pot plant. Poor thing, I muse. But there is still a *little* bit of life in it, and maybe it could be revived with some water and plant food and love, like Frieda's cheese plant. It's thriving now, a miracle of survival following years of maltreatment and neglect.

Water, food and love.

Two years ago, when Paul and I went on the distillery tour, Jean, the guide – of course, I know her name now – told us the crucial ingredients for whisky. 'Just three things, isn't it, Harry?' she'd said, beaming at the elderly head distiller. He'd rolled his eyes at the 'love' part and I'd smiled, assuming he was too down to earth for that kind of flowery talk. Yet that's precisely what's amazing about whisky. It's the result of those simple ingredients left to 'lie around in casks, doing fuck all', as Paul so eloquently described the maturation process. It's a beautiful thing made with patience and care.

And that's *all* it should be. Never mind puffin mascots and terrifyingly expensive new light fittings in the visitors' centre; and certainly *never* try to cut corners in a desire to boost profit. Because then an essential ingredient has been stripped away and it's *not* made with love, and it simply cannot possibly turn out as it's meant to.

My heart quickens as I consider all of this, while Rosalind taps out more notes on her computer. *Don't get emotional,* I remind myself. *Be calm, clear, concise.*

'I'm just wondering,' I start, 'if there's another option I could possibly consider?'

She looks up at me in surprise. 'Well, yes, there are always options of course. What are you thinking?'

'Um . . . I'm wondering if there might be a way that I can take it over, by myself, and somehow try to turn things around?'

She bunches up her mouth. It's hard to imagine her at university, as a young person, when my sister first knew her. She seems like she'd have been a serious-minded adult at twenty years old, flossing twice daily and consuming the recommended eight glasses of water per day. 'Are you thinking of some kind of rescue operation?' she asks.

122

'Erm, well, yes. I'm just wondering about it.'

'On your *own*?'

'If it's possible, then maybe . . .' I pause, aware of the enormity of what I'm suggesting. 'It's got to be better than giving up, hasn't it?' I add. 'The distillery's been there for eighty years. It's what Sgadansay's famous for. I can't just shut down, Roz. *Rosalind.*'

She nods, and her forehead crinkles. 'I do take your point. It does seem terribly sad.'

'So, could I actually do that?' I continue. 'Legally, I mean, so Paul wouldn't be a joint director anymore?'

'Oh, that's entirely possible,' she says, still brisk but a little warmer now. 'Basically, he would be contacted – we could do that for you – and if he was in agreement, we would arrange for him to sign his shares in the company over to you.'

I take this in for a moment. 'But you know I didn't put anything into it? Financially, I mean. It was bought with Paul's inheritance . . .'

'Yes, but you own it jointly and in taking it over you'd be solely responsible for the debts.' I nod. Christ, what a terrifying thought. 'Do you think he'll be relieved to step away?' she asks.

'Looks like it,' I reply. 'He's made it clear that he doesn't want anything to do with me directly – or the business. But . . .' I pause. 'What about the debts? I mean, obviously we're in a financial mess and I don't imagine I can borrow money from anywhere. I have my house, of course, but—'

'I don't think it'll come to that, Suzy.'

'I hope not. But if it does—' I break off, trying not to even imagine myself at forty-eight, having to sell my house and living back with my parents, with Mum remarking, 'I don't know how you can sit around writing about dead

123

people all day. I'd find it depressing!' Obviously, Belinda and Derek couldn't have me, now that I own a dog. *Thank Christ I have a dog.*

'If you're seriously considering a rescue mission,' Rosalind says, leaning forward, 'then your creditors *might* be persuaded to agree to a turn-around period, while you address the problems and get things back on track.'

I blink at her. 'Really? Is that likely, d'you think?'

'It's possible,' she says, 'if you could manage to convince them that it's a viable option. I mean, if they believe that, in the long run, they're better sticking with you and allowing you the time to turn things around. Rather than winding up the company, I mean.'

'Wow.' I take a moment to allow this new information to settle.

'You'd need to come up with a strong proposal,' Rosalind adds, 'and be absolutely upfront about your plans.'

I nod. 'Uh-huh. I could do that.'

Could I? Could I really? Never mind Paul blundering into the whisky business with sod all experience. My own knowledge of booze production amounts to discovering Isaac's secret home brewery in his wardrobe and my brief experiment with making sloe gin.

'And we'd have to agree a timetable of payments to all your creditors,' she continues, 'so they'd feel reassured that you're getting things back on track.'

Bloody hell. It sounds like a heck of an undertaking, but something is starting to grow in me; a tiny seed of determination that I'm *not* going to roll over and give up. Harry's face shimmers into my mind. The proud, distinguished master distiller would know what to do. I need to contact him somehow, I decide. I need his expertise

124

and support; I need him *with* me in all of this. But will he even agree to have anything to do with me?

'I want to do this,' I tell Rosalind now. 'I really want to give it my very best shot.'

A small smile crosses her lips. 'Okay, if you're sure. I'll need a few days to start pulling things together and then we can speak again . . .'

'And what about your fees?' I say quickly. 'We haven't talked about—'

'I'll set all that out in an email,' she cuts in. 'So, if you could give me contact details for your partner, I mean your *ex*-partner . . .'

'I only have his mobile number and he might not respond.'

'We can try,' she says with a note of authority that makes me think: will he dare to ignore her? Or will he be relieved that this might possibly represent a way out for him? After all, this isn't like the wine club, the cycling or any of his other short-lived obsessions. He can't just act like it never happened.

Please, Paul, I will him as I leave Rosalind's office. *Please just do this one thing for me.*

Chapter Eighteen

Alcohol disaster stories might not seem like what I need right now. However as Isaac, Frieda and I reminisce around the garden table, chuckling over the memory of Isaac's audacious home brewery, I'm aware of the recent stresses ebbing away a little.

It's partly the kids being here. They arrived by train within an hour of each other last night, and were thrilled to meet Scout; it really was like guinea pig day all over again. But even better because our time together seems precious these days, as it's so rare.

'You had no idea at all, did you?' Isaac chuckles now, sipping a beer.

'That you had a brewery in your wardrobe?' I smirk at the memory. He'd been fifteen years old and apparently it had been the major project of the summer. 'No, love, because I was a respectful mother who'd never have dreamed of delving about in your wardrobe unless I thought something was up.'

Frieda laughs. She looks so natural and pretty in a white T-shirt and jeans, with her long dark hair loosely tied back and a faint suggestion of freckles across her upturned nose. 'You're so gullible, Mum,' she teases. 'You didn't even suspect anything when they kept going for all those bracing walks?' Isaac and his mates, she means.

'I just thought they were enjoying a healthy, outdoor lifestyle!'

'When actually, they were gathering nettles and smuggling them home in carrier bags stuffed up their sweatshirts . . .'

'If I hadn't smelt something strange,' I remark, turning to Isaac, 'you'd have got away with it for longer.'

'Yeah.' He smiles. 'It tasted disgusting, though.'

'It made you puke, Ize,' Frieda retorts, beckoning Scout, who trots across the lawn towards her and lets her fix on his lead.

We head out on a walk, following the winding path along the river with Scout trotting a little way ahead. 'It feels like he's part of our family already,' she says, linking her arm in mine.

'You're right, it really does.'

'Oh, Mum, I hope no one claims him.'

'I very much doubt it. It's been over a week, love.'

She nods, and I turn to Isaac, who seems to have grown even taller since I last saw him. Lean and long-limbed, he towers over me by a good six inches now. His hair is shorn extremely short, and there's a bit of a tufty little beard going on. But he still has that teenage gangliness; his grey T-shirt is rumpled and his jeans are ripped at the knees. When he arrived yesterday I registered the state of his shoes, mangled and filthy with the soles flapping loose, as if he'd found them lying in the road. He'd laughed when I announced that he needed new ones, and tried to force money onto him. *These are fine, Mum! Stop fussing!*

127

Later, bringing Scout along for the ride, I drive the kids to their dad's where they're staying tonight. Since we broke up, it's always been fairly amicable between Tony and me. We'd just got together too young and were no longer in love – at least, not in *that* way. While Frieda and Isaac were understandably upset at first, pretty soon it became normal for them to live between our two homes. They even handled things well when Tony met Maddy and moved out of town to their rickety farmhouse, then produced four more children.

'I never realised I'd been married to the most fertile man in Yorkshire,' I joked with friends. And I suppose that *did* feel a little weird, especially as our kids were clearly entranced by their younger siblings and loved spending time there. Whenever I dropped them round at Tony's, the house would be filled with shrieks and laughter and the aroma of baking. Someone would be bashing a drum or running around in a dinosaur costume. Of course, I was glad our kids felt part of this bustling family, but my heart ached for them when they weren't with me.

I was lonely, I guess. Perhaps, when I'd met Paul, I'd been seeking a little craziness of my own. He was full of life and always up for a new adventure. If I'd known then what his most recent 'adventure' would entail, I'd have clung to my old life as if it were a raft in a storm. But I still loved him then.

We pull up at Tony and Maddy's where we are greeted warmly and I'm handed a mug of tea within seconds of stepping into the steamy kitchen. Immediately, the children throw down their Lego and paintbrushes as they all swoop upon Scout:

He's so friendly!

Aw, he licked my face!

Mum, Mum, can we get a dog?

At which Maddy pushes back her curly fair hair and laughs. 'Don't you think I've got enough on my plate with you lot?' Although we're not friends exactly, we get along well. She has welcomed Isaac and Frieda into their milieu as if they were her own.

'So you finally gave in,' Tony teases me.

I smile. 'No one's nagged me about getting a dog for at least ten years!'

Maddy grins. 'It's that classic thing, isn't it? Kids fly the nest, Mum gets a dog . . .'

'Yes, admit it, Mum.' Isaac chuckles, draping an arm around my shoulders. 'Scout wasn't a stray, was he? You went out and bought him 'cause you miss us so much.'

It's true that I miss them. But I also feel boosted by their visit and spend a long, productive Sunday writing more obituaries. Scout likes to lie at my feet as I work, chomping away on Paul's fantastically expensive cycling shorts. I've particularly enjoyed seeing him gnawing contentedly on the gusset. Happily, Dee reported that he'd behaved beautifully at her place (chewing only an 'ugly' tea towel), and here at home he's been delightful – apart from shunning his new deluxe wicker basket, £39.99.

By Monday the weather has brightened, luring me out to my garden. By this point in March I'm usually eager for nature to get a move on, and for the cheery lupins and clematis to burst into bloom. But with everything that's been going on, I've neglected things out here. So, while Scout sniffs around, I fork over the borders, plucking out weeds as I go.

I've just broken off to make coffee when my phone trills on the kitchen worktop. Rosalind's name is displayed.

My heart rate quickens as I answer it. 'Well,' she says, not bothering with any preliminaries, 'you'll be glad to hear that I've managed to speak to Paul.'

'Oh, really? That's great!' So, he's still alive at least. His mate George hadn't just been spinning me a yarn about him having 'gone out to lunch'.

'Yes,' she goes on, 'and, as you said, it looks like he just wants to step away from the business now.'

I frown. 'So, um . . . does that mean . . .'

'It means we can start the process of him signing his shares in the company over to you.'

'Oh!' Ridiculously, I'm seized by a desire for a strong alcoholic drink and it's not even 11 a.m. 'Well, that's good news,' I manage, 'isn't it?'

'It's certainly a step in the right direction,' Rosalind says. 'I'll email you now, so could you go through it all carefully and we can talk again later?'

'Yes,' I exclaim. 'Yes, of course. Oh, this is . . .' What *is* it exactly? I'm going to be the sole proprictor of an ailing distillery. I actually feel a little faint now, like a Victorian lady, requiring smelling salts.

'Are you *sure* this is the route you want to take?' Rosalind asks. 'I mean, are you ready for this?'

I take a deep, steadying breath. 'Yes,' I say firmly. 'Yes, I am.'

The tiny seed of hope inside me begins to swell. A cool breeze wafts through the open kitchen window and the lawn, which needs a cut already, is dappled in golden light.

After her call, I pace about, letting her words settle. There's no point in trying to write anything now. Instead, I make a cup of tea and sit in the garden as I drink it.

It's true, I decide; I *am* ready for this. I might not have had the kind of career where you rise through the ranks, like Belinda has, but I've always worked hard, and I've raised two kids to young adulthood and made a decent living of writing about dead people.

Scout is gazing up at me with a look that seems so trusting, as if he knows I'll take care of him and everything will be fine. And it's clear to me now, what I need to do.

I need us to be surrounded by purplish mountains and the glittering sea. We need to stride along that silver sand beach and breathe the crisp island air deep into our lungs.

Scout and I need to go back to Sgadansay.

Chapter Nineteen

Two Weeks Later
Ricky

The ferry rolls and tosses in the choppy sea. It's late afternoon on a stormy Sunday and the smell of soup and fried eggs hangs heavily in the lounge area. I've fetched teas for me and Meg (the café had no hibiscus), an Irn Bru and a Tunnock's Caramel Log for Arthur – so shoot me – and I'm trying to maintain a cheerful demeanour as I chatter on about the numerous splendours that await us on Sgadansay.

'The beaches are lovely,' I tell Meg. 'The one nearest Dad's is called Silver Beach, and then around the headland there's a lighthouse and a bit further on there's a little cove that not many tourists know about. We call it the Secret Beach. There's a cave there, isn't there, Arthur?'

'Uh?' He flinches as if only just remembering I'm there. Meg, too, is looking less than enthralled. Her face is pallid and there's a sheen of perspiration on her brow.

'You know, the *cave*,' I prompt him. 'Remember we used to build a fire outside it? And play that pirate game?'

'Mmm,' he murmurs, looking bleakly out of the

window. Of course, kids rarely appreciate being reminded of the things they *used to* enjoy. They're too young for nostalgia. Still, he could show a bit of enthusiasm for our trip. He could give some indication that we're on our way to somewhere fantastic – on a holiday – and not, say, jail.

So far on the journey, he's been immersed in playing a game on his phone. I realise that, at ten years old, he doesn't really 'need' a mobile – but he'd gone on about everyone else having them, and when Ralph, Kai's dad, had found one 'going spare' in their house and offered to give it to him, I'd relented. Whilst I didn't relish the idea of Arthur being permanently glued to it, I'd figured that he does have his football, and I didn't want to be the kind of parent who's pointedly *against* phones.

Meg, too, is gazing out of the window, although it's mostly steamed up. 'There's a castle, too,' I continue, quite the chirpy tour guide. 'It's a ruin – fifteenth century – and it's been used in loads of films, like, um . . .'

She turns and gives me an expectant look. Unable to remember the names of any of the films right now, I rescue the situation by neatly flipping into the role of TV weatherman: 'The forecast is pretty good. I know it's bad today but it looks like it'll get brighter with some sunny spells, maybe a bit windy but by next weekend – by your birthday, Arthur – it should be pretty decent . . .' I'm aware now that all I need to do, to round things off nicely, is to talk about projected precipitation levels, wind speeds and cold fronts.

'That's good,' Meg says, with something like a cold front hanging ominously above her head. She turns back to the window and traces a shape in the condensation with a finger. From where I'm sitting it could be interpreted

133

as a dagger, and I worry now that she's considering fetching a knife from the café and stabbing herself. But it's probably just a random collection of lines.

'Down by the harbour,' I witter on, 'there's little place called the Seafood Shack. They do amazing fresh mussels—'

'Erm, Ricky?' She turns to me again, looking decidedly peaky now as the boat continues to lurch like a child's plastic toy. 'D'you mind if we don't talk about mussels right now?'

'Oh, erm, yeah.' Of course, what my girlfriend needs when she's clearly feeling seasick is for me to start on about molluscs. 'I'll get you some water,' I add, jumping up and marching back to the café.

We'd been outside on the deck of the ferry for the first half hour, which is actually better than being trapped inside when the crossing is rough like this. I'd tried to explain that it's good to be able to see the horizon (as well as breathe in fresh air instead of the cooking smells). That way, I'd mansplained, you avoid confusion between what the inner ear can sense, in terms of motion, and what the eyes can see. Because that's what triggers nausea.

She'd thanked me curtly for my explanation before adding, 'I do know a little bit about human anatomy, Ricky.' Of course, she ear-candles for a living. Arthur and I had followed her, mutely, as she'd retreated to the lounge.

I hand her a glass of water and give Arthur the Caramel Log he'd requested. Meg glowers at it as I've just slid him a packet of cigarettes. When stuff like this happens – and I catch these gusts of disapproval – I can't help wondering whether it's going to work out for us after all. But then, mostly it's fine and I try to avoid having those 'where is this going?' conversations with myself. We just have different views on things, that's all.

Things like oven chips and plastic tomato-shaped ketchup dispensers and whether I'm soft for not marching Arthur off to bed at 7.30 p.m. every night, as if he's four years old.

'How're you feeling now?' I ask as I sit back down next to her.

She sips her water. 'A bit ropey, but I'll be fine. It's a long crossing, isn't it?'

'Yeah. Another hour to go. Sure you don't want to go back outside and get some air?'

She shakes her head mutely. As the weather worsens I silently curse it behaving in this way, as if it's a child throwing a tantrum in a supermarket because it hasn't been allowed a bag of Haribos. I'd willed it to be *good* today, for the sun to be shining and for Arthur to seem happy and excited about spending a week on the island like he used to. But he didn't seem excited when we were packing, and who could blame him? We were on Sgadansay together just a few weeks ago, and right now he was meant to be with Kai's family at that villa in Spain.

Meg brushes a strand of hair from her face, seeming to gather herself as she smiles wanly. 'Looking forward to this, Arthur?'

'Yeah,' he says unconvincingly as if she'd said, *Looking forward to having that massive injection, Arthur?*

'Not long till your birthday either,' she adds. I will him to at least try to pretend to be cheerful.

'Yeah,' he says again.

'It's on Saturday, isn't it?' she carries on, gamely.

'Yeah, not long to go now!' I say unnecessarily because he knows what blinking day it is and how many there are in a week.

'What d'you think you'll do for it?' Meg asks.

135

He shoots me a quick look. 'Probably just hang out and watch some stuff,' he replies.

'Yeah, we can watch movies,' I say.

'But Granddad doesn't have Netflix.'

'Erm, no, he doesn't.'

'Or a DVD player,' he adds helpfully.

'Oh dear,' Meg says.

'He does have a TV,' I remark, 'but it's black and white and takes about forty-five minutes to warm up—'

'Really?' Meg says, looking shocked.

'No, not really.' I muster a smile. 'He actually loves his telly nearly as much as the pub.'

'So he *does* have hobbies?' she asks, raising a brow.

'Of a kind, yeah. Mainly drinking beer and whisky and muttering at politicians on the TV. But I don't think there are Scout badges for those.'

Arthur gives me a faintly exasperated look, and I wonder now if it's not the cancelled Spain trip that's causing him to act this way, but the stage he's reached: too old for hunting for cowrie shells and building fires on the beach to cook sausages on. There's a collection of buckets and spades that he keeps at Dad's. I guess they're redundant now.

As we settle into silence, I try to convince myself that once we arrive, everything will be okay; different maybe, but *fine*. My son's growing up, that's all. It's just part of his development to edge away from me and realise I'm not so great after all, with my shabby attempts at putting on birthday parties for him with a bought cake. I'm sure Dad will be pleasant and welcoming to Meg, and I know he and Arthur will enjoy hanging out together as they always do. Dad seemed happy when I told him he was coming with us after all.

I open the newspaper I brought for the crossing (Meg has felt too queasy to read it) and, out of habit, turn to the page I always go to first. 'Why d'you read those?' Arthur asks.

'The obituaries? They're just interesting,' I reply.

'But they're about dead people, Dad.'

'You can still be interesting when you're dead,' Meg remarks, glancing round briefly before turning back, morosely, towards the window.

'They're like a whole life condensed,' I add, 'with the dull parts missed out. It's just the fascinating bits . . .'

Arthur peers down at the page. 'The fascinating bits about a jellyfish expert.'

'Well, yeah.' I chuckle. 'That *is* fascinating, don't you think?'

He snorts in mock derision. 'I s'pose so, Dad. If you say so.'

'What about that animal encyclopaedia you kept borrowing from the school library?' I remind him. 'You were obsessed with the jellyfish part. They can clone themselves, you kept telling me. And they don't have brains . . .' I push the newspaper towards him. 'You should read about this guy, he's *exactly* your kind of person—'

'I'm not that interested in them anymore,' he announces.

'Jellyfish,' I remark with an eye-roll. 'They're *so* last season, drifting around in their brainless way—'

'Yeah,' he says, finally cracking a smile. 'It's all about marsupials now—' Now both of us are laughing. Thank Christ he's cheered up. The weather has too. The sea has calmed, the sky has brightened, and someone's opened a lounge door so the eggy smell is fading away.

Across the lounge, a woman with long dark hair seems to be talking to someone down by her feet. I assume it's

137

a child at first, then notice her small brown and white dog who seems reluctant to come out from under the table. 'Come on, boy,' she says gently. 'We're almost there.' Arthur, who's noticed them too, nudges me.

'That looks just like the dog we met on Silver Beach. Remember?'

I nod. 'Yeah, he does.' We both glance over as she finally manages to coax him out from his hiding place. Pulling along a large wheeled suitcase with one hand, and clutching his lead in the other, the woman makes her way across the lounge, and out onto the deck, with the dog trotting along beside her.

Arthur turns to Meg. 'Dogs get seasick just like people do,' he explains. 'It's that inner ear thing Dad was going on about.'

'Really? Poor things,' she says without feeling.

He nods and wipes away a patch of condensation – and the dagger drawing – from the window. 'Look,' he adds. 'There's seals over there, lying on the rocks.'

'Oh, yes, there are loads!' She brightens at the sight of our welcoming party.

'We see them all the time here,' he adds, clearly aware that this is something of a novelty for Meg.

'Really?' she says. 'What kind are they, d'you know?'

'They're common,' Arthur replies.

'Yes, but what *kind* are they?'

'No, that's what they *are*,' he says, clearly enjoying knowing more about them than she does. 'Common seal is the species and there are grey seals on the island as well.'

'Oh, I see!' She sips more water and glances out again. 'I can see the town pretty clearly now.'

'That's where Granddad lives,' Arthur says.

'His street's probably the most photographed one on the island,' I add.

'Why's that?' she asks.

'It's a terrace of fishermen's cottages and each one's painted a different colour. Dad can just about tolerate tourists standing on the other side of the road, getting the whole terrace in,' I add, gathering together the newspaper and a selection of unread books and magazines in preparation for arrival. 'It's when they come up close and want to get all the details – the window boxes and door knockers and stuff – that his blood starts boiling.' I stop, wondering what's possessed me to portray him as an embittered old man when my girlfriend's about to spend a week with him.

'Really?' Meg exclaims.

'Yeah, he's got a *furious* temper,' Arthur says gleefully as the ferry docks at the quay.

Chapter Twenty

Suzy

Although the Cormorant Hotel isn't particularly pictur-
esque, it *is* dog friendly and that's what matters. Crying
out for a fresh coat of whitewash, it's set a few streets
back from the harbour front. But something about its
cosy granny's-front-room vibe feels comforting as I check
in, especially after the choppy ferry crossing, when I'd
sat close to a family who hadn't exactly seemed enthralled
about their trip either. Poor man, I'd thought as he tried
to cheer up his partner and son – or maybe stepson – by
enthusing about the island's castle and beautiful beaches.
At one point, the woman looked as if she might throw
up. A few of the passengers already had, as I'd heard
some noisy retching behind closed cubicle doors in the
loos. I hadn't been feeling too perky myself.

My hotel room is plainly furnished, with a single bed,
and is tucked away up in the eaves. I hadn't been able
to find a cottage or apartment to rent; at least, not in
town with reliable Wi-Fi and a mobile signal. I'd wanted
to be within walking distance of the distillery too, as I
plan to immerse myself in every step of the processes this

time. I hope the team will tolerate me being around and help me to understand how things are done.

Although I'd been keen to relocate to Sgadansay immediately, Rosalind had persuaded me to hold fire for a couple of weeks. At home in York, she'd pointed out, I'd be within easy reach of her office. In fact, I suspect she was worried that hotfooting it to the Outer Hebrides before I was fully prepared wasn't exactly the wisest thing to do. We had a follow-up face-to-face meeting at her office (the pot plant appeared to have not been watered in the interim) where she explained that my initial meetings with the creditors would happen via Skype or Zoom. Was I comfortable with that, she'd asked?

'Yes, of course,' I'd fibbed. It was like when the dentist asks if you're 'okay' while she descales your teeth with her pokey implements and blaster machine. *Yep, I'm having a lovely time, thanks, while you tear at my gums!* 'You're used to them, with your work?' she remarked. Perhaps she'd forgotten that I'm a writer of obituaries. What did she think I did? Skyped the dead?

However, I've got through them so far, and felt that I was at least making some progress as I dropped off a set of house keys to Dee, who'll ensure that *my* houseplants are tended and keep an eye on the place. I've booked in here for a week initially, and left my return ferry ticket open as I'm not sure how long I'll stay. Everything feels vague and open-ended but that's the way it'll have to be.

'Take things a step at a time,' Rosalind counselled just before I left, 'and don't do anything rash.'

I look down at Scout, who's conducted a preliminary sniff-around of our room. I won't be alone, I remind myself. As long as he's with me I am never truly alone.

'Fancy a walk?' I ask him. His ears prick up, and he wags his tail; of course he does. He doesn't care that it's drizzling when we step outside or that the sky hangs over us like a grey tarpaulin. He's probably just grateful to be off the ferry where, again, he cowered and trembled the whole journey.

It's late afternoon and most of the shops on the main street are closed. It's Sunday after all, and this is how Sundays used to be, and on Sgadansay there's a strong sense of being propelled back in time, to when life was gentler and slower. They even have half-day closing on Wednesdays like in the olden days! Paul could hardly believe it.

We head for the harbour where the fishing boats' masts chime soothingly. A lorry pulls up at the quayside and a man unloads crates with a clatter. The drizzle peters away and, as if the tarpaulin sky has been torn apart, a shaft of bright sunshine beams down upon us. I catch the scent of shellfish and remember that I haven't eaten since that bowl of soothing vegetable broth on the ferry, which partly settled my stomach. My taste buds seem to tingle as we march towards the emerald green hut with its wonkily hand-painted Seafood Shack sign.

'What can I get for you?' asks the ruddy-faced man in the kiosk. My gaze skims the array of shellfish gleaming on ice beneath the glass counter: cockles, mussels, langoustines and hand-dived scallops. I'm so ravenous I could devour them all.

'Ummm . . . I can't decide.'

'Just arrived, have you?' he asks, obviously picking up on my accent. I smile at him, pushing away any fears that he, like every other local here, is somehow connected to the distillery.

142

'Yes, just this afternoon.' I pause. 'Um, I think I'll go for a portion of mussels.'

'Good choice,' he remarks, sizzling some butter in a pan and slinging in a generous scoopful. Once they're cooked and smelling heavenly he loads them into a cardboard carton, and crams in a wodge of thick wholemeal bread and a quarter of a lemon.

Perched on a rock, I devour it all greedily. Seals pop up in the shimmering sea as I lick my fingers clean of brown butter.

Although it's tempting to stop by at Mary's Store for wine – which *is* open on Sundays, until 7.30 p.m.! – I'm aware that I'd probably tipple the whole bottle during the long evening ahead and I want to be clear-headed tomorrow.

Back at the hotel, I glance briefly into the bar. It looks cosy enough with its dark wood panelling and sepia-tinted photographs of island scenes. The barman, who looks no older than Isaac, flashes a quick smile as he polishes a glass with a cloth. One teensy little wine wouldn't hurt, I suppose. However, there are no guests in there, and no music is playing, and I don't fancy sitting there alone, in awkward silence, or for the bartender to feel obliged to chat to me. So I head up to my functional but not exactly cosy room, wondering what I could do to make it feel more welcoming.

Whenever Dee goes away on her own – which she does, frequently, as a bold independent traveller – she takes scented candles and something to squoosh onto her pillow and immediately she feels at home. But it would never occur to me to pack candles or pillow spray. Instead, I just click on the bedside lamp and boil the kettle for a cup of tea. When it's ready, I stretch out on the bed, edging over to make room for Scout as he jumps up to join me. It'll be a bit of a squeeze, if he insists on spending the night here, but we'll manage, I decide. And now, as I sip my tea and he snuggles closer, resting his head on my thigh, the room starts to feel a little homelier.

So here we are, I reflect, as his breathing settles into a slow rhythm. Just the two of us, here for God knows how long, for the purpose of persuading the distillery's employees that I'm doing my best to turn things around. It'll involve lengthy meetings with individual employees – and the whole team all together again. The very prospect causes my heart to lurch, and to take my mind off it I move to the flimsy desk where I start to unpack my paperwork. It's not quite 7 p.m. and the long evening stretches ahead. Luckily, I have Scout to walk again later, plus a few hours' work to crack on with.

I flinch at my phone's chirpy ringtone. My heart sinks; it's my parents' landline. I'm not sure I'm up to updating Mum on everything right now. She was horrified when she heard I was planning to take on the business alone, and couldn't understand my need to go back to the island so soon, if ever.

Wouldn't it be easier just to wrap it up and be done with it, Suzy? As if it were as simple as taking an ugly vase to the charity shop.

I sigh and accept the call. 'Hi, Mum.'

'Hi, love.'

It's not Mum, but my father. He has made an actual phone call. This is virtually unheard of. 'Dad? Is everything all right?'

'Yes, love. Everything's fine,' he murmurs. Why is he speaking so quietly? Perhaps it's just that I'm unused to hearing his voice on the phone. 'Just wanted to make

144

sure you've arrived safely,' he adds, so softly I can barely hear him.

'Oh! Yes, I'm fine thanks, Dad. So everything's okay, is it? Is Mum all right?'

'Yep, she's just having a bath, love.'

'Ah, right.' I can't help smiling.

'I wanted to wish you luck,' he adds. I'm still in shock. Whatever next? Will he be WhatsApping me? Setting up a Facebook account? I can't remember the last time we communicated in between seeing each other face to face.

'That's really kind of you,' I say, my vision fuzzing a little.

There's a pause. I hear faint sounds in the background and picture Mum emerging from the bathroom in her rose-patterned dressing gown. 'I'm very proud of you, love,' he continues, his voice even quieter now, 'taking this on all by yourself. Takes some gumption, that.'

'Thanks, Dad.' I swallow hard, waiting for him to add something like, 'But we're worried about you', or: 'What'll you do if it all goes wrong?'

'Have you brought that little dog of yours?' he asks.

'Yes, of course.' My heart seems to lift as I ruffle Scout's head. 'He hates the ferry,' I add. 'It seems to make him really unwell.'

'Poor thing,' Dad says. 'Not too keen on boat travel myself. I'm looking forward to meeting him, though . . .'

My smile widens. 'I'll bring him over next time I see you.'

There's a small lull. The background noise has stopped. 'That'd be nice, love. I've always wanted a dog.'

'Have you? I never knew that!'

He chuckles. 'Yes, but, you know. Your mum was never keen. And you can't have everything, can you?'

145

'No, I guess you can't.'

'So, anyway,' he says, in a brisker tone now, perhaps keen to wrap things up before Mum catches him talking to me, illicitly. 'I'm sure you'll be fine, Suzy, love. You're a clever, resourceful woman and you know best what to do.'

Do I really? I think as we finish the call. *Do I really know best?*

It's a bit too late to worry about that now.

Chapter Twenty-One

Ricky

'Your street's so *instagrammable*, Harry,' Meg announces to Dad as he brings a pot of tea to the living room.

'It's what?' Dad looks perplexed. He seemed a little shy when we arrived, greeting Meg hesitantly as if she might have come from the council to inspect the premises, and I was permitted a brief sort of half-hug. But he and Arthur embraced properly, as they always do.

'It's social media, Granddad,' Arthur explains. 'It's a way of sharing what you're doing with your followers.'

Dad nods gravely, apparently taking this in. In Harry Vance's world, 'social' means a few drinks at the Anchor and 'media' amounts to the BBC news, supplemented – for the really hard-cutting stuff – with the *Sgadansay Gazette*. 'D'you have social media, Arthur?' Dad asks.

'Yeah, 'course I do.' He smiles.

'He's a bit young for it really,' I add, 'but I couldn't see any harm in it.'

'Oh, it *is* awfully young,' Meg remarks in a surprised tone. Christ, it's only Instagram we're talking about, not vodka.

'So who are these *followers*?' Dad wants to know.

Arthur shrugs. 'Just, y'know, my friends and stuff—'

'Do you have them too?' Dad turns to Meg, who's perched neatly on the edge of the ancient armchair as if wary of fully settling into it.

'Yes,' she tells him patiently, 'but mine aren't just my friends. It's actually a lot broader than that.' I catch her looking down at the purple mug she's holding as if trying to muster the strength to sip from it. It bears the logo of a local drain excavation company. I don't think any of Dad's mugs have white interiors.

'You know them, though, don't you?' He studies her with a mixture of wariness and awe.

'Not in real life, no,' she replies, at which he looks even more confused since, as far as he's concerned, real life is the only life there is.

'So what do they want?' he asks. 'These followers, I mean?'

Meg's mouth twitches. 'They just want to see pictures of your lifestyle. It's a way of sharing your aesthetic – a kind of window into your world.'

'Oh,' he remarks, and as our conversation swerves towards more familiar territory of the weather (islanders discuss it obsessively), I can't help wondering what Dad's Instagram would be like.

So far, I've avoided mentioning the distillery. Understandably, it only seems to rile him to the point of simmering fury, and that's the last thing I want to do while we're here. Instead, I quiz him about Sgadansay gossip, and we learn that Mr Ross's cat was found 'flattened in the road' and someone I don't even know had to have a section of colon removed – all the uplifting local news. Once that's all been covered, Dad announces

148

that he'll 'get the tea on' (the evening meal is always tea here; never dinner or, God forbid, supper). I follow him into the kitchen and offer to help. However, he says he doesn't *need* help and I slope away like a dog sent out of the room.

'Show Meg where the bathroom is!' he calls after me, as if she might have continence issues. Arthur trots upstairs happily – he loves his little box room here – and Meg and I follow behind with our suitcases.

'This is . . . cosy,' she murmurs, stooping to avoid cracking her skull on the eaves. As I grew up in this house, I'm familiar with its quirky angles and do that automatically.

I smile at her. 'Dad seemed a bit shy with you. I forget he can be like that sometimes.'

'He's probably just not used to meeting new people,' she remarks which, whilst true, still rankles a little. I tell myself that she probably didn't mean to sound patronising. As she peruses the room I wonder what she's making of the yellow woodchip walls, the green tasselled lampshade over the centre light, and the washed-out purple duvet cover that's been in use since I was a child. We haven't seen much of each other since her parents' party; crazy-busy with work, she'd explained. I know she sees clients at home sometimes outside her normal hours. I haven't mentioned the polyamory thing again; it's in her past and I guess it's none of my business. Nor have I gone into details of what happened to Arthur's mum, beyond the basics, because I haven't wanted to get into how I could have done things differently and made everything better.

When she asked me that night, I brushed her off with, 'I've told you already. We split up and she disappeared.

I've tried to track her down but eventually I had to give up.'

'There's more to it than that,' she insisted. 'I can tell.'

'I really don't want to rake it all up, Meg.'

'You're so bloody private!' she'd exclaimed, turning away irritably before falling into a deep sleep. And the next morning, she hadn't mentioned it again.

There's some clanking about downstairs now. 'Just going out to the chippy,' Dad shouts up.

'Dad,' I call back, 'if we're having fish suppers I'll go and get them—'

'No, only chips. I've got the rest sorted.' The front closes, and he's gone.

Back in the living room now, I scan the place for signs that Dad has allowed things to deteriorate since Arthur and I came up a few weeks ago. That time, he'd seemed determined to show that he was doing okay, that he wasn't missing his job *one bit*. And thankfully the place is still neat and tidy, if a little oppressive. With all its dark wooden furniture, the room feels like a tiny antique shop that never properly fills with light.

An inviting aroma is drifting through, of something warming in the oven. Meg wanders through to the kitchen. 'Ricky?' she calls out. 'Come here a minute, would you?'

'What is it?'

'I want you to see this.' She appears in the kitchen doorway and gives me what I can only interpret as a look of mild disgust.

Christ, what's Dad left lying about in there? Don't say it's an old pair of underpants or, worse, some titillating reading material. I've never imagined him as a consumer of that kind of stuff, but maybe the lack of a job to go to has made him start acting out of character.

Looking faintly seasick again, Meg turns back into the kitchen. I hurry through to find her glaring down at the offending item.

'Oh,' I say, laughing now. It's not a porn mag sitting there in plain view on Dad's kitchen table. It's just a hardcore Scotch pie.

She gives me a pained look. 'D'you think that's what we're having for dinner?'

'It's a bit small for four of us,' I reply.

'It's not the size of it, Ricky. It's just . . . I've never eaten a mutton pie in my life.'

'They're actually really good,' I remark. 'Me and Arthur always get one at the football—'

'We're not at the football now, are we?'

'It's only mutton,' I venture.

'Yeah, mutton and about a gallon of grease. If you squeezed one you could lubricate the engine on that ferry—'

I'm laughing now – I can't help it – as she flings open the oven door and jabs a finger at four similar pies warming on a tray. 'Why did he leave that one on the table?' she barks.

'Um, maybe it's spare in case anyone fancies two?' She scowls at me. 'Just have the chips then,' I add. 'Don't feel obliged to eat it—' I stop as the front door opens and Dad strides in with a carrier bag containing cartons of delicious-smelling chips.

Arthur trots downstairs, announcing, happily, 'Scotch pies!' as Dad tips baked beans from a can into a Tupperware bowl and blasts them in the microwave. *Ping!*

'Erm, can I help?' Meg asks, still looking squeamish.

'No, you're fine, love,' Dad says briskly, now extracting a white sliced loaf from the bread bin. He plucks four

151

slices from the packet, whacks them onto a chipped plate and spreads them liberally with margarine. As I lift plates from the wall cupboard, Arthur opens a drawer and grabs a bunch of ancient cutlery, which looks as if it might have been rescued from a shipwreck.

Dad serves dinner up, and as the male contingent tucks in, Meg prods hesitantly at her pie's pastry lid. Clearly mustering courage, she nibbles at a tiny forkful and swallows it down. As for Dad, for whom having a stranger in his house is in fact a massive deal, he is clearly making an effort in his own, gruff way. After all, baked beans come under the banner of 'vegetable' and normally we'd just be having pie and chips.

'So, what d'you do for a job then?' he asks her, which strikes me as some kind of miracle. Dad isn't a *so-what-do-you-do?* kind of man. As Meg pokes at her rapidly cooling chips, she explains what an alternative therapy practitioner actually does. Dad seems fine with the massage and even the acupuncture parts, but I suspect she's lost him as she describes the concept of ear candling.

'I place one end of the candle into my client's ear,' she explains, 'and light it.'

'You put a lit candle in someone's ear?' Dad gasps.

'Not the lit end, no. The pointy end—'

'Why would you do that to someone?' he exclaims as if she's just described her preferred method of assault.

She places her cutlery beside her barely touched dinner. 'I use *hollow* candles,' she explains. He fails to look reassured by this. 'And the flame creates suction that helps to draw out the impurities,' she adds.

I catch Arthur trying, unsuccessfully, to suppress a grin. We've discussed this candling thing between ourselves, and whilst I didn't want to give the impression that I was

152

running down my girlfriend's profession, I had to admit that I was doubtful about its effectiveness. At best, I imagined that the client would be lucky to avoid injury.

'And people pay money for that?' Dad asks.

'They do,' Meg says, 'and they always seem a lot lighter, and happier, after a session—'

'Probably because you've taken the candle out,' Dad quips, which makes Arthur splutter, and when I turn to Meg I see that she's managed to muster a smile too.

The mood has lifted, and as I clear the table I decide that Dad might take a little time to warm up, but he'll soon get to know my girlfriend and become used to having her around. As for Meg, she'll understand that there are no grazing tables or toasted coconut granola around here, and as long as she doesn't try to stuff a candle into Dad's ear, everyone will get along fine.

Chapter Twenty-Two

Suzy

Scout slept at the foot of my bed last night. He stretches, yawning with an audible yowl as I get up to make an instant coffee, and I lift him up into my arms so we can watch the island waking up from our window. It's not yet seven-thirty and the sky is mottled purple streaked with gold.

After I've dressed and showered we head out for the morning walk that's already become a natural part of our day. Only now, the leafy residential streets of York have been replaced by narrow lanes that cut between the shops and fishermen's cottages, leading us to the harbour and onwards towards the silvery beach. The sky is brightening, the purplish tones turning to mauve, then a pale, clear blue. By the time we return to the hotel, bright April sunshine is beaming brightly onto its flaking facade.

'Is it okay to bring my dog in?' I ask the girl on duty in the breakfast room.

'Of course it is,' she says, looking surprised that I'd even thought he might not be allowed. She looks no older than fifteen and, after bringing my oddly

154

comforting bendy white toast, poached eggs and coffee, she disappears. Despite this being the start of the Easter holidays, no other guests show up for breakfast and we haven't yet seen – or heard – any evidence of anyone else staying here.

Back in my room now, I conduct a meeting via Zoom, during which I explain to a senior man at our bottle suppliers that I am in the process of trying to take over the business by myself, as well as focusing hard on getting things back on track. 'But you've lost key personnel,' he points out, not unreasonably.

'Yes,' I say, 'our head distiller resigned, unfortunately. But I'm on the island now – that's one of the reasons for me being here, to see what I can do about that. And, in the meantime, the team here are all experienced—'

'But this new branding,' he cuts in, 'with the little *bird*. Was that your idea?' He has swept-over grey hair with distinctive grooves in it, as if it's been combed with a fork, and has a way of addressing me as if I am ten years old. I can handle being patronised right now – at least he doesn't call me a fucking idiot – and I'm buoyed up enough to explain, 'It wasn't actually, but rather than focusing on the mistakes that have been made, I'm keen to start with a clear slate and look to the future.' Meaningless management speak, perhaps; the kind beloved of a former boss at the recruitment consultancy where I worked, joylessly, for several years. But I actually mean it.

He clears his throat. 'Well, I have to say, it's good to deal with someone who's actually *communicating* with us . . .'

'I'm glad you feel that way,' I say. 'You can call me absolutely anytime.'

'That's helpful to hear,' he says gruffly as we finish the call.

During the past few years I'd started to notice Paul's head-in-the-sand approach to the more challenging aspects of life. At first I'd viewed this as a positive trait; I'd even enthused to friends about how 'free-spirited' he was. In contrast, Belinda once admitted that she'd been attracted to Derek because he'd seemed 'solid and dependable'. Whilst they were precisely the qualities I looked for in a washing machine, they're not what I look for in a man, and I was thrilled to meet someone for whom life was basically about having fun. Paul lightened me up and reminded me that life wasn't all about persuading the kids to eat peas and dealing with an endless torrent of household admin. He was like a breath of fresh air to me.

We'd caught each other's eye at a mutual friend's party. The music had been pretty much limited to 'ironic' Nineties boy bands, and Paul spun me a yarn about having been in a boy band himself. He certainly had the looks, I decided; but of course he'd been winding me up, and by the time we'd agreed to share a taxi home, he'd had me in stitches laughing.

We kissed in the taxi. I don't mean proper snogging; Christ no. I was forty years old and Paul was forty-two, and anyway, there wasn't time for any of that as my road had appeared far too quickly (how had we arrived there so fast?). It was just a tender kiss on the lips that lingered for just long enough to send my head into a spin.

It was all I could do to not grin inanely as I strode in to be faced with the babysitter. 'Fun party?' she asked, packing her college work into her bag.

'Yeah, it was pretty good,' I said, trying to convey that I'd done nothing more exciting than stand around nibbling

156

pretzels. Four years I'd been single since the split from Tony, and our divorce had come through a couple of years ago. Here was the promise of thrilling adventure – and I jumped right in.

Scout nudges at my ankle to signify that another walk is required. It's just gone 11 a.m. as we circuit the town, and as we arrive back at the hotel, Cara texts me: *Hope your journey was okay. Horrible weather for your crossing yesterday! D'you fancy popping over for lunch sometime? It would be lovely to see you.*

Love to, I reply. *When's good for you?*

Today would be great, if you're free? About one-ish? My heart lifts at the prospect. I'm planning to spend the afternoon at the distillery and if there's anything I could do with seeing today, it's a friendly face.

I pat the bed – Scout's cue to jump up and join me – and pull him in for a belly tickle as I tell him, 'Guess what? You and me have a date.'

Chapter Twenty-Three

'This is lovely,' I exclaim as Cara sets out a spinach tart, plus bowls of potato and green salad on the worn oak table. 'But you needn't have gone to all this trouble for me.'

'It's no trouble at all,' she insists. 'Would you like some wine?'

'Better not,' I say reluctantly. 'I'm due at the distillery after this.'

'And you don't want anyone to think you're filling your days with boozy lunches,' she says, pulling a mock-stern expression.

'Yes, exactly.'

Cara smiles and sits opposite me. It's not just the lunch that's surprised me, but also her living quarters here, which are far nicer than the impression she'd given. Tucked away to the rear of the former teashop, the combined kitchen and living room are sparsely furnished with a quirky mix of brightly painted furniture, and the exposed brick walls are painted chalky white. 'It's beautiful,' I say, gazing around. 'So bright and joyful. You said it was a wreck of a place . . .'

'Well, it was pretty shabby when I moved in,' she says, tucking her bobbed hair behind her ears. 'But the landlord said I could do what I wanted so I ripped out some horrible old units and stripped it back to the bones – like a bare canvas.' She laughs self-deprecatingly. 'If that doesn't sound too pretentious.'

'Of course it doesn't,' I say. As she greeted me and Scout warmly at the side entrance, I have yet to see her studio, which is housed in what was the original tearoom at the front.

'So, how's Scout been settling in?' she asks as we start to tuck in. 'Does he like his new home?'

'Oh, he's been brilliant,' I reply, checking her expression. 'I'm so sorry about Barney,' I add. 'I hope it doesn't feel weird or upsetting for you, having Scout here.' As soon as we'd arrived, and he'd conducted a preliminary sniff-around, he'd settled happily on Barney's plush floor cushion.

'Not at all,' Cara says firmly. 'You know, I realised the end was coming and I wouldn't have wanted him to go through more months of illness, being prodded and poked and God knows what.' Her eyes moisten and she musters a brave smile. 'I had to make the decision that it was better to say goodbye.'

'That must have been awful for you.' I put down my fork, unsure of what else to say.

'It's okay,' she continues with a quick shake of her head. 'These past six months, since I've been here, were probably the best of his life. Running wild on the beaches, and up into the hills . . . he couldn't have wished for a better time, really.'

'I'm glad you feel that way,' I murmur.

She clears her throat. 'I did have to put away all his

159

things – his chewy toys, his cushion.' She glances towards it. 'I just put it out again today for Scout.'

'Oh, that was kind of you,' I say, taken aback yet again by her generosity. 'And thanks for putting those lost dog posters around town—'

'That was no trouble. And at least you can be pretty sure that no one's looking for him now.'

'Yeah, that's good to know. So I guess he probably isn't from the island, which means someone must have left him behind here. That's the only explanation I can think of.'

Cara nods. 'He's so lucky to have found you.'

'I'm lucky too.' I smile. 'And actually, I'm happy to be back here. It might sound a bit mad but it seemed less daunting somehow, having him with me this time.'

'Oh yes, I can imagine,' she says. 'So, how long are you planning to stay?'

'I'm not sure exactly. I'm booked into the hotel for a week but I'm sure I could extend that. I mean, it's hardly thronging with guests . . .'

She grimaces. 'Bit bleak, is it?'

'It's okay actually,' I say truthfully. 'It's the first time I've slept in a single bed since I was twenty-one, but I'm not complaining.'

Cara chuckles. 'And what about the distillery? What's happening there?' I fill her in on my meetings with Rosalind, the tricky business of Paul and his part-ownership of the company, and my virtual meetings with the creditors, many of whom Paul had simply stopped paying, due to the disastrous cash flow situation.

'Wow,' she murmurs, placing down her fork. 'It's a lot to take on. How d'you feel about it all now?'

'Terrified?' I say with a hollow laugh.

'I'm not surprised. God, I wouldn't know where to start . . .' She gets up and we clear the table together.

'Anyway,' I add, 'the distillery's going to dominate my every waking moment from now, so let's not talk about that. How about your work? What's that like?'

She smiles brightly. 'Would you like to see my studio?'

'Of course, yes. I'd love to.' She leads me through to the arched doorway to the former tearoom. Like her living area, it's all exposed, whitewashed brick with beautifully printed fabrics tacked to the walls. There are hand-painted vases of cheery daffodils and fabric swatches attached to an enormous cork pinboard.

'These are lovely,' I exclaim, going over to admire the prints more closely. 'There's something incredibly soothing about them.' They are mainly in the island's colours of blues, heathery purples and faded greens.

'Thanks,' Cara says. 'You can probably guess where my inspiration's coming from just now.'

'Well, I can see they're based on the landscape here, but they're almost abstract, aren't they?' I wonder now if it's presumptuous to comment when I know very little about art – apart from the fact that, in galleries, I always zoom towards the modern stuff. And now I'm picturing Paul and me, on the Sgadansay ferry when the whole debacle began. 'It looks like one of those old religious paintings,' I'd told him, as we surveyed the view. 'All it needs are some floating cherubs and a scattering of naked muscular gods.' While I can appreciate the genius of those incredible paintings, I'm more drawn to bold, contemporary images like these.

'That's exactly what I try to do,' Cara says. 'I like playing about with shapes and colours and there's no shortage of inspiration on the island . . .'

161

'So you're glad you moved here?' I ask.

She hesitates for a moment. '*Most* of the time,' she says. As she doesn't seem keen to elaborate further, I look around the studio again. At one end is what I assume is her screen-printing equipment, and behind it are neatly ordered shelves bearing jars of brushes and bottles of paint, or perhaps inks, in vivid colours. At the other end is a day bed made up with plump pillows and a dazzling, clearly handmade patchwork quilt. I've never been in a real working artist's studio before and had imagined Cara's to be splattered in paint and with dirty rags strewn everywhere. However, there are only a few daubs of colour on the grey polished concrete floor. I suspect she likes her life to be neatly ordered and find myself wondering again what it's really been like for her to move to the island, alone, without knowing a soul.

'D'you sell your work here?' I ask. 'On the island, I mean?'

'Not yet,' she replies. 'I get by through licensing designs to companies and selling through my online shop.'

'I'm so impressed,' I tell her truthfully, 'that you've come out here and created all of this.'

'Oh, I s'pose I'm quite proud too,' she says with a self-deprecating laugh as Scout potters through to find us.

I crouch down to greet him and he jumps up at my knees, panting expectantly. 'This has been lovely,' I say, 'but I guess we'd better face the distillery team . . .'

'Well, good luck,' Cara says.

'Thank you.' I smile at her with a rush of gratitude. 'And thanks so much for lunch today. You can't imagine how much it's helped to see a friendly face.'

'It's helped me too,' she says as she sees us out. 'I can end up talking to the walls here, working all by myself.' I look at this slightly built woman in her crisp white

162

T-shirt and skinny dark jeans and wonder now just how lonely she's been during the past six months.

'I can imagine,' I say.

'Erm, I was wondering,' she adds, 'if you'd like a bit of help with Scout now and again, while you're here? If you're busy with meetings and spending time at the distillery – stuff like that. I mean, if you need someone to walk him—'

'Oh, I love our walks,' I say, 'and I'm planning to take him to the distillery with me. I can't imagine anyone would mind . . .' I break off as it dawns on me that Cara is asking not just to offer her help but because she *wants* to spend time with Scout. 'But actually,' I add, 'if you're sure, that'd be great. I still have my regular work to keep up with, and it means I could do a full day—'

'You have an actual job as well as the distillery?' she exclaims. 'I'm sorry, I didn't even think to ask—'

'Oh, that's okay,' I say quickly. 'The distillery part wasn't planned. My real job – at least, the one I chose for myself – is writing obituaries.'

'Wow, I bet that's fascinating! But how are you finding the time?'

'I manage,' I say, 'and my writing work helps me, actually.' I pause and shrug. 'At least, with that part of my life, I feel like I know what I'm doing.'

She ruffles the top of Scout's head. 'He could stay with me now if you like. That way, you could fully focus on what you've got to do this afternoon . . .'

'Actually, that'd be brilliant,' I say.

She grins and turns to address Scout, as if to ensure that he fully approves of our plan: 'Hey, little man, we'll go for a beach walk, okay? You and me are going to have such fun.'

* * *

As I stride through the town, I try to quell my nervousness by reminding myself of all the *good* stuff that's happened. After all, we've only been here for a day, yet I've already conducted a couple of meetings from my little room in the eaves and, crucially, seem to have made a real friend here – as has Scout.

My heartbeat quickens as I pass the bow-fronted bookshop with its cheerful red exterior, the blue-and-white chip shop, which seems to be bustling at all times of day, and an old-fashioned pharmacy, its gold-lettered signage glinting in the early afternoon sun. Such a beautiful town, utterly unspoilt and apparently barely changed for decades. In the distance, the ferry is making its slow, stately journey towards the mainland.

'Proper Scotland', as Mum called it, when she'd grilled me about why Paul and I were set on visiting this far-flung island. It strikes me now how different my life would be if I'd insisted that we hadn't visited Sgadansay after all, but holidayed in Majorca instead. Maybe Paul's wild notion of buying the distillery would have been forgotten, along with the wine club membership and his short-lived attempts to play the trumpet.

However, it happened, and I am slap-bang in the thick of it, and now my mouth is sandpaper-dry as the distillery comes into view. I'm conscious of breathing deeply, of pushing back my shoulders and walking tall as I stride towards the entrance.

Don't get emotional, I tell myself firmly as I open the door and walk in.

Chapter Twenty-Four

Ricky

Until our last visit I'd never really noticed Dad ageing, but since he left the distillery he hasn't seemed like his usual hearty self. Although I've managed to persuade him to come on our walk to the lighthouse, it seems to be taking more out of him than usual. But then, he's seventy-eight, I remind myself. And everyone grows older – even Harry Vance.

'I miss Bess,' Arthur remarks.

Dad nods. 'Aye, me too.' I glance at him as we walk; it's the first time I've heard him acknowledge it. But of course he misses her. He'd no more have been spotted out minus his trousers than without her trotting along at his side.

Arthur turns to me. 'D'you think we'll ever see that dog again?'

'Which dog?' I ask, confused.

'The one I was playing with last time we were here—'

'That was weeks ago,' I remind him, surprised that he's still thinking about him. 'He's bound to have been found or handed in somewhere by now.'

Arthur shrugs and seems to scan the scrubby ground to our right, as if almost expecting to spot him. Occasionally, at times like this, I wonder if I've made the right decision in not letting him have a dog of his own. After all, plenty of people with full-time jobs manage to have pets too. Maybe we could have found a way to make it work.

The lighthouse comes into view and Arthur brightens. 'Look, Meg! There it is . . .' Like with the seals on the rocks, he seems keen to show off the island's attributes to her. I'm grateful to see a glimmer of his childlike enthusiasm again.

'That so cool,' she remarks, pulling out her phone and taking numerous photos as we approach. Bright white with a solid red stripe, it's perched on the jagged rocks that my friends and I would scramble over when we were kids and – with a lack of much else to do – even as teenagers.

When we're close enough, Meg takes a selfie in front of it, presumably for her Instagram, #lighthouse. She seems to be enjoying herself, which is something of a relief as she was pretty subdued after dinner last night.

Maybe she'd been craving the city already, after being on Sgadansay for something like six hours. When I'd suggested an evening stroll to the harbour she'd muttered something about needing to make a phone call. She'd proceeded to conduct it down at the bottom of Dad's back garden, lurking by the wheelie bins like a guilty smoker. 'Client stuff,' she'd said, by way of a vague explanation. What kind of client stuff did she need to discuss at 9 p.m.? However, the mood is brighter today, the sky a wash of clear blue, and everyone – even Dad – greets my suggestion of a pub lunch with enthusiasm.

By the time we arrive back in town, and step into the

166

cosy fug of the Anchor, the usual handful of regulars are either clustered around the bar or tucking into controversial pies and chips at the scuffed tables. The deep-fat fryer has clearly been busy. We briefly chat to Rab the fisherman, Len the taxi driver and Mrs Pert, who still owns the hairdressing salon Mum used to frequent. Nothing seems to ever change here.

While Arthur, Dad and I order fish and chips (they really are excellent), Meg requests a salad, which comes laden with copious coleslaw. But at least there's greenery too – at least, a couple of token leaves – and the pub's ancient interior is clearly deemed worthy of her Instagram feed as more photos are taken.

Dad's local has barely changed since I was a teenager Like me, my parents were born and brought up on the island, both on far-flung crofts; small farmsteads where a living would be scratched out through the growing of crops and sheep farming. Moving to the town was a big deal for them when they got married. Suddenly, they were in close proximity to thrilling amenities such as a post office, a shoe shop and a newsagent's whose window display still consists of sun-faded jigsaws; I wonder, in fact, if they're the same ones that were there when I was a kid. They certainly look it.

'That'll get the customers in,' I joke as we pass it on our way back to Dad's.

Meg chuckles. 'You could get one for Arthur's birthday, Ricky.'

'You know, I'd be tempted if I hadn't brought his present with me.'

'You got him that laptop, right?' she murmurs. Dad and Arthur are a little way ahead, pointing at things, locked in conversation.

'Yeah, it's what he wanted,' I reply, adding, 'Actually, you know what he'd really love?'

She blinks at me. 'Not still asking for a dog, is he?'

'God, yeah, I don't think he'll ever give up on that,' I tell her, although – understandably – she's been unaware of that. Keen to avoid being that tedious bloke who's always blathering on about his kid, I tend not to share too much with her about Arthur's life. She doesn't need to know that he's been on at me to let him get a buzz cut like Lucas's, or that he scored a heroic (and indeed match-winning) goal in his last game. There's my Arthur life and my Meg life, the latter of which, I have to admit, has been concerning me lately – and still is now, even on our holiday. Because, for every hint that she might actually be enjoying herself, there have been episodes of what I can only describe as weirdness.

Back at Dad's place, I head straight to the kitchen to make a pot of tea. Dad drinks gallons of the stuff daily; it's something of a biological mystery why he doesn't spend three-quarters of his day in the loo. So of course he fancies a cuppa, as does Arthur (he never drinks tea at home). However, when I ask Meg whether she wants a cup, her gaze alights briefly on the pink wafer biscuits I've pulled out of the cupboard – they're Dad's favourite – and she says, 'Oh, I'm okay, thanks,' in a faintly beleaguered way, as if she's had enough to contend with today with the coleslaw mountain.

'Just got some calls to make,' she adds. Then, quick as a whippet, she's off out to Dad's garden again, closing the back door firmly behind her. When I glance through the window I see her pacing about, head bent down, perhaps reassuring a client that she's only away for a week and will attend to their ear candling next Monday.

Dad is already installed on the sofa, with the TV blaring, and Arthur is plonked there, cross-legged, at his side. Having taken their teas and the pink wafers through to them, I glance out again to see that Meg seems to have finished her call. She's just standing there, looking pensive, kind of gazing into space.

Christ, I hope it's not depressing her, being here. Although she's dressed casually in a black sweater and jeans, she still radiates 'city person' from her every pore. 'Is there a cashpoint here?' she'd asked Dad earlier, just before we went to the pub.

'Aye, of course there is,' he'd replied, looking as baffled as if she'd enquired, 'Do children go to school here? Can they *read*?'

Taking out my own tea, I stroll towards her. 'You okay?' I ask.

'Yeah, I'm fine.' She smiles tightly.

I look around the garden, even though there's not much to see: just Dad's wonky old shed and the spindly wooden chair he uses when he wants to read his newspaper in the sunshine. 'What did you think of the lighthouse?' I ask.

'Oh, it was beautiful,' she says, 'especially against that bright blue sky. I got some brilliant pictures.'

'Can I see?'

'Sure.' She pulls her phone from her jeans pocket and taps the photos icon. Angling it towards me, she scrolls with her thumb. There are so many pictures of the lighthouse, some with her standing in front of it, her light brown hair blowing attractively, and others just with the structure itself.

'These are great,' I murmur. 'Have you already posted one on your—' I stop as she flinches, as if jabbed with a pin. She pulls back her phone, but too late; I've already seen it.

One of those pictures wasn't of the lighthouse. It wasn't of the beach, or the Anchor, or even the ice-cream-coloured cottages in this street.

It was of my girlfriend lying naked on the bed.

Chapter Twenty-Five

For a moment I wonder if I imagined it. Or maybe it was some kind of fluky thing and just 'happened', to do with her phone? I mean, they're always doing weird stuff. Wasn't there are a thing, a few years back, when Rick Astley's 'Never Gonna Give You Up' kept blasting out of people's mobiles, driving everyone mad, and no one could stop it? I'm not a phone person like Meg is, wedded to the thing, using it for everything from accessing workouts to tracking her sleep.

However, I'm not entirely unfamiliar with how they work. And now I think about it, as she stuffs it into her pocket and turns back towards the house, I'm pretty certain that must have been a recent photo.

'Meg?'

She looks round at me. 'Yeah?'

'What was that picture?'

'What picture?' She affects a look of bewilderment.

'I saw a naked photo of you there. Unless I was hallucinating or something?' I try for a laugh, to make light of it.

'Oh, that's ancient,' she mutters with a dismissive shake of her head. 'It's nothing.'

I frown and try to read her expression. 'But that duvet you were lying on, it's the one here. It's the purple one in our room.'

She splutters. 'Ricky Vance, you must be the only straight man alive who'd see a picture of a naked woman lying on a bed and comment on the duvet cover.'

I shrug, deciding it's probably best just to let it drop. I mean, I'm not the prying type and I do realise that people's phones are immensely personal. Maybe hers just 'went off' when she was lying there, having a little catnap? Maybe it hovered about two feet above her naked body, kept aloft by some freakish warm air current and decided to take a photo of its own accord?

'It was a mistake,' she adds.

'You took a picture of yourself naked by mistake?'

'Yeah,' she says curtly. 'You know, it happens!'

For a moment, that does seems feasible. While hardly a rabid photographer, I do take the odd photo and occasionally I've done that thing where you flip to selfie mode accidentally – and instead of framing Sgadansay Bay I've been confronted by my looming face on the screen, and the undeniable evidence that I should probably have shaved and could do with more sleep. But what had she intended to photograph in the bedroom? The yellow wood chip ceiling? The tasselled lampshade?

'Was the picture . . . *for* somebody?' I ask.

'For God's sake,' she exclaims. 'What is this, an inter-rogation?'

'Okay, okay—'

'Look, I took the picture for *myself*, all right?'

'For yourself?' Just when I think I'm growing slightly

closer to understanding the intricate workings of the female mind, something like this happens.

'Yes, Ricky. I just wanted to see what I looked like after that massive dinner last night.'

I stare at her. That massive dinner? Like, a couple of bites of a mutton pie and about five chips? 'Can I see it again?' I ask.

She sighs loudly as she extracts the phone from her pocket again, finds the image and thrusts it at me. 'Would I *dream* of denying you, Ricky?'

I take it from her and blink at the picture. Her long, slender legs are bent at the knees and her free arm is draped seductively behind her head. She's pouting, and her eyes are languid, half-closed, and she looks incredibly sexy. 'You're posing,' I remark.

'Of course I'm posing,' she says with a dry laugh. 'Any woman wants to look good in a photo, doesn't she? Not like a shot putter who's fallen flat on her back.'

I hand her phone to her. 'Okay. Look, whatever you do is your business.' Her mouth seems to tighten and she glances towards the house, as if there's something happening in there that she really must attend to. 'But if something's going on,' I add, 'could you please tell me what it is?'

She just stands there and looks at me.

'Meg?' I prompt her. 'Can you talk to me?'

She blinks and crinkles her lower lip. Maybe Dad's turned off the TV – I don't know – but everything feels very quiet and still. 'Something's . . . sort of *happened*,' she murmurs.

Now her lower left eyelid is vibrating slightly. 'What kind of thing?' I ask.

She looks down at Dad's scrubby lawn as if it's suddenly fascinating to her and says nothing.

'Are you pregnant?'

'God, no, I'm not pregnant!' She looks aghast.

'What, then?'

She sweeps her hands across her face and back over her fine hair, as if trying to mentally collect herself. 'There's . . . something. I mean . . . someone. I should've told you, Ricky. I mean, I was going to, I *planned* to . . .'

At first, I'm not quite sure if I've heard her properly because it doesn't make sense. If there's someone else, then why on earth has she come to Sgadansay with Arthur and me?

'You mean . . . you've been seeing somebody?'

She nods mutely.

'Who is it?'

'Um, just someone I know from way back and, well . . .' a hopeless shrug, as if it was inevitable really '. . . it's kind of sparked back up again.'

I'm still having trouble taking this in. Sparked back up again? What does that mean? I think of fireworks, and how you're not meant to go back to one that hasn't lit properly in case it blows up in your face. 'You mean you've been sleeping with him?'

'Sort of, yes.' She nods again and her cheeks redden. 'I'm sorry, Ricky. Really, I am.'

We stand there, just looking at each other in Dad's back garden. A seagull's dropping splats close to my feet and the bird squawks loudly, mockingly. 'And that photo on the bed . . . did you take that for him?'

'Let's not get into that again,' she mutters.

'So you were taking naked pics of yourself in my dad's house to send to your boyfriend?' I glance round at the house and spot Arthur pottering about in the kitchen. I will him to stay there and not come out.

174

'He's not my *boyfriend*,' she says firmly. 'He's just someone who means a lot to me—'

'Who you're having sex with—'

'Ricky,' she snaps, apparently outraged.

'Is it that padded body warmer guy? The one with the statement moustache—'

'Gerald?' she splutters. 'No, of course it's not Gerald!'

'Who is it, then?'

She's still gripping her phone as if it's essential to life. 'It's one of my hibiscus guys.'

'What?'

'He owns a deli. I met him through doing my tea thing . . .'

'But you said it was someone from way back?' As if it makes any difference.

'He *is*,' she insists. 'He's the first guy who took an order from me and we had a little fling, before I met you. We were just friends after that. Brihat's been really brilliant and supportive—'

'What's his name?'

'Brihat. It's a Sanskrit name,' she explains.

'Oh, did he give it to himself?' I bark, realising how bitter I'm sounding now. But I can't help it.

Her expression turns defensive. 'Yes, he did actually. What does it matter?'

'Was it to sound more like a yoga kind of guy?'

'Well, yes,' she snaps, 'because it's more spiritual than Colin—'

'Colin!' I splutter. 'Yeah, I can see why he changed it.'

She glares at me, then her face softens. 'Look, I didn't plan to tell you here. It's the last thing I wanted to do, to ruin the trip—'

'I s'pose it's not ideal really,' I cut in, 'when we're on

175

holiday.' Holiday? What am I saying? Meg likes her jaunts to involve yoga, meditation, exotic juices and salads scattered with edible flowers. That's probably the kind of trip Brihat would take her on. And I've brought her to a Hebridean island to eat pies.

A huge crow lands on the fence and stares at us as if curious to see what'll happen next. But I don't know what'll happen because I'm at a complete loss as to what to do. Clearly, we can't go into all the ins and outs – unfortunate phrase – of her 'sparking up' with her spiritual friend, not with my father and son a few feet away in the house. But nor can we carry on with our jolly holiday as if it's never happened.

Fucking hell, we've only been here for twenty-four hours. How the hell are we going to struggle through the next six days?

'Is it that polyamory thing?' I ask, and Meg shrugs and nods.

'I just want to be free to see other people, Ricky. It's more . . . *me*.'

I stare at her. 'But I thought that was meant to be out in the open, not sneaking and lying—'

'Well, I knew how you'd react—'

'Oh, sorry for being a bit upset!' I snap.

Meg steps away from me. 'Okay, okay. Forget I said it. Forget everything. I think I should go home, all right?'

'When?' I exclaim. 'You mean, like, today?'

'Yes, like today.'

'But how?'

'On the *ferry*,' she says with unnecessary emphasis, as if I am an imbecile.

'But . . .' I look around the garden, feeling like all the wind's been knocked out of me. 'It doesn't leave until seven, and it'll be nearly ten o'clock by the time you get to Oban and—'

'I think I can manage,' she says.

What about Arthur? I'm thinking. *And Dad?* I know it's ridiculous and more about my pride, and how I'm going to explain it to them.

Me and Meg had a bit of a disagreement and she's gone home.

Jesus fuck.

'I'll be able to get a train back to Glasgow tonight, won't I?'

'Erm, yes. I don't know. You might miss the last one. What'll you do then?'

'Get a hotel in Oban.' Great. Lovely. So that's everything all sorted then. 'I'm sorry, Ricky,' she adds, walking back to the house now. 'I'll go upstairs and grab my stuff.'

'What, now?' I call after her. 'But the ferry doesn't leave for, what, three hours—'

'I'll sit there and wait then,' she announces, glancing back at me as she adds, 'I've brought a birthday present for Arthur and I'll leave it on the bed. I hope he likes it.'

Chapter Twenty-Six

Suzy

The distillery tour hadn't been like this. Back then, in the mists of time, when I'd still loved Paul and thought we'd just gone on holiday for *fun*, Jean had greeted our tour group with a twinkling smile as she'd patiently explained how whisky is made. We were given samples to try, plus fingers of sugary shortbread to nibble on. We'd posed, grinning, as our obliging guide had taken photographs of us in front of the gleaming copper stills. We were told how that particular metal removes any sulphurous traces from the fermentation, and why the stills are shaped like gorgeous curvaceous, coppery onions.

'Thank you,' I told Jean at the end of our tour. 'We've learnt such a lot.'

Of course now I realise I know virtually nothing at all. But how quaint and delightful everything seemed that day, with the cooper ('Our barrel boffin,' as Jean put it) explaining that the wooden casks originally came from Spain, where they'd have contained sherry, or from the grain whisky distilleries of Kentucky.

Today Kenny, who's busily repairing barrels, barely

grunts in response to my hesitant hello, and Jean looks up distractedly from the office with a mere, 'I'm here all day if you need anything.'

'Thank you,' I say. 'I'm just going to sort of . . . be here and . . . you know.'

She adjusts her gold-rimmed spectacles and peers at me from behind her orderly desk. There are framed photos on it because of course, no one 'hot desks' here; it's her personal space and I assume they're her three grandchildren, beaming broadly in their blue school uniforms. I catch a hint of her rose perfume – plus powerful 'I am actually extremely busy' vibes – as I take myself off to the malting room to make a nuisance of myself there.

In the vast, vaulted space, barley lies quietly germinating on the floor. It's tended by Liam, the lumberjack shirt man who'd been so angry during my first meeting here.

'Hullo,' he says gruffly, as if I have come to pick fault with his practices. Of course I wasn't expecting a big smile and a hug, like I'm some long-lost pal. I'm regarded with similar coolness and suspicion as I get in the way of the women in the box packing area, and the man who manages the kilns, where the barley goes to be – well, *kilned* is all I know about that part of the process.

It's understandable that my questions are answered curtly, especially when I casually ask about Harry's situation now (I have learned that he was widowed several years ago). No one wants to be seen to be fraternising with the enemy, I realise. But I'd hoped there might be a glimmer of warmth, and that at least some of the team would understand that I have come here to put things right.

I hover about in the bottling room, feeling like the kid at the party who's only there because the birthday girl's mother insisted on it. 'For God's sake, Emily, just invite her. It'll look mean if you don't and she's not *that* bad.' The bottling machine clanks away and I observe from a distance as a woman fills other bottles from an urn by hand.

It's probably not even called an urn. It's probably called a *strommuch*, a *squidden* or some equally mystifying term; Christ, my head is swimming with unfamiliar words like 'rummager' (something inside the still, I've gathered, and not an eager person at a jumble sale). I listened as hard as I could when Liam explained, reluctantly, what 'grist', 'mash' and 'draff' mean. I pretended I understood when another man said there was a problem where the worm tub connected to the grist arm (or was it the other way round?).

I haven't even been able to remember everyone's names yet. I could have name badges made for everyone, but fear that the very suggestion would see me being stuffed into a barrel and rolled out to sea.

In reception now, I find the maintenance man – I *think* he's called Stuart – up a ladder as he does something to the skylight. Feeling helpless, I clutch my notebook to my chest. 'Can I hold that for you?'

'Hmm?' he mumbles because, I realise now, he has several nails clamped between his lips; nails he's about to use for an important task. In interrupting him, I could have caused him to choke.

'I, er, wondered if I could help?'

'What with?' he asks, having pulled the nails from his mouth.

'Erm, anything really! I just thought, maybe . . . anyway.'

He stares at me as if I've just asked him to accompany me to the ballet. Taking this as a 'no', I shuffle past the terrible display of puffin paraphernalia that still blights the entrance area, looking cheap and ridiculous and entirely out of place.

Outside the building now I catch the waft of cigarette smoke from a young employee who, registering me, springs back in alarm.

'Hi.' I beam at her to show how un-scary I am.

''Lo.' The woman – raven-haired with a complexion like cream – takes another quick draw of her cigarette.

'Quite chilly today, isn't it?'

'Aye.'

A cool silence hovers between us. 'How are things going?' I ask.

She eyes me warily as if figuring out how to respond. *Considering the business is virtually fucked and I'm probably going to be out of a job soon, things are going really, really well.*

'All right,' she says. She drops her butt into a pot on the ground and scoots back inside as if I might horsewhip her for taking a few minutes out of her working day.

I check the time on my phone. 3.30 p.m.; Christ, only a couple of hours have passed since Cara's lunch. It feels like *weeks*. Is it possible that time has slowed down, almost to a halt? The morning was sunny and bright, but now the sky is darkening moodily, and the Atlantic wind is getting up.

I hover at the main door, wondering whether to do the rounds of the distillery again, telling everyone in turn that I'm leaving for the day now, like some terribly drawn-out exit from a party, when no one cares anyway. I think they call it a 'French exit' when you just leave.

So that's what I do. Having slunk in to grab my bag from reception, I hurry back outside, thinking, that went

181

well; clearly everyone warmed to my ineffectual comments, and will be wondering who the hell I thought I was. The Queen, touring a factory? Saying, 'So how long have you worked here?' and 'Can you tell me what that machine does?' I can sense salt spray on my tongue and relief emanating from the distillery now I've gone.

Suzy Medley has left the building! Thank Christ for that.

But then, after the deepest sleep I can ever remember, I wake with a renewed sense of optimism. The sun is already shining brightly and Scout is snuggled close to my side. I am due to drop him off at Cara's today; she loved having him yesterday and was keen to invite him over again. I hope he won't mind. Hang on, what am I saying? He was running around Sgadansay all alone for God knows how long. Of course he won't mind.

We set off on our walk before breakfast. The sky is a pale, cloudless turquoise and the bay is sparkling as if sprinkled with glitter. My mouth waters at the thought of bendy toast and poached eggs brought by the young waitress who chats to me a little now. While the hotel is hardly bustling, I have spotted the occasional, mainly elderly fellow guest, and the brisk, copper-haired woman on the front desk offered a treat to Scout yesterday. Just as thrillingly – terrifying too, considering the debts – Rosalind has emailed to confirm that Paul has agreed to sign his share of the company over to me.

So, once the documentation has all been dealt with, the Sgadansay Distillery will be all mine.

Am I really regarding this as significant and life-changing as the hotel receptionist offering Scout a biscuit?

I don't know what to feel anymore. Sometimes it seems as if my emotions are strapped to a roller coaster, and the shady-looking fairground guy is having a smoke and has forgotten to activate the stop button. Still, there's much work to be done, so after breakfast I make call after call to our creditors, to update them on progress. Once that's all done, and I'm craving air, Scout and I head over to Cara's.

'She's looking forward to seeing you again,' I tell him as we make our way through the winding streets. I catch the eye of a young woman holding her toddler daughter's hand, and they both smile, and I realise I'm not remotely embarrassed at having been caught talking to my dog. Doesn't everyone do that? It would feel weirder to *not* communicate.

Scout greets Cara by running around in ragged circles as if he doesn't know what to do with himself. 'Look at him! He's attached to you already,' I say as she beckons me in.

'Well, it goes both ways,' she says with a smile. 'D'you fancy a cuppa or something? D'you have time?'

'That'd be lovely,' I say. So she makes us tea, quizzing me gently as I update her on distillery matters, then she shows me pieces of fabric she's been printing: beautiful slices of dusky purple and green, evoking the hills.

'These are wonderful,' I say. 'Are you going to make them into something?' I sense myself flushing. They're *art*, for goodness' sake, and I'm talking about them as if they're going to be turned into cushion covers.

'I'll mount and frame them,' she explains. 'I've just heard one of the galleries here is going to show them. You know the Bay Gallery?'

'I've seen it, yes. That's brilliant news!'

'Oh, it's a relief really,' she says with a grimace. 'I need to step things up here and open up the studio and start classes, like I did back home. I mean, I had so many plans

183

when I first came here. I planned to get scarves and tote bags into production for the outlets I used to sell through. But, you know—' She stops suddenly.

'Well, you've been busy,' I remark.

'Yeah, busy going stark-raving mad.' She exhales loudly.

I study her face. 'Really? I thought you'd settled in fine. You've done this place out, and it's beautiful—'

'It's a beautiful place to go quietly round the bend,' she says with an off-kilter smile.

'I didn't realise you felt like that,' I murmur.

Cara sips her tea. 'Well, I didn't want to blurt out all my woes when you have so much on your plate.'

'Hey,' I exclaim, 'I've blurted out all mine to you.' I pause. 'Was it hard being here throughout the winter?'

'Oh, God, yes.' She nods. 'I mean, I was prepared for it being cold and dark and wet – all that. What I hadn't been ready for was the awful loneliness, you know? Feeling so isolated here, so cut off, with just Barney for company . . .'

'I'm so sorry,' I say.

Her face brightens. 'But you know what? I'm not just saying this, but things are getting better. Spring's amazing here, isn't it?'

'Yes, it's stunning.'

'And it's made me feel more hopeful.' She pauses. 'I'd been shutting myself away, working too much, not really making an effort to get to know people here. You know when I took those lost dog posters around town?'

'Yes?' I nod.

'People were so kind and lovely and it turned out lots of the local shopkeepers and café owners had been curious about us – about me and Barney, I mean – and I think maybe I'd come across as a bit standoffish until then.'

184

'I can't believe that,' I say truthfully.

She shrugs. 'I'm actually pretty shy, you know. You'd think, at thirty-eight, I'd have got over it . . .' She places her mug on the old worn oak table.

'Cara, I'm ten years older than you and I haven't either.'

Grinning now, she crouches down to fuss over Scout. 'Anyway, I'm getting myself back on track now and this little man—' she plants a kiss on his head '—he's a brilliant little sidekick, isn't he?'

'Yes, he really is.'

Her smile broadens. 'God, I'm talking as if he's mine. I'm being ridiculous. I just so enjoyed being out with him yesterday—'

'Cara, it's okay,' I cut in. 'He obviously loves coming here too.' I pause. 'We can keep on doing this if you like, while I'm here on the island? Kind of sharing him, I mean . . .'

'Oh, are you sure?' She beams at me.

'Yes, of course. I mean, we could work out something regular, or just see what suits us day to day?'

'That sounds best. I'd love that,' she enthuses, her cheeks flushed pink now. 'I really would.'

'Okay,' I say, 'let's do that.' I look down at my dog – or rather, *our* dog, for the duration of my stay, at least – and wonder now if he could possibly help to fill the Barney-shaped hole in her life. 'We're *sharing* you, Scout,' I tell him. 'I hope you're okay with that.'

And it feels fine, I decide as we leave, perhaps because he just arrived in my life, so really, he isn't mine. At least, he could just as easily have been Cara's if he'd turned up at her place, wet and quivering on that lousy night. He could have been anyone's.

I stride through the town, inhaling the delicious aromas from the bakery and then, a little further on, the heady scents from the blooms busting from their galvanised buckets outside the florist's. Everything looks so fresh and alive, I can't resist taking a few photos with my phone.

The Seafood Shack man smiles and waves as I pass. I'm filled with happiness, and the emotion feels so rare and precious that I want to hold it close, to stop it blowing away on the breeze.

I stop and select a picture on my phone. It's not of the shimmering bay or the floral display, but of Scout leaping majestically across the beach with all four feet in the air. And right now – even though another trip to the distillery awaits me – I feel a little like that myself.

Chapter Twenty-Seven

Medley Family WhatsApp

Thought you'd like to see how much Scout loves it here.

Frieda: Brilliant pic Mum. He's so cute!

I can't take credit love. A friend took it. I've met a woman called Cara and we've set up a kind of dog share arrangement.

Frieda: You're farming him out already? MUM!!

It's not like that. Honestly – he loves it. I'm planning to spend mornings in meetings in my room and most afternoons I'll be at the distillery. Cara's dog died recently and she's loving having Scout around and taking him for big walks. So it works for everyone.

Frieda: Suppose that's okay as long as she's a nice person.

Of course she's a nice person! I wouldn't leave him with just anyone would I?

Isaac: Guess so. You were always picky about our babysitters.

Frieda: After that time you found all those bottles in our garden.

She'd had a party!
Isaac: Just a couple of friends round she said.
Let's not dwell on that. But is it any wonder I hardly ever went out?
Frieda: The others were nice, Mum.
I did my best. Anyway how are things? Jobs going okay?
Isaac: It's full on and pretty shit.
What, the Mexican take-away? I thought you said it sounded good. Didn't Matis work there for a bit?
Isaac: Yeah but it's shit.
Frieda: You haven't set the microwave on fire?
Isaac: No I'm being micro-managed.
By who?
Frieda: By WHOM :)
Isaac: By my micro-manager.
Frieda: Maybe you need micro-managing.
Isaac: To put cheese and lettuce in a wrap?
There's a lot that could go wrong with that, Isaac.
Frieda: Your wraps sound a bit basic. I won't be going there.
Isaac: It's okay for Frieda serving scones in a teashop.
Frieda: Hey it's hard work!
Isaac: Making sure they get the right kind of jam?
Well I'm sorry you have to work, Isaac, but you know Dad and I support you as much as we can.
Isaac: I know. I appreciate it.
Frieda: We both do Mum. And everyone on my course has a part-time job.
Isaac: But not as shitty as mine.
Okay, better go in a minute. I'm nearly at the distillery.

188

Frieda: How's it going there?

All right I guess. But I'm starting to realise it'll take years to understand it all properly.

Frieda: Aw you'll soon pick it up!

Thanks love, but I really need help. Remember I told you about the master distiller?

Isaac: The old guy who flounced out?

Well he left, yes, but it was understandable. And I need to get him on board again.

Isaac: Get him on board? You've gone all management Mum.

I am the management!

Frieda: She'll be asking for some blue-sky thinking next.

Isaac: Or if either of us has a window.

Ha-ha. The thing is, I have his home address. It's still on the staff database.

Isaac: Go see him then.

I can't just turn up can I? Out of the blue?

Isaac: Why not?

It'd be rude. I've no right to do that.

Frieda: Maybe you could write him a letter?

What would I say? I don't want to make him angry or upset.

Frieda: Mum, you're the writer. You know what to say.

Isaac: Remember all those thank-you letters you made us write after Christmas and birthdays?

Yes and what a fuss you made every time! If I could've forged your writing and done it myself, I would have.

Isaac: I wish you had.

Me too, I'd probably look ten years younger now.

Frieda: I hated writing those letters. It was so hard knowing what to put.

Was it really that bad? I hope it hasn't caused any lasting psychological damage.

Isaac: I'm okay, I just get flashbacks sometimes.

Frieda: Me too. What to say about those horrible pink shorts from Aunty Belinda? 'How hard can it be!' you always said.

Isaac: Dear Aunt Belinda, thank you for the disgusting shorts. Mum took them straight to the charity shop.

I really have to go now!

Frieda: Good luck and write that letter.

Isaac: Yeah, Mum. How hard can it be?

Chapter Twenty-Eight

Ricky

I could have spun Dad and Arthur some yarn about an emergency back home. I might have been able to cobble together something about one of Meg's parents having had an accident, or a fire at her flat or clinic, but I wasn't comfortable with lying. And anyway, I figured, why I should I? There were hurried goodbyes, and Dad and Arthur just stood there, looking bewildered and shocked.

I drove Meg to the ferry, even though she'd said she could quite easily walk, thank-you-very-much. She also insisted she'd be *fine* sitting for three hours in the waiting area, which consists of a few benches and a roof but only has a wall running along one side. Everyone knows the wind whips right through it. Even the small group of hardened teenage smokers who congregate there find it a bit too bracing sometimes.

But what else could I do? We were hardly going to sit there huddling together for warmth. She hadn't even wanted me to get out of the car. 'No need to stop,' she'd announced as we'd approached, as if she'd have preferred to open the door and hurl herself out while I drove past at speed.

Back home, I gave Dad and Arthur a potted version of what had happened (omitting the parts about the naked photo, the copious lying and the shagging of her yogi lover). The rest of the evening, and the whole of yesterday, was predictably pretty grim, made all the worse when Ralph called to say that Brenna's mum had passed away. So they'd been right not to go to Spain after all. Kai phoned Arthur and they had a chat in his room. I tried not to overhear but couldn't help catching the occasional phrase: 'She was really nice, your gran. Bet you'll miss her.' And: 'Meg's gone home. It's really weird. I think she's dumped Dad.'

'Did you argue?' Arthur asked later last night when I went up to say goodnight.

'No, it was nothing like that,' I said quickly, as if it had all been completely amicable. And now, a whole two days since she left, Arthur has taken to loitering around me with silent questions still hovering between us.

I pause making sandwiches in Dad's kitchen and turn to look at him. 'D'you fancy packing this lot up for a picnic?' I ask.

'Yeah, all right,' he says without enthusiasm.

Great! Fantastic! A picnic will make everything all right. 'Dad,' I call through to the living room, 'how about taking our lunch to the beach?'

'What?' he barks. I glance through to see him sitting bolt upright, intently studying last week's *Sgadansay Gazette*, which I know he's read from cover to cover already.

'Me and Arthur were thinking it'd be really nice to make the most of the weather today and pack a picnic. What d'you think?'

192

He lowers the paper a little. 'I'm all right, son. You two go ahead.'

Bloody hell, I'm at a loss as to how to cheer up the funereal atmosphere that I feel responsible for creating, if only through my connection to Meg. But then, it can't all be her fault, can it? I rack my brains for evidence that I dragged her here against her will and that's why she's left me. But then, she'd been seeing that bloke *before* I forced her onto the ferry that made her feel so sick, and before my father had failed to grasp the benefits of ear candling.

It was probably happening the whole time we were together. I wonder if her boyfriend's into polyamory too, and I was just too staid for her with my monogamous ways? Maybe they'll cycle off into the sunset together, on their pushbikes with wicker baskets on the front, for copious herbal infusions with their numerous lovers. I bet Brihat doesn't have a plastic tomato-shaped ketchup dispenser.

Determined to rescue the rest of the day, I pack up lunch for Arthur and me and, feeling like quite the Famous Five adventurer, virtually haul him out of the house. 'You're walking too fast, Dad.' He glares at me.

'Oh, sorry. I didn't realise.'

He shoots me a sideways look as we fall into step. 'Are you all right?'

'Yeah, I'm fine!' I say brightly.

We fall into silence for a few minutes. Then: 'D'you think you'll get back together?'

'What, me and Meg?' As if I've barely given the issue much thought. 'I don't think so, to be honest.' I picture her Kilner jars of petal tea and granola sitting on my kitchen worktop and wonder if she'll want them back.

We've reached the shore now. Silver Beach is probably

one of my favourite places in the entire world, but right now I can't see a single spot on it where I'd like to sit. Although the day is sunny and bright, it's also windy; the perfect conditions for our sandwiches to acquire a fine coating of sand. But, hey, we're on holiday, and picnics are cheering, holidayish things!

'Where d'you wanna sit?' Arthur asks, eyes narrowed.

'Erm, how about down there on the rocks?'

'Yeah, all right.' He is trying to be kind, I realise. He's fully aware why I insisted on coming down here, after yesterday when we did little more than mooch around town, where I bought him a stack of comics that were too young for him, and then tried to further raise his spirits by insisting we went into the church for a 'look around'. Because that's what a ten-year-old kid wants to look at on his holiday, isn't it? A dusty organ and some stained glass. After that thrilling diversion we went back to Dad's and watched a western (my father's favourite genre – in fact, the only kind of film he'll tolerate). It might as well have been a Blue Peter expedition for all the attention I was paying to it.

Arthur and I perch on the damp rocks and I pass him a ham sandwich. It's made from Dad's favoured white bread, from a waxed packet, and budget meat, at the opposite end of the ham spectrum from the air-dried charcuterie on Meg's Mum's grazing table. A seagull swoops down, as if about to snatch mine, but swerves away at the last moment, squawking in what could possibly be derision.

As we sit and munch stoically, pretending this is far preferable to eating in relative comfort at Dad's kitchen table, I try to figure out what we could do after this – and tomorrow and the day after that. At least on Saturday we'll be celebrating Arthur's birthday so that should perk things up. The parcel Meg left for him is a rigid, neatly gift-wrapped box. I wonder if it'll be weird for him to open it now she's gone.

'Dad?' Arthur wipes his mouth with the back of his hand.

'Yeah?'

He frowns at me, his eyes radiating concern. 'Did Meg dump you?'

'It wasn't really like that,' I reply.

'What was it like then?'

I fix my gaze on the horizon and shrug. 'We just weren't really right together, that's all.'

'Oh.' Then: 'Did you consciously uncouple?'

I splutter and, despite everything, I laugh. 'Where did you hear that phrase?'

He shrugs. 'I dunno. I've just heard it. So, was it a shock, then?'

'Erm . . .' I look at my son, who's fixing me with a steady gaze that's tinged with something like sympathy now. 'Oh, *you* know. Kind of, I s'pose.' As if, at not quite eleven years old, he knows anything about being left.

'Yeah,' he murmurs, nodding sagely, and something shifts uneasily in my gut. Of course, his mother dumped him. At least, it could be interpreted as that. Occasionally, when an opportunity seems to present itself, I broach the subject with him. I don't want him to think he can't talk about her, that she's a taboo subject. But he never seems to want to. And when she *is* mentioned, he changes the subject quickly – or rushes off, making out there's something urgent he needs to do.

'But it's happened,' I add, 'and I'm okay, honestly. So I don't want you worrying about anything because we're fine, aren't we?'

He nods and raises a smile. I slide an arm around his shoulders and he leans into me. 'Yeah, we are, Dad. We're fine.'

I clear my throat. 'But I'm sorry it's gone a bit weird. This holiday, I mean.'

'It's all right,' he says.

We sit for a moment, with him resting his head against me in a way that he hasn't done since he was really little. I don't want to move, even if the heavens open and it starts bucketing down. It looks unlikely right now, as the sky is still a pale, clear blue, but they say you can experience four seasons in one day here, and they're not wrong; you can be sunbathing one minute and battered by hailstones the next.

'Dad, look!' Arthur jerks away from me and points down the beach.

'What is it?' I follow his gaze, assuming for one mad moment that Meg's come back. She's sorry, she made a terrible mistake and she loves me madly! My panic at this tells me something, I realise: that the last thing I'd want is for her to appear right now and try to make everything okay. Because it *wasn't* okay, not really. Sure, we had fun, but a lot of the time I was conscious of being judged – for letting Arthur have a phone and Coco Pops, and for fixing my pupils' instruments without pay.

'Shouldn't you be doing that in your teaching time?' she'd asked. There was never time in my teaching time, I'd explained. 'I just think kids should take better care of their instruments, that's all,' she'd added with a disapproving frown.

Well, that was life, I'd tried to explain. No one damaged a violin deliberately. Accidents happened and who could blame a dog for mistaking a bow for a plain old stick?

196

What I'd really wanted to say was that my pupils didn't have the kind of privileged upbringing she'd enjoyed, with private tutors for a raft of activities and holidays to the South of France. Many of them wear shabby or outgrown school uniforms – if they even *have* uniforms – and have no holidays at all.

Jesus. A whole year, Meg and I were together, because I fancied her and she was nice to my son without being *overly* nice, and I enjoyed being with someone, and having another adult to talk to, and do stuff with, after years of rattling about by myself.

I'm still peering into the distance, wondering what's caught Arthur's attention. He's hurried off now, clutching his Caramel Wafer, towards the sea. 'Dad!' he calls back. 'It's that dog again! Look!'

I scan the shore, then spot the small brown terrier-type with a flash of white on its chest. Although it's running freely I can see now that there's a woman strolling along, still some way off, holding a lead. She has dark bobbed hair and is wearing one of those yellow fishermen's jackets that are actually nothing to do with fishing at all.

'Are you sure?' I call after him.

'I think so, yeah . . .' Arthur stops as the woman approaches and greets the dog. 'Is he yours?' he asks.

'He's a friend's actually,' she replies, 'but I walk him for her. We kind of share him—'

'Was he a stray?' my son cuts in.

'Arthur,' I say, speeding up to join them, 'I don't think this is the same one. The other one was thinner—'

'Actually, yes, he *was* a stray,' the woman says, pushing her windblown hair from her face.

'I thought I saw him on the ferry as well,' Arthur adds.

The woman smiles warmly. 'You probably did. My

friend brought him back here on Sunday, but she found him here, on the island. We think he must've been abandoned but we don't really know what his story was. So she decided to keep him—'

'See, Dad?' Arthur turns to face me, a note of triumph in his voice. 'We could've done that. We could've kept him and now he'd be ours.'

Chapter Twenty-Nine

Suzy

I'm not putting off writing that letter to Harry. However, after yesterday's distillery visit my head was crammed with yet more baffling terms, and all I was good for was going through my notes, then lying down with a cup of tea and Scout curled up at my side.

I'd met Vicki, our environmental consultant. Slim and athletic – I'd guessed her at late thirties – she'd seemed surprised that I knew so little about minerals, precipitation and geological formations. 'Our water,' she'd said with a note of admonishment, as if I'd handed in sloppy homework, '*is* Sgadansay whisky.' Then she'd proceeded to tell me in *extreme* detail about our unique water source – a fast-flowing stream from up in the mountains – then up on her computer screen had appeared cross-sectional diagrams of the land structure and so much information about porosity, peat deposits and 'sphagnum' (a kind of moss, I learned) that my head had started to reel. By the time she'd finished I'd filled an entire pad with scribbled notes and rudimentary sketches.

I was immensely grateful to Vicki for being willing to

spend so much time with me, and relieved that my change of tactic seemed to have worked. Instead of lurking apologetically, as if almost guilty for being on the premises, I'd forced myself to be bolder and to fire questions – *heaps* of questions, as Paul had on that distillery tour. Then I'd gone to pick up Scout from Cara as usual (already, our routine feels so natural), and she told me about the red-haired boy she'd met on the beach: 'He loved Scout! And he was convinced he'd seen him before, a few weeks ago, on the beach . . .'

'When he was running about lost?' I asked incredulously.

'Yes! But he'd run off before he and his dad could take him anywhere safe. Oh, he was so sweet with him, Suzy. He was throwing sticks for him and knew all these facts about dogs. His dad said he was desperate for one of his own.' I'd smiled at that. He sounded just like Frieda.

And now, on this cool, grey-skied Thursday morning, I'm installed at the desk by the window in my hotel room, trying to wrestle my thoughts to the matter in hand. *Just write the letter,* I tell myself. All I need to do is lay out the situation now and why I need Harry to come back. Don't sweat the small stuff!

But how to be apologetic, humble and gently persuasive (without grovelling or begging) whilst retaining a respectful tone? Should I try to sound authoritative or admit that I've been a blundering fool? It's tougher than any obituary I've ever written. It's harder, even, than those thank-you letters Mum insisted I wrote after every Christmas and birthday. My kids might moan that I was a stickler for them, but at least I left them to get on with the job without sticking my oar in.

My mother didn't. She'd insist on checking what I'd put before it was deemed suitable for sending: 'You can't just say, "Dear Aunty Lynne, thank you for the lovely belt. I really liked it. Love, Suzy." No, I had to go into copious detail: it was a *beautiful plaited suede belt*, and would go perfectly with my favourite jeans and I couldn't wait to wear it to the disco with my lemon top. And then I'd have to ask about how her Christmas had been, or where she was going on holiday; my letters were so long and convoluted they should have been divided into chapters, and almost made me resent the actual plaited belt. It's a wonder I ever wanted to become a writer after that.

I start to type, agonising over my opening sentence, which I *never* do with my work. Within minutes I seem to have reached a dead end. I get up and make a cup of tea and pace about, then read bits of it out to Scout as if he might be able to offer helpful suggestions. He just blinks at me, looking nonplussed. I hunch over my laptop and rework it until even commonplace words like 'grateful' and 'expertise' look like meaningless clusters of random letters. Oh, I know what I *really* want to say: *Dear Harry! I'm so bloody sorry! Please, please come back!* But that won't do.

Finally, it's finished At least, I've done my best. In the absence of a printer I copy it out neatly, in my very best handwriting, just as I did with those thank-you letters in order to garner Mum's praise. I fold the sheet of A4 crisply and slide it into an envelope. As we leave the hotel I remind Scout that he won't be going to Cara's today; she's spending the whole day screen printing, and we're giving her some space.

She said she's feeling all fired up and that just being around Scout has helped her enormously. I'd never have imagined that a woman who seems so cheery and friendly, who'd upped sticks to a remote Hebridean island, and with whom I ate a fish supper just hours after we'd met, could be lonely. But it shows that there's often much more to a person than is apparent when you first meet them.

Maybe Harry will be willing to meet me and talk things over, at least? After all, I don't even know the man. But I do know that news travels fast on the island, and that by now he'll know that Paul's no longer involved. Perhaps he's been sitting patiently all this time, waiting for me to get in touch.

I stop and double-check the map on my phone. Harry's street is a fifteen-minute walk away. Cutting away from the town centre, I follow the map to a terrace of almost impossibly pretty cottages. Each house is painted a different colour: lemon, lilac, cream, pale orange and pink. And the end one is a beautiful sun-faded blue: Harry's house.

I pluck the letter from my bag and study the envelope. *Mr H. Vance,* I wrote neatly on the front, as if the respectful formality might sway him. I cross the road, with Scout trotting along at my side, and approach the cottage furtively, checking left and right. People are just going about their business: neighbours chatting, a young mum trying to coax her toddler into his buggy, a teenage couple walking arm in arm. A loud woman with violently bleached hair announces to her friend how pretty the street is and takes a few pictures with her phone.

'Stunning, isn't it?' She turns to me.

'It's lovely, yes.' Off they march, still discussing how quaint everything is and wouldn't it be amazing to see what those cottages were like inside? 'D'you think,' she bellows, 'anyone would mind if we knocked and asked if we could have a quick peek?'

'These are people's homes, Brenda! Don't be daft.'

'Yeah, but they're so *cute*!'

I inhale deeply, trying to affect a casual manner as if I am just standing here for no apparent reason in front of Harry's house. Then I speed-walk to his front door, push the envelope through his letterbox and hurry away.

Chapter Thirty

Of course, Paul wasn't all bad. He had some lovely qualities – otherwise we wouldn't have stayed together for eight years. He was kind and funny (and also handsome, the bastard) and great at throwing together delicious dinners from the odds and sods in the fridge. And he'd always been a trouper with Frieda and Isaac, brushing off their hormonal moods with a lightness I'd never been able to emulate. They might have eye-rolled in response to his harebrained schemes, but there'd been a mutual fondness too.

He'd been their friend, and even mopped up their vomit, for goodness' sake – caused by stomach bugs and, in Isaac's case, by drinking that home-made nettle beer. And my God, he gave great gifts! I don't mean expensive as he was always pretty broke (apart from when he 'invested' in all that Lycra cycling gear; amazingly, he'd been able to find the money for that). Anyway, I'd never expected or wanted anything extravagant. But while friends of mine moaned about low-effort presents (gift tokens, dull knitwear or plain old cash), Paul always managed to squirrel out something thoughtful and special. And although I don't *think* I miss him as a partner, occasionally I'm hit with something like a sharp punch to the gut.

We're not together anymore, I realise, like it's only just happened. As if I've woken up to find him gone. The man who dutifully drove my children to and from sports fixtures and parties, and with whom I had date nights at home, the way the magazines say you should when the kids are still young and you can't get a babysitter. When you make an effort to cook something special, light candles and wear your nicest clothes, and pretend you're in a restaurant.

It happens now – the punch thing – as Scout and I leave Harry's street and make our way to the beach. We descend the worn stone steps to the sand and I unclip his lead, his signal to run off. The day has brightened already, the bleary grey sky lightening to pastel blue.

Nuggets of sea-glass gleam amongst the pebbles and shells. A wave has washed over them, making everything look varnished. I pick up a piece of amber glass, smooth as a sugared almond. One birthday, Paul asked a friend of his to make me a bracelet of semi-precious stones. My favourite colours – blues, greens and amber – were linked together on a fine silver chain. It was beautiful. I haven't worn it since he left.

Spotting a gnarly piece of driftwood, I try to shake off such thoughts by throwing it as hard as I can. Scout runs for it, grabbing it in his jaws and dancing in the shallow waves as if delighted by his own cleverness.

'Dad, look! That's that dog again!'

At the sound of a child's voice I turn to see a boy with a shock of reddish hair in the distance. His father shoves his hands into his jacket pockets as his son runs towards us. 'Scout!' the child yells. Scout hurtles towards him as if they are long-lost friends. They greet each other in a delighted tumble and I can see now that the man is smiling expectantly as he approaches.

'They know each other?' I say with a grin.

'Yeah.' The man nods. 'We met Scout yesterday, but he was with your friend—'

'Oh yes, Cara was looking after him. She told me she'd met you. And I heard you'd met Scout a few a weeks ago . . .' In all the excitement Scout has dropped his stick and is crouching, waiting for his new friend to throw it.

'Yeah, we think so.' The man nods. 'I felt pretty guilty, actually. Letting him run off like that . . .'

'Well, it ended happily.' I glance at Scout and smile. 'And look – he's fine and healthy.'

'Yes, I can see that,' he says. He has an attractive face with kind, deep-brown eyes and short dark hair flecked with a little grey. The soft island accent is faintly detectable.

'D'you have one of your own?' I ask.

'No, but Arthur would love one. That was always a big draw for him, coming out here for his holidays. To spend time with his granddad's dog. And his granddad too, of course,' he adds quickly. 'But Bess passed away last year so I suspect it's not quite the same for him anymore.'

'Oh, that's sad,' I say.

'Yeah.' He nods. 'So, your friend said Scout just turned up at your house?'

'At the holiday cottage I was staying at, yes. No one reported him missing, so I decided to keep him.'

'Great decision,' he says, and I glance over as Scout and Arthur dart in and out of the sea. Arthur's trainers must be soaked. It's heartening to see a parent not minding about stuff like that. 'You're not from round here, then?' the man asks.

'No, I live in York,' I reply. 'How about you?'

'We live in Glasgow but I grew up here – it's where I'm from. We're staying with my dad. Are you here on holiday?'

'Erm, I'm sort of working here,' I reply.

'Oh, what kind of work?' he asks.

'Just, uh, something I'm setting up,' I say, vaguely, as Arthur comes back and we all start to make our way along the beach. Thankfully, his father doesn't quiz me any further.

'He's such a nice dog,' Arthur announces.

'Thanks,' I say with a smile. 'He's loving all the attention. He'd play stick all day long if you let him.'

'Yeah. We were doing that yesterday.' Arthur turns to me with a hopeful grin. 'I'd like to walk him sometime,' he adds.

'Well, I'm sure I'll bump into you again,' I say. He's a good-looking boy with deep brown eyes like his father's, but his hair colour is strikingly different.

'No, I mean for *me* to take him for a walk,' he explains.

'Arthur,' his dad says, laughing, 'you can't just ask to take other people's dogs out.'

'Yeah, you can,' he says firmly. 'There's this thing, this website, where you can borrow dogs, like if you can't have one of your own. If you live in a flat or something and they're not allowed.' He pauses. 'Or if your dad won't let you have one.'

His dad smirks. 'That's right, Arthur. What a despicable father I am.'

I catch a brief scowl from his son. 'Remember I mentioned it? That dog borrowing website?'

'Er, yeah, I think so,' he says.

'You said you'd look into it and we'd maybe join?'

'Uh-huh . . .'

'And you never did?' Arthur adds with a note of admonishment.

The man laughs. 'Yep, that's yet another thing I've never got around to. It's a wonder I've been allowed to raise you, really.' He gives me a *kids-eh* kind of look.

'Well,' Arthur says, 'maybe we could borrow Scout?'

'You're lovely with him,' I say quickly, 'but I really enjoy doing the morning and evening walks, and Cara's helping to look after him during the daytime . . .'

Arthur's face falls. 'Oh, okay.'

'Anyway,' his father says, placing a hand on the boy's shoulder, 'we're only here for a few more days, remember?'

'Till Sunday,' he says, his cheeks colouring as he digs the toe of a trainer into the wet sand.

There's a slightly awkward lull, which I break by calling Scout over and clipping on his lead. 'Well, I'd better get back,' I say. 'It's been lovely meeting you.'

'You too,' says the man. We part company and I head straight for the steps, wondering now what harm it would have done to say, 'Yes, okay, you can walk him.' I mean, Arthur's not a little kid. He looks about eleven and I'm sure he wouldn't do anything stupid. I could've let him borrow Scout on the condition that his dad went along too.

It just felt a bit much, that's all – sharing him with yet another person so soon, especially someone I don't even know. Frieda would be horrified! But Scout seems to be a particularly sociable dog, at ease with new people (he certainly was with Cara), and Arthur really wanted to do it. Maybe, I reflect, as we wander back into town, he's missing his granddad's dog terribly? Yes, that'll be it. His dad said that had been a huge part of the appeal of coming here. That's why Arthur wanted to walk Scout.

It's only Thursday, and if they're here for three more days I'm sure we can arrange something. Prickling with guilt now, I turn back and walk briskly towards the beach. But when I arrive back at the steps, and gaze left and right along the wide sweep of sand, Arthur and his father have already gone.

Chapter Thirty-One

Ricky

'Granddad, we met that dog again! We were playing stick and he was so sweet, he—' Registering my father's thunderous expression, Arthur stops abruptly.

'Dad? What's wrong?' I dump my rucksack on the sofa as my father thrusts a piece of paper and an envelope at me.

'This came through the door. I just found it. It was hand delivered. Bloody cheek!'

I take it from him, studying the envelope first, on which his name has been neatly written: *Mr H. Vance.* Then I turn my attentions to the handwritten letter.

Dear Harry,

I hope this letter finds you well and that you don't mind me contacting you directly. I am aware that you were an extremely experienced and valued member of the Sgadansay Distillery team and wanted to put you in the picture as to what is happening now with the company.

As you may be aware, my former partner, Paul Leighton, is no longer associated with the business. As sole proprietor I am fully focused on getting the distillery back on track. I realise many mistakes were made during the past two years and I wish to assure you that I am doing everything in my power to rectify them . . .

'I mean,' he chokes out, 'the bloody nerve of it!'

'Yeah, I know, Dad,' I murmur, reading on:

. . . I also realise that you left the company in unhappy circumstances. I would welcome the opportunity to arrange a meeting with a view to welcoming you back into the team . . .

I look at Dad. 'She wants you back?'

'Aye! That's what she's saying right there.'

I skim through the last lines:

. . . As our greatest asset, I hope you will consider meeting with me so I can explain the situation further. I am also planning to arrange a team meeting at the distillery and would greatly value your presence there. I can of course arrange this at a time of your convenience—

I break off. 'She's inviting you to a team meeting. And she wants to meet you personally as well.'

'I *can* read,' Dad says irritably. I'm aware of Arthur wincing as he gives me a quick look.

'Yes, I know, Dad,' I murmur. I study his face. 'We could meet her together, if you like? Just to see what she has to say?'

'No, we'll *not* see what she has to say,' he snaps. I exhale slowly and skim through the final lines: *We are at a crucial stage in our dealings with the creditors and I know that your return would be greatly welcomed by everyone connected to the Sgadansay Distillery.*

With warmest wishes,
Yours sincerely,
Suzy Medley

211

Beneath her name, she has neatly written her mobile number and that of the Cormorant Hotel. I fold the letter in half carefully and hand it back to Dad. 'That's . . . incredible really,' I murmur.

'Yeah, you could call it that,' he says.

I peer at him in the gloomy living room, trying to read his face. 'You're not interested in meeting her, then?'

'What do *you* think?' he snaps.

'Um, I don't know really. But I s'pose there's no harm in—'

'Did you read it?' he blurts out. 'Did you just read that thing?'

I step back. 'Yes, Dad. I read it . . .'

'She wants me back so the creditors can see that she's doing stuff. That she's trying to put things back to the way they were—'

'Yes,' I say, aware of Arthur sitting quietly now, picking at his fingernails. 'But maybe, if you just—'

'She wants to use me as bait,' he announces, 'or a carrot—'

'Dad, I'm sure it wasn't meant like—'

'Why are you sticking up for her?'

'I'm not! Jesus, Dad . . .' I stare at him, frustration bubbling up in me now. I know it's not me he's angry with, and it's understandable that he's reacting like this. But it takes an almighty effort to speak calmly when his face is inches from mine, his eyes filled with fury. 'I'm *not* taking her side,' I say firmly. 'Why on earth would I do that? I don't even know the woman. All I'm saying is, it might be good for you to at least—'

'I'll tell you what'll be good for me,' Dad announces, snatching the envelope and letter from my hand and scrunching them up in his fist. Arthur stares, open-

212

mouthed, as his grandfather storms through to the kitchen. I hurry after him and watch as he stamps so hard on the pedal bin's pedal that it cracks.

'Granddad, your bin!' Arthur cries out behind me.

Dad flings the letter and envelope into it. 'Never mind that,' he shoots back, angry red patches springing up on his cheeks. 'What'll be good for me is for that damn woman to leave me the hell alone.'

Chapter Thirty-Two

Suzy

'Fancy an early pub supper?' Cara asks when I turn up to collect Scout. 'The Anchor does an amazing cullen skink on Fridays.'

'What's cullen skink?' I ask. Yet another mysterious term.

She laughs. 'It's a lovely, creamy, smoky fish soup. Once you've tried it, I promise you'll never forget it.'

I jump at the chance, grateful for Cara's company as a distraction from obsessing over Harry Vance. All day I've been checking my phone for missed calls, willing him to get in touch, even though I only dropped off his letter yesterday. He's probably taking his time, mulling things over. And why *should* he feel obliged to respond right away? Perhaps, I mused, over a quick lunchtime sandwich with Vicki, he's making me sweat it out.

However, I relax as soon as Cara and I are installed in the Anchor's snug. The pub is delightfully cosy with its evocative sepia photographs of islanders from days gone by: mending boats, landing catches of fish and working on the land. While the wind moans outside, the fire crackles and glows invitingly and, as Cara had promised, the pub's famous soup is a comfort blanket for a chilly April evening.

'Have you decided how long you're staying here?' she asks, placing her spoon in her empty bowl.

'At least another couple of weeks,' I reply. 'I'm starting to love it here. I really am. A friend back home is keeping an eye on my house so there's no real reason to rush back.'

'I'm so glad to hear that,' she says. Then, after a pause: 'I was thinking . . . look, I don't want you to feel obliged, and I realise it might not suit you at all. But I was wondering, instead of booking more nights at the hotel, you'd be really welcome to come and stay with me. In the studio, I mean. There's a bed there, and if you needed peace and quiet while I'm working you could set up at the kitchen table . . .'

'Oh, that's so kind of you, but—'

'I know it's pretty basic,' she adds, 'so please don't feel bad if you'd rather not.'

'The Cormorant Hotel's pretty basic,' I say with a smile. 'And your studio's lovely. But would that really be okay, us being under your feet—'

'I'd love you and Scout to be there,' she says firmly.

I look at her, overwhelmed by her generosity. 'Cara, that sounds great. But I'd have to pay you. I mean, I'd be paying for a hotel room anyway.'

'Absolutely not,' she says firmly. 'I couldn't accept that. To be honest . . .' She exhales. 'Well, I've told you how lonely it can be, working on my own. And having Scout for his visits has made such a difference . . . D'you think he'd like to stay at mine?' We peek down to where he's been dozing peacefully under the table. As if sensing our attention, he wakes himself with a vigorous shake, then potters between us with tail wagging.

I catch Cara's eye and we laugh. 'I think we can take that as a yes,' I say.

It's just gone seven when we part company at the end of the street, having agreed that I'll move into Cara's on Sunday when my hotel booking comes to an end. Although most of the shops have closed for the day, the bookshop is still open. I glance in to see a huge, fluffy tabby cat snoozing on a cushion on the counter. Unable to resist, I open the door a little and ask if it's okay to bring in my dog.

'Of course it is,' says a young woman in denim dungarees. 'Oh, he's a lovely wee thing. Is he a he?'

'He is,' I reply. 'He's called Scout.' She crouches down and makes a fuss of him while I browse the shelves, selecting a novel and a guidebook of walks on the island. Maybe one day I'll have time to explore some more, to get to know the place and feel like I really belong. The thought of going back to York is faintly unsettling; it feels so very far away. But I'll have to at some point, of course. Although Isaac and Frieda both hope to go travelling this summer, they'll want to spend some time at home before they go. Frieda's graduation is coming up too. It feels as if I am living two very separate lives.

Scout and I leave the shop and wander past the Seafood Shack on the quay. The wind has died down and the evening is beautifully still, the sea as calm as a mirror. Cormorants are diving for fish and a yellow-beaked seagull perches on a litter bin, eyeing the scene regally.

In the distance, I spot that man and his son – Arthur – from the beach. They're eating chips from brown paper bags and seem to be locked in intense conversation.

I catch the man's eye and he smiles in recognition as they approach. 'Hi,' he says. 'Lovely evening, isn't it?'

'It's beautiful,' I say as Arthur greets Scout with enthusiasm.

'Can I give him a chip?' he asks with a grin.

'Sure, he'd love that,' I say, touched by the way Arthur is with him. He leads Scout to a nearby bench, takes a seat and pats the space next to him – Scout's cue to jump up.

I smile at his father. 'Those two are so sweet together.'

'Yeah.' He laughs. 'Look, um, I'm sorry he went on about borrowing him. I hope it didn't make you feel awkward.'

'Not at all,' I say quickly, 'and he didn't go on. He's so good with him. In fact, I went back to the beach to say that of course he could walk him sometime. But you'd already gone. I don't know why I said no. It was just—'

'It's fine,' he insists. 'You don't go around handing your dog over to complete strangers, do you?'

'No,' I say, 'but I'm sure you're trustworthy. I mean, I don't think you're likely to steal him—'

'Much as Arthur would like us to.' He grins and his deep brown eyes glint in the evening sunshine. His easy-going manner is attractive, and I find myself wondering what Arthur's mum is like, and if they're together. He's certainly an appealing, handsome man.

'Well, um,' I continue, 'what I wanted to say is, I'd be absolutely fine about it as long you or another adult went along too. I mean, I'm sure Arthur's very sensible, but—'

'Oh, I understand,' he says. 'I'd be with him, definitely. I'm Ricky,' he adds.

'And I'm Suzy,' I say, without hesitation – because what else can I do? It's a common enough name, and I've

217

already decided I was just being paranoid about locals connecting me to the distillery. 'So, if Arthur would still like to walk Scout,' I add, 'maybe we could arrange that?'

Ricky's face brightens. 'That'd be great. But the thing is, we're going home to Glasgow on Sunday—'

'Oh, yes, you did tell me,' I say as Arthur and Scout wander back towards us.

He looks up at his dad. 'Wish we were staying longer.'

'Do you?' Ricky smiles. '*That's* a bit of a change of heart.'

Arthur shrugs. 'I still like it here, Dad.'

'Yeah, I know you do.' As Ricky rests an arm around his son's shoulders, I wonder if they've reached the point at which Arthur has become less than enthusiastic about his trips here.

'I'm taking Scout to the beach now,' I tell them. 'You're welcome to come with us, if you like?'

'I'd love to!' Arthur enthuses.

'Great,' Ricky says. 'Let's do that.' He pauses. 'If you're sure you don't mind us tagging along?'

'No, of course not,' I say.

'Shall we go and get Granddad?' Arthur asks, turning to his father. 'It might cheer him up. He was in a bad mood last night, wasn't he, Dad? I've never seen him as mad as that—'

'Oh, I think we'll leave him in peace,' Ricky says briskly as we head down the worn stone steps to the shore.

Chapter Thirty-Three

Find your pack, feel the joy, ran an advertising slogan a few years ago. It was for a sportswear brand and showed dozens of dogs charging delightedly across a field. It seemed a bit corny back then, but now I'm feeling Scout's joy as he pelts across the wide arc of sand, oblivious to being watched.

Arthur, who's running in pursuit, has found an abandoned tennis ball. 'They're having such fun,' I say as he throws it for Scout to fetch.

'Yeah,' Ricky says with a warm smile. 'It's great to see.'

I glance back at him, wondering what the scenario is with the bad-tempered granddad. Of course, I'm not going to ask. But I hope it's not something Arthur did that provoked his anger last night. He seems like such a good-natured kid. 'You said he'd love a dog of his own,' I add.

'God, yes. Every birthday and Christmas it comes up, guaranteed. He's hoping I'll reach that tipping point and finally crumble.'

'We ended up with guinea pigs,' I say, chuckling in recognition. 'That was our compromise.'

'Smart move,' he says. 'How many d'you have? Kids, I mean . . .'

'Yeah, the guinea pigs are long gone, sadly. I have a son and a daughter, both away at uni now. They've been teasing me that I got Scout as a child substitute . . .'

'They've rumbled you, then.' Amusement glimmers in his dark brown eyes, and we fall into a comfortable silence for a few moments. The sun is setting now, sliding towards the flat horizon where the sea meets the pink-smudged sky.

'So, you're not going to give in?' I ask. 'Over the dog thing, I mean?'

'I can't,' Ricky says with a shake of his head. 'We live in a flat and I'm out all day at work. It wouldn't be fair at all.'

I register the 'I', rather than a 'we'. So I assume he's separated or divorced. 'What d'you do for a job?' I ask.

'I'm a peripatetic music teacher. I mean, I go to different schools, teaching violin, cello, double bass . . .'

'Oh, yes, I remember the peri from my school. A lovely man – long suffering, actually. I think most of us only took up an instrument to get time out of classes—'

'Yeah, that happens,' Ricky says. 'So, what's your instrument?'

'I don't have one,' I reply. 'My sister had played the clarinet for a while so it was passed on to me, but I never really had the knack for it.'

'Did you go through the grades, all of that?'

'Only one. I have a deep fear of performing or speaking in front of people, and playing those pieces for the examiner nearly finished me off.'

'Music exams aren't for everyone,' Ricky concedes. 'In fact, most of my pupils choose not to do them and that's fine with me. The last thing I want to do is stress them out and put them off playing.' He pauses. 'So, what kind of job d'you do?'

My heart seems to jolt. *I'm sort of working here,* I told him when we first met. *Just something I'm setting up.* Does that count as a lie? 'I'm a writer,' I reply. 'I write obituaries, mainly for newspapers . . .'

'Wow.' He looks at me in surprise. 'I've never met anyone who does anything like that before.'

I laugh. 'Well, it is a bit niche. But I'd always found them fascinating . . .'

'Oh, I do too,' Ricky says. 'Arthur thinks it's weird, but I always read them.'

'Kids think *anything* their parents do is weird,' I remark, and he laughs.

'You're right there. There's something about them, though. I like the quirky ones best. You know, the ones about people you'd never have heard of otherwise?'

'Unless they'd died, you mean?' I smile.

He nods. 'That sounds awful, doesn't it?'

'It's true, though,' I say. 'They're my favourites too and I always try to do them justice.'

'I'm sure you do.' He looks thoughtful for a moment. 'I read one on the ferry about this marine biologist, a world expert on jellyfish—'

'That was Lionel Foster,' I say with a tinge of pride. 'I wrote that.'

'You're kidding!' he exclaims, and I notice again how attractive his smile his; wide and generous and crinkling his eyes.

'Well, mine was the only one in a newspaper,' I add. 'There were others in specialist scientific publications, of course. I mean he was *the* go-to jellyfish guy . . .'

221

'So I gathered,' he says, still seeming quite taken aback by the connection. 'Is that why you came here? To get away from it all and write?'

'Er, sort of,' I say quickly, not wanting to go into the whole distillery business now. After all, Ricky grew up on the island. He's bound to know someone who's connected to it and I'd hate our enjoyable chat to swerve down that route. 'So, d'you enjoy teaching?' I ask.

'I love it,' he replies. 'Arthur doesn't so much. Unfortunately, his school's one of the primaries I visit.'

'You mean you teach him?'

'No, I tried to coax him – gently – when he was younger, but sport's his thing, not music. I mean, it's a bit mortifying for him that I teach there.' He smiles in a *what-can-you-do?* kind of way as his son wanders towards us. 'Isn't that right, Arthur?'

'It's okay, I s'pose,' he says with a shrug.

'What kind of job would you like your dad to have?' I ask.

'A normal one?' He catches his dad's eye, and they laugh as we wait for Scout to potter back to us. The sunset is breathtaking now, the sea reflecting the intense pinks and golds of the swiftly darkening sky.

'There's a kind of hierarchy of coolness among music tutors,' Ricky adds.

'How does that work, then?'

He grimaces and rubs a hand across his short dark hair. 'Drum teachers are acceptable – almost human, really. Woodwind falls somewhere in the middle and strings are definitely at the bottom . . .'

'Really? I had no idea!' I glance at him, imagining that he's an excellent teacher. 'This has been lovely,' I add. 'I don't think I've ever seen sunsets like the ones here.'

'Yeah, it's famous for it,' Ricky says, then Arthur cuts in: 'Can we walk Scout again? I mean, can we borrow him?'

'Arthur—' his dad starts.

'Of course you can,' I say quickly.

'Can we do it tomorrow?' Arthur grins hopefully. 'We go home the day after—'

'It's your birthday tomorrow,' Ricky cuts in.

'Yeah, I know, but that's okay, isn't it?' He shrugs again. 'I mean, what else are we doing?'

'Well, er—' Ricky starts as Arthur adds: 'Maybe we could bring Granddad?' He turns to me. 'Is that all right, if he comes as well?'

'Of course it is.' I can't help smiling that he feels the need to ask permission to invite him along. 'Shall we meet here tomorrow morning, then? Is eleven okay?'

'That's perfect for us,' Ricky says, placing an arm on Arthur's shoulder. 'And that's a good idea, to ask Granddad along.' He glances at me as we make for the steps. 'My dad really hasn't been himself lately,' he adds. 'And although he won't admit it, I know he really misses having a dog.'

Chapter Thirty-Four

Ricky

Arthur seems pleased with his reconditioned laptop plus a football strip, a couple of books and enough chocolate to give Meg an actual heart attack, were she here to witness this. However, there's still a strained atmosphere around Dad's place. I just wish that woman had never dropped off her letter for him. *She had the nerve to put it through my bloody door!* he's muttered more than once. As if the thought of her hand even hovering by his letterbox is enough to make his simmering irritation rise to a rolling boil all over again.

Plus, there's the weirdness of Meg rushing off, a situation Dad has barely mentioned (emotional matters don't really feature on his radar) apart from to ask, in a slightly hurt tone, 'Didn't she like it here?'

Of course she did, I tried to reassure him. It was nothing to do with that. But he's seemed to take it as a personal slight, and I'm grateful now that we've planned to walk Scout later this morning. I can't help feeling that Dad's spending too much time brooding in the house.

Perhaps in an attempt to please him, Arthur gathers

up all the torn wrapping paper (a first!) and stuffs it into the broken pedal bin. Dad has given Arthur a couple of crumpled tenners and a birthday card, and Kai has phoned him, but I gather they're all – understandably – still distraught over Kai's grandma dying and the conversation seemed stilted and was short-lived.

Now, having had breakfast, Arthur opens the present Meg left for him. It's a crisp, white, expensive-looking box containing a bottle of aftershave. Aftershave, for an eleven-year-old kid! He probably won't be acquainting himself with a razor for another four years. If it was meant purely as fragrance I can safely say that my son would be no more likely to spray himself with car paint.

'Wow,' I murmur. 'That's . . . an interesting choice.'

'Yeah.' Arthur pulls a grim expression and passes me the accompanying card to read:

Happy birthday, Arthur! I know boys of your age start dousing themselves in Lynx and God knows what so I thought I'd get in first with something lovely that you can enjoy wearing. I had it blended specially for you according to your tastes.
Love, Meg xxx

What tastes were they? Fish fingers and Caramel Logs?

'That's some fancy stuff you've got there, son,' Dad says, cracking a smile at last.

'D'you want it, Granddad?' Arthur asks with a grin, nudging the bottle towards him across the kitchen table.

'No, I bloody well do not!'

Arthur chuckles. 'Do *you*, Dad?'

'Erm, no thanks,' I say quickly. 'It'd feel, um, kind of . . .'

'Weird?'

'Yeah, just a bit. Um, maybe you should just keep it. You might like it one day. Remember how you used to hate tuna? And cheese? You *hated* cheese. And now—'

'Dad, this isn't like tuna or cheese!' He's laughing now.

'It'd smell better if it was,' Dad remarks, smirking. I chuckle and glance towards the window, relieved to see that, although our famous Atlantic winds seem to be in full throttle, at least it's not raining.

'We've arranged to walk a dog today,' I tell him.

'Aye, Arthur mentioned it.' Dad smiles at him. 'That's nice for you.'

'Then we're going to pick up my birthday cake,' Arthur adds, grinning now.

I stare at him. 'You know about that?'

Arthur nods. 'I heard you on the phone in the garden. When you ordered it, I mean. My bedroom window was open,' he adds.

'Okay,' I say with a sigh. 'But it was meant to be a surprise!'

He sniggers. 'Sorry, Dad.'

I shrug. 'Never mind. So, how about getting out of your pyjamas and properly dressed? We should be going soon . . .'

'Okay!' Arthur beams at me and pelts upstairs.

I glance at Dad as I clear away the breakfast things. 'You know, sometimes I think he's already hurtling into puberty and becoming all world-weary and cynical. Then something like this happens.'

'Yeah.' Dad nods. 'He's a good kid. You've done a good job there, son.'

This unexpected praise affects me perhaps more than it should. But Dad has already turned his attentions to the aftershave, which he picks up and studies, holding the squarish bottle at arm's length, as if it's a souvenir a neighbour has brought him back from their 'foreign travel' and he's not sure about it at all. My father has never been abroad and has never expressed any desire to do so. His diet is so quintessentially British that he even regards pasta as something startlingly 'different', from a faraway land, rather than being so ubiquitous it has its own aisle in the supermarket.

'He doesn't eat pasta at all?' Arthur asked once, incredulously.

'Well, yeah – he's fine with tinned spaghetti,' I replied. 'But not the kind you boil in a pan.'

He laughed in disbelief. 'What about pizza? Does he like that?'

'God, no, that's far too exotic.'

Arthur spluttered. He loves pizza, but I also suspect he enjoys his Granddad's quirks and stubbornness. 'Is that right, son?' Dad marvelled when Arthur explained that ten different languages are spoken at his Glasgow primary school. I could tell it both baffled and intrigued him as Arthur then proceeded to list them all. At Dad's school, there was just English, of course – and Gaelic.

Now Arthur has reappeared in a sweater and jeans, raring to go. 'Are you coming with us, Granddad?' he asks.

'Aw no, you two go. I've stuff to be getting on with here.' As if to reiterate his point, he goes to fetch the carpet sweeper from the hall cupboard; an ancient yellow plastic model, which he proceeds to rake back and forth vigorously across the living room rug. He moves on to the hallway, clearly intent on an energetic bout of cleaning which, although the house isn't dirty, is certainly rarely witnessed.

Arthur and I trail after him. 'I'll do that later,' I say. 'Just leave it for now.'

'No, you're fine, son.' He rakes some more. After Mum died, Dad 'retired' the hoover in favour of the sweeper – I suspect because it doesn't use any electricity.

'Come on, Dad,' I say, checking the time on my phone. 'We're meeting down at Silver Beach. The day's brightening up and it *is* Arthur's birthday.' I glance at my son.

'Please, Granddad,' Arthur says hopefully. 'I really want you to come.'

My father exhales slowly and stands there, gripping the carpet sweeper as if weighing up whether the housework can wait. 'All right then,' he says.

Arthur beams at him. 'Great! C'mon then, let's go. I can't wait for you to meet Scout.'

Chapter Thirty-Five

Suzy

I worked late again last night, fired up by the thought of moving into Cara's studio and Arthur being excited to see Scout one last time. Perhaps I worked *too* late, as even when 1 a.m. rolled around and I crawled into bed I wasn't properly tired. And then, as if to sabotage any prospect of sleep, my happy thoughts were slowly replaced by the troubling matter of the distillery's accounts. Although our original accountant – sidelined by Paul – is diligently working through things with me, figures still swarmed around in my head like malevolent biting insects.

Why are things so much more worrying in the middle of the night? I lay there, staring at the ceiling, fretting about how I am going to keep my family afloat. As well as gradually whittling down the distillery's debts, I'll also have Rosalind's bills to settle. Plus, what about Harry? Stupidly perhaps, I've all but promised the creditors that our 'renowned expert' will be returning to help to steer us out of the storm and into calmer waters. But so far there's been no response to my letter. The very real possibility that Harry will simply ignore it is something I'm trying not to dwell upon.

My night-worries slid ominously back to the matter of my family. When it comes to supporting our kids, Tony has never been difficult about paying his share, but I can't ask him to contribute more than he does already – not with four more children of his own to bring up. Yet there are frequent small emergencies where our pair is concerned. I'll deduce that Isaac needs history textbooks, or a utility bill paying urgently, or it'll become apparent that Frieda lacks a proper winter coat. And those shoes of Isaac's, which he refuses to replace! Is it a badge of honour, this thing of shuffling around in disintegrating (and, I have to say, reeking) footwear?

Finally, with my head now filled with rotting shoes and freezing student flats, I must have somehow tipped over into sleep. Because next thing I knew, Scout's wet, cold nose was probing my ear and it was morning – raining, yes, but who knew how the days would turn out here? It could easily be sunny by lunchtime.

We braved the steady rain together and returned, damp and clammy, for breakfast. By now those barely decipherable accountancy figures had settled into something more orderly in my mind.

Back in our room, I looked through some notes for an obituary I need to write today for a ballet dancer who died two days short of her hundredth birthday. There is a raft of emails to deal with, and Mum has texted. I replied quickly, reassuring her that I am fully in control and *everything is going to be okay*. I also texted Dee to give her a quick update of how things are here; thankfully all is fine back home. And now, at 10.45 a.m., I glance over to Scout, who's waiting expectantly by the door.

'You have another date today,' I tell him. 'You're extremely popular around here and that's because you're such a lovely boy.' I go over to hug him, my spirits lifted by his warmth, his furriness, his *everything* really.

We set off and make our way through the narrow streets towards the beach. I spot Vicki from the distillery across the street. She smiles, and I smile and wave back. Perhaps I am no longer the antichrist around here? Tempting aromas of coffee and freshly baked loaves waft from the cluster of cafés, and a few fishing boats are bobbing a little way out to sea.

Already, Scout has stopped to do something like fifteen pees along the way. It seems like a terribly inefficient system when one lengthy widdle would have done the job. I guess the territory-marking aspect must be important. He also tries to munch at some greenery from a terracotta plant pot outside someone's front door, but I manage to coax him away. This vegetation-eating thing seems nonsensical as it only makes him sick. I've already had to wipe up a couple of small puddles from the grey carpet in my hotel room. Maybe it's the canine equivalent of knocking back those horribly potent alcohol shots that young people appeared to be partial to for a while, and which always seemed to end in vomiting – or, at the very least, copious tears (does anyone drink that stuff anymore? When I was a teenager the preferred alcoholic beverage was snakebite and black, *far* more sensible).

Now Scout is mooching onwards, pausing only to snaffle a couple of chips off the pavement as we stride towards the beach. I hope Arthur is still excited about walking him and hasn't gone off the idea. After all, it's his birthday. He might be too thrilled by his presents to want to come out.

Scout and I trot down the old stone steps to the beach. Frondy black seaweed is strewn across the wet sand like a lacy cobweb. I look around for Ricky and Arthur but the only people in sight are a lone jogger and an elderly lady with a tiny white dog, barely bigger than an ear muff. A second, matching dog appears from behind a rock; a *pair* of ear muffs, pottering along in the light drizzle.

We wander across the rippled sand towards the sea. When I glance back, I spot Arthur, Ricky and an older man in the far distance. I'm a little taken aback by how happy I am to see them again.

I am actually getting to know people – making connections of my own – here on Sgadansay. A few weeks ago, that would have hardly seemed possible. I'm reminded again how it was always Paul who befriended strangers on holiday; how he'd collect everyone's numbers and even arrange reunions. He was always far more outgoing than me. Yet here I am, soon to move into Cara's studio, and about to lend Scout to Ricky, Arthur and Ricky's dad. Perhaps I didn't know myself as well as I thought I did. I also seem to have become a keen scholar of Hebridean geological formations, having swotted up on Sgadansay's metamorphic rock – the oldest in Britain! – with its bands of mica and quartz. I've pored over facts about the island's mosses, which infuse the water and create our whisky's barely detectable smoky taste.

Arthur has spotted me now. 'Scout!' he yells, his face breaking into a wide grin. He starts running towards us and Scout tears towards him in delight.

'Hey, little man!' Arthur exclaims, slightly breathless as they meet in an excited blur. He looks up at me. 'Can we borrow him this time?'

'Yes, that's fine,' I say. 'I can go off and do some work and meet you later. Oh, and happy birthday!'

'Thanks.' He beams at me. 'How long can we have him?'

'I'll figure it out with your dad,' I reply, turning towards Ricky and the older man as they approach.

'Hi,' Ricky says with a wide smile.

'Hi.' My own smile has frozen. Ricky, Arthur and even Scout seem to melt away as there is only one face I see.

It's the man who looked crushed at my first meeting at the distillery. The man who'd resigned in disgust after Paul had blundered in and insisted on doing things *his* way.

Apparently, Harry had kicked against Paul's every decision. 'He's stuck in the past,' Paul had thundered, following one of his trips to the island. 'He's going to have to understand that things are changing. So he can either get on board or fuck off.' I hadn't met Harry then, apart from briefly, on that distillery tour, when we hadn't even spoken directly. I'd thought it was harsh but Paul wouldn't listen to anything I had to say. After all, hadn't I said from the start that he would take charge, that I hadn't wanted 'another strand'?

I'm sorry, I want to tell Harry now. *I shouldn't have believed Paul when he said everything would be okay and we could manage without a head distiller.* But all I can manage is a croaky 'Hello, Harry' as my cheeks blaze.

'Oh,' he says curtly. 'It's *you*. Ricky never told me that.' He shoots his son a fierce look.

Ricky stares at his father, then at me. 'You two know each other?'

'Erm yes, we do,' I start. 'I'm sorry, Harry. I didn't realise it was you—'

'You're right, we know each other,' Harry snaps. 'This is Suzy Medley. The Meddler—'

233

Christ, is that what they call me? Tears spring into my eyes.

'You're the distillery woman?' Ricky exclaims. 'But . . . why didn't you say?'

'I'm sorry,' I start. 'I—'

'Was it you who wrote that letter to Granddad?' Arthur gasps.

'Yep, she did. Enjoy your walk then,' Harry mutters before I can answer. Then he stuffs his hands into his jeans pockets and marches away.

Chapter Thirty-Six

Ricky

To think I was worried about Dad's fitness. He's stormed off now at the speed of a man half his age. I was poised to hurry after him but I know there's no point. When he's like this he's best left alone. Anyway, it would upset Arthur, on his birthday, and now all I can think of is to try and salvage his day as best as I can.

'I'm sorry,' Suzy is saying. 'Honestly, I had *no* idea Harry's your dad. Will he be all right, d'you think?'

'He'll be fine,' I say distractedly. 'I just . . . why didn't you tell me that's why you're here? You said you're a writer, that you came here to—'

'Ricky, I'm really sorry,' she says, looking genuinely distraught. 'I *am* a writer. That part's true. I was just . . .' She rakes back her long hair and her face flushes. 'I was enjoying our walk last night and, well . . . the whole distillery business is obviously pretty contentious and I didn't want to go into it all with you . . .' She tails off.

I glance down at Arthur and then back at Suzy. Despite everything I can't help feeling sorry for her. She doesn't seem like the heartless monster she's been made out to be.

'I'm sorry,' she says again. 'I know I should've said.'

Arthur rubs at his nose. 'Granddad's just upset,' he murmurs.

'Yes.' She nods. 'I'm guessing now that it wasn't a good idea to drop off that letter.'

'No, he threw it away and broke the bin,' Arthur announces.

'Oh God, did he?' Her eyes widen.

'Well, um . . .' I grimace. 'It's all still pretty sensitive, the way he felt forced out by your partner—'

'Paul's nothing to do with it anymore,' she says quickly. 'I'm taking it over by myself.'

'Yeah.' I nod. 'You said so in your letter and Dad already knew that anyway. I mean, people talk around here—'

'But he was still angry,' Arthur says, his expression grave.

'Okay, Arthur,' I say quietly. Scout is sitting patiently between us with ears pricked, and Arthur bobs down to stroke him. I glance over towards the steps but of course, Dad is long gone.

'Can we still walk him?' he asks.

'You're welcome to,' Suzy starts, 'if you like . . .'

I exhale. 'Oh, I don't think it's the best time, Arthur,' I mutter.

'Yes, you'd probably better go and see if your granddad's all right,' Suzy adds quickly, at which Arthur's face seems to crumple.

'He'll be all right, won't he, Dad? He'll just go home and make tea. And it *is* my birthday . . .' He grinds a trainer toe into the sand.

'How about we go and see if your cake's ready at the bakery?' I suggest in an overly bright voice.

'*Please* let's walk Scout,' he mumbles. There's an awkward silence, broken only by the plaintive cries of the gulls.

'Well, okay then,' I say. 'But we'd better not be too long.'

'Aw, Dad,' Arthur says with a sigh.

I look at Suzy. Already, I can understand why she didn't go into the whole distillery business last night. It had been a lovely evening and, well, she wasn't obliged to tell me all about her life. It was just chitchat and I'd found myself enjoying her company. And Arthur had loved it. He'd been full of enthusiasm when we'd gone back to Dad's. 'How about we walk him to the rocks and back?' I suggest, turning to Suzy. 'All of us, I mean? I just think it's not worth you going away, and then coming back again—'

'Yes, of course,' she says, mustering a smile.

'You mean we're not borrowing him?' Arthur says, clearly put out by the injustice of it all.

'Look, it'll have to do, okay?' Impatience has crept into my voice even though none of this is his fault. I'm just pretty eager to get back to Dad's. And so that's what we do, with Arthur and Scout running off ahead, our ominous presence seemingly forgotten within minutes.

Suzy glances sideways at me as we fall into step. 'I'm really sorry about the whole situation with your dad,' she starts. 'And I'm doing everything I can. To get things back on track, I mean.'

'Yeah, I've heard that,' I say truthfully. There's been quite a bit of talk around town about how involved she is, how she's full of questions, badgering everyone and constantly scribbling notes. But the whole situation still seems bizarre. Why would you go onto a partnership with someone and sit back while they screw everything up?

Up ahead, Scout is running in crazy zig-zags. Arthur has brought that manky old tennis ball he found, and Scout charges after it, catching it neatly in his mouth. 'So, how did it all come about?' I ask Suzy. 'You and your partner buying the distillery, I mean?' She looks at me as if wondering how best to start. And then she tells me, as we walk, how it had been his idea, and how impetuous he was, and why she'd pushed her fears and doubts aside as everything had slid rapidly downhill.

'It was Paul's inheritance from his dad,' she explains. 'He was set on wanting to do something amazing with it, and when it came down to it I couldn't bring myself to stand in his way.' I nod, letting all this new information settle. The day has brightened now, the blustery wind having dropped to a gentle breeze. 'Can I ask you something?' she adds.

'Sure,' I say lightly.

'D'you think there's any chance your dad would agree to meet up with me?'

I stuff my hands into my jeans pockets, trying to figure out the answer myself. It would make sense, of course. She's certainly helped me to understand things better and I know it would help him too. If nothing else, he might be a little less angry. This simmering fury – the bin breaking, the angry carpet raking – can't be good for him. 'The thing about Dad,' I start, 'is that once he's made up his mind about someone, that's that.'

'Really?' Disappointment flickers in her greenish eyes.

'I mean, obviously he's bitter about what happened,' I add. 'So I guess it's understandable.'

'Yes, of course it is.'

'But he's cut people out of his life for far less,' I continue. 'About twenty years ago a local guy did a shoddy job of

238

re-felting his shed roof. They were friends, and they used to have the odd drink and stuff. But Dad never spoke to him again.'

'Wow,' she murmurs. 'So there's not much hope for me, then.'

'I don't think so, no.' We settle back into silence for a few moments.

'Well, look,' she says finally, 'if he won't meet me one-to-one, d'you think he'd come along to a meeting at the distillery? Not to take part or anything, but just to be there?' She looks at me expectantly. 'I'm holding one for all the staff on Monday,' she adds. 'I think a huge part of the anger and frustration came about because no one had the full picture of what was going on.'

'Yeah, you're probably right.' I nod.

'I'd be hugely grateful if your dad would agree to come, Ricky.' She smiles then and, for a moment, I wish I didn't feel the need to head back to Dad's. Because I *like* this woman, this Suzy Medley. She didn't lie to me exactly. In fact, she strikes me as being honest and decent and she's just trying to do her best.

'I'll mention it to him,' I tell her.

'Thank you,' she says. 'Thank you so much—'

'But I'm sorry, I can't promise he'll agree to come—'

'No, of course not. I understand that,' she says as I wave to Arthur in an attempt to catch his attention.

'Hey,' I call out, 'we should head back now!'

'Already?' he yells back.

'Yeah. C'mon, son.' We turn back, with Arthur lagging way behind us and Scout meandering along at his side.

We reach the steps and wait for them to catch up with us. 'Did you enjoy that?' I ask him.

'It was a bit quick,' he replies. 'Can we do it again, properly?'

'We're going home tomorrow,' I remind him.

'Yeah, I know that,' Arthur says. 'I mean, next time we visit Granddad.' He turns to Suzy. 'D'you live here?'

'Oh, I'm just staying here for a while,' she says. 'I'm not quite sure how long for.'

The twinge of regret takes me by surprise. We'll probably never see her and Scout again. 'Well, good luck with everything,' I say.

'Thanks.' Her smile is warm and wide now, no longer hesitant. 'Enjoy the rest of your birthday, Arthur.'

'Thanks,' he says with a smile.

'We'd better pick up your surprise cake that you're not supposed to know anything about,' I add. 'And then we'll get back to see what Granddad's been getting up to.'

Chapter Thirty-Seven

'Jesus, Dad. We'll need to get you looked at!'

My father is perched on the edge of the armchair, groaning and clutching at his chest. All I've been able to deduce so far is that he slipped in the bath. What was he doing having a bath in the middle of the day? He rarely has them anyway. He seems to think they're wildly extravagant – to be savoured only on special occasions, like steak. 'Looked at by who?' he barks, his face milk-pale.

Who does he think? The postman? 'The doctor, of course!'

'I'm all right,' he insists. 'Just leave me. I'll be okay in a minute.' He flaps me away as if I'm a bluebottle, buzzing around his face.

'Dad, I'm not *leaving* you. This could be serious.' Arthur and I had come back to find Dad clutching at the bannister, struggling to make his way downstairs. Still wet, with hair dripping, he'd managed to pull on his dressing gown but his face was contorted in pain. It now transpires that he'd returned from the beach to throw himself into an energetic bout of gardening. Angry weeding, I'd imagine. The furious hoicking out of dandelions, and perhaps some vicious jabbing with the fork. He'd worked himself up into such a sweat that he'd gone for a shower – it's an antiquated over-the-bath type – and that's when the accident had happened.

Why hadn't we just come straight home with him instead of walking with Suzy and then going to collect the cake?

'Where's the pain?' I ask now. 'Is it your ribs, d'you think? Around your chest? Let me see . . .'

'Are you gonna be okay, Granddad?' Arthur is hovering, agitated, at my side.

'I've just winded myself, son,' he mumbles.

'Dad, *please* let me have a look.'

Reluctantly, he lets me open his dressing gown. The sight of his chest, thin and pale with a few straggly greying hairs, tugs at my heart. Some bruising is evident already. 'The surgery's not open on Saturday, is it?' I ask.

Dad shakes his head. 'I don't need the doctor.' No, of course not. A seventy-eight-year-old man injures himself to the point at which he can barely move without flinching – but heaven forbid he might require medical attention.

He turns away, pointedly avoiding my gaze the way a child might whilst being told off. My God, how did he get to be so maddening? How did Mum put up with him all those years? I look around the living room. Apart from the bulky three-piece suite, there's also the highly polished sideboard, a nest of tables that no one ever uses and another table that will probably sit in its stowed-away configuration, adorned by a lacy doily, forever. When it's fully extended it's too big for the room, and was only

242

ever used on special occasions when Mum was still here and the best china came out. Back home, Arthur and I don't have a 'best' anything.

'Could you make Granddad a cup of tea?' I ask Arthur. He nods and scuttles off, dutifully, to put the kettle on. However, even when it's brought to Dad, loaded with his customary three spoons of sugar, it doesn't seem to have its usual restorative effect. Still pallid, he is sweating now, his brow visibly moist.

'We'd better take you to hospital,' I say.

'Don't be ridiculous! It's not for this kind of thing.'

Arthur and I exchange a quick glance. 'It's not for people who are hurt?' I ask. 'What *is* it for then?'

He huffs some more and I detect that, as well as the pain of the fall, there's also resentment lurking about us having walked *that woman's* dog. Dad clearly views the matter as an act of treachery on my part.

'We're going to hospital,' I say firmly.

'I told you, I'm not going!' He tries to get up from the chair and groans loudly. 'Uhh, bloody hell . . .'

'Come on, Dad, please,' I say firmly. 'Arthur, go upstairs and get Granddad some jeans, pyjama bottoms . . . anything you can find.'

He makes for the stairs. 'And a top and some pants?' he asks.

'Don't worry about pants.' Dad glowers at me as if affronted by having his underwear discussed at all. 'If you can find some,' I add quickly. 'And grab a jumper and his slippers.'

'I'm not going in *slippers*,' Dad thunders, as if it's a wedding we're about to attend. However, he acquiesces and, minutes later, I have managed to ease my father into his clothes, and then my car, and we pull up at the hospital

243

across town just as the sky darkens dramatically and heavy rain starts to fall.

Sgadansay's main medical facility is quaintly known as a cottage hospital. It looks like somebody's house – albeit a fairly substantial one – with a rose garden at the front and a summerhouse that I can't imagine anyone ever uses.

The waiting room has sage green walls and vases of faded fake flowers on the windowsills. Two snowy-haired women are chatting about Mrs McLeod from the bank's retirement party, and who's going to make the meringues for it; it seems meringues are essential. The women register Dad's presence with nods and smiles; it's clear that they know him, as virtually everyone does. He turns his back on them abruptly, emitting powerful *do not talk to me* vibes. Thankfully their conversation about party catering soon resumes.

Dad gazes down at the floor, looking pale and glum, and slightly eccentric in checked fleecy pyjama bottoms, his felty grey slippers and a light-blue cable-knit sweater that I think I might have given him several Christmases ago, and which appears distinctly unworn.

'I'll do the meringues if Sandra will at least make a flan,' one of the women says.

I glance at Arthur, who's sitting to my left. Although I'm trying to remain positive, I have to admit that his eleventh birthday probably hasn't been one of his best.

He was pleased with the laptop, the football strip and books, and the cash from his granddad, but then there was the weirdness of the aftershave.

I'd promised he could borrow Scout, but he didn't get to really.

His chocolate cake turned out to be a carrot cake as the bakery had mixed up our order with someone else's.

Arthur had pretended it was fine, but as his father I know his true feelings about vegetables hiding in cakes.

And now he's sitting in a hospital waiting room, leafing miserably through a copy of *Woman's Weekly* while his granddad is seen by the doctor (Dad flatly refused for me to accompany him into the consulting room). Finally, the doctor appears with Dad looking even thinner than usual at his side, as he explains that my father has in all likelihood fractured a rib, although they haven't X-rayed him because they don't have the facilities here. For that, he'd have to be air-ambulanced to the mainland.

'So what happens now?' I ask, alarmed. Dad is already making for the door.

'Mr Vance is fit and in excellent shape for his age,' the doctor says, 'and our ribs are remarkably good at healing themselves. But he will need to rest and take things easy for quite some time.'

'So he can go home now?'

The young man has swept back dark hair and a smooth, almost poreless complexion. It's hard to believe he's been through medical school and that my father allowed this youth to examine him. 'Yes, as long as someone's with him for the next twenty-four hours,' he says. 'But we'll need to know if there's any change in him – for instance, if he gets dizzy or vomits or if the pain worsens.'

I look at my father. His hand is already clamped on the door handle. 'Are you okay with that, Dad?'

He nods. 'I s'pose so.'

'You've had quite a trauma, Mr Vance,' the doctor adds, frowning.

'He really has,' I say, thanking the doctor quickly and following Dad outside as he makes straight for my car, with Arthur marching along at his side. It's still raining steadily but I suspect that's not the only reason he's so eager to leave. It's in case anyone else spots him and says, *Oh, I saw Harry Vance at the hospital, there must be something wrong with him, maybe he's not invincible after all.*

'Dad,' I venture as we drive home, 'you know this means Arthur and I won't be going home tomorrow, don't you?'

He whips round to face me. 'But don't you have to?'

'Well, not really. I mean, there's still another week of Easter holidays and we don't have any plans. So I think it's best that we stay for a few more days, just to make sure everything's all right.'

Dad exhales through his nose. 'You don't need to do that.'

'Well, maybe not,' I say lightly, 'but I'd actually like to, Dad.' I flick him a quick glance in the passenger seat. He looks all askew in his peculiar outfit with his pale grey hair sticking up in tufts. What I really want to do is pull over and hug the awkward bugger, but it would probably hurt him and even if it didn't, he'd try to shove me off. 'Is that okay with you?' I ask.

'Uh, yeah, I suppose so. Yeah.'

I suppress a smile and catch my son's nonplussed expression on the back seat. 'How about you, Arthur?' I prompt him. 'Another week's holiday, eh? That's not so bad, is it?'

'No,' he replies, brightening now. 'Does that mean we can borrow Scout?'

Chapter Thirty-Eight

Suzy

It's my father I'm focusing on as I stride towards the distillery on this blustery Monday morning. Dad, who actually picked up the phone and called me. *I'm sure you'll be fine, Suzy, love. You're a clever, resourceful woman and you know best what to do.* And he'd waited until Mum was in the bath to do it. I'd have been no more shocked if he'd gone and got a sleeve tattoo.

And now, as I follow the narrow lane through the oldest part of town, past the boutique gallery and the bow-fronted bookshop, it's my daughter who filters into my mind. She's graduating in June. As a trained outdoor leader she'll be fully qualified to navigate wildernesses, with clueless strangers wittering that they've lost a mitten and moaning that there isn't a pub. And if Frieda can do that, then I can handle the meeting I've arranged with the entire distillery team.

Apart from Harry, that is. He didn't call my mobile or try to reach me at the Cormorant Hotel. And of course, after talking to Ricky on Saturday I can fully understand why. *My letter made him so angry he broke his bin.*

I'm not even staying at the Cormorant anymore. I'm installed in Cara's cosy studio instead. Although I'd grown quite fond of my little room in the eaves, it's lovely to wake up and see her beautiful hand-printed fabrics pinned all over the walls and not just a fire-evacuation-procedure notice. Plus, she is easy-going company and I hadn't realised quite how lonely I'd become, working away by myself. We had breakfast together this morning: still-warm rolls I'd picked up from the bakery, with local raspberry jam and Cara's excellent coffee. We also polished off the remains of the sensational dark chocolate Easter egg I'd bought her from the local sweet shop. 'You'll be ready for anything now,' she'd said with a smile.

My heartbeat quickens as the distillery comes into view. The solid stone building sits close to the shore. Up in the hills behind it, I can just make out the wiggly line of the stream – or *burn*, as Vicki called it, because no one says 'stream' around here – that supplies us with our precious water. Cara plans to head up that way with Scout today. Weirdly, I have never felt uncomfortable about him spending so much time with her. There was no, 'Might he start preferring her to me?' Because I trust her, of course – and it just feels right.

I think of Ricky and Arthur, and how Arthur had taken such a shine to Scout. Shame they went back to Glasgow yesterday. I wish they'd been able to borrow him as we'd planned. But of course, nothing had gone to plan that day.

As I approach the distillery I find myself hoping that Ricky understands that I really am doing my best, and that I'd give anything for things to have turned out differently. Because, I realise now, it seems to matter very much that he doesn't think badly of me – and not just because of his father.

He's a decent man, I think. Thoughtful and kind and because, after all, he still walked with me along the beach despite his dad storming off. He gave me a chance, it seems. A chance to explain, although I can't really – at least, not all of it.

I can tell the entire team *why* things went wrong. But I can't put it into words why I truly believed that Paul would be able to make a go of the distillery. After all, his previous business interests – the ones that were promised to 'make us a fucking fortune, Suzy!' – had all gone tits up. I guess I just let him have his own way because I loved him and wanted him to be happy. But of course, it was a mistake.

I hope to God my own kids exercise more care with their future relationships. So far, neither Frieda nor Isaac have seemed in any hurry to involve themselves in anything serious, and I can't help thinking that's a sensible way to go about things. Several friends – Dee, for instance – are long-term single, with no interest in dating, and nothing seems to be lacking in their lives. Cara doesn't seem to be looking to meet anyone either, and she hasn't mentioned any previous partners.

I pause outside the distillery and try to smooth down my hair, which has been buffeted by the wind. Remembering how my attempts to appear sleek and professional in Dee's suit and heels had backfired ('Margaret-fucking-Thatcher!'), I glance down at my blue denim shirt and plain black trousers: smart enough, hopefully, without trying to create any kind of impression.

I look around the bay in all its dazzling beauty and lick my parched lips. *Don't get emotional,* I tell myself firmly as I open the door and walk in.

*   *   *

Jean looks up from her orderly desk in the wood-panelled office; the nerve centre of administration. 'Hi, can I make you a tea or coffee?' she asks crisply.

'Thanks, but I'll make it,' I say. 'What would you like?'

'You've got enough to think about,' she says with a dismissive flap of her hand. As she beetles away to the staff kitchen, I make my way back to reception where the meeting will take place. While I hadn't expected the genteel sixty-something lady to punch me in the face, I'm a little taken aback by the fact that she's being *slightly* more approachable today.

Vicki approaches with a stack of files clutched to her chest. 'Hi,' I say brightly.

'Hi,' she says, returning my smile. 'All ready for this?'

'I *think* so. Thanks for spending so much time with me last week,' I add. 'I really appreciated it.'

'Oh, that's what I'm here for,' she says in her Home Counties accent. I've since learned that the previous owner had been thrilled to coax her all the way out here to work on a consultancy basis. Obviously, Vicki knows a thing or two about rock porosity and moss. But with a little research I've discovered that her PhD thesis was on the environmental fate of contaminants of emerging concerns in river catchment systems – or something like that. When Paul had been at the helm I hadn't even known we *had* an environmental consultant, although he had mentioned 'a scary woman from down south who rambles on about water a lot'. I wouldn't call her scary at all. Highly capable, obviously, and someone I'd far prefer to have on my side, rather than against me; but there's a warmth about her, shining through her fierce intelligence. Perhaps she just gave Paul short shrift on his visits.

'Here you go, Suzy.' Jean hands me a Sgadansay Distillery mug (bearing the original pre-puffin design) and I thank her profusely. 'You're welcome,' she says, placing a plate of several varieties of biscuits, all fanned out neatly, on the low table. Might these be used as missiles when I start my presentation? She hovers around as I unpack my folders and laptop.

'So, how's it all going?' she asks in a guarded sort of way. I notice that her gaze keeps darting this way and that, as if she's still a little wary of being spotted collaborating with the enemy.

'It's, well . . . things are progressing,' I reply.

Jean nods. 'That's good to hear.' She has neatly styled silvery hair and a pink, powdered complexion. I can imagine her as a kind grandma, reading stories, excelling at baking. 'I'm sure you're doing your best,' she adds.

I look at her in surprise. Her comment feels like an unexpected gift.

'Thank you,' I say with a smile. I glance over at the wall display of puffin paraphernalia: brochures, posters and tea towels all pinned up on a board. She checks her tiny gold watch. 'You said you needed Stuart to set up the screen for you?'

'Oh, I'm sure I can do it,' I say quickly. Vicki is still loitering and I don't want to look like some idiot who can't manage to set up the most basic equipment. But Stuart appears, ruddy-faced and wearing overalls; he'd been one of the shoutier attendees at my first meeting here. Instructed by Jean, before I can even get a word in, he fixes the screen into place.

'That's brilliant,' I enthuse. 'That's just what I needed. Thank you so much.' *For Christ's sake calm down, Suzy. It's just a screen on a wall.*

251

'No bother,' Stuart mumbles. The team is starting to filter in now, clutching mugs, taking seats, selecting biscuits from the plate. Vicki sits pertly, right at the front. The badly drawn puffins stare down at me.

And I begin.

Chapter Thirty-Nine

Ricky

Of course Dad wouldn't go to the meeting today. He'd spent Sunday, the day after his fall, in bed and Arthur and I had taken it in turns to sit with him or bring him mugs of tea, until his temper had frayed and he'd snapped, 'Can't I get a minute's peace around here?' So Arthur and I had relocated to the garden, where he'd guzzled two Easter eggs (one from me, one from Dad) and we'd chatted companionably about this and that.

About how we thought Kai might be doing, and what his other mate Lucas might be getting up to, and whether Arthur's mum ever thinks about him on his birthday, stuff like that. I was surprised he'd mentioned her and could only assume that he was feeling a bit stirred up about things, with Meg leaving and his granddad having his fall. Or maybe the lack of so much as a card from his mum hurts him every birthday, more than I've realised? It's not as if I've ever felt able to ask, 'Are you okay about her not sending you anything?' Christ, it's hard to know whether to try to gauge what he's feeling or just say nothing and hope he's all right.

'I'm sure she does,' I said, even though I knew – and Arthur knew – that it was a pointless thing to say. Because neither of us know what Katy thinks about anything.

Sometimes I wonder if Dad finds it a bit strange that Arthur and I have managed to muddle along together all these years, without his mother. When I was a kid, Mum took care of everything to do with me and the house, the family, all of that. It wouldn't have occurred to Dad to acquaint himself with the iron or the potato peeler. Much later, when Mum became ill and he had to step up and take on some domestic duties, I heard that they'd had tinned mushroom soup every day for a week and she'd had to put her foot down and ban it.

'For goodness' sake,' she told me on the phone, 'you'd think he could manage to fry an egg!' My heart had gone out to both of them: to Mum, who needed looking after, and to Dad who was no doubt trying to figure out what they could eat, and how the washing machine worked. These past ten years he's had to learn how to fend for himself.

Thankfully, he seemed to sleep soundly last night. At least, he hadn't reacted to me peering around his bedroom door sporadically to check up on him. I took him breakfast in bed, consisting of tea, white buttered toast and his painkillers. Once that was done he announced that he was 'all better now', and he tottered downstairs, gingerly, to watch TV. It was blaring all morning, alternating between news and some magazine show with shouty presenters. Although Arthur had been a trouper, I could tell he was getting fidgety, alternately poking at his phone and staring out at the billowing clouds.

And now it's mid-afternoon and the day has turned sunny and a little hazy, and Dad has agreed to sit out in the garden to read the paper. 'You two should go out,' he remarks.

'We *are* out,' I say. Arthur has been helping me with a spot of weeding.

Dad peers at him as he plucks a plant from the narrow border. 'That's not a weed!'

'Sorry, Granddad.' Arthur springs back and wipes his soily hands on his jeans.

'Why don't you both go to the beach or something?' Dad mutters, frowning.

I look at my father, aware that he's still clearly in discomfort and he didn't mean it the way it had come out; implying that Arthur was being a nuisance. 'I'm not sure about leaving you here by yourself,' I remark.

'Why not?'

'Because you had a fall, Dad . . .'

'I've told you,' he says gruffly, raising the opened newspaper in front of his face, like a shield. 'I'm fine now.'

With a sigh I put an arm around Arthur, but he shrugs me off and wanders back to the house. 'Can I get you anything?' I ask Dad.

'No-I'm-all-right-thanks.' He lowers the newspaper a little so I can just see his dark eyes. Whilst he looks tired and beleaguered, his steeliness – that brittle exterior – is very much still there.

'Okay, if you're sure.' I'm conscious of him studying me over his newspaper.

'Is Arthur all right?'

'Yeah, he's fine,' I reply. 'But I was thinking . . .' I hesitate, wondering how best to put it in order to mini-mise the risk of him flaring up again. 'You know how he loved being with that dog the other day?'

'That woman's dog?' His eyes narrow.

'Yeah.' I nod. 'Well, I thought it'd be nice for him to do that again.'

Dad's gaze is drilling into my forehead. 'Go ahead then.'

'Would you be okay with that?'

He shrugs. 'Yeah, I s'pose so.' He glances towards the house. 'Look, son . . . I didn't mean to snap at him just then.'

'Oh, Dad. It's okay. He's fine about it.' I reach out and squeeze his bony arm, and he flinches.

'D'you know where she's staying?' he asks.

I shake my head. 'You don't have her mobile number, do you?'

'I think it was on that letter of hers, but I slung it out.'

'Oh yes, of course. Never mind then.' I turn and make my way back towards the house.

'Ricky?' he calls after me. 'I s'pose someone at the distillery would know, wouldn't they? Jean, maybe? She knows everything.'

I nod. 'She certainly does.'

'You could give her a call, or go round . . .'

'Mmm, yeah,' I say, pretending to consider this, but by the time I'm back in Dad's kitchen I've already decided it's too risky for me to show up there and ask. What if word got around that it was probably Dad who wanted Suzy's number? The whole island would be buzzing with rumours that he desperately wants his old job back. I can't think of a way of asking for Suzy's contact number without sparking an international scandal.

My gaze drops to the pedal bin. I open it and carefully pick out the crumpled birthday wrapping paper, then a few tins, an instant coffee jar, a newspaper with jam all over it and some other random bits and pieces. The deeper I delve, the more unpleasant it becomes and by the time

I've reached the bottom it's pretty clear that Suzy's letter to Dad isn't there.

Of course it's not. Dad must have emptied the bin since then. Upstairs in his room, Arthur is chattering away on his phone – probably to Kai or Lucas. I glance outside to see that Dad is up on his feet now, poking at the borders with his hoe. I'm not prepared to start rummaging about in his wheelie bin while he's there. I'm also aware that even entertaining this thought probably signals that I'm not fully in control of my faculties right now. But I suspect that, once Arthur has finished his conversation, he'll slide back into gloom and we'll just hang around with that uneaten carrot cake still sitting out on the kitchen worktop.

'Will you have a bit?' I asked Dad earlier.

'No, you're all right, son,' he said, edging away from it as if I'd scraped it off the pavement.

Then a miracle happens. At least, a miracle by Sgadansay standards. Dad leans the hoe against the fence and ambles back towards the house. He nods at me as he passes and heads straight upstairs to the bathroom. I hear tinkling, then the taps being turned on. *Detective Vance surmises that his father is washing his hands.*

I dart outside to the wheelie bin and flip it open, checking the vicinity as I lift out a knotted black bin bag, trying not to think how Meg would react if she could see me now. I bet Brihat does Pilates on holiday. He doesn't rummage through bins, opening bags and poking around in them, wincing at the smell.

Fuck Brihat, I think, rebelliously, as my hand lands on a screwed-up sheet of white paper. I open it up and pick a small brown slug off it.

Back in Dad's kitchen I sluice it down at the sink, then

grab my phone from my jacket pocket. Dad is still pottering around upstairs, and I can hear him chatting to Arthur now in the box room, perhaps trying to make up for snapping at him earlier. I'm not sure why it seems so important that Dad doesn't find out I've been delving about in his outside bin. I just suspect it's a scenario he'd object to.

I step back out into the garden, poised to make the call. Maybe I'm really losing it now because this mission seems to be about something far more important than simply offering to walk Suzy's dog. It's the only way I can think of to cheer up my son, not just today but, hopefully, for the rest of this long, long week ahead. To make it special for him, when he should've been in Spain with his best friend, not on Sgadansay with his dumped dad.

I take a deep breath and tap out Suzy Medley's number, willing her not only to accept my call, but to say *yes*.

Chapter Forty

Suzy

There was no hail of custard creams at the meeting. There weren't even any stony faces. Instead, as I went through my PowerPoint presentation, everyone just sat quietly and seemed to take it all in.

Yes, a PowerPoint presentation – another first for me (although, admittedly, I'd rehearsed it with Cara and Scout as my audience, back in her studio). I'd put it together to explain the steps I'm taking to restore our fine reputation, such as:

- A reintroduction of our distillery's traditional label design and branding. We're returning to the beautiful antique illustration of Sgadansay harbour, as if the puffin episode had never happened.

- A return to our precise production methods with no corner-cutting and associated fears about the quality of future batches. Neglected equipment will be given the necessary attention and upgraded where necessary.

- A concerted marketing effort to reassure our customers that there will be a return to our core values.

- Coverage in newspapers and magazines about the Hebridean whisky industry (with particular focus on Sgadansay).

- Full and regular consultation with the entire team so we can pull through this difficult period together.

'It's like we're re-launching,' I explained. 'But instead of promoting something shiny and new, the focus will be on a return to tradition, to the way things have been done for decades. Because malt whisky isn't about newness and gimmicks, is it?' I felt almost foolish saying that, as a newcomer to all of this, in front of these people who spend their entire working days attending to the quietly germinating barley and kilns. Who was I to stand there spouting off, as if I was some kind of expert?

I caught Vicki's gaze. For a moment I was that terrified twelve-year-old and she was the examiner, showing no emotion as I squeaked my way through my grade one clarinet pieces accompanied by my pounding heart. 'It's about tradition,' I ploughed on, 'and I want to reassure you that I fully respect that.'

There was some muted discussion among the team as I reached for my glass of water. I glanced down to see that I'd developed a nervous rash on my neck. *Attractive.* 'Are there any questions?' I asked.

Liam from the malting room put up his hand. 'How come all this is happening now? This newspaper stuff, I mean?'

I pushed back my hair from my clammy forehead. 'Well, um, I hasn't happened yet, but—'

'So it's just something you *want* to do,' he said, looking unimpressed.

'Is there any chance of it happening?' Stuart asked. 'I mean, of getting stuff in the papers about us?' He shrugged. 'Why should they? We're just one of dozens of distilleries . . .'

'Well, I'm hopeful,' I said. I paused and looked around the room. 'And I do have some contacts who might be able to help us.'

'What contacts?' Liam asked with a frown.

'I work for newspapers,' I replied. 'I'm a writer, I write obituaries . . .'

'You write about dead people?' exclaimed Stuart, perking up now.

I nodded. 'Yes, I do. I know it seems completely at odds with what I'm doing here—'

'Oh, I don't know about that,' he said with a smirk. 'Whisky, dead people . . . it's all spirits, isn't it?' There was a ripple of laughter and I sensed my neck rash starting to ebb away.

There were more questions about orders, and our creditors, and some kind of glitch this morning with the bottling machine that I had to pass on to Misha, who's the expert on that. I thanked everyone profusely, and the team members drifted off until only Stuart was left.

'Thanks for all your help today,' I said.

He nodded. 'Ach, no bother. That's what I'm here for.' He took down the screen and we put back the chairs in their usual positions, stacked up in a corner. 'That was all right, that,' he added.

I glanced over at him, not quite sure what he was

referring to. It had to be my talk, didn't it? I couldn't think of anything else. And, whilst it wasn't quite crazed enthusiasm, it was a nudge in the right direction. 'Did you think so?' I said. 'Thanks, Stuart. That's good to hear.'

He shrugged and scratched at his greying hair, and I reached for the plate with just a lone finger of shortbread left on it. 'Would you like this?' I asked.

He seemed to study it for a moment, then he shook his head and chuckled. 'No, you have it. I think you deserve it after that.'

Back at Cara's, Scout greeted me with his usual whirlwind of tail wagging and licks. As Cara wanted to know all about the meeting, she broke off from her work – cornflower blue and sunset orange canvases were strewn about everywhere – and I made coffee and flopped down on the sofa next to her. 'Sounds like it went really well,' she enthused.

'I guess so. We've definitely moved on from the first meeting, anyway.'

Her blue eyes glinted as she smiled. 'No one looked like they wanted to punch you.'

'No.' I chuckled. 'It was all very hushed and polite with everyone sitting there with their teas and coffees and biscuits.'

'So, they seemed happy about what you're doing? About going back to the traditional labels, all that?'

'Yeah.' I paused. 'All that was fine. But, you know – I do wonder if it's enough to turn things around. I mean, it's not as if I've come up with anything terribly ground-breaking—'

'Does whisky *need* to be ground-breaking?' she asked.

I got up, prompting Scout to start darting around

excitedly, anticipating a walk. 'I don't know, Cara. Christ, the more I learn, the more I realise I don't know anything really. Only that this business seems so traditional and gentle from the outside, with its barrels and copper stills and a man quietly raking the barley about . . .' I called Scout over before he stuck his nose in a paint pot. 'But it's actually fiercely competitive,' I added. 'I mean, there are 120 distilleries in Scotland. So, in some ways, I can see why Paul wanted to stand out and be different.' I caught myself and laughed. 'Christ, I can't believe I'm saying that.'

Looking to my ex for inspiration was my cue to get out and walk it all off, so Scout and I left Cara to get on with her work and headed off into the hills. A couple of hours have passed now, and I'm feeling calmer, and grateful for the sense of space around us. We follow the winding path that cuts between mounds of springy heather and trickling streams. The air is sharp and invigorating and we glimpse several red deer in the distance, who stop and stare for a second before bounding away.

The path finally leads us back to the road, where I spot a huge rock jutting from the grass verge, marking the end of an unmade, single-track lane. It's the lane that leads to the cottage I'd stayed at, when I'd come to hold that first meeting, and where I'd sat munching my Pringles and slugging my cheap white wine, convinced that my life was a mess.

And then Scout had shown up, wet and trembling, and suddenly things had seemed a little brighter – even when he'd peed on the pouffe.

As we reach the rock I remember that you can get a mobile signal when you stand on top of it; at least, according to comments in the cottage's visitors' book.

So I loop Scout's lead around a fence post, clamber up and wave my phone around until a bar of signal appears. And I see that I have a missed call; a number that's not in my contacts.

I glance around at the cottage as I call it. It looks like a family is staying; children are shrieking excitedly as they run around the garden. Then: 'Hello?' a male voice answers.

'Hi,' I start. 'I have a missed call from this number—'

'Oh, is this Suzy?'

'Yes, that's me.'

'It's Ricky. I hope it was okay to call you—'

'Yes, of course,' I say, a little confused. Surely he's not calling on behalf of his father? Harry hasn't struck me as someone who'd shy away from making his own phone calls.

'It's a bit of a weird one,' Ricky explains. 'Dad had an accident—'

'Oh no! What happened? Is he all right?'

'Yeah, he's recovering well. He was having a shower and he slipped in the bath. Cracked a rib, the doctor reckons . . .'

'That's terrible,' I exclaim. 'I'm so sorry to hear that.'

'Thanks.' He pauses. 'So we didn't go home on Sunday after all. It just didn't feel right to leave Dad here alone while he's recovering.'

'Oh, God, yes. I can understand that.' I glance at Scout and he blinks up at me expectantly. 'Is there anything I can do to help?'

'Actually, I think there might be,' Ricky says. He hesitates for a moment and it strikes me how pleased I am to hear from him. Of course, it's awful that his father has had a fall but, for some reason that I can't quite

264

figure, I'm happy that Ricky and Arthur are still here. 'Y'know, Arthur's taken a real shine to Scout,' he adds.

'Oh, that's so nice. He's really good with him.' An ancient-looking tractor approaches, and I lift a hand in greeting as the driver catches my eye. He gives me a curt nod in response. Of course, around here it's probably quite normal to conduct a phone conversation while balancing precariously on a rock. 'If you have the time,' I add, 'you'd be really welcome to take him out. To borrow him, I mean—'

'Really? That's actually why I was calling. I mean, Arthur's been great – really patient, at least for an eleven-year-old kid. But, you know. He's stuck here with me, and there's not a heck of a lot going on around here, as you've probably gathered . . .'

'I guess not,' I say.

'We'll probably stay until Sunday,' Ricky continues, 'but obviously, we can fit in with you—'

'How about tomorrow, then?'

'Really? That'd be great. Arthur'll be delighted when I tell him. So, what sort of time?'

'Say, ten-ish? Or is that too early?'

'No, that's perfect.' He pauses. 'Same place as before? Or would you rather we came and picked him up—'

'I'll meet you at the beach,' I say, 'if that suits you.'

'Brilliant.' I sense him smiling. 'I won't bring Dad this time,' he adds.

I push my hair from my eyes. 'I'm sorry that was so awkward.'

'Oh, don't worry about that,' Ricky says quickly. 'I did mention your meeting today,' he adds. 'But, y'know, Dad's still recovering, and he's not really getting out much . . .'

'I didn't expect him to come anyway,' I say truthfully.

'But, um . . . anyway, I heard it went pretty well,' he adds. 'That, you know. It kind of helped.'

My heart seems to turn over. 'Really?' I say. 'Where did you hear that?'

'It's just the way it is around here,' Ricky says. 'Good news travels fast.'

Chapter Forty-One

I know it sounds flaky but I have never planned very much in my entire life. For instance, *obviously* I never set out to be sole director of a whisky distillery in the Outer Hebrides. I'm not even cut out to be a boss, not really. Although yesterday's meeting seemed to go well – and I'm no longer treated as if I'm an unpleasant odour wafting around the place – standing up in front of an audience isn't something I'd ever choose to do, or find enjoyable. I've just stumbled into it. It's the kind of situation that's always made my sister despair of me because she seemed to have her whole life pretty much mapped out by the age of eighteen.

University, law degree, well-paid graduate job, smart house, marriage to Derek-with-the-meaty-thighs, bigger house. They'd started dating at sixteen and she said she'd always known he was 'the one', that he 'ticks all my boxes', a phrase that always made me feel slightly queasy. But then, who am I to judge? My sister seems perfectly content with her life.

In contrast, Tony and I had never really planned to

move in together. We'd just decided it would be a brilliant idea after a few drinks one night. Next thing we were cohabiting at twenty-five years old like bona fide grown-ups.

Even getting pregnant with Frieda was accidental (such a happy accident, though; I *loved* the baby stage). Then along came Isaac two years later and still we all blundered along. However, it was inevitable that Tony and I would break up, because we'd rushed in way before we were ready to settle down, before we even knew ourselves really. We 'grew apart', as people so often say – usually because it's true. No wonder Mum and Belinda roll their eyes at me because, when I stop to consider it, I've always tumbled from one thing to the next. Two years from fifty and I'm still rattling along, like someone who's throwing any old random items into her supermarket trolley in the hope that they'll miraculously come together to make a meal.

I didn't plan to be a writer either, as I'm explaining now, in answer to Ricky's question on this crisp, bright Tuesday morning. 'It just sort of happened,' I explain as we wander in the direction in which Arthur and Scout have run off together. 'It was a bit of a fluke really.'

'What kind of fluke?' he asks, stepping over a tangle of amber-coloured seaweed.

I tell him how, fuelled by a rare burst of confidence, I'd taken it upon myself to write an obituary about a woman called Nora Pickles. She'd set up a bakery and tearoom in the 1950s in the North Yorkshire market town where I'd grown up, and where my parents still live. Nora's Tearoom had flourished and soon there'd been similar establishments in all the main touristy towns in the area. It had been a favourite family activity, to go to

Nora's on special occasions, and Dad had always opted for a huge choux pastry bulging with cream and slathered with glossy chocolate icing, so outlandish and messy that he'd have to tackle it with a knife and fork.

'For God's sake, Peter!' Mum would hiss, all vexed and embarrassed in case anyone saw. Whilst I was always content with the Victoria sponge that Mum, Belinda and I always had (as it came as part of the afternoon tea deal), I'd liked the fact that Dad always veered his own way, cake-wise.

'He sounds like a bit of a rebel,' Ricky remarks with a smile.

'Yes, I suppose he is in his own quietly measured way.'

'Mild rebellion then.'

'Yeah. That's it exactly.' I chuckle.

'But what made you write the obituary?' He seems genuinely curious.

'Oh, I'd always loved writing – bits of prose, poetry, that kind of thing, just for myself. So I thought I'd give it a go.' I catch myself and shrug. 'That sounds a bit mad, doesn't it?'

'Not at all. Not if you enjoy writing . . .'

'My mum and sister think it's morbid, that I do this for a job. That I sit around "waiting for people to die".'

Ricky laughs. 'You'll never be out of work, though—'

'Yeah. Like undertakers or headstone engravers . . .'

'So what happened then?' he prompts me.

'I sent it off to a newspaper,' I explain. 'It was just a local one but even so, I didn't think there was any chance that they'd publish it. But they rang me, saying how much they liked it, so I wrote another one about her – longer, more in-depth – and this time I sent it off to a national paper. Again, I didn't think I'd hear anything back. I

269

mean, Nora was famous throughout our part of Yorkshire, but most people would never have heard of her.'

'Did they publish it?' he asks.

'Yes, they did. And for some reason it seemed to attract far more comments online than their usual obituaries – of more famous people, I mean. And they decided they wanted to start including more obits of so-called normal people. So that became my thing – "doing the normals", as they put it. Then they started asking me to do the famousness too.'

'That's amazing,' Ricky says, looking impressed, 'but it wasn't really a fluke, was it?'

'What d'you mean?'

He shrugs as we stroll across the rippled sand. The tide is out and the beach feels huge beneath the wide blue sky. 'It was because of your hard work, wasn't it? And your ability to write.'

'Oh, I guess so,' I say dismissively. 'What I mean is, I'd never planned to do this for a living, or even imagined that it'd be possible.'

'So, what had you planned to be?' He glances at me and it strikes me again how attractive his eyes are; deep brown, like the darkest seaweed that's strewn across the beach.

'I never really had a thought-out career plan,' I reply. 'I wasn't madly in love with school, actually. I didn't do terribly well.'

'Neither did I,' Ricky says. 'It seemed to be about remembering unmanageable quantities of information and being able to handle exams. So, a career as a clarinetist wasn't beckoning you?'

I laugh, surprised that he's remembered that detail. I'm relieved, too, that we're not discussing the distillery again.

It's far less stressful to talk about other stuff, and besides, I'm keen to find out more about his life. 'Absolutely not,' I say, laughing. 'What about you? I mean, how did you get into music?'

He pulls a rueful expression. 'I'd like to say I simply fell in love with it. But, actually, there was a time at my primary school when a whole pile of instruments were donated by some benefactor. So our head teacher decided to set up an orchestra.'

'What did you choose?' I ask. 'The violin?'

He shakes his head. 'Choosing didn't come into it. The woodwind, brass and the smaller stringed instruments were all snapped up quickly. But no one wanted the cello . . .'

'Why not?' I exclaim. 'I love the cello—'

'Yes, but it's so big and unwieldy, you know?'

I nod. 'Yes, of course.'

'Unlike a flute or a clarinet that could at least be hidden in a schoolbag,' he adds. 'But Dad and Mr Ross, the headmaster, were friends, and at some point they'd decided that *I'd* take the instrument no other kid wanted.'

I smile in sympathy. 'Poor you.'

He smirks. 'Yeah, I was pretty put out. But there was no arguing with Dad once he'd got an idea into his head. I suspect it was a matter of pride to persuade me to learn how to play it. So I started lugging it back and forth from school like, um . . .'

'. . . A socially awkward cousin?' I suggest.

'Yeah.' His handsome face breaks into an even broader grin.

'One who's refused to go home.'

'*Exactly* that.'

We're both laughing now. 'Bet you wish you'd been quick enough to grab a trumpet,' I add.

271

'God, yes.' Arthur and Scout are way ahead now, dashing between the rock pools. The likeness between Ricky and his son is apparent: both are slim and tall with long, strong noses and intensely dark eyes. But Arthur's shock of red hair must be inherited from his mum. Once again I find myself wondering about her; whether Arthur lives between their two homes or what their arrangement is.

'Did your parents encourage you?' I ask. 'With your music, I mean?'

'Mum did,' Ricky replies. 'Dad, not so much. That's not a reflection on him, though. It's just what the men in our community were like back then.' His eyes glint with amusement. 'I mean, they were hardly wandering about with their children strapped to their bodies in harnesses like they do now . . .'

I chuckle. Back in York, our local park is filled with young fathers herding wild-haired children whilst doling out rice cakes and simultaneously growing their beards. 'Maybe classical music wasn't his thing?' I suggest.

'Yep, not at all. It wasn't really mine either. But I s'pose I developed a kind of grudging appreciation of those old dead guys . . .'

I smile as Arthur looks around and shouts, 'What old dead guys?'

'Composers,' Ricky calls back, and as his son responds with an exaggerated shudder I'm aware that they're supposed to be *borrowing* Scout – rather than having me tagging along – and I really should leave them to it.

'Well, I s'pose I should get on with some work,' I say with a trace of reluctance.

'Oh, yes, of course. Shall we bring Scout back to you? We don't even know where you're staying—'

272

'I'm at Cara's at the moment. She's the one who was walking Scout, the first time you met him . . .' He nods. 'How about phoning me when you're ready?' I suggest. 'Then I can come and meet you.'

'That sounds great.' I can't help registering his lovely, softly lilting Hebridean accent again. 'And thanks for this,' he adds. 'For letting us walk him, I mean.'

'You're really welcome.' With those deep brown eyes and wide, generous smile, he's not exactly offensive to look at either, and it strikes me that I'd be quite happy to hang out with him and Arthur for their entire walk, thank you very much.

I almost laugh out loud at how ridiculous I'm being as I leave the beach.

Chapter Forty-Two

Ricky

'Is this going to be a regular thing, then?' Dad wants to know.

'What?' I ask.

'This *walking her dog* thing.' He shudders as if it's some weird kind of cult I've become involved with.

'Well, we're only here till Sunday,' I reply as Arthur dips toast soldiers into his runny boiled egg (not that he calls them soldiers anymore; that'd be unthinkable now he's eleven. He merely slices his toast into thin pieces suitable for dunking).

'Aye, I know that,' Dad says, gripping his mug of tea firmly. 'What I'm saying is, it seems to be kind of a *thing* now.'

'We just like it, Granddad,' Arthur says as he jumps up from the table and makes for the kitchen door. 'You should come with us sometime. When you're all better, I mean,' he adds quickly. Dad just mutters something under his breath. Still in pyjamas, Arthur darts off to get dressed so we can head out and pick up Scout – this time from Cara's place across town – as we arranged with Suzy yesterday.

274

I get up and wash up our breakfast dishes. 'We won't be long,' I tell Dad. 'A couple of hours or so max.'

'Be as long as you like,' he huffs, getting up from the table. I dry off my hands and follow him into the living room where he is flicking idly through the stack of *Sgadansay Gazettes* that sits on the nest of tables. There seems to be a kind of 'holding period' required before they can be safely thrown away. After all, you never know when you might urgently need to refer to a six-week-old article about the repainting of the town hall's clock tower.

'You know,' I start hesitantly, 'she's actually okay.'

Dad peers at me. 'Who is?'

'Suzy. Suzy Medley.'

'*Is* she?' he says, his voice laced with disbelief. Having selected a newspaper from the pile – seemingly at random – he installs himself in the ancient tweedy armchair and starts to leaf through it.

'Well, yes,' I say, perching on the sofa arm. 'But if you're uncomfortable about it – about us walking her dog, I mean – all you need to do is say—'

'No, no, don't let *me* stand in your way,' he declares, rattling the newspaper.

'Dad, can we go now?' Arthur has reappeared at the bottom of the stairs in faded jeans and a favourite scruffy old navy fleece. He's clutching the orange tennis ball he found on the beach that first day we walked Scout. I know he'd prefer to walk him by himself, without me being there, and of course he's old enough to manage that without doing anything stupid. But I'd reassured Suzy that I'd always be there too – and anyway, I enjoy being out with my son on the beach. And, admittedly, it's good to get a little breather from Dad.

I guess I'm enjoying getting to know Suzy a little too

because she is *nothing* like I'd imagined. Yesterday, when we met up again after our dog walk, we'd chatted for a few minutes, waiting for Arthur and Scout to finish their stick game. 'C'mon, Arthur!' I'd called out. Either my voice was carried away on the breeze or he was feigning deafness. Or maybe I hadn't shouted *that* loudly as I was happy to sit and talk to her. Whatever it was, I found myself sitting next to her on the rocks, finding out a little more about how the distillery purchase had come about.

Suzy admitted that she'd always been a bit of a 'soft touch', as she put it, letting her ex-partner drift from one ill-thought-out scheme to the next. He'd even been a guide on ghost tours around York, she told me: 'Which lasted about two weeks.'

'What happened with that?' I asked. By now she'd explained that he wasn't her kids' dad, and I was wondering why this obviously bright, attractive woman had involved herself with him in the first place. Obviously he was flaky and directionless. But worse than that, he'd basically run off and left her with a colossal mess to clear up.

'He found it monotonous,' she replied. 'Same old spooky stories night after night. He couldn't stand being given a script to follow. If there's one thing Paul hates it's being told what to do—'

'So, could you have stopped him anyway?' I asked. 'Buying the distillery, I mean?'

'I could've kicked up more of a fuss,' she'd said with a shrug.

I looked at her, finding it hard to imagine her as a fuss-kicking kind of person – although she's not weak, far from it; that much is obvious. She certainly doesn't match the image I'd formed in my mind from what I'd heard about this couple from Yorkshire who'd bought the distillery with seemingly no more knowledge of whisky production than how to fly in the air.

I'd pictured someone ruthless and hard, caring only about profit and not giving a shit about the havoc she and her partner had caused here. But she's not like that at all. Not remotely.

In fact, I like Suzy Medley. I like her more every time I see her and I keeping thinking that maybe, in other circumstances, we might even have become friends. But I have no intention of saying that to Dad.

I don't plan to ask if she'd like to come on the walk with us either, when Arthur and I arrive at Cara's as arranged. Cara welcomes us warmly, and when Arthur seems interested in her studio she takes us through to show us her work, and Suzy brings me a coffee and Arthur an orange juice.

'I don't normally do recognisable places,' Cara explains when Arthur makes straight for a screen print of the lighthouse. 'They're usually more abstract. But I love the lighthouse. Don't you, Arthur?'

He nods. 'Yeah, I do.'

'It's so bold and striking,' Cara adds, 'with the red and white against a blue sky. It looks the way a child would draw one.' Arthur nods again and sips his juice. 'I mean, a little kid,' she adds quickly, as if worried that she might have sounded patronising. 'Not someone your age . . .'

'*I'd* draw one like that.' Arthur smiles and turns to Suzy. 'Have you seen it?'

She looks almost apologetic. 'It sounds mad but I haven't yet. I've kept meaning to. But I've never been round to that part of the coast . . .'

'D'you fancy coming with us today?' I ask. 'I mean, you're probably busy but—'

'Oh, why not?' she says quickly. 'I could do with a break from staring at my laptop.' She looks at Cara. 'D'you fancy coming too?'

Cara shakes her head. 'I'll just crack on here. But *you* go. It's a glorious day and it seems like a shame to miss it.'

And so we leave Cara's and head out of town, with Arthur and Scout marching ahead of us as if we aren't even there. 'Is your dad okay about this?' Suzy asks.

'About us walking Scout?' I catch her hesitant expression. Her long dark brown hair is blowing around her face.

'Yes,' she says. 'I just thought . . . you know. He mightn't like it.'

'Um, he's *accepting* it,' I say noncommittally; a tiny fib because I don't want her to think she's causing me any conflict with Dad.

'How's he doing?' she asks. 'Is he recovering from his fall?'

'Yeah.' I nod. 'He's amazing really, for his age. He just needs to take it easy for a little while.'

Suzy nods and smiles. She's wearing faded jeans, a baggy blue sweater and walking boots. Apart from her Yorkshire accent she could pass as a local. My mind is brimming with questions about her plans for the distillery – but I don't want her to think I only asked her along so I could quiz her about it. I know most of the people who work there, after all. They're forthright and outspoken, so I can imagine she's had a fair old grilling already and I don't want to add to that.

'You and your dad seem pretty close,' she remarks as the path veers away from the road and follows the edge

278

of the coastline. Way down below us, waves are foaming pure white against the jagged rocks.

'I s'pose we are, in a way,' I say. 'I mean, there's only me. Mum died ten years ago.'

'I'm sorry,' Suzy murmurs.

'It's okay. Dad does all right.' Well, he *did*, but I'm not planning to get into that now.

'Does he visit you often?' she asks. 'In Glasgow, I mean?'

'God, no. Hardly ever. A couple of times maybe, since Mum died.' I pause. 'They'd come a bit more often then. Mum was better at dragging him off the island than I am.' I catch her eye and she smiles. 'Every three or four years, they'd make the journey down and stop off to see various relatives all over the country. It was a pretty major expedition – like a band embarking on a world tour.' She chuckles. 'But Dad can never relax in Glasgow,' I add. 'Even at my graduation he was on tenterhooks the whole time.'

'Why?' she asks.

'Oh, he was convinced he'd be robbed at knifepoint everywhere we went.'

'What, at your graduation?' she gasps.

'*Especially* there,' I reply, laughing now. 'With all the students and their proud parents, decked out in their finery with their jewellery and hats and those little decorative head things, what are they again—'

'Fascinators?' She crooks an eyebrow and her greenish eyes catch the sunlight, almost stopping me in my tracks.

'Is that what they're called?' I ask.

'I think so, yes—'

We are both laughing now. 'Well, he was convinced it was a prime picking ground for thieves.'

As the lighthouse comes into view – a solid column of red and white, in stark contrast to the nearby spindly trees – Arthur stops and swings around to face us. 'Meg took *so* many pictures of this,' he announces. 'Didn't she, Dad?'

'Er, yeah!' I reply.

'For her Instagram,' he adds with a smirk. 'She was *always* looking for stuff for her Instagram.'

'Yeah, she was.' I'm conscious of Suzy looking at me now. Christ, now I'm going to have to give her some kind of explanation. I can't just let the name hover in the air like this, like some kind of mysterious spectre: *Meg-of-whom-we-must-not-speak*.

Suzy slips her hands into her jeans pockets as we walk. 'Erm, we actually came here with someone,' I say. Arthur and Scout are forging ahead again now, making their way over the rocks close to the lighthouse. While Arthur bounds from one to the next without hesitation, Scout has clearly reached his limit and stops and sits, waiting expectantly, for Arthur to come back.

'Did you?' Suzy says.

'Yeah.' We walk in silence for a few moments. 'She was, erm, someone I was kind of seeing,' I add, aware how ridiculous this is starting to sound. *We came here with someone. She was someone I was kind of seeing.* I'm making it sound like I had psychiatric supervision. 'It didn't really work out,' I add quickly, registering Suzy's puzzled expression now and regretting even starting this. After all, what does she care about my personal situation?

'What happened?' she asks.

'Well, er, we broke up—'

'Oh! Oh, I see,' she murmurs. 'I'm sorry, I shouldn't have asked . . .'

'It was our second day here!' Arthur shouts helpfully.

'Wow,' Suzy says, looking a little shocked. Christ, I hadn't even realised he was within earshot. Whenever I ask him to pick up his dirty socks or load the dishwasher he doesn't seem to hear a word. Yet when I'm having a private conversation from something like ten metres away he doesn't miss a word.

'She was meant to stay the whole week,' Arthur adds.

'Okay, Arthur, thank you!' I call back.

Suzy steps deftly over a jagged rock. 'So, did she go home?'

'Uh-huh.' I nod. 'Back to Glasgow.'

She catches my eye again, looking as if she's about to ask more, but then decides not to. 'That's a shame,' she adds, and I nod, aware of something peculiar happening.

I don't usually share personal stuff. Of course I talk to my old college mates who are still kicking around Glasgow, and the friends I've met through Arthur's mates, and his football and karate clubs, and my teaching. There are plenty of people to have a drink with, but we hardly ever discuss anything terribly important; in fact, most of them don't even know about Arthur's mum, apart from the obvious fact that she's not involved in his life.

With most men, if there's something that could potentially be a bit difficult or sad or emotional, they give it a wide berth – as if it's a puddle of sick on the pavement after a Friday night.

And yet, as Arthur and Scout jump from the rocks back onto the path, I realise that I want very much to tell Suzy what happened here, and during the weeks leading up to our trip. I want to explain how it had seemed like we were getting along fine, and how it had all gone wrong and she'd hated Dad's pie and it had all come out about Colin – sorry, *Brihat* – and she'd left Arthur the aftershave for his birthday, and all of that.

I'm not sure why it's Suzy I want to tell. Perhaps it's because I hardly know her, and she's obviously smart and non-judgemental, and I don't *think* she'll assume I'm some sad fucker who's such terrible company that his girlfriend could only endure twenty-four hours of holiday with him before legging it home.

Or maybe it's because she just seems like the kind of person you can talk to. And perhaps I don't talk enough – to anyone – about the things that really matter.

And so I take a deep breath and wait until Arthur is properly out of earshot. And then I tell Suzy all about Meg and me.

Chapter Forty-Three

Suzy

I know it can't last because Ricky and Arthur are leaving on Sunday. But already, it almost feels like Scout belongs to all of us. To me, Cara, Ricky and Arthur. We all love him and he seems to love all of us. I wonder now if, as well as those millions of scent receptors, dogs also have the ability to love a whole bunch of people unconditionally, with no limits on numbers. He greets each of us with the same completely bonkers, tail-spinning display of delight. And it lifts my heart to see it.

Ricky called this morning to ask if they could take him up into the hills, making a fun day of it with a picnic. 'I think Dad wants us out from under his feet,' he added.

'Of course you can,' I said, surprised by how pleased I was to hear his voice again. How it makes me smile.

'D'you want to come with us?' he asked lightly.

Now I was thinking he probably felt he *needed* to ask me, because of yesterday, when we'd walked to the light-house and he'd told me all that stuff about Meg. And I didn't want him to think he had to ask me along every time – to feel obliged. 'Thanks,' I said, 'but I've got tons to get on with today.'

So they came round to pick up Scout, and now they've gone I've settled down to work at Cara's kitchen table. I've had a positive response from my newspaper contacts, and one of the food supplement editors has suggested I write a series of columns about the inner workings of our island distillery. I'm filled with ideas on what I'll write about – like our unique water source and the barrels we use from sherry producers in southern Spain. I plan to include mini profiles of our team members, such as Kenny, who's a mine of information on those ageing sherry casks. He seemed a little surprised – but pleased, I think – when I first mentioned this, and announced that he'd better get a haircut if his picture's going to be in the paper. 'My mum will probably buy up all the copies on the island,' he said with a grin.

After a couple of hours I head out for a walk along the beach. The tide is out and it's a beautiful day, dazzlingly bright. I can just make out the tiny white flecks of sailing boats far out to sea. Closer to shore, fishing boats in weather-bleached reds and blues bob lazily in the sparkling water. The first time I came here I thought the town was almost impossibly quaint with its muddle of shops selling stout walking boots, fishing equipment and old-fashioned boiled sweets from jars. Paul and I were thrilled by the Seafood Shack, the bakery and the newsagent's with its faded jigsaws and trays of penny sweets. How quaint, we thought! But I know now that there's far more to the island than what I first saw as a wide-eyed tourist. It's a real, living community, bustling with life.

From the beach I stroll back into the centre of town.

In a harbourside café I open my laptop at a windowsill table. Fuelled by enthusiasm and strong, malty tea, I launch into a flurry of writing, pausing only to sip from my mug and glance out at the searing blue sky occasionally.

A woman with blonde hair pulled into a high, bouncy ponytail comes over to offer me a refill from a teapot. 'I won't be much longer,' I say, after thanking her. 'I've been taking up this table for ages.'

'No, you're fine,' she says. 'We're not too busy just now. Are you here on holiday?'

'No, I'm working here,' I say.

'Oh, whereabouts?'

'At the distillery,' I reply without thinking. She nods and smiles and goes to take the order of a young couple with rucksacks who've just come in. After a detailed discussion of the various cakes on offer, they ask her for recommendations of places to see. She mentions the ruined castle, the lighthouse and the various walks along the coastline and up into the hills. It strikes me that I know all of those places, almost as if it's my home – a place where, gradually, I am starting to feel accepted.

'What about the distillery?' the man asks. 'Is it okay to just drop in and visit?'

'They used to do tours,' the woman replies, 'but they seem to have stopped now. I'm not sure why.'

'Ah, that's a shame.'

She looks over at me. 'D'you know anything about that, love?'

'Um, we hope the tours will be starting up again soon,' I reply.

'That's good to hear.' She turns back to the couple. 'You really should visit the lighthouse. And if you fancy trying to catch mackerel, some of the boats do fishing trips.'

The young man thanks her, and when she disappears to the kitchen he murmurs to his partner, 'People are so welcoming here.'

It's true, I decide. Apart from the initial hostile reception, I've been grateful for the warmth of people I've met in shops, cafés and even at the Cormorant Hotel; all the friendly hellos when I've been walking Scout, and the dog biscuits given out. And then there's Cara, of course, welcoming me into her home – and Ricky.

Now he's popped into my mind I realise I'm smiling, replaying that part of our walk yesterday when he'd told me all that personal stuff. Obviously, he'd been pretty shocked to find his girlfriend had been cheating on him – but he didn't tell me in an embittered, scorned kind of way. There were funny parts too – like when we were speculating whether she keeps a jar of toasted coconut granola at her other boyfriend's house too (I had to agree with Ricky that it sounded like he'd have his own). And Arthur saying to his friend, loudly on the phone, 'Dad got dumped!' and then asking, 'Did you consciously uncouple?'

We both ended up laughing on the way back to town and I was honoured that he'd opened up to me. Now I'm wondering where he, Arthur and Scout are now, and wishing I was there too.

I catch myself, conscious of my heart beating a little faster as I close my laptop. Get a grip, I tell myself silently as I fish out my purse. Yes, he's an interesting, attractive man. But he's going home on Sunday, he came out of a relationship about five minutes ago and anyway, I didn't come here to start having *thoughts* about someone. That's the last thing I need cluttering up my brain.

He's just a man who borrows Scout, I remind myself.

And he does it to make his son happy, that's all. I leave the café, inhaling a deep lungful of sharp salty air, determined to steer my thoughts back to the matter in hand.

I blundered into owning a dog, and a distillery, with no planning or prior knowledge. The distillery part has been somewhat more challenging than getting to know Scout. But I'm getting there – mainly by asking copious questions.

Can you tell me a bit more about heat conduction please, Vicki?

So, how do you think we could improve the layout of the packing room?

Would you mind drawing a diagram for me, so I can understand it better?

I can't claim to be a world expert on malting, maturation or the harvesting methods of our locally grown barley. However, I do know more than I ever thought it possible to know about crop rotation (once our farmer Martin gets started there's no stopping him). And, gradually, all of the facts and processes are starting to make sense – so perhaps I am capable of understanding how things are done; and, crucially, why things went wrong.

After a couple of hours at the distillery, during which I have pored over our accounts in an airless cubbyhole, I step outside for a breath of air. Perching on a low stone wall I fish out my phone from my pocket, feeling boosted enough now to call my mother.

I listen patiently as she tells me about the despicable new people over the road who apparently keep 'taking' her and Dad's parking space (as it's on the street, my parents have no legal claim over it). 'I sent your dad over to have a go at them,' she adds. Poor Dad; he's not the confrontational type. I've known him tell a waiter that it didn't matter when he'd brought the wrong thing; *I'll just have this, it looks very nice anyway.* Then my mother: *I wish you'd stand up for yourself occasionally, Peter!*

'Anyway,' she continues now, having giving me a rundown of the various parking crimes in the vicinity, 'how's it all going on that island of yours?' As if I own the entire place.

'Fine,' I tell her. 'There's still an awful lot to sort out, but—'

'You should give Belinda a call,' she cuts in. 'She'll know what to do—'

'Mum, she's helped me already,' I say, aware of a vein starting to throb in my temples. 'She put me in touch with a brilliant legal expert. She—'

'You'll be lucky to catch her at the moment, though,' Mum warns. 'The amount of work she has on – I don't know how she does it. But you know what she's like, keeping all those plates spinning . . .'

Which plates are these? Granted she has her high-ranking job. Yet she and Derek employ a cleaner – who comes in *three* times a week – plus an ironing lady, a gardener and a handyman who attends to anything else that needs doing, including changing their halogen kitchen lightbulbs and possibly massaging Ralgex into Derek's meaty thighs, which he always seems to be spraining and clearly enjoys displaying in minuscule shiny shorts. So, as far as I can calculate, that amounts to *one* plate.

'I've just spoken to her actually,' Mum rattles on, in full flow now, 'and you'll never believe what she was doing . . .'

Riding Derek like a donkey? 'I can't imagine,' I remark.

Mum pauses, cranking up the tension. 'Making naan bread. Can you believe, with everything she has going

288

on, that she manages to bake naan that's as good, if not better, than anything you'd get in a restaurant?'

'Amazing,' I drawl, thinking: why would anyone bother to do that? Then, briskly, 'I'll be in touch again soon, Mum. I just have to finish some work.' The call ends somewhat abruptly – like Belinda, Mum is always madly busy – and I step back inside, making my way to Jean's office. It's only in recent weeks that I've discovered that she became the main point of contact for disgruntled contractors as well as overseeing our online shop, the cleaning team, first aid and health and safety matters and God knows what else. Basically, Jean McDonald runs the place.

The dark wooden door is ajar but I knock anyway. 'Yes?' she says pertly.

'Erm, Jean, I'm heading off pretty soon.' I pause. 'But I wondered if you've got time to have quick cup of tea with me?'

She looks surprised. 'Yes, of course. I'll go and make it.'

'No, no, I'll do it,' I say, zooming off to the staff kitchen and ferrying our drinks back to her. I place the mugs on her desk and perch gingerly on the chair opposite her. 'I just wanted to thank you,' I start.

'What for?' She has a Sunday school teacher's manner; no nonsense, but not unkind.

'For basically keeping things going here,' I say. 'For doing way more than your actual job.'

'Oh, that's quite all right,' she says.

'I really appreciate it,' I add. She nods, pressing her lips together, and a small silence hovers between us.

'Well, if there's anything you need I'm here to help.' Such a Jean thing to say; brisk, efficient, capable.

'Actually, there is something,' I say.

Her fine, fair brows shoot up. 'What is it?'

I get up from the chair. 'Would you mind coming out to reception with me?'

'Er, no problem.' Looking quizzical, she follows me out of her office to the main reception area.

The gigantic display board still dominates the whole space. Jean glances at me, then follows my gaze towards it. I catch a glimmer of amusement – of mischievousness really – in her soft grey eyes.

The board is covered in puffin paraphernalia: posters, brochures, calendars – even tea towels. A flock of badly drawn seabirds, masterminded by Paul on one of his visits here. *It's our new identity, Suze. We need it to smack people in the face the minute they walk in.*

Jean is smiling now. It's as if she can read my mind. 'Shall we?' I ask.

She nods and touches her beaded necklace. 'Oh, yes,' she replies.

We start slowly, unpinning the items one by one and placing them on a nearby table. But then I rip down a poster more forcefully, and it feels so good, I tear another one down. Catching my eye again, Jean smiles naughtily and reaches for a gatefold brochure, which she not only tugs off the board but also rips cleanly in two. We are chuckling like naughty teenagers.

'What's going on here?' Now Stuart has appeared, and we're in a flurry of ripping and tearing as he stares, mouth open. Brochures and posters are flying everywhere.

'Help us out, Stu,' Jean commands, so he joins in too and soon the floor is covered in ripped pictures and flung-down tea towels.

'We thought it was time to get rid of all of this,' I explain, belatedly.

'Yep, you're right there.' He stops and looks down at the tattered papers. 'I've nothing *against* puffins,' he adds.

'Neither have I,' I say quickly. 'I think they're beautiful.'

Stuart nods. 'But it was never right, was it? That new label and stuff. The *modernising*.'

'No, it wasn't,' I say. 'It was a big mistake.'

'Bloody right it was.' He catches my gaze and I detect a glimmer of amusement in his eyes.

Then off he goes, and Jean and I gather everything up and stuff it all into the bin.

'No more puffins,' I say when we're done.

She nods and smiles. 'That felt good, doing that.'

'Well, thanks for helping me.' I pause. 'I guess I'd better get back and see how my dog's been doing. Friends have taken him out and they're due back pretty soon—'

'Um, just before you go,' Jean says quickly, 'I wanted to say . . .' She smooths down her short, fine hair. 'A lot of us here, we've been worried about losing our jobs and what that's going to mean for us. I don't mean just us older ones,' she adds. 'I mean the younger ones too.'

'Yes, I can understand that,' I murmur.

'What I mean is,' she goes on, 'it's a common misconception that every young person who lives here is desperate to get off the island, to escape to the cities for a more exciting life.' I nod, waiting for her to continue. 'Of course, some do,' she adds. 'They're off the minute they leave school. They're virtually *running* for the ferry, dying to get to Glasgow or Edinburgh or London or whatever. But they're not all like that.'

'Yes, I can imagine,' I say.

'I mean, a lot of young people are happy here. It's their home. It's where they belong. And they love it.' Shockingly, her eyes have filled with tears. I'm stuck for

291

how to respond but of course, I know why she's telling me this. And, although I'm grateful to her for speaking out, I also feel helpless that I can't *promise* everything will turn out okay.

She pauses and adjusts her spectacles. 'You can understand that there hasn't been a lot of goodwill for the current management.'

'Of course, yes.' I nod.

'But for the *company* there is,' she goes on. 'For the heritage and the history, I mean. No one wants to see this fail, Suzy.'

She's used my name. I feel quite choked and I'm about to thank her for telling me all of this – for caring enough to ensure that I understand. But, brisk as anything, she's already marching away in her sensible brogues as she says, 'Anyway, I'd better crack on. There's a couple of glitches with the online shop and they're not going to fix themselves.'

Chapter Forty-Four

Ricky

I love Sgadansay. Even as a teenager I still loved it even though I was desperate to get away. Like, you still love your parents even though you don't want to live under the same roof as them anymore. You don't want them dictating the rhythms of your day or for your mum to be washing your underpants. You want to be yourself – or at least to have a decent stab at finding out what that might possibly mean.

This time, I don't want to leave. I keep telling myself it's because of Dad, and that I'd like to hang around a bit longer, but it's not just that. I mean, he's pretty much back to his usual self, going at the carpet with the sweeper like he's trying to rake the pattern off it and virtually fighting me off when I say I'll do it.

It's because of Scout, I try to reason with myself. After all, being able to spend so much time with him has been sheer joy for Arthur. So, yes, there's that.

But that's not the real reason either.

'So, how long d'you think you'll stay here?' I ask Suzy as we stroll along the water's edge. These past couple of days, she's come along on our walks ('We're not here for much longer,' I told her. 'We'd like you to come too.' I was careful to say 'we' and not 'I'). But the truth is, *I've* wanted her to come. Just for the company, of course. I love hanging out with Arthur, but obviously, Scout's far more appealing than his tedious old dad and it's nice to have someone to chat to.

'A few more weeks, I think,' she replies. 'It's so much easier to do things from here, being close to everything and being able to get to know everyone better. And apart from that, it's been brilliant for writing, away from all the distractions of being at home. It's kind of refreshing.'

'Yeah, I can imagine that.'

Suzy smiles, and as our eyes meet for a moment everything looks brighter. I catch myself and wonder what's happening to me. Less than two weeks ago Meg was here. Maybe it's sent me a bit mad, that whole thing; the 'sparking back up' and all the lying. It's probably just as well school starts on Monday. I'll be back to the manic whirl of teaching and my head'll be too full of Arthur's packed sporting schedule and the impending June concert – Christ, will Joey get to grips with that cello part? – for any other distracting thoughts.

'How about you?' she asks. 'When d'you think you'll be back?'

'I'm not sure, but definitely over the summer at some point. I'll need to make sure Dad's not getting himself into any more bother.'

She nods, and as we slip into an easy silence I wonder if she seems a little sad that we're leaving. No, that would be ridiculous. She has her hands full. Every minuscule detail of everything is discussed here, and I've heard that she flits around the distillery, observing keenly, calling meetings and getting involved in everything from helping to process orders to tidying up the grounds, tending the plants, even scrubbing down the signage so it looks bright and inviting again. She won't think about us for a minute.

'D'you worry about your dad?' she asks suddenly.

'Um . . . yeah, I s'pose I do. I mean, especially after his fall. That shower's not safe – I keep telling him that . . .'

'But what do *you* know?' she teases.

'Yeah. Obviously, I'm still his little kid who can't tie his shoelaces properly. I mean, I had the cheek to suggest he gets one of those rubberised mats for the bath. You know, the non-slip kind?'

She nods, grinning.

'And d'you know what he said? "For God's sake, son – they're for old people. I'll not be needing one of those!"' Her eyes glint as she laughs.

We are approaching the steps now, and Scout is zipping back and forth, showing no sign of tiring. I glance at Suzy, taken again by how she looks like she belongs here, so natural and at ease and, well . . . *beautiful.*

It's just the two of us today. Arthur and Dad wanted a last wander around town together; it was my father's suggestion, and I know from previous visits that they'll have gone for fish and chips. And then – as part of Dad's campaign to make sure Arthur has no teeth left by the age of fifteen – he'll have taken him to choose a load of boiled sweets from the sweet shop.

'Well, I'll miss you,' Suzy says, adding quickly, 'I mean, I'll miss you both. It's been lovely for Scout, having all this fuss and attention.' She seems to flush a little.

'We'll miss you too,' I say lightly as we climb the steps away from the beach. We stop, and I scan the street, aware that I'm avoiding saying what I want to say: *shall we stay in touch?* I feel oddly self-conscious and out of place, which is ridiculous, as I've never felt that way here; the island is in my bones. And why would Suzy want to stay in touch anyway? I'm aware of her presence, so close to me, as I raise a hand in greeting to a couple of familiar faces across the street.

'So, are you going to find your dad and Arthur?' she asks – signalling, I guess, that she needs to get on with stuff.

'Um, they're actually coming here,' I reply.

'Oh, God, are they?' It comes out in a rush. 'I'd better go then, hadn't I, before your dad—'

'No, don't rush off.' Without thinking I've taken hold of her hand.

Her lips part and her gaze seems to hold mine, and for that moment everything else seems to fade away. There are no cars or people or seagulls squawking. There's no clanking from the boats' masts or the guys yelling to each other from the shellfish boats.

There's just Suzy Medley and me.

'Harry's coming to see you,' I say, aware of my heart thumping.

'But why?' She looks shocked, but she's smiling.

'To talk to you,' I reply.

Now her smile broadens and she's blurting out, 'Did you persuade him? Oh, you did, didn't you?' Her eyes are sparkling and – possibly without thinking – she throws her arms around me. 'Thank you, Ricky. Thank you so much!'

We pull apart and it all comes out a bit scrambled as I explain: 'I talked to him, yes, but you know what he's like, he never does anything he doesn't want to do. So I think he must have wanted to really, because he's seen how happy Arthur is around Scout. I mean, he talks about nothing *but* Scout—'

'Good old Scout,' she says, laughing.

'And I think Dad realised that, well, you're a dog person – like him . . .'

She nods, as if waiting for me to go on. But I don't say anything else. I can't, because my mind is so full of her, and just as I'm trying to get myself together, to say how much I've enjoyed spending all this time together, Arthur shouts out: 'Dad!'

I step away from Suzy to see my father and son marching towards us. 'Hi,' I say in an overly bright voice.

'Hi, Arthur, Harry—' Suzy starts.

'Hullo,' Dad says, hands stuffed in the pockets of his waterproof coat.

'We had fish suppers,' Arthur announces happily, swinging his khaki rucksack by a strap, 'and Granddad's bought me sweets and Top Trumps.'

'That's great,' I say, deciding now that they can't have seen us holding hands, then hugging – but what does it matter if they did?

'I remember Top Trumps,' Suzy says, smiling. 'My kids loved them. I didn't know they were still around.'

'Yeah, they're brilliant,' Arthur enthuses. In fact he used to love them too, though I assumed he'd outgrown them a few years ago. But then, as Suzy said, what the heck do I know?

'Well, um, it's good to see you, Harry,' Suzy adds as Arthur crouches down to fuss over Scout.

Dad raises an eyebrow. 'Yeah. So, anyway, about your letter,' he says bluntly.

'I, um . . . I *really* hope you didn't mind me dropping it off to you . . .'

I glance at Dad. His expression is indecipherable and I find myself willing him to at least be pleasant to her, to give her a chance. 'I s'pose not. You said you wanted to meet up with me?'

'Um, yes,' she says, her cheeks flushing pink now. 'I mean, if it's okay with you. Maybe we could arrange to get together and have a chat about everything? At a time that suits you, I mean?'

Dad purses his lips and glances up and down the beach, then finally seems to look at her properly for the very first time. 'Well,' he says, 'how about now?'

Chapter Forty-Five

Two Months Later
Suzy

It tears at my heart to leave Scout on Sgadansay. I just have to keep reminding myself that he'll have a far better time on the island than having to endure those ferry crossings again. Besides, I'll be darting all over the place. There's Frieda's graduation in Cumbria, then Belinda and Derek are putting on a big dinner for Mum and Dad's golden wedding anniversary. And – as Belinda has been at great pains to remind me – Derek has a bad reaction to dogs. As if Scout so much as putting a paw in the same *county* would trigger his allergies. So I reassure myself that I've made the right decision as I sip milky tea on the deck of the ferry, and then drive south, where I pick up Tony and we head onwards to Cumbria for our daughter's graduation.

Isaac comes over for it too. It's such a joyful day and it feels so right and comforting for all four of us to be together. In the whirl of celebration and happiness, the distillery recedes into the distance. I barely think about barley or barrels or the boxing room.

'Guess we didn't mess up too badly,' Tony says with a smile at our family dinner later in a local restaurant. And I have to agree. However, I do think about Ricky. Of course I do. I think about that moment when he held my hand – in fact, I wonder now if I imagined it – and I picture him at *his* graduation, with all those dressed-up parents ('A flurry of fascinators!' he'd joked), and Harry, all tensed up as he was handed a glass of wine, in case somebody picked his pockets.

'He must have been proud of you, though,' I'd remarked on one of our beach walks. 'What about all those school concerts you performed in? Seeing you up there on stage with your cello? I couldn't watch my kids in a nativity without blubbing into tissues!'

Ricky had grinned at that. 'Honestly, I think he went out of duty – because Mum made him,' he explained. 'From the outside it always looked like he was boss, but he wasn't really. Mum was strong as an ox when it counted. So he'd always go along, dutifully. But he'd be one of the first parents springing up out of his seat when it was over, making for the exit, fag lit – he smoked back then – when he was barely out of the door, probably thinking, "Thank fuck that's over."' And he'd laughed. 'There was only so much Elgar my dad could take.'

The day after her graduation we leave Frieda preparing for a celebratory camping trip with friends, and drive Isaac back to Liverpool, where he and his mates are keeping their student house on for next year. Tony and I have booked ourselves into a couple of rooms at a nearby Travelodge. Maddy, his partner, has never been difficult about us spending time together when there's family stuff going on. In fact, if it wasn't for their brood of kids back home, she'd have come to Frieda's graduation too.

Tony and I both love the city and cram in as much sightseeing as possible during our two days there: museums, art galleries, the Mersey ferry. 'You're such a pair of tourists,' Isaac scoffs as he peels potatoes back in his kitchen. He's insisted on cooking dinner for us instead of us all eating out. Keen to show off his newly acquired domestic skills, we suspect. Eager to show that there'll be no microwave/kettle dramas on his watch. The mood is happy and light as he pours us tepid white wine from a box and potato peelings ping onto the cracked lino.

His housemates, Rex and Matis, drift in and out with girlfriends and friends; there's a constant procession of young people and everyone's charmingly polite: their chatting-to-parents personas. Somehow, Isaac has pulled it together to make roast pork. The only accompaniments are roast potatoes and a jar of apple sauce but I have to say, it's delicious. Our son, now twenty, appears to be entirely capable of cooking a meal without injuring himself or burning down the house. We all cram around the scuffed table, and neither Tony nor I mention the pizza boxes, plus a lone pineapple core, lying on the floor next to the overflowing bin. At least, not until the young ones are out of earshot when he nudges me and whispers, 'At least someone's getting one of their five-a-day.'

They'll get better, I decide. They'll leave uni and get proper jobs, and further down the line they might even acquire more than one set of bed linen and start paying attention to use-by dates on food. But there's plenty of time for all of that. Acres of time to grow up and be sensible and discover that life can swerve off in unexpected directions, and there's no handy guidebook to it, for anyone.

* * *

From Liverpool I head to Leeds for a meeting at Rosalind's office. 'I have to say, I'm impressed,' she says, flashing a brief smile across her desk.

'Thank you,' I say, allowing myself a moment's pride.

'We both knew how difficult it was going to be to change everyone's perception,' she adds. 'But you're definitely managing it. All this media coverage seems to be helping, doesn't it?'

'Yes, I think it is. I've set up some press trips so we'll have journalists coming up to spend time on the island. I thought it was worth investing in that – putting them up for a few days in the art deco hotel there, giving them a lovely Sgadansay experience—'

'That is a good idea,' Rosalind says.

'Harry, the master distiller, is back with us now,' I add, 'and when he heard about this he offered to take them on tours around the island.' In fact, it was a bit of a surprise. I hadn't imagined him as the tour guide type. But then as he'd told me, gruffly, 'We might as well have someone taking them around who knows what they're talking about.' And no one knows the secret beaches and coves – the most interesting, tucked-away parts – like Harry.

'This all sounds great,' Rosalind concedes, 'and it looks like we're on target to meet those quarterly figures.'

'I'm so pleased,' I say. Although it's not a natural talent, I've forced myself to get my head around the financial matters. Spreadsheets no longer fill me with dread. When our accountant calls me for a meeting I'm no longer seized by an urge to run away.

'D'you think it's helped,' she asks, 'basing yourself out there on the island?'

'Definitely,' I reply. 'I wasn't sure how it'd be but, you know, I loved Sgadansay that first time Paul and I visited.

I mean, I *really* fell in love with it. I knew it was a special place.' An image flashes into my mind of that glorious silver beach, with Cara, Ricky or Arthur throwing a stick or a tennis ball for Scout. It catches me by surprise and I sense my heart lifting. Again, it feels as if I might have imagined Ricky taking my hand, and the look we exchanged when I was sure I felt *something* between us; or maybe I dreamt it.

'The main thing is,' Rosalind continues, 'you've restored a lot of faith in the company.'

'I think a lot of that is to do with Harry,' I say. 'Paul called him a dinosaur and said he was stuck in his ways. But he's not at all.' It's true; even Jean has mentioned that he seems to have returned to work with a newfound vigour, and he's set on developing special edition whiskies and perhaps even 'diversifying a bit', as he put it (in typical Harry fashion he wouldn't expand on that. I guess, like our whisky itself, he'll be ready when he's *ready*).

'But actually,' Rosalind adds, 'you're the one who's turned things around, getting orders back up and creating a positive feeling around Sgadansay again.' She meets my gaze and her face seems to light up for the first time since I've seen her. Even this drab little office looks a little brighter. 'So don't shy away from taking some credit, Suzy,' she says firmly. 'Really, it's all been down to you.'

Perhaps that's why letting go of my house, albeit temporarily, doesn't feel difficult. I brought my family up here, and we raised guinea pigs in the garden – but even after a few days I'm itching to get back to the island again, and there's no point in this place lying empty. It's not forever, anyway. It's for . . . well, we'll see. I can no longer think too far ahead.

A friend of Dee's youngest daughter is studying at the university here, and has apparently been living in a bit of a hovel. As she's staying in York to work over the summer, she was apparently delighted by the possibility of living here with friends for a knockdown rent. It'll help me, too, as I'm aware that I can't stay at Cara's indefinitely and I already have my eye on a tiny rental cottage on the edge of town. Dee has been popping in here regularly, and my indoor plants – and garden – have clearly been cared for, and my non-essential mail has been neatly stacked up in the hallway with her usual efficiency (any urgent stuff she's been forwarding to me).

'Thanks so much for taking care of things,' I tell her when she comes round for lunch in my garden.

'Well, thanks for letting the girls move in,' she says. 'They're so excited.'

'They seemed it,' I say, picturing their gleeful faces as I showed them round. June sunshine beats down on us and bees hover around the herbaceous border. 'I'm glad they'll be here,' I add. 'I can't *quite* believe I'm moving out, though. Not really. I mean, when it all started . . . d'you remember we called it his gazpacho thing?' She knows what I mean; how Paul would become madly enthusiastic about things we'd seen or eaten on holiday, and would want to carry that feeling back home under grey Yorkshire skies.

'Yeah,' she says. 'From that time you went to Majorca and he was mad about the chilled soup . . .'

'Uh-huh. We kept going back to the same restaurant and he ordered it every single time.'

'And then he made it when you got home.' She grins at the memory.

'But it was just a bland, tomato-based chilled liquid and he tipped most of it away . . .'

'Anyway,' she cuts in, 'never mind Paul. How about Ricky? Have you been in touch since he went home?'

I smile. Obviously, his name has come up. I've told her about how he is as a dad, and a son, and a friend to me. I've told her all about Arthur and how brilliant he is with Scout; such a sweet and earnest but still endearingly enthusiastic kid. 'No,' I reply, 'but I'll text him. I will.'

'You should!'

'But . . . what for?' I ask. 'I mean, what'll I say?' I know I'm sounding like an awkward kid myself.

She grins at me. 'Couldn't you just ask how he's doing? How he's settled back into life after his holiday?'

'Yes, that'd sound completely natural.' I snigger. In fact, I have been poised to text, just to say hi. But since he left I haven't quite summoned the nerve, which seems ridiculous as I've found the courage to tackle far more daunting stuff.

Anyway, I keep telling myself, he could contact *me*.

'So, what's the story with Arthur's mum?' Dee asks now.

I shrug as I gather up our plates. 'I'm really not sure. All I know is that she hasn't been in his life for a very long time. She disappeared when he was six, apparently. But that's all Ricky's told me and I'm not planning to quiz him about it.'

She frowns. 'She's alive, though, isn't she?'

'I assume so,' I reply. 'But honestly, I've got the feeling that I just shouldn't go there, when we've been chatting, so I haven't.' I pause and top up our glasses with chilled rosé. 'It's a bit odd, though. I mean, he seems like a pretty open person about all kinds of stuff – like his ex going back home, all that . . .' But not Arthur's mum, I reflect. And, considering how much we've talked, she seems like a pretty significant omission.

'And it was Ricky who persuaded his dad to come back and work with you?' Dee asks.

I nod and smile. 'Well, yes. He finally told me he'd actually had far more to do with Harry's change of heart than he'd first admitted.' And I tell Dee how Harry had kept saying, 'Don't mind me!' whenever Ricky asked if he was *really* okay about him walking Scout and spending time with me. And how Ricky had said, 'You keeping saying *don't mind me,* but *I* mind. I mind how you feel about it.' Finally, Harry had cracked and barked that he was absolutely-bloody-fine, thanks very much. And Ricky had said, 'If you're *that* fine, Dad, why not meet her properly?'

'So it was a kind of showdown?' Dee ventures.

'I suppose so, yes. But Ricky knew his dad would be happier back at work, being respected, doing what he was good at. He was never a man for hobbies, Ricky said. He'd gone to seed a bit, hanging around the house, obsessively raking at his carpets with this ancient sweeper thing. Ricky said he—'

'"Ricky said",' Dee repeats, teasing me, and I catch her expression and laugh.

'Stop it,' I say.

'C'mon, Suze,' she says, eyeing me over her glass, 'there's something between you two. I can just tell.'

'D'you reckon?' I sip my wine and look at her. 'I mean, how d'you know?'

'I just think . . .' She pauses. 'Yes, maybe he did it for his dad, because he knew it'd be good for him. But I think he mainly did it for you.'

306

Chapter Forty-Six

After she's gone I deep-clean the house and box up the remains of Paul's possessions. There isn't much, as he'd left in his own car – in a cloud of smoke, I imagine, like in cartoons – and had managed to stuff it with most of his things. It's tempting to drop off the rest at the charity shop without contacting him, because I really *don't* want to hear excuses, apologies or whatever else he might happen to come out with. However, deciding I'd better give him the option, I message his friend George in London who replies: *Paul says thanks but he doesn't need any of that stuff.* Like he wants to wash his hands of everything to do with us.

In fact, I'm glad. It's easier this way. So the odd bits of clothing, a pile of 'get rich quick' type manuals, the trumpet and the cycling gear (at least, the items not gnawed by Scout) are dropped off at my nearest charity shop, where the elderly lady is delighted: 'This is amazing,' she enthuses, admiring the gleaming instrument. 'It looks like it's hardly been played!'

Back home there's more boxing up of all the stuff I

need to shove out of the way for the students moving in. This all goes up into the loft, which prompts me to bring down all the baby and toddler equipment Tony and I stashed up there all those years ago: cots, trikes and highchairs that I'd never got around to passing on. And now, of course, I don't really know anyone with young children so this, too, is dispatched to new homes via charity shops and Freecycle.

I'm aware of beavering away in order to stop dwelling on whether or not I should drop Ricky a friendly text. I'm conscious that he's busy, and I'm busy too; all this *busyness*. And anyway, the thought of anything ever happening between us is ridiculous. Apart from the geographic issues, we are two middle-aged people with our own lives to get on with. It was a little hand-hold on the beach, and a hug, and that was that. Straight afterwards, Ricky had whisked Arthur away – so quickly I'd wondered if he was embarrassed or something. Harry and I had gone for a drink together (not at the Anchor; perhaps he hadn't wanted his friends to see him fraternising with me in his local). We'd gone to the Ship instead – on his suggestion – and that's where we'd discussed my distillery plans and he'd agreed to come back and be my right-hand man.

But I hadn't seen Ricky or Arthur again after that. And the thought that I mightn't ever again triggers an actual ache in my gut.

In my second week back home, Frieda returns, fresh from her camping trip and is soon joined by Isaac for their grandparents' golden wedding anniversary.

We arrive en masse at Belinda's, and she does her usual thing of greeting us with enthusiasm whilst teetering back slightly as if there are *dozens* of us all tumbling into her house. There are hugs all round – I brace myself for Derek's customary wet-lipped kiss – but the minute we all settle I know something's up; something is *different* around here.

'I've just had a lot on,' Belinda tells me distractedly as we lift steaming trays from the catering-sized oven: deliciously scented roast lamb, an unfeasibly large chicken and a nut roast for Frieda, plus roast potatoes and numerous vegetables all perfectly cooked, as I knew they would be.

I glance at my sister as she mops at her brow with her Cath Kidston oven glove. Does she just mean her usual, plate-spinning kind of scenario? Maybe. But this feels different somehow. Unusually, she's been knocking back wine as she prepared the meal. I've noticed that so far, Derek hasn't lifted a finger.

'So what's been happening?' I ask.

'Oh, me and Derek have just had some *stuff* going on lately.' She transfers mint sauce from a jar into a white porcelain bowl. Bought mint sauce, I note. Normally she makes her own with mint from the garden.

However the dinner is wonderful and naturally, I don't quiz Belinda on what kind of 'stuff' she was referring to. The table is cleared, more wine tippled and Mum is holding court about her various fundraising triumphs for local charities, while my father gazes at her in undisguised admiration. He loves her so much, I reflect. After all, she's a powerhouse, and however hackle-rising I find her, I have to admire her energy and drive. Without her fundraising efforts, I'd imagine that their local, once-derelict swimming pool would never again have seen a droplet of water – not to mention the aqua fitness classes and all of the other stuff that goes on there.

309

'Your granddad keeps telling me to take my foot off the gas,' she announces to Frieda and Isaac, who are watching her with bemused expressions (when did she start saying things like 'foot off the gas'?). 'But I can't,' she goes on, tipsily, 'or nothing would get done, would it, Peter?'

'No, love,' Dad says, patting her hand. Then, after a pause: 'The whole *town* would grind to a standstill without you at the helm, Junie.' He catches my eye momentarily with a mischievous glint and Mum turns to me.

'How's your work going anyway, Suzy? You haven't really said . . .'

'The distillery?' I ask. 'Or my writing work?'

'Your writing,' she says quickly, turning back to Frieda and Isaac. 'I don't know how your mum can write about death all day—'

'I think it's really interesting,' Frieda announces, loyally.

'Yeah, me too,' Isaac says, adding as he turns to me: 'Better than a real job anyway. Isn't it, Mum?'

'*Loads* better,' I say, catching his eye, so grateful that he and his sister are here, defusing things.

'It's going really well, Mum,' I tell her.

'The distillery is too,' Belinda pipes up, and I stare at her, amazed. 'Well, so I hear anyway,' she adds quickly, 'from what Suzy's been saying.' In fact, I haven't actually told her very much; just the odd titbit during our occasional phone conversations. I wonder now if she's been reading about it, googling stuff. Because a lot's been written about us now, in specialist drinks publications but also in the business and travel sections of national newspapers; about the distillery's rapid demise, and it being taken over by one half of a former partnership and how things seem to be flourishing again on Sgadansay.

310

'That's nice, love,' Mum remarks, as if I've just won a tenner on a lottery ticket.

Now, as Derek launches into a spiel about how he's doing *terribly well* too, with his various 'projects', my sister grabs at my wrist and leads me out to the conservatory at the back of the house.

'Sorry about that.' She motions for me to sit beside her on the wicker seat.

'What for?' I stare at her.

'For, well . . . Derek, going on like that. Turning it all back onto him. That's *so* typical . . .'

'That's okay,' I say, still bewildered. 'I didn't even notice.' I wonder now if I've missed something, being the only sober person in the room (only because I'm driving later; in any other circumstances I'd be compelled to anaesthetise myself in the presence of my brother-in-law). Perhaps it's one of those occasions where you need to be on the same plane as everyone else, alcohol-wise, in order to pick up on all of the nuances?

'And I'm sorry about the other stuff too,' Belinda adds.

'What other stuff?' Genuinely, I have no idea what she's talking about.

'I mean . . . how I've been about the distillery and Paul and everything,' she blurts out, all in a rush.

'You've been . . . *fine*,' I say hesitantly.

Belinda grips the stem of her wine glass and takes a big swig from it. She usually has her shoulder-length hair coloured mid-brown, but I've noticed she's letting the grey come through. 'I haven't really. I've been dismissive, haven't I? And not exactly supportive. I mean, for one thing, your relationship ended—'

'Oh, Bel.' I reach over and hug her. 'What happened between Paul and me was so enormous, and such an

311

almighty screw-up, that the actual dumpage part hardly feels significant. And I'm fine, honestly.'

She musters a weak smile. 'I never really thought he was right for you, to be honest.'

'Thanks for that.' I raise a brow and smile too.

'But I liked him,' she adds.

I can't help smirking at that. 'Yes, I did too. But you're right – he wasn't the man for me.'

'You seemed so in love with him, though—'

'I probably was – but I don't really know. I mean, I've never been as confident as you. And maybe it's taken me until the age of forty-eight to realise that, whenever a man has made it clear that he's keen, I've been so surprised and delighted that I've tried to mould myself to fit them. Even with Tony, I did it. I always have. But now, there's someone—'

'You've met someone?' she exclaims.

I look at her, already wishing I hadn't blurted that out. 'It's nothing,' I say quickly. 'I've just made a friend, that's all . . .'

'On the island?' She drains her glass and grins at me, eyes wide, anticipating gossip.

'It's nothing, honestly.' Of course it's nothing, I tell myself firmly. How could anything possibly happen? Ricky lives in Glasgow, and besides that, Harry Vance is his father – and although he's back with us now, I'm aware that I need to tread carefully around him. I'm certainly not planning to hurl myself at his son. Christ, it'd probably be on the front page of the *Sgadansay Gazette*.

'I never knew that about you,' Belinda adds.

'Knew what?' I ask.

'The "moulding yourself" thing. You've always seemed very much your own person to me, doing your own thing.

And all my male friends used to go on about my gorgeous little sister—'

'Oh, come on,' I retort. 'That's *not* true.'

'It is!' she exclaims.

I look at her, my incredibly high-achieving sister who has this huge, immaculate house, and a wardrobe of smart designer outfits in colours like teal and taupe, and always seemed to have everything all sorted out. 'I'll tell you something,' I add. 'I always thought that trying to meet someone is a bit like shoe shopping. It's such a horrible, soul-sapping business that whenever I've spotted some I like – that I *really* like – I've forced my feet into them even if they're too small, completely the wrong shape and painful. It's like I can't accept the shoes aren't right for me. I'm convinced it's my *feet* that are wrong—'

'And then you end up with blisters and bleeding toes, possibly crippled,' she remarks with a trace of glee.

I laugh. 'Yeah, I guess so. But you're not like that. You always knew Derek was right, didn't you?'

'Um . . . maybe.' She looks down at her empty glass. 'I s'pose so.'

I frown. 'Bel, what is it? What's been happening?'

She rubs at her face and jumps up from the seat. 'Nothing. Nothing at all. I guess we should get back to the party—'

'Belinda?' I stand up too. 'Is something going on with you two? Because you seem—'

'I was just wondering,' she says blithely, already marching ahead, 'if I could come up and see you sometime? On the island, I mean?'

'Yes, of course you can. I'd love that!'

She stops in the doorway. Her cheeks are blotchy and her eyes are a little pink. 'D'you mean both of you?' I

313

add. 'Because there's the dog issue, obviously. With Derek's allergies . . .'

'Oh no, it'd definitely just be me,' she says firmly, flouncing ahead of me to the living room now. 'To be honest, Suze, I could do with a little break.'

Chapter Forty-Seven

Two Weeks Later

It felt like such an adventure that first time I came to Sgadansay with Paul. Even the lack of phone signal on much of the island seemed somehow exotic. As we drove off the ferry, Paul was clutching the paper map he'd had the forethought to buy, and was giving directions from the passenger seat.

'Follow the road inland,' he said. 'It's about fifteen minutes away.' We passed clusters of cottages, a tea shop, the smokery and a church. Then the buildings petered out into rolling hills with the craggier peaks visible hazily in the distance. He switched on the car radio, but the signal was so faint he turned it off again and we settled into a pleasant silence. We passed through a village with neat front gardens, the odd boat in a driveway, and a red telephone box. I spotted a village hall, its white paint peeling slightly, with a rust-coloured corrugated-iron roof. In less than a minute we were out in the wilds again with nothing around us but sheep.

Although the island is far more familiar to me these days, I still feel a surge of something when I first arrive.

Ricky and Arthur may be in Glasgow but it's okay, I tell myself, because Scout is here – and Cara. I knock lightly on the side door and Cara answers it, greeting me with a tight hug as Scout shoots out. 'Hey, we've missed you!' she announces.

'I've missed you too,' I say, smiling. I bob down and gather Scout into my arms, his whiskers tickling my face as he jumps all over me. 'It's so good to be back,' I add, and it is. It feels like home.

'Heard from Ricky?' Cara asks later, when we're settled in front of her wood-burning stove.

I shake my head. 'I wasn't expecting to really.' She gives me a look because she knows, I think. But I can't say it because there's nothing to say really.

'Maybe he'll be back in the summer holidays?' she adds. 'When do schools break up again?'

'I'm not sure,' I say, although of course I've looked this up, and I know that, in Scotland, the summer term finishes soon. But to admit that I've checked, and that I'm hoping they'll come back soon, would be to admit to *myself* that I'm hoping. And anyway, there's still a whole heap of work to be done, which is why I'm here after all.

To put things right and, more than that, to push us forward. That's what I'm focusing on. There's an ambition welling in me that I've never experienced before; certainly not in my job at the recruitment consultancy. That didn't truly excite me. But this does. I'd never imagined I'd be excited about barley – or *water*, for that matter. How had I never realised that water is such a thing?

*   *   *

316

Scout and I leave Cara's, and I settle into my new life on the island, in a tiny one-storey rented cottage now, as I couldn't impinge on her any longer. She'd been going out the odd evening, and seemed a little flustered and evasive when she came home.

'Did you have a nice time?' I'd ask her.

'It was great, thanks,' she'd reply, then explain that she was having an early night or planned to get stuck into some painting, or printing, in her studio. A slight awkwardness had crept in. I hated to think she might feel obliged to ask me along on a night out, or feel bad if she didn't, as if we were student housemates. But there was *something*, I knew it. Maybe she was just ready to have her place to herself again, and who could blame her? She'd been more than generous to me and Scout.

My cottage is basic and plain but also beautiful with its bare, rough stone interior walls, just like Cara's place, and a tiny garden out the back. There are a few beleaguered shrubs that I hope to resurrect. The lawn is soggy and waterlogged, but I'm planning to ask the landlord if I can dig channels on either side to drain it. That'll keep me busy. I also have Rosalind's plant, which I've brought back with me. She seemed quite startled when I asked if I could take it, but I'm planning to return it to her, renewed – the way Ricky told me he mends his pupils' instruments and then hands them back.

'Well, you have a good track record for nursing things back to good health,' Rosalind said, with a flicker of a smile.

Meanwhile I've been spending most of my time at the distillery, learning new things every day. Like the fact that, according to Vicki, here on the island we have the ideal ingredients for gin. The perfect water and botanics that could give our own spirit a unique flavour, she means. 'Have you heard of sugar kelp?' she asks one afternoon as she hands Harry and me mugs of tea in the distillery's reception area.

'Not really,' I say. 'Is it a kind of seaweed?'

''Course it is,' Harry exclaims, in a *don't-you-know-anything?* voice.

I catch Vicki shooting him an exasperated look. 'Why would Suzy know that, Harry?'

He shrugs and blows across the top of his mug.

'Maybe you could look into it, Harry?' I venture.

'Oh, I know how to distil gin,' he says blithely, as if it's nothing – like Isaac and his mates gathering nettles to brew beer. They thought all they'd have to do was stuff the whole load in the cask, with water and bicarbonate of soda nicked from my kitchen cupboard, and that would be that.

'What's special about sugar kelp?' I ask Vicki.

'It has a distinctive sweet and salty taste,' she says. 'There's nothing else quite like it. And there are huge beds of it around the coast here that can be harvested sustainably at the right time of year.'

'That's right,' Harry says, as if we're talking about picking lettuce.

'Could *we* do that?' I ask him. 'To use as a flavouring, I mean?'

He nods. 'Yep, there's a diver I know who does that.'

'What, harvests seaweed?' I gasp.

He nods. 'Aye, of course.' I know better than to bombard him with questions, but I have to ask, 'Harry, d'you really think we could produce a gin? One that's unique to us?'

318

'I think that'd be fantastic,' Vicki says quickly. 'It's been mooted before, and I've always said we're ideally placed to do it – but you know how things were around here. Very traditional, with nothing ever changing . . .'

'Well, maybe now's the right time to try it?' I glance at Harry. 'I know it's a lot to ask, but could we start to think about that? Just in a small way, to see how it goes?'

'I'll have a think,' he says. Then he gets up, signifying that he has far more important things to get on with than sit around chatting to us. Harry isn't really a tea break kind of man.

Chapter Forty-Eight

The gin idea is pushed firmly out of my mind as Belinda arrives on Sgadansay. Windswept and looking bewildered, she stomps into the cottage with her smart wheeled suitcase, then flings it aside, virtually collapsing onto the sofa. 'My God, Suze,' she announces. 'That ferry crossing!'

'I know,' I say sympathetically. 'It's pretty rough today.'

'Is it always like that?' She frowns, as if it were someone's fault, and there might be a number she can call to lodge a complaint.

'Not always, no,' I say. 'You were just unlucky, especially at this time of year.' When I offer her water she wafts me away. But a glass of wine is accepted gratefully. It feels so strange to see her here, out of context, what feels like a million miles from her immaculate home, with her usually sleek blow-dry all tousled from being on the deck of the ferry because sitting inside made her feel ill.

She is here for four days – I have relocated to the box room to give her the decent double bed – and I am a little apprehensive about how it'll be.

We haven't spent this much time together, solidly, since she left home over thirty years ago. And besides that, Belinda isn't used to places like Sgadansay. Usually, she and Derek go to Florida or the Maldives and stay in swanky complexes where exotic fruit platters and endless chilled drinks are brought to the poolside. But there are no obliging waiters bringing treats to your lounger on Silver Beach. There aren't even any loungers.

When we wake up next morning the island is already bathed in bright sunshine. We head out towards the ruined castle, where Belinda insists on taking numerous selfies of us arm in arm, in front of the crumbled remains. I'm quite touched that she wants pictures of us together. 'Well, we've never done this before, have we?' she asks. 'Been away together, I mean, just you and me?'

Something seems to twist around my heart as she takes Scout's photo too. Although she's not a dog lover really, she's admitted that he's 'sweet'.

'No, we haven't,' I say. 'But you know you can come here anytime now . . .'

'And face that ferry journey again?' she splutters.

'It's not always like that, Bel!'

'I think I'll fly,' she says, grinning, as we make our way back to the coast.

An hour or so later we reach the narrow path that runs along the edge of the cliff. 'This is stunning,' Belinda exclaims. 'My God, it's like another world!' She gazes out to sea, taking yet more photos, and turns back to me. 'Why doesn't everyone come here? I mean, why isn't Sgadansay packed with tourists?'

I smile, sensing a rush of pride as if the island is mine. 'It's not for everyone, is it? The wildness, I mean? The mad weather—' The words are no sooner out of my

321

mouth than a fierce gust of wind catches her scarf and tosses it out to sea.

'Oh, never mind,' she announces. 'I'll get another one. Is there an Oliver Bonas here?'

I look at her, and we laugh like we've never laughed before – at least not as far as I can remember – as we step carefully down the steep narrow path, overgrown with ferns, to the secret beach Ricky told me about.

It's a golden cove, sheltered on both sides by steep cliffs, and with what could be described as a cave at the furthest end; a natural indent in the rocks. I remember Ricky telling me how he, Arthur and Arthur's mum used to come here and light fires, cook sausages and play pirates.

Belinda and I sit together on a large, flat rock and she links her arm in mine. I know there's something going on with her; of course I do. But I don't want to press her on anything. I just want her to see Sgadansay as I do, in all its wild, unpredictable glory. And I know she'll tell me when she's ready.

So we pass the days together quite happily, and she meets Cara and we all walk Scout together. One afternoon, Cara mentions that Vicki will be joining us too. I catch her expression; I know their paths will have crossed (*everyone's* does on Sgadansay). And I've introduced them, when we've met around town. But as they chat easily, chuckling at shared jokes as we stride along the beach together, it's clear that there's a spark of something between them. Cara seems relaxed and happier than I've ever seen her. And I don't quiz her about it; there's no need. But it explains Cara's mysterious evenings out, when I was still living at her place.

On Belinda's last evening I take her to the island's

poshest hotel, where locally caught seafood is brought to us on a vast oval platter. We have just finished, and are drinking coffee from tiny cups when she looks at me intently. 'So, you liked him, didn't you?' she ventures.

She means Ricky of course. I've told her a little more about him since she's been here; about our short-lived dog share and how he coaxed his father to come back and work with us. 'Of course I did,' I reply, not wanting to get into this; at least, not with my sister. I try to push away a niggle of hurt that he hasn't been in touch since his visit here.

'Maybe he'll be back soon,' she adds.

'Maybe,' I say vaguely.

'Well, as long as he's not like Paul,' she remarks with a glint in her eye.

I frown at her. 'Why d'you say that?'

'I'm only kidding,' she says quickly. 'Don't be so sensitive. You're always like this. You take things the wrong—'

'Belinda,' I cut in, 'please don't tell me what I'm like. Let's not get into how stupid and irresponsible I've been—'

'Oh, Suze.' She reaches for my hand across the white tablecloth. 'I didn't mean—'

'What did you mean then?' I'm aware of my heart thumping hard now, and know I'm over-reacting.

'I'm sorry,' she says.

'It's okay,' I murmur. 'I'm sorry too.'

'It was a stupid thing to say.' A lull hangs over us until the predictable wrangling over the bill. Belinda finally relents and lets me treat her.

She links her arm in mine as we stroll back to the cottage. It's new, this linking thing. In fact, I've noticed lots of new things about Belinda when she's far away from her kitchen island and Derek bustling around in the background, popping his vitamins, stretching out his hamstrings. And again, I wonder what's going on with her, back home. I know she didn't come here just to admire the beaches and savour the just-caught Hebridean seafood.

I remember Dee telling me how a patient often blurts out the real issue – the 'Oh, and there's another thing' – just as they're about to leave the surgery. And as my sister is packing up next morning in preparation for catching the ferry, it comes out.

'There's a bit of a thing going on with Derek at the moment,' she says, all in a rush, as I hand her a mug of coffee.

'What is it?'

'Oh, it's just . . . *you* know.' She sits on the bed and pushes back her hair distractedly. 'His gambling thing.'

'What gambling thing?' I move her neatly packed suitcase aside on the bed and sit next to her. 'I didn't know he did that,' I add. 'D'you mean it's a problem?'

Belinda nods. 'It's been going on for years, but it only came out at the start of this year just how bad a mess we were in.' She purses her lips. 'I'm an intelligent woman, aren't I, Suze?' Her eyes are wet now. I put an arm around her shoulders.

'Of course you are! You're far smarter than I am.'

'I don't know about that,' she says bitterly. 'God, Suzy. I don't know how I had the nerve to go on to you about the distillery when I sat back and allowed it to happen. I let him take control of our finances because he was always adamant that he was better at managing them than I was – with his investments and all that.'

I stroke her hair gently. '*Are* there any investments?' I ask.

324

'With the bookies, yes. But I don't think they're the kind that a financial adviser would recommend.'

We look at each other and I hug her. 'I'm so sorry, Bel. I had no idea.'

'Hmm. Well, no one did. They still don't. You're the only one I've told – apart from Rosalind, of course . . .'

'Rosalind?' I stare at her. 'You've been seeing her too?'

'Yeah,' she says quietly. 'That's why I tracked her down, to help me sort out the mess. We'd lost touch since uni but she's been brilliant, actually.' My sister musters a faint smile. 'She's a bit of a whizz, isn't she?'

'God, yes,' I say. 'So, what are you going to do?'

'About Derek?' She shrugs. 'I'm not sure. It depends on . . .' She breaks off, jumps up and zips up her case. 'Don't say anything to Mum, will you?'

'Of course I won't!' I exclaim. 'But, Bel, is there anything I can do? I mean, even if you just want to talk about things?'

'Thanks,' she says briskly. 'It'll all work out. I'm sure it will. But hadn't we better set off? The ferry leaves in—'

'We have ages yet,' I cut in. I've already reminded her that it's not like an international flight; we don't need to show up two hours early. But Belinda is adamant and so we set off, with her making it clear that the matter is closed, she'll be *fine*, and it's been lovely having all this time together; and I have to agree that it has.

I see my sister off onto the ferry. The sea is thankfully calm but I'm still reeling with her news that her husband has squandered all their money. It's hard to process when I've spent a lifetime feeling queasy whenever our two lives have been compared: Belinda and Derek, financially advised to the hilt, and therefore able to enjoy a retirement sipping negronis on loungers whereas I'll probably spend my dotage boiling up cabbage.

Back home, in the need of a head-clearing walk, I clip on Scout's lead and we set off. We're approaching the beach when my phone rings. I'm almost expecting it to be Belinda, even though there's no signal at sea; but it's an unknown number.

'Hi, is that Suzy?' It's a man's voice.

'Yes?'

'It's Oskar, from the animal sanctuary. How are you? How's Scout doing?'

'He's fine, thanks,' I say. 'He's settled in so well. He's a *brilliant* dog . . .' I pause, trying to dismiss a growing sense of unease. He's probably just checking up how we're doing, I reassure myself.

'That's good,' he says. 'Look, um, I'm sorry to call you out of the blue like this. It's a bit of a weird one, actually.' He clears his throat.

'What is it?'

'We've had a call,' Oskar says. 'A call from a woman who said he's hers.'

'What?' I exclaim. 'After all this time?'

'I know. It's really bizarre. Shalini and I couldn't believe it.'

I crouch down to stroke Scout, and glance around anxiously as if someone might appear from nowhere and try to snatch him away from me.

'She called this morning,' Oskar goes on. 'She feels terrible about leaving him on the island like that, but her situation was difficult . . .'

'Who is she?' I blurt out.

'Her name's Lorraine Sampson. She lives in the Midlands somewhere and they'd been on Sgadansay on holiday—'

326

'And she'd just abandoned him? And it's taken her all this time to even make a phone call—'

'Yeah, like I said, it sounds like things were difficult.' For her, maybe, I think angrily. But what about her dog, running about lost and hungry on a cold, wet night? 'She didn't go into much detail,' he adds, 'but she sent me a picture of him – and she called him Pip.' Pip? The nerve of it! 'And as far as I could tell from the photos she sent, and ones I took of him, it's definitely him. I told her he's with you but I haven't passed on your contact details, obviously. We never do that.'

'Thank you,' I say, still feeling stunned and faintly nauseous now.

'Can I send you hers, though? Her mobile number, I mean?'

'Yes, of course,' I say. 'Do send it.'

'Okay,' Oskar says, 'and . . . look, I'm sorry I can't do more to help. But will you call her?'

I exhale fiercely as Scout and I make our way briskly towards the beach, as if the sea wind will blow all of this away. 'I . . . I'm not sure,' I start. 'I just never expected this to happen—'

'Well, look, Suzy,' he says, 'I think Scout is very much yours now. But I'll leave it to you to decide what you want to do.'

Chapter Forty-Nine

Ricky

It feels different this time, even though I've been doing it all my adult life – coming back to Sgadansay to see Mum and Dad, and then just Dad. And now – I might as well admit it myself – I'm not *just* here to see my father. Which is why, after settling in and leaving Arthur and Dad installed in front of a western together, munching crisps, I head straight over to Suzy's new place.

'You didn't tell me you were coming!' she exclaimed when I called her earlier.

'We thought we'd surprise you,' I said, wondering now if I'd done the right thing. Because, I have to say, she didn't sound delighted. 'It was Arthur's idea,' I added.

'Oh, right!'

'Um . . . is everything okay?' I asked.

'Um, yeah. It's fine.'

'D'you fancy a drink later?'

'I'm not really in the mood for going out,' she replied. 'I saw Belinda off earlier and—'

'Shall we just leave it tonight then?' I tried to sound

as if that was fine with me, and it had only been a suggestion. Perhaps she was upset over her sister leaving?

'No, do come over,' she said, but even as she told me where she's living now, I knew something was different.

And now I'm here, and it still feels a little odd, even when she chuckles over the fact that my father knew we were coming, obviously, but had kept it secret. 'Erm, something's happened, Ricky,' she says suddenly, as she hands me a mug of tea.

I study her fine-boned face. It suits her, being here; she has a hint of a tan and her green eyes gleam like sea glass. But I can sense a flicker of something in them; stress or something. I don't know. 'Is it do with the distillery?' I ask. She shakes her head, and my heart lurches; she's met someone out here, then. She's fallen in love with someone. I remind myself that nothing's ever happened between us, and if I thought it had, I must have just imagined it.

She gets up from the armchair and comes to sit next to me on the sofa, stretching out her long legs. 'Scout's owner's been in touch,' she says flatly. 'With the rescue centre, I mean. They've sent me her number. Lorraine something. And I don't know what to do, Ricky . . .' She looks at me, eyes wide and brimming with tears.

'Oh, God, Suzy.' I put my arms around her and pull her close. And then, without thinking, I kiss her gently on the mouth. And she kisses me back. And just then it feels as if there's nothing else; just me and her, together, with nothing to worry about at all.

We pull apart. She rubs at her eyes and pushes back her long dark hair. 'Hey,' she says, smiling. 'I feel a bit better now.'

I smile too and kiss her again. 'I'm glad.'

'I've missed you,' she adds. 'I thought about getting in touch, but I wasn't sure—'

'Yeah, me too,' I say. 'I thought about it so many times. I've had my phone in my hand, and I've scrolled to your number—'

'Oh, God. I've done that too. Your dad almost caught me once, at the distillery—' She breaks off and laughs, then winds her arms around me. It feels so good, so right to be close to her.

And perhaps that's why it's happened now, when it's never happened before. Why I've been overcome by an urge to come back here. I've tried to fight it, reminding myself that Arthur's life and my job are in Glasgow, and it's our home. But now, I start to tell her, an opening has come up for a music educator on Sgadansay, to set up teaching programmes, courses and events, for the local community but also to attract more visitors out here. The distillery tours have started up again, but we need more going on here; we need new ideas to make the island a vibrant and thriving place for kids, teenagers, adults – for everyone.

'Will you apply for it?' she asks.

'I want to, yes. But I haven't said anything to Arthur or Dad yet. I mean, I'm not sure how Arthur will feel about it. But he was keen to come back this time. Keener than I can remember, actually – probably because of Scout . . .'

Her smile seems to light up her face. 'That's lovely to hear.'

I nod. 'But it'll probably be hugely competitive. The job, I mean . . .'

'You want to do it, though?'

'Yes, I do. Very much.' She beams at me and kisses me so passionately my head seems to fill with fireworks. And maybe that's why I tell her the other thing; because she's sparked something in me and I know it'll be okay, and that she won't judge me. She's the kind of person you can talk to, I guess. And so I do. As we sit together, sipping tea on her sofa in her tiny cottage, I start to tell her about Arthur's mum.

'She was a pharmacist,' I say. 'Incredibly bright and driven and so ambitious. We met when we were thirty but I could tell she'd have been a fully formed adult at the age of eighteen. D'you know anyone like that?'

'Yes, my sister,' she says. 'She had a mortgage by the age of twenty-seven – *and* a cleaner. I was still ironing my clothes dry when I needed them for a night out.'

'You mean the great clouds of steam thing?' She nods and smiles, and I go on: 'And then, gradually, Katy stopped being so driven. She kind of . . . *changed*. She seemed up and down emotionally – and secretive too. I should've known something was going on.' I pause, grateful that she's here, listening to me. Already I can sense the relief at getting it all out there, out of my head. 'You mightn't think it'd be possible for a pharmacist to steal drugs from work,' I add, 'but that's what she was doing.'

'Oh, God,' Suzy murmurs. 'And you had no idea?'

'Not for a long time, no. If I found any, she'd brush it off and say they were a bona fide prescription for anxiety. I knew she pushed herself hard, she was always a high achiever, and for a while I thought it was just about that. But, you know.' I shrug. 'I'm not that dumb. At least, I hope I'm not. I'd started to think she had a problem, and eventually she admitted she did. She'd always said she wasn't ready to be a mother, and the years went on and I started to accept that it probably wasn't going to happen for us. I mean, I'd always imagined

I'd be a dad someday. But Katy didn't think she'd ever feel ready.'

Suzy takes my hand and squeezes it gently. 'How old were you when Arthur was born?'

'Thirty-seven. Same as Katy. He wasn't planned, but I was delighted and actually, she seemed happy too. She managed to get clean and I admired her for that. She didn't do meetings or anything – she just went cold turkey.'

'That must've been hard for her,' Suzy says.

'Yeah.' I exhale slowly. 'It was too hard, as it turned out. Arthur was born and she went back to work a few months later, and it came out that she'd got straight back onto it, forging prescriptions, nicking stuff, stuffing drugs into her bag or her socks or wherever she could without being noticed.'

A sense of calm seems to settle over us. We sip our teas and Scout rearranges himself on the hearth rug. 'What happened?' Suzy asks. 'Was she caught?'

'Yep.' I nod. 'A locum saw her stashing some stuff in her bag at the end of the day, and when she went to the loo he checked it. And then it all came out – the forged scripts, the copious missing drugs. There was a hearing and she was struck off the pharmacists' register. Only for a year, amazingly, but that was it for her. She never went back. Arthur was about four then, and she wasn't working. Instead, she was out at all hours because of course, she had to get her drugs from somewhere else then.' I rub at my eyes, realising they're wet.

'Oh, Ricky.' Suzy pulls me close and I breathe in the scent of her hair. She smells wonderful; of the sky and the hills and the sea.

'There were rages,' I add as Scout potters over towards us. 'Like, she'd really lose it if the flat was messy or Arthur was playing up. One night she took a heavy iron frying pan and smashed up his karaoke machine.'

'My God, that's terrible—'

'I know I should've done more to try and help her,' I continue, 'but I didn't. I was at the end of my rope by then, trying to keep up a pretence that everything was normal and that we were a happy, functioning family.'

'Did she try to get help?' Suzy asks.

'No, and I didn't really help her either. I mean, I didn't do enough.'

'What could you have done, though?'

'I don't know. Something that might have stopped all the rows and her just leaving like that. Maybe if I'd been a better partner and not driven her away, Arthur would still have a mum—'

'I'm sure you didn't drive her away,' she exclaims. 'Where did she go anyway?'

'That's the thing,' I reply. 'No one knows. She just disappeared, leaving no contact details or anything. And she's never been in touch, not even with Arthur. I tried to trace her, of course, and reported her as a missing person. But there was nothing. It's been nearly five years now.'

We fall into silence for a few moments. Scout jumps up onto the sofa and settles comfortably in the small space between us. 'What d'you think happened?' she asks.

I look at her, so glad I'm here with Suzy, and feeling oddly light, now I've told her everything. 'Believe me, I've run through every possibility in my head, including the worst one. But what I try to keep telling myself is that Katy just didn't want to be found.'

Chapter Fifty

The summer unfolds and Arthur takes to hanging out with a bunch of local lads here, enjoying a freedom he never has back home. He's become close with a couple of the boys, and they've started calling for him, asking him out for games of football on the beach or in the park at the other end of town. Of course he's old enough now to roam about with his mates, just as I did then. And it strikes me that, on this visit, he's hardly mentioned Glasgow at all.

Maybe it's because his football back home is all time-tabled and pretty rigid. It's basically all about training sessions and fixtures with other schools. But here on the island, he can head out and play whenever he wants to; there are no adults organising everything. Arthur seems to love that. He's always been a pretty independent kid.

In fact, it almost feels as if this is where he belongs now. The whole 'home' thing certainly doesn't even seem as straightforward as it was just a few months ago.

Dad has been a big part of that. Although he's never been your archetypal all-singing granddad with a repertoire of magic tricks, he's always been extremely patient with Arthur, making it clear that he doesn't merely tolerate but actually welcomes him trotting about on errands with him. And Arthur knows everyone here: the fishermen, the shop and café owners and all of Dad's friends. And that's thanks to Dad, for letting him tag along, an eager little sidekick from faraway Glasgow, which could be Rio de Janeiro when you're living out here.

I still know many of the faces around here too. In fact they often talk as if I only moved away last month. (*How's it going in Glasgow, son? Still playing that music?*). When I was Arthur's age I had already formed a clear vision of what life on the mainland, in a city, must be like: filled with McDonald's and cinemas and spotting famous people in the street. The girls at school regarded Miss Selfridge as some kind of otherworldly concept and the boys talked about Rangers and Celtic games like the stuff of dreams.

On the mainland, I reckoned, you'd be able to do whatever you wanted. Everyone knows each other here. You couldn't get away with anything without it being reported straight back. I'd scaled a lamppost once, drunk on whisky stolen from a friend's parents' drinks cabinet. Mum had heard all about it before I'd even staggered home.

And the teasing I got from lugging my cello about!

Hey, Ricky, that's a bloody big fiddle, ha-ha!

Play us a tune, Rick!

Have you got a licence to carry that thing?

I yearned to escape back then, to disappear into a world where you could be anything and no one would care.

And now I'm ready to come home.

* * *

Frieda and Isaac arrive for a holiday before they both go travelling – together, as it turns out, which seemed to amaze Suzy when she found out. She said they were always bickering when they were little but they seem close now, forever teasing and taking the piss out of each other. But they're thoughtful kids too (is that all right? To think of them as kids?). Frieda is often out hiking up into the mountains, coaxing Suzy and her brother along and, on one occasion, Cara and Vicki too – planning their trips like the fully fledged mountain leader she aims to be. And Isaac is clearly fascinated by our island's history; the lighthouse, the remains of early settlements, the ruined castle, all of that. There's a closeness between the three of them that's touching to see. I hope Arthur's still as happy to hang out with me when he's their age.

On their last day here, Suzy puts on a huge lunch at her place. There's quite a crowd of us: Frieda and Isaac, of course, with whom Arthur seems to be pretty enthralled, plus Cara and Vicki, and me and Dad.

And Scout, of course. The dog who brought us all together.

After lunch we all take him out on a walk, right round the headland to the secret beach. Dad marches along, looking much more like his old, hearty self, back when he had Bess trotting alongside him. I catch him watching, with a big smile on his face, as Scout zips into the sea and straight out again, hurling his soggy self at me and, as if I'm not wet enough already, giving himself a thorough shake.

It's early evening when Suzy drives Frieda and Isaac to the ferry. They'll spend the night in a cheap hotel in Oban, take an early train to Glasgow and fly to Paris from there, and their summer adventure will begin. Six weeks of hopping all over Europe. I'm musing over how adventurous they seem, far more than I was at their age, as Arthur and I start to clear Suzy's kitchen table and stack the copious crockery and glasses into the dishwasher. Glasgow seemed like enough of an adventure for me, maybe because I'd never really been anywhere as a child. People didn't even have annual summer holidays back then. At least, they didn't on Sgadansay – although occasionally we'd trundle down in our van to Dad's older sister's house on the Solway Firth. Still in Scotland, yes, but the air was soft, the landscape gently rolling. It felt so exotically warm it could have been the Mediterranean to me.

Arthur hands me a stack of plates. 'That was fun today, wasn't it?' I remark.

'Yeah, it was great.' I've noticed lately that the hormonal grumpiness seems to have dissipated. Maybe he hasn't quite reached that stage yet. Or it might have just been a blip. 'Could we live here?' he asks suddenly.

I turn and stare at him. 'You mean *here*?'

'Yeah, on Sgadansay,' he says. 'I like it. And Granddad's here and he's not getting any younger.' I laugh at his turn of phrase.

'Nope, and neither am I.'

'And Suzy and Scout are here,' he adds, and I detect something in the look he gives me.

'Yeah, I know.' I put an arm around him and lead him through to the living room where we sit down together. 'I'm actually thinking I'd like to be here too,' I add. 'There's a job going here, one I could do – that I'd really *like* to do . . .'

'You should go for it, Dad!'

'Yeah, but it'd be a massive move, Arthur.' I pause and look at him, wondering if he's meaning this seriously or it's just a whim. 'What about your friends? What about Kai and Lucas and all the stuff you do back home? Your footie team?'

'There's football here,' he says, 'and I have friends here as well. And wouldn't Granddad like us being here all the time?'

'I'm sure we'd drive him mad,' I say, laughing. But our conversation is still shimmering in the air when Suzy reappears in the doorway. 'Hey, are you okay?' I ask.

'I'm fine,' she says with a brave smile.

'It must be hard, saying goodbye to your kids.'

She nods mutely, and that's when she does it, in front of Arthur too; she comes over and hugs me, and her eyes are shining with tears. 'It was terrible,' she says, pulling away and laughing off her emotional turn. 'You'd think I'd be used to it by now. But it just gets worse!'

A tear rolls down her cheek. Arthur is too busy sneaking Scout a scrap of leftover chicken to even notice what's going on right under his nose. I have to summon every ounce of willpower not to gently wipe her tear away.

'Ricky,' she murmurs, beckoning me out of the kitchen and through the cottage to the tiny porch. 'I was thinking, when I saw the kids off at the ferry. Scout's real owner caught that ferry knowing she'd left him behind.'

'But *you're* his real owner now,' I say firmly. 'She made that choice, Suzy—'

'Yes, I know.' She takes both of my hands in hers and meets my gaze. 'But she needs to know he's okay, at least. And I have to find out why she did it.'

'Yes, but what if she wants him back? What'll you do then?'

'I don't know,' she says firmly. 'Honestly, I have no idea what I'm going to do. But I'm going to call her tonight.'

338

Chapter Fifty-One

Suzy

I'm scared and worried and feel quite sick. But there's something else going on too, apart from my fears over who really 'owns' Scout; a need to know what happened here on the island last spring. *I have to know why she did it.* Maybe that's why I love writing about people – and not just the recently deceased: I'm curious about what makes them who they are and do the things they do. Why would anyone abandon a dog?

And the minute this woman – this Lorraine Sampson – starts to speak, all of my anger and fear dissipates. 'I just wanted to know what happened to him,' she says, her throaty voice punctuated by frequent dry coughs. 'I didn't want to leave him behind but my boyfriend was adamant that we had to catch the lunchtime ferry. He had a job interview in Birmingham the next day. Pip had run off,' she adds. 'I'd spent three hours looking for him and Danny said that was it, we were leaving, and if I didn't come too it was all over with us.'

'But why didn't you report him lost?' I ask, clutching

my phone to my ear. 'You could have called the vet's, or the police—'

'I didn't want to get into all that,' she says quickly. 'I thought we'd be in trouble for leaving him—'

'So you just dumped him?' I exclaim.

There's a coughing episode that takes a few moments to die down. 'I was in a bit of a state. I didn't know what else to do.'

A small silence hangs between us. I'm not about to lecture her, because it's not my place to do so and clearly, she must have felt bad. At least, she hasn't forgotten him. But what does she want to do now? Come all the way up here and collect him?

'He wasn't even microchipped,' I add.

'No, we never got around to that.'

It's the law, I want to tell her, but stop myself. I don't want to sound like the police.

'So, what made you call the Oban sanctuary?'

'I couldn't find one on the island. That seemed like it was the nearest one.'

'Yes, but you left him *months* ago,' I remind her. 'I'm sorry, I'm still finding it hard to understand—'

'I thought it was better to just leave it,' she replies. 'Danny never liked him anyway, the way he kept chewing things – his trainers and jumpers and all sorts. He was always eating Danny's stuff, never mine. And I thought the island seemed so lovely and friendly and someone would probably take him in, and maybe he'd be happier there than with us, with Danny always shouting at him . . .' She pauses. I'm aware of a dull throbbing in my head. 'But I kept thinking about him,' she adds, sounding tearful now. 'My little Pip. I miss him so much, you see. I even dream about him running around and all his funny little ways. The way he loves playing stick and chasing tennis balls. Me and Danny have split up now anyway—'

'Well, look,' I say firmly. 'I want you to know that he's very happy now. With us, I mean.'

'With you and your family?' she asks, and her voice brightens.

I consider this, and I'm about to say no. Instead, I explain: 'We're a sort of family, yes. We all share him. There's me and my friends, Cara and Vicki, and another friend called Ricky and his son and granddad . . .'

'That's a lot of people!' she remarks.

'Well, yes. He has lots of people who care for him—'

'Like a kid with divorced parents?'

I pat the space on the sofa and Scout jumps up beside me. 'Not really,' I say. 'We all just love him. That's all.'

'That's nice,' she says, sounding a little choked now.

'Lorraine,' I add, 'it might sound unusual but it really works. It means he has lots of company and fun and walks, all of that. He seems happy. He *is* happy, I can promise you that. So, if you're thinking of—'

'Oh, I'm not planning to come all the way out there to fetch him,' she says quickly. 'God, no, I wouldn't dream of upsetting him again. I know I can't just abandon him and expect to have him back.' Her voice wavers – I think she's crying – and I'm overcome by a wave of sympathy for her, despite what she did. 'I just wanted to know that he's safe and loved,' she adds. 'And it seems to me like he is.'

341

Chapter Fifty-Two

Four Months Later
Arthur

She wrote to me. I never in a million years thought she would, but she did. Maybe it's because we live on Sgadansay now. Mum loved coming here for holidays. The fires on the Secret Beach, the pirate game – she started those. They were her idea. After she'd gone, me and Dad carried them on, trying to act like everything was normal. But it wasn't the same without her.

She got in touch with a letter, sent to Granddad's house. We'd just finished breakfast when we heard the post falling through the letterbox. Granddad went through and came back with the envelope. 'It's for you, Arthur,' he said, looking surprised.

Dad looked at me and then at Suzy. She and Scout had come over to see if we wanted to go on their morning walk. We see them a lot these days. I love that and so does Dad.

I examined the envelope and my heart started beating really hard. My name and Granddad's address had been written neatly on the front. Everyone was dead quiet as I opened it and read:

October 11

My darling Arthur,

So much has happened I don't know where to start. I just want you to know that not a single day has gone by that I haven't missed you crazily. I made a lot of mistakes. I wish I could turn back the clock and make things different, and have been a proper mum to you these past five years. Sadly I can't. There's nothing I can do to make that happen. But what I can do is try to make things right from now on.

Arthur, I've been all over the place these past few years. I don't just mean emotionally. I mean in different parts of the country too: London, Bristol, Brighton, the middle of nowhere in Wales. I had a friend and we travelled about, doing odd jobs working in bars, clubs, things like that. It felt okay for a while, but as time has gone on I realised that I wouldn't feel right anywhere unless I could be with you.

I don't expect to slot back into your life as if nothing has happened. I'm sure Dad has moved on (I hope he has).

I looked around the kitchen table. Granddad, Dad and Suzy were sitting there as if they didn't know what to do with themselves.

'Arthur?' Dad said quietly. 'Are you okay?'

I nodded and rubbed at my eyes. 'Yeah.'

'Is it from—?'

'Yeah.' I nodded again. I looked back down at the letter and read on:

All I'm asking is to see you, my love. I made enquiries and I found out that your dad has a job on the island now. So I assume you're both living there. How brilliant for you! I know you always loved Sgadansay.

Can I come up and meet you sometime, Arthur? Could

you ask Dad if that's okay? It would make me so happy
to see my beautiful boy again.
  Love,
  Mum xxx

Dad got up and rested his hands on my shoulders and Suzy reached over and held my hand. I like Suzy. I *really* like her. Meg was okay, and the others I can hardly remember, although there was one who used to buy me T-shirts and got her friend to dress up as Santa for me. *That* was a bit awkward.

I was only about six when Mum went away and I'm eleven now. I'm at the school here on Sgadansay and it's pretty good. I actually like school now. Sometimes I even do my homework. Me and Dad live in the house at the other end of the street from Granddad – the yellow one. Dad teaches music here on the island (not at my school thankfully), and runs courses and stuff. He also has a side business repairing instruments. Not just stringed instruments either. He knew the basics, from his teacher friends back in Glasgow, but he's learning more and more and now he can repair woodwind instruments too.

'Did you know penicillin was first discovered incubating in a nine-year-old's oboe?' he asked me last night, while he fiddled with a disgusting-looking mouthpiece. He thinks he's so funny. 'Dad jokes' – there should be a book of them.

Anyway, that was all yesterday. All day, I didn't know what to say about Mum's letter or how to react or anything. We just sat about in Granddad's living room, and it seemed like no one else really knew how to react either. But I was glad they were there. And I was glad, too, that we're in the October holidays so there was no work for Dad or school for me. I just wanted to be with my family.

Eventually, Suzy did have to see to some distillery stuff, but she came back and asked me if I'd like to take Scout for the night, so he'd be with me. He slept on my bed. That helped a lot.

And now it's morning and it's just Dad and me, having breakfast. Well, Scout's here too but he doesn't get his breakfast until after his walk.

I glance at Dad across the table. He looks pale and pretty stressed. 'D'you know what you want to do?' he asks gently.

I shrug, not to pretend I don't care but because I really don't know. 'Not sure,' I say.

He gets up and comes round and hugs me. I'm actually crying now. It's embarrassing, but I can't stop myself. Tears are streaming down my face. 'Dad,' I choke out.

'It's okay,' he says gently into my hair. 'Whatever you want to do is fine, son.'

'I know,' I tell him. 'Maybe I will see her, just 'cause she wants to—'

'Arthur,' he says, 'it's not about Mum. It's about what *you* want. And you don't have to decide anything. I mean, there's no rush . . .'

'Yeah, Mum hasn't exactly rushed,' I say, but I don't mean it really. I mean, I'm not angry. I don't know what I am. I'm okay, I suppose, being with Dad. Better than okay really. And I don't even remember that much about Mum. Well, I do, but some of it I try *not* to remember – like the karaoke machine. But it wasn't all bad. Some of it, like the pirate game, was really fun.

'If you think you want to see her,' Dad says, 'I'm happy to come with you, if you like.'

Straight away, I know that's not what I want. To sit there in a café or something with my parents, I mean. 'No, Dad,' I tell him, as it all starts to make sense in my head. Like with a jigsaw when you suddenly spot the piece you need.

I sit down on the floor and lift Scout onto my lap and stroke him, enjoying the feeling of his soft, warm body and his gentle breathing. It's amazing how calming dogs can be.

'Dad, I don't think I want Mum to come here,' I say, looking up at him.

'Really?' He looks sort of worried.

'I mean, not now. Not yet. But maybe one day.' I pause. 'I was thinking I'd write and tell her that. But I don't want to seem . . . *y'know*.'

'Hey, I don't think you'll seem like anything,' he says gently, giving me a hug. 'But if that's what feels right, then that's probably the best thing to do for now.'

I nod, feeling a bit choked up again. 'I'm not great at writing letters,' I add.

'They're not easy,' he says, nodding. 'But I'm sure you can do it, and if you want any help, just tell me . . .'

'I was thinking I'd write it and then maybe Suzy could read it?' I say quickly. 'Just to make sure it sounds like I want it to?'

Dad smiles. 'That sounds like a good idea.' He clears his throat and rubs at his chin and then adds, 'Whatever you need, you know we're here for you.'

I catch those words, and the way he said them: *we're here*. Dad and Suzy. And it gives me a warm feeling and I think, actually, I can probably manage to write that letter on my own.

Chapter Fifty-Three

Springtime
Suzy

Obituary for the *Sgadansay Gazette*

Harry Vance was born and brought up on Sgadansay and was well known to many as Head Distiller at the distillery. As a young boy, living on the family's croft with his parents and sister, he excelled at both football and science . . .

I show it to Ricky and he sits down to read it. There's lots I wanted to put in it but I want to keep it neat, and to the point, like Harry himself. So I didn't mention that Harry left the distillery, and then came back, all guns blazing – in a good way, I mean. Full of ideas. We have our own gin now; Arthur had suggested calling it Scout Gin, with a picture of him on the label, but after the puffin episode we decided to play safe. So it's Sgadansay Gin. And it's Harry's baby. It was his idea to develop and launch it and it will always be his.

Ricky reads the obituary right through to the end. We

are at his place, a cottage similar in layout to Harry's but painted bright white inside, so much lighter and airier. 'This is really good,' he says. I stand behind him, place my hands on his shoulders and kiss the top of his head. Scout potters over to us and looks up, as if waiting. Waiting for his walk.

Mum was wrong, I always thought, when she said writing obituaries must be morbid. I don't find that. They're about amazing people, the things they've done, the mark they've made on the world and the people who loved them. They are a celebration of life.

'I'm so glad you're happy with it,' I say. 'D'you think your dad will be too?'

'God, I hope so,' Ricky says, getting up when there's a sharp rap on the door. 'Typical Dad, wanting to vet it . . .'

And now Harry appears in the living room – because of course he just walks straight in – with a hefty-looking book under his arm.

'Hi, Harry,' I say.

'Hi.' He raises a brief smile and places the book on the coffee table. I realise now that it's an album of some kind – of photographs maybe. Its burgundy leather cover is embellished with gold.

'What's that, Dad?' Ricky asks.

'Oh, I was just doing some clearing out,' he says with a shrug, 'and I found this. Your mum must've kept it.' He turns to me. 'I thought you might want a look at it?'

'Oh, thank you. And, um, this is for you, Harry,' I add. 'You said you wanted to me write it for you—'

'Yep, that's right,' he says as the front door opens again, and Arthur appears in the doorway, having gone out to buy a loaf.

'What're you reading, Granddad?' he asks.

Harry flaps a hand distractedly.

'Granddad decided he wanted Suzy to write his obituary,' Ricky explains, going over to put an arm around his son's shoulders.

Arthur frowns, looking baffled. 'But I thought they were for when you've, like, died—'

'Aye, I'm not dead yet.' Harry grins at him. 'But I wanted to see it. I wanted to have some . . . input, y'know?'

'You're not ill, are you?' Arthur stares at him.

'Nothing wrong with me, son,' Harry mutters. As he continues to read, I pick up the album and turn the pages. It's a scrapbook really, crammed with cuttings from various newspapers, but mostly from the *Sgadansay Gazette*, all yellowing now, depicting Ricky as a boy, his face set in rapt concentration as he plays his cello. There are photos too, of a younger Ricky – all cheekbones and angles, and so strikingly handsome – and cuttings from national newspapers from when he'd won prizes for performances as a young man. Everything is captioned in careful, forward-sloping handwriting.

Ricky performing at the Municipal Hall.

Our Ricky winning prize for best performance, June 30, 1981.

Musical concert August 27, 1982. Top prize.

Ricky's Graduation. A memorable day.

I glance at Ricky, who's been looking at the book at my side. 'Your dad's writing,' I mouth, and he nods, and I know exactly what he's thinking: so Harry did care after all. He just wasn't terribly good at showing it.

The morning has brightened now. It's one of those crisp, brilliantly sunny April days that would freeze the pants off you. 'Look, Granddad,' Arthur announces, peering through the window. 'Someone's photographing our house.' We all turn and look at the woman in red jeans and an Aran sweater who's holding up her phone right in front of the cottage. Then she marches off down the street, stopping at the other end of the terrace.

'She's probably doing it for her Instagram,' Arthur says, turning to his granddad.

'For her followers,' Harry adds with a nod.

'Yeah, Granddad,' Arthur says, clearly enjoying baiting him. '*Thousands* of people are going to see your house.'

Ricky laughs, and then, telling Harry and Arthur we're going to walk Scout, he takes my hand and we step out of the cottage. No wonder people love this street. It's beautiful. Who wouldn't want to share this?

The air is so cold and fresh, it's almost dizzying. At the end of the street is the sea, shimmering in the sunlight. Scout potters along at my side. We don't need a lead anymore. He just trots along beside us, such a good boy.

Dogs are so clever, I decide. They can sniff out drugs, find missing people and transport brandy in little barrels under their chins.

And they can bring people together, I think, as Ricky catches my eye and smiles his warm, broad smile that lifts my heart. They can definitely do that.

He takes my hand. 'Where d'you fancy going?' he asks.

I look up at the blue, blue sky and at the sea glittering before us. 'It's such a beautiful day,' I tell him. 'Let's go to the beach.'

Acknowledgements

Huge thanks to Rachel Faulkner-Willcocks, Tilda McDonald, Molly Walker-Sharp, Phoebe Morgan, Sabah Khan, Helena Newton and the wonderful Avon team who brought this book to life. Special thanks to Caroline Sheldon and Rosemary Buckman for being reassuringly brilliant during such a challenging year. Thank you Jan Currie and Robin Thompson for help with Gaelic terms, and to Jackie Loughery and Calum Barker – a font of knowledge on distillery matters. Cheers, Calum! Huge gratitude to Aimee McMorrow who answered my endless questions about teaching music in schools, to Agata at Perthshire Abandoned Dogs Society (PADS) for doggy info, and to Ross Fitzsimons for advice on legal shenanigans. Much love to Tania Cheston for reading this book (in her usual insightful fashion) at an early stage, and to my daughter Erin for proofreading when my locked-down brain was boggled. Cheers to Elise Allan's creativity coaching group: Christobel, Annie, Anne and Mif – you're all so boosting and inspiring. Thank you Anita Naik for the obituaries idea (you've probably forgotten you even mentioned that), to Deborah Bradley and Marion for the guinea pig names, and to Emma Jane Lambert – mum to Arthur – who gave me the idea for Arthur's name in the book. It fitted him perfectly. Finally, heaps of love to Jimmy, Sam, Dexter and Erin – and Jack, our beloved collie cross, who has owned our hearts since 2011 and is never knowingly under-tickled.

Follow me on Instagram @fiona_gib
twitter@FionaGibson
Website: www.fionagibson.com

Sometimes life can be bittersweet . . .

FIONA GIBSON

WHEN LIFE gives you LEMONS

...just add gin and tonic!

When life gives you lemons, lemonade just won't cut it.
Bring on the gin!

When the kids are away . . .

'Warm, funny and poignant' *Daily Mail*

THE
MUM
WHO GOT
HER LIFE
BACK

An empty nest has
never been so much fun!

Fiona Gibson

**The laugh-out-loud *Sunday Times* bestseller is back
and funnier than ever!**

Everyone has a last straw . . .

THE
MUM
WHO'D
HAD
ENOUGH

Everyone has a last straw . . .
Fiona Gibson

An unmissable novel, perfect for fans of Milly Johnson
and Jill Mansell.

What happens when The One That Got Away shows
up again . . . thirty years later?

An unmissable novel from the voice of the modern
woman!

Forget about having it all. Sometimes you just want to leave it all behind.

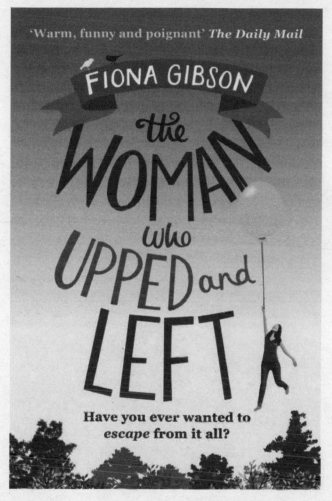

'Warm, funny and poignant' *The Daily Mail*

FIONA GIBSON

the
WOMAN
who
UPPED and
LEFT

Have you ever wanted to
escape from it all?

A warm, funny and honest read that's perfect for when you've just had enough.